New Life at the Krossroads

Bill,
May all of life's crossroads lead you to joy —

Marge

New Life at the Krossroads

MARJORIE E. DUFAULT

iUniverse, Inc.
New York Bloomington

New Life at the Krossroads

Copyright © 2010 Marjorie E. Dufault

All rights reserved. No part of this book may be used or reproduced by any means, graphic, electronic, or mechanical, including photocopying, recording, taping or by any information storage retrieval system without the written permission of the publisher except in the case of brief quotations embodied in critical articles and reviews.

This is a work of fiction. All of the characters, names, incidents, organizations, and dialogue in this novel are either the products of the author's imagination or are used fictitiously.

iUniverse books may be ordered through booksellers or by contacting:

iUniverse
1663 Liberty Drive
Bloomington, IN 47403
www.iuniverse.com
1-800-Authors (1-800-288-4677)

Because of the dynamic nature of the Internet, any Web addresses or links contained in this book may have changed since publication and may no longer be valid. The views expressed in this work are solely those of the author and do not necessarily reflect the views of the publisher, and the publisher hereby disclaims any responsibility for them.

ISBN: 978-1-4502-2945-6 (pbk)
ISBN: 978-1-4502-2948-7 (cloth)
ISBN: 978-1-4502-2946-3 (ebook)

Printed in the United States of America

iUniverse rev. date: 6/2/10

This book is dedicated to Katie
You will live in my heart forever.

Acknowledgements

As always, I wish to thank my family and friends, all of whom continue to encourage me in my writing. You know who you are and you know that I love all of you dearly.

Special thanks to Linda Davis who created my wonderful cover painting; Francine, my editor extraordinaire; and to Tom Nelson for permission to use the DDD setting for the "snippet" in my epilogue.

Disclaimer

Although there is a Krossroads Diner located at the intersection of Highway 60 and Highway 801 in Farmers, Kentucky, all references to the diner, the people involved and the history of the diner itself, are purely of my imagination. While all major characters within the story are purely fictional, several are inspired by people I have known. If you recognize yourself in any of the characters, I hope you will be pleased with my interpretation of your persona.

Segment on Diners, Drive-Ins and Dives used with permission.

NEW LIFE AT THE KROSSROADS

By: Marjorie E. Dufault

Prologue

Granny Pickles smiled when she heard the front door burst open. She called out, "I'm in the kitchen girls. I have some fresh-baked cookies and milk ready for anyone who's interested."

Expecting to hear two pair of feet charging toward the kitchen, she was prepared to greet her two granddaughters with warm hugs. All she heard was a loud thump, followed by silence. Heading to the living room, she found her youngest granddaughter slumped on the couch, a stack of books on the coffee table – obviously the source of the loud thump.

"What's the problem, cupcake? Where's Amy?"

"Amy's at cheerleading practice," she replied in a monotone voice of indifference. "They had a special practice this week to get ready for homecoming. She said you knew about it."

Granny vaguely remembered something about an extra session, but had forgotten the exact day. Karen's posture was pure dejection. Elbows on knees, chin in hands, she lifted her head just enough to look her grandmother in the eyes and abruptly declared, "I hate school!"

Granny was aware that nine year old Karen was not the best of students. As a retired schoolteacher, she also knew it had nothing to do with a lack of intelligence. Karen's bright golden eyes were constantly alert, and her keen sense of observation absorbed knowledge like a sponge – *if* a subject attracted her interest. Therein lay the problem with school. Most subjects didn't interest her, so she merely did what it took to get by. What she loved more than anything was spending time in the kitchen with Granny. She would rush through her homework and then head to the kitchen to help Granny prepare dinner.

In her gentle, schoolteacher voice, Granny said, "I don't think you mean that, cupcake. What's really wrong?"

Pointing to a loose paper on the top of her books, Karen said, "We have to do a stupid science project from this dumb list that Ms Foreman gave us."

"When is this project due?" Granny asked, studying the list of seven items that began with a simple experiment involving floating an egg, to a rather complicated project involving electromagnetism.

Color flooded Karen's cheeks as she answered in a low murmur. "Tomorrow."

Knowing her granddaughter well, Granny raised her eyebrows as she spoke. "How long have you known about this?"

"Two weeks," she mumbled, knowing to lie wasn't an option.

"Well then, I suppose we won't have time to cook tonight."

Watching the tears well in her granddaughter's eyes, Granny opted not to scold and simply asked, "Have you decided which of the projects you want to tackle?"

Karen pointed to the first one on the list. With a furrowed brow, Granny sat down pulling Karen onto her lap. "Is that how you are going to go through life, cupcake? Settling on the easy way? Why even the Good Book tells us to take the narrow door, not the big wide easy door."

Then, taking Karen's chin and gently raising her face, she continued. "Throughout your life you will have to make decisions that determine who you are…who you will become. Decisions are like crossroads. Every time you come to one, you have to make a choice. Will you settle on the well worn path where everyone else's tracks make it easy; or will you take the more difficult path and help create a new road that will allow you to shine rather than live in the shadow of others? It's your choice."

Granny pointed to the first experiment and said, "Settle?" then to the last one, "or shine?"

Chapter 1

"You bastard!" Karen Beckham's face glowed red with rage. Tears streamed down her cheeks and her golden eyes reflected a combination of pain and disbelief.

"I didn't do this to hurt you, Kar-O. It just happened."

"Well, forgive me Chase for taking it personally. I just don't recall this part being in the *game plan*."

The bitterness in her voice made Chase cringe.

"What the hell am I supposed to do? She's pregnant…and I do love her Kar-O."

The pain on Karen's face reflected only a fraction of the ache that coursed through her entire being. Swallowing back the choked moan that had caught in her throat, she spoke in a calculated effort through clenched teeth.

"The first thing you can do is to stop calling me Kar-O. I've always hated that and you know it. The next thing you can do is get the hell out of my house before I pick something up and throw it at you."

They were standing in the kitchen, and a large French knife sat dangerously close to her hand, causing the color to drain from Chase's face as he backed toward the door.

"I'll leave…but it's our house, Kar…en. Call me when you're ready to discuss this calmly."

"We'll see whose house it is after I talk to my lawyer…and don't count on me calming down any time soon."

As soon as she heard the door slam she picked up the knife and continued chopping vegetables. Tears streamed down her cheeks and with the back of her hand she brushed them away before bursting into trembling sobs. After a few minutes, shaking her head to clear it, Karen continued chopping wildly at a carrot on the cutting board while talking to herself.

"Well what do you expect, Karen Odessa Christian. For six…no…make that eight years you have been nothing more than a puppet – with Chase pulling the strings and making every decision regarding your life. What man wants a puppet for a wife?" Looking down at the chopping block she realized that the carrot was more pulverized than chopped, so she laid the knife aside and took a deep breath.

"Pull yourself together, Karen. You've got to figure out what to do."

Reaching behind her, she turned off the oven and then slowly walked over to the temperature controlled wine storage unit behind the bar. She already knew which wine she would select. Chase's treasured Palmers Bordeaux, Vintage 1989. It had been a fifth anniversary gift from his boss. According to Chase, it increased in flavor, as well as value, over the years. He guessed it had cost well over three hundred dollars. They were saving it for a *special occasion*. Maybe their tenth anniversary, Chase had suggested.

"Well this is about as special as it gets!" she mumbled as she uncorked the rich red wine. "This is the day that I come back to life. My Pinocchio day!"

Laughing bitterly at her own little joke, she headed for the couch, bottle and wineglass in hand. For over an hour she sipped wine in an attempt to numb the pain. Her thoughts were a jumble of past regrets and questions about her future. Pouring the last of the bottle into her glass, she cautiously stood up, walked over to her desk and picked up a legal pad and pen. Sitting down at the dining room table, she began writing. At the top of the page she scribbled in bold large letters: All the things I've put on hold because they didn't fit into *Chase's* game plan.

With angry determination, she began compiling a list. She wasn't certain which came first, finishing the wine or the list, but at some point she returned to the couch where she fell into a deep, dreamless sleep…or perhaps she had simply passed out. The mantle clock read three-thirty when Karen awoke with a pounding headache. Stumbling up the stairs and into the bathroom, she took two goodies powders, and then lay down on her bed, fully clothed.

Chapter 2

Karen's eyes popped open when the phone rang. She abruptly sat up, which caused her head to spin, so she closed her eyes again. On the fourth ring, the answering machine picked up. She listened to her own voice cheerfully announce that "Karen or Chase can't come to the phone right now. Please leave a message at the tone and we will get back to you as soon as possible." The frantic voice that came on the line was her boss, Judy.

"Pick up Kar. If you're there, pick up."

Moving like a sloth, she cautiously reached across to the side table and pressed the speaker button.

"I'm here Judy," she said in a groggy rasp.

"Why? Why are you there? The Goodwins are due here at nine and you promised you could have them out of the office by ten."

"I'm…not feeling well. Can you handle them for me?"

"But you have all the papers with you and I have a nine o'clock appointment as well."

"What about Martha. Is she there?"

"Well yes, but if she has to do the paperwork she'll expect to get half credit for the sale. You won't make the Million Dollar Club without this sale and tomorrow's the last day."

"How close is Martha?"

"About the same as you, but…"

"Give her the whole thing. Consider it an early wedding gift."

"Are you out of your mind? What's really going on Kar? I don't like your tone."

"Just do it Judy. Please – for me. I'll explain everything later. The contract is in my computer. You can print up another copy. You know my password."

She hung up before Judy could say anything further.

Forty minutes later, showered and still battling the remains of last night's headache, she headed for the kitchen to put on a pot of coffee. As she passed the dining room table, she spotted the legal pad. Vaguely remembering making some kind of list, she stared at the pad in confusion.

After reading her words at the top of the page, she snickered at the two bold underlines beneath Chase's name. The list read;

1. Having a baby
2. Going to church regularly
3. My career choice
4. Spending more time with my family
5. Choosing my own friends
6. Living outside the city
7. Buying the home I want
8. Having a baby!! (Again, bold underlines.)

At the bottom of the page was the word "Crossroad;" and beneath it was a large cross. Printed across one line was the word *settle;* across the other, *shine.*

She didn't remember doing this, but the memory of Granny Pickles' little lesson on choices was clear in her memory.

Karen paused to reflect on the list realizing that for almost eight years, since first dating Chase, she had settled. Chase had made every decision in their lives from the day they met. He planned every date, every event, and every move they made. He even made certain that their wedding was exactly what *he* wanted. Her mother thought it was wonderful that he was so involved.

After they were married, he would cut her off when she expressed her desires saying, "Maybe in time. Meanwhile we have to stick to the game plan." The fact that she had never been privy to the overall game plan appeared to be irrelevant. But she never questioned Chase's decisions. Looking back, Karen wondered how she had fallen into this pattern of being manipulated.

Chase Beckham had literally run into her in an employment office. He was returning from an interview with a large corporation that sold computer software; she was inquiring about a cooking position in an upscale restaurant and had just been told that she lacked the required skills – her only experience having been in fast food restaurants during high school. The kind consultant read her disappointment and told her to check out the diner three doors down. She handed her a slip of paper with a man's name on it and told Karen to mention her name.

"The owner's a friend and I happen to know he's looking for kitchen help. It might be a good place to start."

Karen was reading the name on the paper as she headed for the door just as Chase came charging through, knocking her flat on the floor. He apologized profusely, asked if she was okay, and then introduced himself, announcing proudly that he had just landed a primo job.

"Guess I was so excited I didn't see you on the other side of the glass."

She allowed him to help her up, taking his hand saying, "I'm Karen Christian and I didn't have such good luck...oh...I didn't mean to imply it was mere luck. You obviously have the proper skills...qualifications..." Blushing, she stumbled over her words and finally managed to end with "Congratulations."

"Thanks. I gotta get this over to her." He nodded his head toward the receptionist. "Nice meeting you."

Twenty minutes later she was sitting in a booth at Handi's Midtown Diner filling out an application when Chase walked through the door.

"Fancy meeting you again," he said as he took the seat across from her. "Can I buy you a cup of coffee? I sorta owe you after knocking you down. Is that an application for here you're filling out?"

He wore the same broad smile as earlier. With deep blue eyes, sandy colored hair and an athletic build, he was charming, handsome, and filled with enthusiasm. Karen had never expected to see him again and shyly returned the smile as she accepted his offer.

She got the job at the diner and Chase came by every day at lunchtime for the next month. By the end of the second month, they were dating.

In the beginning, she was so infatuated by his charm, good looks, confidence and enthusiasm, that she was willing to do anything to make him happy. By the time they got married, she was so used to him making all the decisions that she had forgotten how to think for herself. She never recalled having actually discussed a *game plan* at any particular point. It was just out there!

The first mention of the game plan came when she said she wanted to start a family right away. This was immediately nixed, "until we are well established and can afford to raise our children properly." She now realized this meant; without denying Chase all the things he enjoyed. When she wanted to continue her job as a cook at the diner, he convinced her to take a course in real estate.

"That's where there's money to be made. You'll do great and we'll be able to buy a house sooner."

He constantly reminded her that he was older and more experienced, so she acquiesced to his opinion and got her real estate license three months before they were married.

They were living in an overpriced apartment that she hated when she found a perfect little starter home just outside of Portland. The house was about twenty years old with twelve hundred square feet of living space and a detached garage. It sat on two acres of land, dotted with lovely old trees. Granted, the house needed work, but it was a buyers' market at the time, and they could have bought it for under seventy-five thousand dollars.

Chase's response?

"It'll take years to turn this into something that's re-saleable. We need to wait until we can afford something in a nice suburb where we can double our investment in only a few years."

The house they ended up buying was in an upscale golf course community. The three level monstrosity was far more house than she wanted to maintain, its only redeeming quality being a spacious, well-equipped kitchen. She liked the house as an investment, but knew it wasn't where she wanted to raise a family – which they now couldn't afford because of the astronomical house payments.

Chase's family lived in Oregon City. There was little contact with his parents or his two siblings. Karen couldn't figure them out and stopped trying after he told her to, "Stop worrying about it. Not all families are as touchy, feely as yours. We respect each other's privacy, that's all."

When Karen visited her sister, it was mostly alone. Chase always complained that Amy's three children were far too lively and wore him out with their constant chatter. With her parents, he was all charm, but he rarely joined her at family gatherings. Since he spent so much time on the road, he would opt out by saying he needed to spend some time at home...just relaxing. "But you have a good time and tell everyone I said hi," he would say as he practically pushed her out the door. *Relaxing* usually meant an afternoon on the golf course.

None of her close friends from high school or the diner felt comfortable around Chase, and soon their circle of *friends* consisted mainly of his business contacts and co-workers. It seemed every time they entertained, it had to do with a business deal; or he was schmoozing his bosses.

"It's for our future, Kar-O. If I can get that regional sales manager's position, I won't have to travel so much. We may even be able to start a family if we stick to the game plan."

Working in real estate meant Sundays were mostly work days for her and time on the golf course for Chase. With all the new sub-divisions springing up, she would have to sit in one of the sales offices almost every Sunday for an "Open House." She usually spent the morning preparing snacks that were served to potential buyers – ninety-five percent of whom were just lookers. The only thing she enjoyed about Sundays any more was preparing the snacks. She got the impression that the lookers searched out what sub-division she was working just so they could pig out on her imaginative creations. She was on a first name basis with several couples. The only redeeming factor was that they were usually more interesting to talk to than Chase's acquaintances.

When Chase came home early last evening, she should have known something was wrong as soon as he said that he took off early so they could talk. It was "of the utmost importance." Seeing his furrowed brow, she feared he had lost his job or been transferred.

"Is something wrong, Chase?" she inquired, attempting to keep a calm, reassuring tone to her voice.

Without answering her question, he said, "Let's go into the living room. I'll fix us a drink."

"I have something in the oven that I need to watch. You can tell me whatever it is right here. I don't really want a drink, but you go ahead and make one for yourself."

"I'll pass as well, then."

She couldn't decipher the tentative look on his face and attempted to sound lighthearted as she spoke. "Just say what you have to say, Chase. I'm a big girl. I can handle it."

"It's serious, Karen. I really wish you would…"

"For God's sake, Chase, you're scaring me. I don't want to leave the kitchen. How is sitting in the living room going to change what you have to say?"

His abrupt reply almost made her knees buckle.

"I want…I need a divorce."

"You…need…a…divorce? What the hell does that mean? You need a divorce!"

Slumping down on a barstool, Chase buried his face in his hands. His next words came out in a muffled groan.

"I've been having an affair…actually it's more than that. I've fallen in love with someone else."

The final blow had of course been that his personal assistant, Debbie Whoz-za-ma-jig-it, (she could never remember her last name) was pregnant. Pregnant with the child that Karen had been denied for six years.

That's when she had exploded at him.

Drawing herself back to the present, Karen once again looked down at the legal pad. Picking up the pen, she firmly circled *shine*.

Chapter 3

The first thing Karen did was to place a call to a real estate lawyer she knew, certain he would be able to give her the name of a good divorce lawyer. After hearing her story, he assured her that the woman he was currently dating was an excellent divorce lawyer. "She could squeeze a goose egg out of a robin if you are so inclined."

"I'm still numb, Jack. Sorta past my anger and ready to get on with my life. I want it fast and clean."

She wrote down the number, called, mentioned Jack's name, and was able to get an appointment for the following morning. Then she set about putting together her current accessible assets.

Karen had never touched the education trust fund set up by Granny Pickles. When she had told Granny she didn't think she wanted to go to college, Granny laughed her adorable little cackle saying, "It's an education fund, cupcake, not a college fund. I intentionally named it that because I know there are all kinds of ways to get an education. Some people get it by traveling, some by working, and others by giving. How you use it is up to you. All I ask is that however you use it, let it be a learning experience – something you want and enjoy." Going online to check the balance, Karen realized her investments had done well. It would be a good start.

Chase had always insisted that they each have their own checking account for personal needs in addition to their household account. Both of their paychecks were on automatic deposit, allocating eighty-five percent to the household account and fifteen percent to their personal accounts. She immediately called payroll to request that her check for the coming Friday would all go into her personal account explaining that she would be in tomorrow to fill out the necessary forms.

Her upcoming check was in excess of four thousand dollars and she already had twelve thousand in her personal checking and saving's accounts. She had once determined that if she could save twenty-five thousand dollars on her own, she would get off the pill and get pregnant whether Chase was ready or not. Combined with her trust fund, it could supplement their income while she had to be on maternity leave. Throughout their marriage, she spent very little on herself, choosing to buy her clothes at sales and outlet mall stores and she never indulged herself the way Chase did with his allowance.

Chase, on the other hand, purchased only first quality for himself. Once, the wife of his company's president complimented Karen on her "lovely cocktail dress." Karen made the mistake of bragging that she had found it for less than half price at an outlet mall. Chase evidently overheard the conversation, and when they got home that evening, he lectured her on what was proper and improper conversation to have with his colleagues. "I don't give a damn where you buy your clothes or what you talk about with your diner league cohorts, but with my friends, I'd appreciate it if you wouldn't try to make me sound like a cheap-ass."

Remembering these types of incidents only stirred up bitter emotions, consisting mostly of anger at her own idiocy. Determined to set the past aside, she continued her task and tried to concentrate on the future. Her future.

The rest of the day was spent packing all her clothes and personal belongings into her SUV. It was paid for and in her name. Chase drove a sporty Mazda coupe that was in his name, also paid for. Both their names were on the Benz; the designated *family car* – which Chase never allowed her to drive. It carried a large loan balance, as did the mortgage. *Chase's problem*, she thought bitterly.

Shortly after six, her packing almost complete, Karen heard the front door rattle. She had deliberately locked all the doors and latched the chains knowing that she didn't want to face Chase. Her SUV was in the garage, and she had disengaged the automatic door opener so he couldn't get in that way.

"Open the door, Karen!" He yelled, "I need to get some of my things."

"Tell me what you need," she replied from the other side of the door. "I'll toss them out the window."

"You'll do no such thing. Dammit, open this door or I'll break it down."

"If you try, I'll call the police."

Silence...then, "Be reasonable, Karen. I have to get some clothes."

"Tell me what you need, then go wait in your car. I'll put them on the porch and you can come get them after I'm back in the house."

"You're being childish."

"I don't want to see you…I don't want to be anywhere near you…ever again. You can either do as I ask or go without. Your choice."

A few minutes later she heard his car door slam and the engine start up. She peeked out the window as he drove away, then, with an anguished sob, released the pain filled, angry tears she had been holding in check.

Chapter 4

It was quite late when Karen knocked on Amy's door. More than surprised at her sister's appearance, Amy listened without comment throughout Karen's tearful telling of yesterday's events. The expressionless look on her face belied the turmoil of emotions that churned in her stomach. When Karen ended by saying that she had an appointment with a lawyer the following day, Amy finally spoke.

"My God, Karen, do you have any idea how guilty I feel right now?"

"Guilty? Why on earth would you feel guilty? Certainly you didn't see this coming any more than I did."

"No. Not this. But I've watched you change over the years. It was easy to see that Chase was a control freak. He sucked the life out of you. I don't know how many times I've complained to Ronnie about it. He never cared much for Chase, but he always made me keep my mouth shut. 'It's none of our business,' he'd say, 'Life has a way of catching up with those sorts of jerks. Better he's the one to show his ass than you pointing it out.'"

Karen thought the world of her big homely brother-in-law with the easy smile and gentle manners. She knew he was probably right. If Amy had attempted to point out Chase's character flaws, she would have defended him, and resented Amy's interference. With a half hearted chuckle, she told her sister, "He's right you know, so drop the guilt. I did this to myself."

"So what are your plans…other than divorcing the S.O.B.?"

"I'm leaving. Leaving Portland and finding a place where I can start my life over."

Somehow, this didn't surprise Amy. Prior to her marriage to Chase, Karen had always been determined and confident in her decisions. Just the fact that she had defied her parent's plea that she give college a try showed far more courage than Amy ever possessed. Her decision to go to work in a diner practically caused them to disown her, but she ignored their threats and moved in with Granny Pickles until they relented.

"Where do you plan on going?"

"At the moment, I have no idea. I'll need your help and your confidentiality. I don't want anyone to know where I am until I'm satisfied that Chase is no longer a part of my life. I don't expect you to understand what I'm feeling right now, Amy. I'm not sure I do. I just know that I have to put some distance between here and the person I've been for the last eight years. I know it sounds cliché, but I have to find myself."

"Not even Mom and Dad?"

"Especially Mom and Dad. They both think Chase walks on water and you know what they think of my impulsive, irrational decision making."

Karen's wan little smile as she continued speaking almost broke Amy's heart. "Chase is the ultimate salesman when it comes to selling himself. That alone should have warned me about the kind of person he is."

"When do you plan on leaving?"

"My car's packed and ready to go. It will depend on what my lawyer has to say. I'll leave tomorrow if I can."

Seeing the resolve on her sister's face, Amy reached over and gave her a bear hug. In a tearful choked voice she said, "I'll help in any way I can, little sister. More than anything, I want you to experience the kind of happiness I have with Ronnie and the kids. But we'll sure miss you. Would you like something to drink before you head back home?"

"Actually, I was hoping I could spend the night…maybe even a couple of nights. I've packed up everything I care to take from the house and I really don't want to go back there. If it's inconvenient, I'll go to a hotel."

"Don't be absurd. Of course you can stay. Mindy hasn't had the opportunity to share her room with her favorite aunt in ages. She'll be thrilled."

The following day, Karen met with her lawyer, who sat quietly taking notes while Karen told her what was happening. She made it clear that all she expected out of the divorce was for Chase to pay the legal fees, and to get her name off the mortgage and car loan. He could keep it all, including the furnishings; or sell it if he was so inclined. She just didn't want to have to deal with any of it. She also wanted to go back to her maiden name.

One thing that Chase had been adamant about, for which she was now grateful, was his refusal to use personal credit cards. The only debt they had was the house and car. He would, of course, be expected to keep up the payments on both if he wished to keep them.

Her lawyer wasn't exactly thrilled by Karen's indifference to their shared holdings. She assured her that she could "take him to the cleaners, and collect alimony to boot."

Karen just smiled a sad, reflective smile, saying she appreciated her willingness to fight for her, but all those *things* would just be reminders of her own stupidity.

All contact after this meeting would be through Amy. Karen executed a power of attorney in Amy's name, and then went to see her parents. Arliss and James Christian were both in their early sixties. They had met and married after each was well established in their careers. Now both were retired, and Karen found the two of them working side by side in their back yard.

After explaining everything to them, she asked for their understanding and patience while she tried to piece her life back together. She assured them that she would let them know where she was as soon as she was permanently settled somewhere and the divorce was finalized.

"That doesn't make sense Karen. Why wouldn't you trust your own parents?" Her tearful mother implored.

"Mom, I don't know what Chase is capable of and what he expects of me. If you don't know where I am, you won't have to lie to him. Amy will know and he won't bother her. She'll keep you up to date. Please Mom, don't make this any harder than it already is."

Her father sat listening without comment. When he finally spoke, his words were directed to his wife. "Arliss, I think Karen's right. This is something she has to get through on her own, and if this is how she wants to handle it, then we need to respect her choice."

He was sitting next to Karen on the couch. Turning to her, he pulled her into a warm embrace and spoke into her thick dark hair. "Just stay safe, baby, that's all I ask."

She felt warm tears touch her hair as he kissed the top of her head.

Chapter 5

It was after two in the afternoon when Karen finally got by the office. Judy met her with a steely glare and after practically shoving her into her office, closed the door as she snarled, "You have a lot of explaining to do Kar. The Goodwin's weren't exactly thrilled to be turned over to another agent. We could have lost that sale. I haven't been able to concentrate on a damn thing all day. I thought we were friends as well as co-workers. This is certainly no way to treat a friend."

Karen let her rant, knowing perfectly well that she would probably feel terrible once she learned what was happening. She watched as Judy's eyes finally met hers and it was as if a light bulb came on.

"Oh God, Kar, something terrible has happened. Is it Chase? One of your parents?"

Karen tried to smile, but was in tears by the time Judy rounded her desk and wrapped her arms around her. She was crying as well as she muttered, "I'm so sorry. I'm so sorry. I am so stupid. I should know you well enough to know you would never…"

"It's okay, Judy. I should have tried to explain a little yesterday; it just hadn't really sunk in yet."

Judy stood in shocked silence as Karen related her story, then sympathetically said, "If you need a little time off to get your head together, we'll handle your…"

Karen didn't let her finish.

"Actually, I'm leaving Portland."

As she spoke, Karen was looking down at her hands nervously fingering the strap of her handbag. When she looked up, she couldn't read Judy's face.

"So that's it. You're just going to pack up and leave. Your family, your friends, your job. Everything. Write us all off as part of your tragic experience. I never took you for that kind of coward."

Judy's voice had turned cold again and her words angered Karen. She had expected, or at least hoped for a little more compassion from her. She wanted her to understand.

"I'm sorry you feel that way Judy. I was hoping we could remain friends. I'll clear my personal belongings from my office. If you need a formal letter of resignation…"

"That's not necessary. Suzy has that form you asked for on her desk."

It was hard to determine whether it was hurt or merely disappointment behind her words. After turning in her company cell phone and appointment book, Karen walked out of the office with an extra burden on her already overloaded emotions.

Her next stop was the bank, where she picked up some traveler's checks, and then Wal-Mart, where she bought a cheap cell phone, after which, she headed back to Amy's. The following morning, she bade a tearful good-bye to Amy and her family. Her last stop before leaving town was to go by the cemetery and place a bouquet of fresh flowers on Granny Pickles grave.

"I hope I'm doing the right thing, Granny. I'm really not running away from something as much as I'm running toward something. I don't know what it is, and I pray I'll recognize it when I find it, but I'm sorta counting on you to help guide me."

Shortly after nine Karen pulled onto Interstate eighty-four, and eleven hours later, she pulled into a motel just North of Salt Lake City. She had no idea where she was ultimately headed. Somewhere in the back of her mind she thought she wanted to get to Anderson, South Carolina, where Granny had lived until she married Grandpa Rickles.

After phoning Amy to let her know she was doing fine, she collapsed on the bed and immediately fell asleep. She hadn't realized how tired she was until she awoke the next morning to find she had slept until nine. Her immediate impulse was to panic when she saw the time, then she fell back into the soft pillows, laughing at herself. She had pushed herself yesterday, stopping only for gas and fast food when necessary. Now she felt there was enough distance between her and Portland to slow down. She hadn't taken time to enjoy any of the beautiful scenery along the drive. *There is no rush!* No one was expecting her anywhere at any given time. A sense of freedom washed over her. She wanted to laugh and cry at the same time.

Taking a leisurely shower, Karen found herself singing for the first time in years. "On the road again, I just can't wait to get on the road again…" She couldn't remember the next line so made up her own words. "To start my life and set my heart back on the mend, I just can't wait to get on the road again."

Laughing at her own clever ad-lib, she stepped out of the shower. "Eat your heart out, Willie." The words, spoken to herself, left her smiling the entire time she dressed. After checking out, she bypassed all the popular chain restaurants and found a homey little café to begin her first day of independence.

It was almost eleven by the time she got back on the road. Originally she had planned on sticking with the interstate highways, but decided to venture off on a more scenic route through the mountains until she reached interstate seventy. She figured she could make it to Denver, but stopped so many times to take in the breathtaking scenery, that she ended up stopping in Vail for the night. After checking into a small older motel at the edge of a charming little shopping village, she realized that she was quite hungry. Walking past the various shops and restaurants lining the street, she once again avoided the larger commercial restaurants in search of a small quaint eatery. To her delight she found an older bar and grill that oozed atmosphere. The menu was simple, but interesting.

It was almost June – off season for the popular ski resort, however, the little bar was doing a brisk business that appeared to be a combination of locals and tourists. Families laughed and chatted while a youthful crowd hovered around a television watching a Colorado Rockies ball game. It was loud and friendly.

"Good evening, pretty lady. Can I start you out with a drink or were you waiting for someone."

"Yes to the first; no to the second. What would you recommend?"

"Pete at the bar makes a mean daiquiri – frozen or over ice. His margaritas are world renowned as well."

"Hmmm. How are his manhattans?"

"Equally good. Up or on the rocks?"

"Up please. Do you have any recommendations on the menu?"

Looking at his watch, he bit his lip. "We don't serve regular dinners after nine. Just appetizers and sandwiches."

Karen looked at her watch. It said eight-twenty. Then she realized she hadn't re-set it.

"Oh, right. I'm still on Oregon time. Guess I missed out on those." She nodded her head toward a Special of the Day board, featuring Venison Stew, Fresh Mountain Trout and Mama's Homemade Chicken Pot Pie.

"Sorry," he said. Then brightening, he added, "You know what? I'm pretty sure we have some of that stew left. Let me get you that drink, and then I'll go check with Smitty. He leaves it on the line for the employees, and quite frankly, it's one of those things that just gets better the longer it stews. By the way, I'm Jason."

"The stew sounds perfect Jason. I'm Karen." She held out her hand as she had become accustomed to doing when meeting clients. Realizing that it wasn't exactly normal to introduce yourself in this manner to your waiter, she started to pull it away, when Jason took her hand.

"Pleased to meet you Karen."

She was blushing and her eyes self-consciously roamed the room to see if others were watching. Then she chuckled at herself. Chase would have been mortified if she had done such a thing in his presence. He always looked down on anyone in a service type job. In his opinion, any courtesy or kindness extended by persons who relied on tips was just a bid for a bigger tip. Sometimes he was positively rude to them.

When Jason left, she began looking around and realized that it had been far too long since she had been in this type of atmosphere. Country music played in the background; people all around her laughed and joked with one another and an occasional loud whoop could be heard from the bar, followed by high-fives and clapping. She felt more relaxed and at home here than she had in years.

She also realized that she should have felt this way at Amy's. But being there always made her aware of how empty her life had become. Suddenly filled with guilt, she admitted to herself how envious she was of her sister's happiness. Her loving husband; her wonderful children; her obvious joy in life. All the things she longed for…and had set aside in order to follow Chase's *game plan*.

She must have had a scowl on her face when Jason returned with her drink.

"Are you okay? You look…pensive."

She smiled. "Pensive is it? Now that's not an observation you normally exact from a waiter."

He laughed. "Social Studies major at Colorado State. I've been coming up here for the last three years to work. The owner is my uncle. He and Aunt Shirley have been running this place for the last thirty-five years. Anymore, the off season is almost as busy as the ski season…especially for a place like this. It's a local's hangout as you may have surmised." He nodded his head toward the crowd around the TV. "By the way, there is some stew left. I tasted it and it's better than when I had a bowl an hour ago."

Despite the time of year, the mountain air was quite cool in the evenings. The stew sounded perfect.

Chapter 6

"That was wonderful," Karen praised as Jason handed her the check. "Any chance I could get the recipe? I love to cook and sorta collect recipes."

"I'll have to check with Aunt Shirley. How long will you be in town?"

"Just passing through. I'll be leaving in the morning."

"Where you headed?"

She almost said, "I don't know yet," but caught herself and said, "Anderson, South Carolina."

"Whew! You got some miles ahead of you. Tell you what I'll do. I'll give Aunt Shirley a call and ask if it's okay to give you the recipe. I know where she keeps it and I have a key to the office."

"That would be super. You won't get into any trouble for doing this will you?"

"No, no. Like I said, I'll get her permission first. I've seen her give recipes to others, and as long as you aren't going to open a competing restaurant nearby...you did say South Carolina, didn't you?"

Fifteen minutes later, she walked out the door with the recipe in hand and a lightheaded feeling that had nothing to do with her earlier drink. Back in her room, she marveled at the fact that this was the first time she had taken a real road trip as an adult. Many days she spent endless hours in and out of her car showing houses, so the driving hadn't bothered her at all. Chase hated driving, yet when they rode together, he refused to let her drive. He would also never make any stops along the way. They flew if a trip was more than a four hour drive.

Seated on the bed with her map, she determined that she would stay on seventy and head toward Kansas City. Then she looked at her watch. Five after ten, Oregon time. She called Amy.

"You're calling late. Did you drive that long today?"

"Not really. I stopped a lot and then had a really pleasant time at a little local bar and grill. Is…is everything okay there?"

"Chase came by this evening. He's furious. He thinks you're running away to avoid the divorce. I assured him that you already filed the papers and that I had power of attorney in your absence, so it shouldn't slow down the process. Then he started ranting about you abandoning the house. I think the only thing he was upset about you taking was your laptop. He said you had all the joint financial information in there."

"That's a load of crap. It's all on the main computer in the office. He's just never taken an interest in the household finances so doesn't know the passwords to the accounts. Tell him it's my middle name followed by our wedding date. That should blow his mind since he's never remembered either in six years. I'm reasonably certain that it's always been Debbie that sent flowers for any special occasions and she probably picked out the anniversary gifts as well. She'll know the anniversary and you can remind him that the O he's so fond of using stands for Odessa."

Amy laughed. "You don't sound bitter. You sound…happy. Are you drunk?"

Now Karen laughed. "Drunk on freedom. I think. I had forgotten how it felt to think for myself. I'm just sorry you have to be in the middle of this. I really didn't think that Chase would drive all the way to your place to bug you."

As she hung up the phone, she glanced at her wedding ring. She had removed the engagement ring, which was worth over five thousand dollars. Amy had suggested it might not be a good idea to be traveling alone wearing such an expensive piece of jewelry, so she left it in Amy's care. Now she removed the band. She had wanted to get them engraved, but was now thankful that Chase had never bothered. *Maybe he knew this was a temporary arrangement!* Slipping it into the envelope for maid service, she wrote on the outside, "Enjoyed my stay, and yes, this is your tip."

Chapter 7

Chase received the divorce papers at his office. Debbie looked at the envelope, saw the return address and promptly took it to him. She stood by and watched his face as he read the papers then removed a smaller envelope. The note inside read:

Chase,
    As shocked and hurt as I was by your request for a divorce, I want you to know that I have no intention of turning this into a nasty battle over material possessions and money. As you can see, I expect nothing from you except that you respect my privacy and do not harass my family as to my whereabouts. Marcia has assured me that we can move forward with the divorce without my presence. I have taken only the things I considered my own from the house. Anything left behind is yours to do with as you please.
    My granny always told me that if someone hurts you, forgiveness is the only balm that can heal the pain. I pray that in time I will be able to forgive you. First I have to determine what true love is in order to understand what we had, and what part I played in losing you.
    K.

Debbie watched the expression on Chase's face go from indifference to a sort of melancholy. Not for the first time, a sense of guilt washed over her as she quietly left his office and returned to her desk. She had always liked Karen.

Over the next few days, Karen stayed on Interstate seventy until she reached St. Louis. A friend had once told her that if she ever got to Kentucky, she had to travel through Lexington. (A lover of horses, her friend assured

Karen she'd see some of the most beautiful horse farms imaginable.) By this time she had decided to drive all the way to the East Coast before turning south toward Anderson. She was having too much fun. Each night she called Amy, who never asked where she was, although she was certain Amy had a pretty good idea that her ultimate intended destination was Anderson.

Just on the other side of Frankfort, she came across an accident on Interstate sixty-four and traffic was being diverted to local highway sixty. She spent the night in Versailles, where the desk clerk assured her that sixty was much more interesting than sixty-four and she could pick up the interstate at any number of places if she so desired.

Having crossed another time zone the prior day, it was after ten when she left the motel. She, again, had to remind herself that she wasn't in any hurry. The desk clerk had been right about traveling the older highway. It took her past many of the large horse farms, the airport, Keeneland, and then through downtown Lexington. Up until this point she had avoided going through any large cities but, thanks to her late start, the traffic hadn't been bad.

It was early afternoon when she pulled into a gas station to fill up and study the map. Having eaten a late breakfast, she wasn't really hungry yet, so decided to get back on the interstate and head toward Ashland. Maybe she would spot an interesting little restaurant at one of the off-ramps.

Fumbling with the radio as she pulled up to a four-way stop, she was almost through the intersection when she realized she had just passed a sign for the interstate and probably should have turned. Immediately, she pulled over in a paved area that had some kind of marker. That's when she saw it.

The old concrete block building with a brick front stood bleak and deserted across the street. Faded black stenciled lettering proclaimed, "Krossroads Diner." Karen stared in wonder – an image flashing before her eyes; *People inside, visible through curtained windows; cars filled the parking area; music, laughter and the savory aroma of freshly prepared food welcomed guests as they opened the door.* Swallowing back the lump in her throat, she crossed the highway and walked over to the boarded up building. *Is this it Granny? Is this where you were leading me? Is this the crossroad that will allow me to shine?*

There were no signs saying the building was for sale or rent. She would have to make inquiries as to whether it was even available. Somehow, she knew it would be. She walked back across the street and read the sign that was posted beneath a large quilt pattern on a wooden board. She had passed several other such quilt block boards hanging on barns or adorning small businesses. Her curiosity aroused, she hoped this would explain what they were about...maybe even give her some information about the old diner. The sign read:

Farmers was first called CrossRoads because it was situated where the road running parallel to the Licking River crossed the road running east and west.

As early as 1792, settlers came to CrossRoads after receiving land grants from the U.S. government.

This quilt pattern, CrossRoads, has been chosen to commemorate the historical contribution of Farmers to Rowan County

Okay, she thought, so the diner was named after a well known crossroad... but why with a K instead of a C? Then, walking over to the large historical marker that stood to one side of the quilt block, she once again stared at the heading in awe. Morgan Raiders' Camp. Granny Rickles maiden name had been Morgan. This was too much. Shaking her head in amazement, she spoke out loud, saying, "When you show me a sign Granny, it's literally a sign. You must have some pull up there!"

"Excuse me?"

The voice came from behind her and she almost jumped out of her skin.

"Were you speaking to me?"

She turned to face a young man dressed in khakis and a bright blue t-shirt that outlined a muscular build. His hair was as black as the cover on the bible he held in his hands, and his eyes as green as the trees that swayed behind him. Karen wasn't certain if the dizziness she felt was caused by her spinning around so fast, the swaying trees, or from just looking at him.

"Ah...actually, I was...talking to my Granny," she stammered.

Looking around, the young man glanced at the packed SUV parked several feet away and saw no one. Seeing the confused look on his face, she pointed up toward the sky. The bible he held gave her the confidence to say, "Up there. We had...have a very close relationship."

The broad grin that spread across his face almost made her knees buckle. He was gorgeous!

"I didn't mean to barge in on your conversation, but I spotted you from over there," he said, pointing to a bench that sat in the woods next to a small church. The large lettering across the front proclaimed, Farmers Christian Community Church. "I was having a conversation with someone up there, myself."

When Simon Crawford had spotted the long legs emerging from the car, he lost all train of thought from the sermon he was preparing for next Sunday. He tried to refocus his mind to the task at hand, but as he watched her lithe body move across the highway to stand staring at the old diner, his curiosity (or was it, God forgive him, lust,) got the best of him. By the time she returned to study the marker, he was close enough to see that she had a lovely face as well.

Karen was now staring at the church with an indiscernible expression on her face. Slowly she began shaking her head and spoke in wonder, her large golden eyes remaining fixed on the building.

"Crossroads! Morgan! Christian! I get it Granny. You don't have to smack me over the head with a two-by-four!"

"Huh?"

Jumping, as if she just realized that someone was standing beside her, she began apologizing profusely. "I'm so sorry. I didn't mean to…that is…I sort of got lost in my own thoughts. It's all so…incredible, really."

"I don't mean to repeat myself, but, huh?"

Her laughter was as delightful as the ping of rain drops on a tin roof. She reached her hand out to him saying, "My name is Karen *Christian*. My Granny's maiden name was *Morgan* and one of her life lessons to me dealt with crossroads. I am *definitely* at a major crossroad in my life and I do believe that Granny is trying to tell me something."

Still confused, but definitely intrigued, Simon took her hand and introduced himself. "The name's Simon Crawford and I am pastor for a small, but wonderful faith-filled group that meets twice weekly at that little church. I'm rather new at my job, but have had to deal with numerous *crossroads* myself, so if you would like to talk about it, I would be delighted to listen."

"Actually, I could use some information. Do you know if that diner over there is for sale or lease?"

"Not really, but I know someone who might be able to help you out. She's a member of my congregation and the best real estate agent in Rowan County. She's also lived here all her life – which she will tell you is forty-nine years, but I happen to know it is in fact, fifty-six. She knows about everybody and everything in this county and its surrounding seven counties. My dad called her a walking encyclopedia when it came to any local history, business affairs or gossip."

"She sounds perfect. I used to deal in real estate myself, so know firsthand how important it is to know your territory. Do you think I could talk to her today?"

Without hesitation, he nodded his head toward the church.

"My little office is in the back of the church. If you like, I can give you her phone number. I…I have a small refrigerator in there," he added reluctantly. "If you're thirsty, I keep it loaded with bottled water and Ale-8."

"What in the world is Ale-8?"

"It's a local favorite. You're obviously not from around here."

"Oregon," she stated simply as they both started walking toward the church.

"Whew! That's a long way off. Do you have relatives in this area? I mean you sound like you're looking to stay around if you're inquiring about a business…or is that for someone else?"

"It's for me. Something I've always wanted to do. Only I wasn't aware of it until now."

He gave her a puzzled look, to which she responded with her delightful laugh.

"Sorry, that was a rather obscure statement. I'll explain it while you're looking for that phone number. Also, I would appreciate it if you could recommend a decent hotel that's close by. I don't recall seeing anything for quite a few miles."

"There's a Comfort Inn just up the road on 801, right before you get to the Interstate. I've sent several people there before. It's clean and they have good, friendly folks working there. A couple of them come to church here."

"Sounds like you're promoting your congregation, Reverend."

"First of all, it's Simon. Most of the older folks call me Reverend Crawford or Brother Crawford, but I really prefer being addressed by my first name. I don't consider myself worthy of a title. I haven't earned it yet."

Humble and good looking. What a concept!

His *office* was little more than a large closet. As a matter of fact, Karen's walk-in closet in her former house was considerably larger. The back of the church was surrounded by trees, making the office surprisingly cool. There was no air conditioner, just a fan in the window. The furnishings consisted of a small desk with a chair, an armchair across from the desk, a dorm size refrigerator and an overloaded bookcase in the corner.

Surveying the small room, Karen commented, "It's no wonder you prefer working outside. This could be positively claustrophobic."

"In fact, it serves its purpose well. When anyone drops in for an unscheduled counseling, they feel like they are in a confessional…at least that's what my good friend, Father Brian tells me. He's pastor for several mission churches in the area and also ministers to two prisons, including one where I serve. Anyway, Brian says it's more conducive to brief, to-the-point sessions."

There must have been something in Karen's expression that made him feel this didn't sound very compassionate. He immediately added, "Don't get me wrong. If I'm counseling someone with real problems, I prefer doing it at home. I have a much larger office there…air conditioned."

Real problems as opposed to the hordes of females who just want to spend time staring at you! Karen thought…*like I'm doing right now.* She immediately refocused on a framed photo sitting on his desk.

"Ah, here it is."

She jumped at the sound of his voice.

Pulling a business card from the small box on his desk, he wrote down a name and phone number, and then handed it to Karen.

"You're welcome to call her from here if you like."

Looking at her watch, she said, "I'll probably wait until I'm settled in a room before calling. How late is she in the office?"

"Oh, this isn't her office phone – it's her cell. She'll answer it 'til midnight… or later if it's someone who needs help. That's just the kind of person she is."

Cocking her head to the side with a puzzled look on her face, she said, "Aren't you playing a little loosey-goosey with someone else's time, Simon?"

His face reddened as the corners of his mouth turned up in a quirky little smile.

"Okay. She's not just a member of my congregation. She's my mother… but the remark about her being the best isn't a biased opinion. She really is the best realtor around."

"So you could have just given me her number without dragging me into your…confessional?"

"Oh no, I really don't know it by heart." The blush deepened as he admitted, "I blame modern technology. Too many of us depend on our cell phone memories rather than using our own. I used to be able to spout off dozens of phone numbers for family and friends. Now I don't even remember my own home number. How pathetic is that!"

"Okay, I'm equally guilty," she laughed, adding, "But I would like to be settled in a room before I get involved in researching the area. Is there a restaurant near the hotel you mentioned?"

"Lunch or dinner?"

"Dinner. I had a really late breakfast so will probably just munch on a granola bar to hold me over 'til then."

That glorious smile spread across his face once again as he opened the side drawer of his desk to reveal a box of various granola bars, candy bars and snack crackers.

"Take your pick."

Then turning behind him, he opened the small refrigerator.

"Water or Ale-8? We can take our tasty snack out to the bench and you can explain your earlier remark as promised."

"One of those," she said, pointing to a Twix Bar. "And I'll try your Ale-8. I'm always open to exploring new tastes."

"Just a warning if caffeine winds you up. It has more than a Coke."

Chapter 8

For twenty minutes Karen talked practically non-stop, beginning with the relationship she had with her grandmother and ending with her broken marriage and subsequent encounter with a bottle of wine and the list that guided her decision to make a fresh start somewhere closer to her Granny Pickle's roots. Perhaps it was the fact that she had spent four days alone that prompted her to open up so freely to a virtual stranger – or perhaps it was the fact that she was simply enjoying being with a man who actually listened to her. He seemed genuinely interested in everything she told him and encouraged her to continue when she feared she was talking too much.

Sighing deeply, she concluded, "There you have it. The story of my life in a nutshell. Now it's your turn. Care to share about your numerous crossroads?"

"Fair's fair," he said, taking a deep breath. "But I warn you, I'm usually the one doing the listening, so I may get carried away. It's not often I can talk to someone who is completely impartial."

"Why do I get the feeling this involves a woman?" Karen teased.

"You're very perceptive. But you should probably know a little about me and my family before I bring her into the picture."

"I've been told that I'm a good listener – and I'm definitely not in a position to pass judgment on anyone if that's what you're worried about."

Simon smiled, took another deep breath and began.

"Along with running a small farm, my father was pastor of this church for almost twenty years. I always knew I wanted to be a pastor as well, but Dad wanted me to be more than a country preacher, which is what he considered himself. He had no schooling beyond high school, before he was drafted. During the two years he spent in Vietnam, he developed a faith that he wanted to share. He and several men in his unit would meet as often as they could and share their beliefs. They were of different denominations, but agreed that as long as you believed in God, followed the teachings of Jesus, and honored the Ten Commandments, it didn't really matter where you chose to worship. When he returned, he began preaching at a little church just up the road. It wasn't affiliated with any denomination, so anyone could preach there. He was good. He had studied the bible and knew it inside-out. According to Mom, he brought more life to that church than they had seen in years. His preaching style was simple and to the point. He had a way of stirring people's emotions. Mom always said he taught as Jesus taught. Pretty soon, the membership outgrew the little building they occupied, so the members built this church.

"Like Dad, I wanted to be open to all denominations, so I attended Washington Bible College for two years followed by a year of mission work in South America. In Sao Paulo, Brazil, I worked alongside numerous priests, nuns and missionaries of various denominations. Then I came home to finish my education at Capital Bible Seminary.

"I never dated anyone in particular until I was a junior in high-school. That's when Staci came along. Her family had just moved here and for the next two years we were a steady couple. "Before I left for college we talked about marriage and a family once I finished my schooling. For the first two years I was away she waited faithfully for my return. We got engaged the Christmas before I left for my mission.

Staci hated the idea of my going to South America. She said she couldn't bear to be separated from me again, so I asked her to come with me. She was just beginning her studies at Morehead College. She was already a volunteer at the hospital and, at the time, wanted to be a nurse. I was certain that she would have been a wonderful asset to our mission. She immediately assured me that she couldn't possibly live in such a remote area without modern conveniences.

"About four months after I was in South America, I learned she had started seeing someone else and had dropped out of the nursing program. Then I received a small package from her containing the engagement ring… nothing else, just the ring."

Simon paused as if this particular memory still brought him pain. Before Karen could comment, he began speaking again.

"I was heartbroken, so threw myself into my mission work, extended my original six month commitment to a year, and then returned home to continue my studies. By the time I graduated, Staci was engaged to a young doctor who had just opened a practice in Morehead.

"Meanwhile, my Dad got sick, so I took over the services here. As it turned out, he had pancreatic cancer, and died within three months after my return. When Staci showed up at the funeral, she appeared as distraught as I was. I realized later that Dad's death was just the topping on the heartache she was already experiencing. Her fiancée had called off the engagement two days before Dad died. When she turned to me for comfort, I was more than willing to oblige. I still loved her and she said she had never stopped loving me.

"After several months, we started talking about marriage again. But when I told her that I wanted to take over my Dad's congregation and make our home here in Farmers, she became very sullen. She said she couldn't see herself as a poor country preacher's wife. A friend of hers in Atlanta knew of an opening for an associate pastor at one of those huge mega churches. She was certain that I would be perfect for the job. It paid well and had many benefits. I said I wasn't interested. She sulked for several days, said I was throwing away my education, and then ultimately told me that she couldn't deal with someone incapable of living up to his potential. A few months later, she reconnected with her former fiancée. They got married shortly after that and moved to Cincinnati. It lasted just over two years.

"Since she's returned home, she has started coming to church here. I get the feeling that she wants to renew our relationship. She told me she learned a lot about relationships from her marriage. I'm just not sure what that means in terms of..."

He stopped talking and sat there with a distant look in his eyes. Karen thought he must still be in love with this girl. Was he having second thoughts about Atlanta? His crossroad?

Suddenly he stood.

"I've kept you here way too long," he said, looking at his watch. "I have an idea," he added abruptly. "How about you go check in the hotel while I finish up here. Then I'll come pick you up in…say two hours. You can come home with me, meet Mom and discuss your business over dinner."

"Oh no. I couldn't barge in on your mother like that."

"Are you kidding? She'll be thrilled that I'm bringing home a potential client. She's used to me dragging home everything from drifters to stray animals, and always cooks way more than the two of us can eat, *just in case*."

Karen couldn't help but react to his enthusiasm. And that gorgeous smile.

"You're sure about this?"

"Absolutely."

Chapter 9

It was five-thirty when Simon knocked on the door. By that time, Karen had freshened up, changed from her shorts and tank top to a soft cotton sundress, and read most of the Morehead newspaper.

The home Simon shared with his mother was a lovely two story frame house on a beautifully landscaped lot located on a hill overlooking Cave Run Lake. Karen had no idea what the real estate prices were in this area, but in Portland, this would be worth well over three hundred thousand. Not exactly where one would expect to find a *poor country preacher*. But then, he said it was his mother's house, and there was a lot of money to be made in real estate. Whatever pay, if any, he received from the church, couldn't be much. Surely he had another source of income if he ever planned on getting married.

Margo, Simon's mother, was a lovely woman who could easily pass for forty-nine. She had the same smile as her son, but the rest of his looks must have come from his father. Her short, light brown hair showed little sign of gray, and her eyes were more hazel than the deep green of her son's. There was also a mischievous glint in them that was missing from Simon's.

After introductions were made, Margo tilted her head to the side, as she appeared to be studying Karen. "My, my. When Simon said he was bringing home a potential client for dinner, I certainly never expected it to be such a lovely young woman."

Karen, who had never blushed easily, felt the heat rise to her face as she meekly replied, "Why thank you," then added, "He also didn't mention to me what a lovely *young* mother he had."

Looking accusingly at her son, she scolded, "Why Simon Edward Crawford, you told her how old I was, didn't you?"

The smirk on his face answered her question.

"Well it's not what you think, Karen. I don't lie about my age out of vanity. It's just…well…it's just that everyone that I have loved the most in this world has died in their fifties. So I decided to just skip over them. When I turn sixty, I'll throw a giant party and announce to the world that I have reached that wonderful milestone. I'll have outlived my parents, my brother and my Dear Ralph."

"That makes perfect sense to me." Karen replied in her most serious tone, swallowing the laughter that threatened to burst forth.

After serving a wonderful meal of a mixed greens salad, country fried steak, mashed potatoes and fresh garden peas and carrots, Margo apologized for not having time to prepare a more elaborate fare and said there was ice cream with fresh strawberries for dessert if anyone was interested.

"Are you kidding me? This was incredible. It's precisely the kind of food I want to serve in my diner. Good southern comfort food, made with fresh local ingredients. Maybe throw in some more exotic dishes once in a while, but mostly stick to basics. As far as dessert goes, I'm going to pass for now."

The eagerness in her voice made Margo sit up straighter. Simon almost laughed as he watched his mother's demeanor transform from gracious hostess to polished business woman.

"Why don't you two ladies go to your office, Mom? I'll take care of the clean-up."

"Please let me help," Karen said. "It's the least I can do to thank you for…"

"Not on your life," Margo interrupted. "Simon is the best pots and pans man around. Aren't you, dear?"

"And it's a darn good thing too. Mom's the world's messiest cook. I think she does it just to make sure I earn my keep."

His mother's indulgent smile as they left the room had Karen once again suppressing her laughter. *This is the kind of banter my family shared. God how I've missed it!*

"But why the Krossroads Diner? It's been closed for many years and the equipment that's still there is probably rusted out and useless. I know of a little cafe in Morehead that's been for lease for about two years. It has good equipment and the location is much better. Its owners closed it down after a bitter divorce and…"

Karen listened patiently as Margo rattled off multiple reasons for *not* pursuing her interest in the Krossroads. When she went so far as to pull out pictures of the Morehead Café, which had a bland, non-descript appearance, Karen finally spoke up.

"I'm afraid it's the Krossroads or nothing. I just have a good feeling about it." *Granny wouldn't mislead me.* "Do you know if it's available?"

"I know who to contact about it, but I really wish you would consider…"

The look on Karen's face made her stop mid-sentence. Biting her lips, Margo thought, *stubborn girl! She has no idea who and what she'll have to deal with.*

Reaching for her rolodex, she pulled out a card that read, "Mason Welters (lawyer for Dilbert Krus.)"

"I'll call Mason first thing in the morning to see if Dil would even be interested. Lord knows there haven't been many inquiries about it since the flood."

"It closed because it flooded?"

"Yes…and no. Maybe I need to tell you about the Krossroads before you make any final decisions." With a deep sigh, Margo began her story.

"The Krus family moved here from Virginia when the original land grants were being given out by the government back in the late seventeen hundreds. It was all wooded land and soon the roads that marked the south and west boundaries of their property became the main crossroad for the numerous lumber mills that sprang up all around this area. The last of the Krus land to be stripped was the section just behind the diner. By that time, around the early nineteen hundreds, the lumber industry died out. Up until then, Farmers – it was called CrossRoads back then – was the largest settlement in Rowan County. Like everyone else, the Kruses went to farming. An old saw mill sat on that corner, so they never farmed that section.

"I don't know if you noticed, but there's a little cottage that sits behind the diner. It was built for Dil's grandmother when they tore down the mill to build the diner back in the forties. She was known to everyone around as 'Ma Krus' and was the heart and soul of the diner – cooked everything in the kitchen by herself until she died at eighty-two. Dil's father handled the grill up front and his mother handled the register in the evenings. When he was old enough, Dil washed dishes and bussed tables during the summers – until he went away to college.

"When Ma Krus died, the diner just wasn't the same. They hired a cook, who was supposed to use Ma's hand-written recipes, which were kept in a three ring binder, but nothing ever tasted the same. Slowly, they lost most of their business, and when the flood shut them down they never re-opened."

Margo's eyes focused directly on Karen and a quirky look covered her face. "Now that's the factual history. What I'm going to tell you now is a combination of fact, hearsay and…let's call it folklore. People around these parts always like to put a folksy spin on local stories."

Karen smiled at the way Margo's voice changed from all business to water-cooler gossip.

"After the flood, Dil's father, Cliff, looked for the cookbook that held Ma's recipes. When he couldn't find it in the diner, he searched the cottage, which had sat empty for almost two years. It was nowhere to be found. He accused Charlie Mae, the cook, of stealing it. She swore on everything that was holy that she put it back in the same drawer where it was always kept before she left at night. After he literally tore the diner apart looking for it, he threatened to bring criminal charges against Charlie Mae. Nothing ever came of it.

"Cliff's insurance didn't cover flooding and no one thought he was really that interested in re-opening the diner anyway. Every night for about six months, if you drove by the diner you would see Cliff sitting at one of the booths, drinking whisky and crying. My Ralph would go tap on the window and call out to try and get his attention, but he just sat there staring straight ahead. Sometimes, his mouth would be moving like he was talking to someone.

"During that time, his wife Mavis wouldn't take visitors, stopped going to church and had withered away to practically nothing. Then one day, Cliff boarded up the diner and he and Mavis moved away. No one knew exactly where, except for Dil, their lawyer and possibly Miriam, their next door neighbor. They sold the house and all the land they still owned, except for the corner where the diner sat. I inquired about it once, but Mason said that Cliff would never sell the diner corner because Ma was still there. He, of course, assumed that Cliff meant spiritually, but several people who had been close to the Kruses said that when Cliff would go to the diner, it was to talk with Ma. He believed she had hidden the recipe book because no one could cook her recipes properly.

"Now here's where the really strange part comes in, and I have to say, I've witnessed this myself. Understand, I don't believe in ghosts or haunting or anything like that, but I sure don't know for sure what I saw that night. Ralph said I was taken in by the ramblings of all the other folks who claim to have seen it. The power of suggestion…or something like that. Anyway, I was at the church late one Christmas Eve helping Ralph set up for services the following morning. When I walked out to my car, I saw a light shining through cracks around the boarded up windows of the diner. I watched for several minutes to see if it went away, thinking it could be a reflection from an oncoming car. The light moved around, but it didn't go away, so I went back into the church and found Ralph. I told him someone was in the diner. When he followed me back out, the light was gone. I made him take a flashlight and walk around the diner with me, but we didn't find anything that could have caused a light to appear through those front windows and all the locks were in place. I've never added my story to all the others, but the locals think that Ma is in there looking for her recipe book. Some think that Mavis took it after the flood because she was tired of the diner and knew Cliff wouldn't reopen it without Ma's recipes."

Concluding her story, she turned to Karen, asking, "Still interested?"

"Even more so." Karen replied enthusiastically. "That name…the people who own it…is it spelled with a K?"

Margo turned the card around so Karen could see the name.

"I've heard they originally wanted to call it the Krus Family Diner, but decided that tying it to the old town name of CrossRoads would attract more attention, so they just changed the C to a K to keep it tied to the family name as well. They actually pronounce their name *cross*, but I don't think that's the true German pronunciation."

Reading the still dubious look on Margo's face, Karen felt compelled to explain to Margo about Granny Pickles, her recipe box, and the *crossroads* lesson.

"I know you think I'm a little crazy, but maybe if I clarify *why* this feels so right to me, you'll understand."

Margo's expression didn't change, but she sat back, ready to listen.

"My granny was born and raised in South Carolina. She was a schoolteacher and the ultimate southern cook. She had a box of recipes passed down through generations of family members from various nationalities. Over the years she added her own creations, and every recipe had a touch of some unique ingredient. At a very young age, I learned to handle the precious recipes with care and respect. Each time I pulled a card from the box; I would wave it past my nose and sniff the air. I could almost smell the appealing aroma of the forthcoming, mouth-watering dish. Granny Pickles would…"

When Karen said Granny *Pickles*, Margo's eyebrows shot up in surprise. The look she wore made Karen burst into laughter.

"Guess I should explain the name," she said, still chuckling at the stunned expression on Margo's face.

"Granny's name is Jean Rickles. During one of our cooking sessions, Granny made the mistake of telling me how one of her students misread her name on the blackboard and called her Miss Pickles. I thought it was hilarious and immediately began calling her Granny Pickles. My sister picked up on the name as well, and since then, she's always been Granny *Pickles*.

Karen was to the point of telling how she truly believed that Granny had led her to the Krossroads Diner, when Simon stuck his head in the door and asked if anyone was ready for dessert. Displaying a tray holding three parfait glasses layered with ice cream and fresh strawberries topped with whip cream, the two women almost drooled. It looked wonderfully refreshing.

"Do we have a choice?" Margo asked.

"I can eat two if either of you refuses."

Chapter 10

Karen spent the following morning in her room perusing the ads for apartments and houses for rent. She didn't see anything that was furnished and knew that having to buy furniture would take a good chunk of the money she needed to put into the diner. She was already assuming that it would be available. The night before, when she had talked to Amy, she asked her to, "Pray with all your might that what I'm about to do is really what I'm supposed to do."

After a long pause, Amy simply said, "Dare I ask?"

"Not now. I'll explain it all to you when it's closer to reality."

"Oh, that makes me feel much better."

There was laughter in her voice, so Karen said, "You'll just have to trust me on this Sis…and don't mention anything to Mom and Dad. I'll call them and let them know that I'm doing great. Happier and more confident than I've been in a long time. Give my love to Ronnie and the kids."

When Amy hung up, Ronnie, who had been watching her expressions and listening to her side of the conversation, lifted his eyebrows and said, "That last bit of conversation was rather ominous. Is everything okay?"

"She sounds wonderful…but she's getting ready to do something that she's obviously a little skeptical about. She asked for our prayers. Lord, I hope she's not getting involved in something she can't handle."

"Amen," Ronnie added.

It was almost noon when Karen's cell rang. Since this was the first time her new cell rang, she started at the unfamiliar ring tone. Amy was the only one from Oregon who had the new number and last night she gave the number to Margo. Knowing that Amy would call only if there was a problem, she said a quick prayer that this was Margo with good news.

"I talked to Mason and we have an appointment to see Dil at three this afternoon. He's in Winchester, so we have a bit of a drive ahead of us. I'll pick you up at one-thirty." Margo's voice sounded excited.

"Where's Winchester?"

"You passed through it coming here if you drove from Lexington. It's maybe forty-five minutes away, but I haven't been there for a while, so I want to give myself time to find his office. I hate being late for appointments almost as much as I hate it when people are late when they have an appointment with me. My Ralph always said I was a bit of an obsessive-compulsive, but I consider it common courtesy to be on time."

Karen had to put her hand over the mouthpiece in case her laughter escaped. She loved the way Margo overloaded answers with her personal observations or other irrelevant musings.

Feigning a cough to cover her muted laughter before speaking, she said, "I agree totally…and now that you mention it, I do seem to recall having passed through Winchester. Nice little downtown area."

"Little compared to Portland maybe. It has about twice the population of Morehead."

Karen waited out front for Margo, who arrived promptly at one-thirty. Dressed in a navy blue suit with a very feminine v-neck red and white striped blouse, red pumps and a matching purse, she appeared both fashionable and professional. Margo smiled her approval as Karen stepped into the car.

Seeing Margo dressed in a navy suit as well, Karen burst into laughter.

"Dress to impress! Great minds think alike," Margo said as she put the car in gear.

Karen noticed that Margo had obviously taken particular care with her hair and make-up. She, on the other hand, wore very little make-up and there wasn't a lot she could do with her mass of dark curls except to pull it back with a clip and pray that the hair spray would prevent too many escapees. She had once thought that she could control it better by having it cut very short, but found that it ended up looking like one of the afro hair styles of the seventies.

"You look lovely, Margo."

Karen watched as color flooded Margo's face.

"As do you…and thank you."

Hmmm…no elaboration.

After a brief pause, Margo gave Karen a sideways glance and said, "Oh, I might as well tell you. It's no big deal anyway…and I doubt that Dil will even remember me. Back in high school, I dated Dil for a while. My folks considered him too *fast* for me. He was two years older, smoked, drank beer and rode a motorcycle. Of course he always picked me up in his daddy's car, but sometimes he would come by my house on his motorcycle. Mama forbade me to ever ride with him. I was crazy about him, but finally decided that it wasn't worth dealing with my parent's disapproval, so broke it off. He spread it around the school that he 'dumped Little Miss Goodie Two-shoes.'

"I rarely saw him after that except when I went to the diner. I was usually with Ralph or my parents, so he would ignore me. Then he went off to college, his parents moved away and I never saw him again. I didn't know he was in Winchester until about six years ago when I had a client that wanted to purchase the corner where the diner is located. Mason put me in touch with him, but I don't think he realized that Margo Crawford was the Margo he had once dated. We talked by phone and the conversation was all business, with the end result being that his dad made it clear the property wasn't for sale."

"Then why are we bothering to go see him?"

"I told Mason that you were interested in leasing if he still wouldn't sell. Besides, his parents are deceased now, so he might reconsider selling."

They spent the remainder of the drive talking about families and Karen finished her story from the night before about all the *signs* that led her to this venture. Margo's computer printed map led them directly to the City Bank building without any hitches.

Located on the outskirts of town in an area populated with chain restaurants scattered amidst office buildings, the bank was a striking newer four story brick structure with a columned entry, marble floors and impressive fixtures. After scoping out the location of Dil's office on the fourth floor, they returned to the lobby. It was only two twenty, so Karen confessed that she hadn't eaten since having a granola bar and coffee that morning. They walked a few buildings over to a fast food eatery that served sandwiches, where Margo drank coffee while Karen downed a tasty turkey sandwich on focaccia bread.

They visited the ladies room before leaving. While Margo fussed with her hair and freshened her lipstick, Karen brushed her teeth. She couldn't help but notice that Margo appeared apprehensive about their meeting and wondered if it was because of the business part or the personal encounter with an old beau. She guessed it was the latter.

Emitting a loud sigh, Margo smiled that wonderful smile she shared with her son, turned from the mirror and said, "Well time to go, Kiddo."

Dil Krus was a very large man. Tall and stout, he had the appearance of one who had played football – and still wore the padding beneath his tailored charcoal gray suit. He had a friendly, gentle face, slightly graying light brown hair, soft blue eyes and an engaging smile. Karen could easily imagine that he had been a real heart breaker in his youth. He stood as the two women entered his office.

"Have a seat, ladies," he said, his gaze never leaving Margo's face.

Karen watched Margo out of the corner of her eye. Her face glowed a bright pink.

"Margo Daly…or more properly, Margo Crawford! You look wonderful," he praised, "How are Ralph and the children?"

The glow left Margo's face, but she maintained a pleasant smile as she spoke. "The children are doing well. Both girls are happily married and Simon is now pastor of our little church. Belinda is expecting a little girl in August and Sandy lives in Lexington. She's working and taking night classes at KU. Going for her masters in economics. Ralph passed three years ago."

A shadow crossed Dil's face as he spoke with genuine compassion. "I'm so sorry to hear that. He was such a good man. I just wish Mason would have mentioned it to me when we spoke this morning."

"I have to say I'm surprised you knew who Margo Crawford is. You didn't seem to recall who I was when we spoke six years ago."

"You're right. I didn't know who I was talking to, but the voice sounded so familiar that I called Mason and asked. He gave me the scoop on you and your family."

The glow was back in Margo's face as she lowered her eyes in a shy, school girl manner that Dil found charming.

Pulling his eyes away from Margo, he turned to Karen. "And you must be the young lady who wants to bring life back to the old diner. I have to say that the prospect is exciting, but I'm not so sure it's a wise business decision."

"Then you are interested in selling?"

"Selling…no. My hands are sort of tied there. You see, my dad stipulated in his will that that corner of land would always remain in the Krus family. He believed that Ma is still there looking for her recipe book. It's ridiculous, I know, but I feel obligated to honor his wishes."

He paused for a moment before continuing with a derisive smile.

"I've heard the stories…the mysterious light that shines through the cracks around the boarded windows," he chuckled, "but if you aren't bothered by a ghost, then I'd be willing to lease the property to you."

Karen fought the urge to jump up, run around the desk and hug the big man.

Throughout Dil's conversation with Karen, Margo maintained a professional composure, hiding her own excitement over both Dil's obvious interest in her and Karen's unrestrained enthusiasm. They were in the office for almost two hours discussing possible terms of a lease; the improvements that would have to be made; who would pay for what and how it would be financed. Karen had shown him her financial statement and said she would be willing to invest all of it in the business, but knew it wasn't nearly enough to do everything that needed to be done. She also had to support herself in the meantime.

"Well, I am a banker, and if you can show me a business plan, a timetable, cost estimates for the improvements and everything you'll need to get opened, I can get you a loan to coincide with the life of the lease."

Reaching in his desk, he brought out a metal box from which he pulled a ring of keys.

"These are the keys to the padlocks on the doors. I don't know if they will still work, but if necessary, you can cut them off. I'll have Mason go with you when you check it out."

His face grew grave as he looked directly at Karen.

"I have no idea what you're going to find in there, Ms. Christian, but after you've looked it over really good, don't be embarrassed to back out. Much as I'd love to see life back in Ma's place, I want you to be completely sure of what you're doing before we sign any papers."

Karen reached across the desk to take the keys, her heart racing with excitement.

"I have such a good feeling about this, Mr. Krus." *Granny wouldn't steer me wrong!*

"Well we've crossed the first hurdle, Kiddo," Margo beamed as they walked toward her car. "What say we run by the house, pick up Simon and go celebrate? My treat."

"Sounds great, but I insist on paying. I really don't think this would be happening if it had been any other realtor in there with me. You're the one that made it happen."

"Not on your life, Sweetie. I pay and that's final. You're the client here."

It became a moot point when they reached the house to find Simon grilling short ribs. He had the table set for three, a salad in the refrigerator, oven roasted new potatoes and corn on the cob all prepared and waiting. There was also a bottle of wine *breathing* on the counter.

Seeing their surprised faces, he greeted them with a broad smile saying, "Well, ladies, are we celebrating or merely gaining strength for the next round?"

"Both," they said in unison.

After listening to everything that happened, Simon insisted on cleaning up while Karen and Margo went to the office to make a list of what lie ahead. It was after midnight when Karen finally reached the motel, only to find that she was far too excited to sleep. She was so anxious to get started that she pulled out her computer, and then realized that without an internet connection she really couldn't do much other than elaborate on the lists she and Margo had already made.

Sitting on the bed, she began typing. Her mind went back to the diner in Portland as she tried to picture every piece of equipment, every pot, every pan, every utensil, and every dish. The list became endless. The later she worked, the more tired she became. Suddenly she was immersed in an overwhelming apprehension. *What am I doing, Granny? I'm in way over my head, aren't I? God help me*, she prayed.

She had no idea at what time she had fallen asleep, but woke with a start when her cell phone rang.

"You didn't call me last night, Karen. My God, I've been worried to death. I stayed up until past eleven, our time, and fell asleep on the couch. Is everything alright?"

Karen was still trying to clear the cobwebs in her head, but managed to mutter, "Sure. Everything's fine. I was up late…working on…" she stopped talking as she looked at the clock on the night stand.

"Oh my God! It's past nine. I'm supposed to be…let me call you back after I've showered and cleared my head. I have to meet someone at ten." She hung up without giving Amy a chance to respond.

Chapter 11

Dressed in a pair of jeans, a short sleeve shirt and sneakers, Karen pulled up in front of the diner at four minutes to ten. Margo had called as she stepped out of the shower to say that she and Mason would be there as close to ten as possible. He had a nine o'clock appointment and wasn't sure if he could get away by ten. Her call back to Amy was brief and left Amy filled with unanswered questions.

Karen had turned the keys over to Margo the night before. Upon arriving at the diner, she saw no other cars, so stepped out of her car and slowly walked around the building. The cracks between the boards and the windows didn't allow for much of a view of the interior. The best possibility appeared to be a small back window that had heavy metal screening over fixed glass. Even on her tiptoes, she couldn't quite see in the window, so she gave up and turned her attention to the little cottage that stood in a wooded area behind the diner.

The windows had been boarded up on it as well, and the exterior was in pretty bad shape. It sat up high off the ground on a cinder block foundation. The entire house couldn't be much larger than the living room of her house in Portland. Former flower beds across the front were overgrown with weeds and wild garlic. The steps leading to the front door were rickety and mostly rotted. Cautiously testing the hand rail, she gingerly stepped on the bottom step and immediately felt it give under her weight. She jumped back just as Simon came around the corner.

"What do you think you're doing?" he scolded.

"I was just testing it." she replied, her voice filled with irritation at having been caught. "I'm waiting for your mother and Mason to come with the keys."

Realizing how she sounded, she immediately apologized. She should be pleased that he was showing such concern for her.

"Is your cell phone dead? She's been trying to reach you."

"Actually, it's in the car. I didn't think to bring it with me. Sorry."

"They're on their way. Should be here in about ten minutes."

Changing the subject, Karen turned to the little cottage and asked, "Do you know if there was much damage done to the cottage from the flood?"

"I don't think the flood got up high enough to actually reach inside the house. The worst damage was most likely to those steps you were foolishly attempting to climb."

There was a smile on his face as he spoke, so she accepted the chide good naturedly.

"I wonder what it would take to make it livable. The framework looks sturdy enough and the cedar shingles on the roof don't look too bad. It would sure be terrific if I could live right here."

"I'm not sure about that. It's pretty isolated – but if that ring of keys has one for the cottage, I'll get my small step ladder from the church and we can take a look."

They had just rounded the corner at the front, when a black Cadillac pulled up next to Karen's car.

"That was a quick ten minutes."

"Guess I should have said ten minutes from the time I hung up the phone, locked up the church and walked over here."

They were both smiling broadly as Margo stepped out of the car dangling the ring of keys.

"Well are you ready for this, Kiddo?" she said, walking toward them.

Meanwhile, the man who emerged from the driver's side of the car was a total surprise to Karen. For some reason she had imagined Mason to be a dried up little old man with beady eyes and a balding head. Margo had said he was in his seventies. The man walking toward her had lots of pure white hair, which contrasted his darkly tanned, leathery skin. The face was furrowed with deep lines that implied this was a man who laughed a lot. His tall lanky body stood perfectly erect and his blue/gray eyes had a mirthful twinkle to them. The features were different, but everything else about him was Grandfather Rickles. At least the way she remembered him before lung cancer ravaged his body.

"So you're the brave young woman who's going to face the wrath of Ma Krus and attempt to revitalize her diner."

The laughter in his voice left no question in Karen's mind as to the fact that he was teasing. Holding out her hand toward him, she half expected him to kiss it - he resonated that degree of chivalry. Margo made hasty introductions as they all started walking toward the diner.

It was Margo who made the first try at the front pad lock after locating the right key. It wouldn't budge for her, so she turned them over to Mason, who didn't have much better luck.

"Don't try it too hard. We don't want to break the key," he said, handing the ring over to Simon.

Meanwhile, Margo had headed back to the car and emerged with a huge pair of wire cutters and a crowbar. Simon wasn't faring any better than his two predecessors, so Mason held up his hand to Margo.

"Don't do anything hasty yet. I have an idea to try first. It would be best if we have a means to lock the place back up afterward." Heading to the trunk of his car, he rattled around in a tool box for several minutes and came up with a can of WD-40. After spraying a liberal amount into the key hole, he allowed it to set for a few seconds, and then tried the key again. It popped right open as everyone cheered.

The heavy door creaked on its hinges when Mason opened it to reveal not only a foul odor, but an interior that looked like a tornado had blown through the restaurant. Holding her hand over her nose, Karen cautiously entered the diner.

The red vinyl on the booths and barstools didn't look that bad, but when Simon pressed his hand into one of the barstools, the vinyl crumbled like dry toast. The fibrous padding spewed up in a cloud of dust, leaving everyone coughing and gasping for fresh air. When they all stepped back outside to catch their breath, Simon took the crowbar his mother had supplied and removed the boarding from one of the windows. The glass was intact, but you could barely see through it. It did, however provide more light to the interior.

Karen was the first to venture inside again. Holding a handkerchief over her nose and mouth, she walked around overturned booths, broken dishes and fixtures as she made her way to the door leading to the kitchen.

The serve-through behind the back counter provided enough light for her to see that it too had been trashed. Cans and jars had been hurled from the shelves, their contents left to putrefy on the floor. They had long ago dried up and the foul odor had to come from something more recently decayed. She didn't want to search any further. Swallowing the golf ball size lump in her throat, she turned around to face three sets of questioning eyes. *Really Granny? Really? Is this what you expect me to do?*

Her unspoken question was answered when her eyes fell on the old cash register at the end of the counter. The last amount rang up on it read 3.79 - her birth month and year. Shaking her head, her eyes rolled upward as she swallowed the lump, smiled and said, "I'll have to completely gut it and start from scratch. Now can we take a look at the cottage out back?"

The cottage turned out to be a pleasant surprise for Karen after the foul wreckage of the diner. It was basically one large rectangular room with a little kitchen set up in a corner to the back. A small bathroom and closet occupied the remainder of the back wall. The only furnishings were an old wire bed springs atop a metal frame on one side of the room and a Formica topped table shoved against the side wall under a window next to the kitchen area. The kitchen cabinet drawers had all been pulled out and thrown on the floor and the doors were open; evidence of Cliff's search for the recipe book in the cottage.

The flooring was old fashioned linoleum that was worn and had curled up around the edges. Faded floral wallpaper covered all the walls. Other than that, it was just dusty and in need of a good airing. There were a couple of places on the ceiling that indicated roof leaks, but none of the woodwork appeared to be rotted or water damaged. Of course, pulling up the linoleum might reveal a whole other story, although the flooring felt firm beneath her feet. The bathroom was extremely small with a bathtub that looked like the kind you find in a camper. Karen envisioned the cozy little studio apartment that Amy had for the brief period she attended college. This appeared to have about the same square footage. *Yes, definite possibilities.*

Simon had followed her in and stood by the door, while Margo and Mason opted to wait outside. He held Karen's hand as she started back down the ladder, wondering if she was seriously considering living here.

"If a house like this sat empty for over thirty years in Portland, it would have been broken into and trashed," Karen said, as she brushed dust and cobwebs from her clothes.

"Well if it weren't for the ghost stories that surrounded the property, it probably would have happened here. Ralph kept an eye on it when he was working at the church and the ghost handled the would-be nighttime intruders." Margo paused and emitted a low chuckle. "My favorite story involved a group of high school boys that were nosing around the place one night. The next day they all swore that a voice had come from the diner saying 'leave now, before I have to hurt you.'" Margo's voice had gone to a deep shaky quiver as she finished her story. "Whichever of them pulled that off must have had a good laugh. But it kept any kids from ever snooping around again," she added. "And as you can see they never disturbed the cottage."

"Do you think that Dil would let me fix it up and live here? I think it has great potential."

A bit surprised that Karen would be interested in living in such a lonely spot, Margo nonetheless assured her, "I don't see why not."

Chapter 12

By the time they met with Dil again, Karen had spent endless hours on Margo's home computer and phone. She may as well have lived with her and Simon, since she ate most of her meals there as well. Several times she had insisted that she provide and prepare dinner, arguing that "I have to keep up my cooking skills. It'll be good practice."

Her meals, mostly from Granny's recipes, always resulted in high praise from both mother and son.

"If this is a sample of what you'll be serving at the diner, I may stop cooking altogether," Margo extolled, after downing her second helping of the honey glazed onions she had served with Granny's peppered pork tenderloin. Then she quickly added, "No, I can't do that. I'd end up weighing two hundred pounds."

Karen had drawn a rough sketch of how she wanted the diner set up, with verbal descriptions of the general décor for the dining area. Using the abundance of magazines that Margo had in her garage, she had cut out pictures and made a decoupage of the colors and patterns she would use. She had also obtained a restaurant supply catalog and made a complete price list of the dishes, flatware, pots, pans, and everything else necessary to equip the kitchen. She hadn't priced equipment yet because Margo was talking to the woman who owned the Morehead Diner to see if she would sell all or part of that equipment. Karen had looked it over and felt that with a good steam cleaning, most of it would work quite well and the layout of their kitchen was pretty close to what she had in mind.

The pictures she had taken of the wreckage that Cliff Krus had left were a complete shock to Dil.

"My God, I had no idea he had done anything like this. I was away at college when Ma died and I didn't realize it had affected Dad this much. I was aware the diner started going downhill afterwards, and had pretty much decided to stay as far away from it as possible. After the flood, I definitely didn't want to go back, but I probably should have at least gone over and checked on it when Dad died."

The despondent look on Dil's face made Karen want to put her arm around him and assure him that it was all right.

Abruptly, he lifted his head from the daunting photos, saying, "Okay, the plan. First thing we need to do is get that mess cleaned out. I'll have Mason hire a crew to get over there as soon as possible. I'll call and let you know when they'll get there. Once the trash is cleared away, we'll get the utilities up and running, so we can start gutting the place. I'm guessing that there's probably asbestos in those ceiling tiles, so I don't want you, young lady, going near it until the air is cleared and it's been completely sanitized and detoxified."

At this point, Karen interrupted. "I really would like to oversee the gutting. There are several things I want to salvage. I'd like to maintain as much as possible of the old diner…and I noticed an old brick smoker built into the back wall of the kitchen. I definitely want that to remain. We can replace the interior if necessary. I didn't look inside to see what was there, but we had a similar smoker in the diner where I worked in Portland, so I know how well they work."

A reminiscent smile crossed Dil's face as he spoke. "I had forgotten about the old smoker…and you're right, it does a great job." Then his face turned serious again. "Now as far as you being in there for the gutting, we'll have to check with the construction crew. In any event, we'll work something out so you can identify what you want to keep. I'll pay for everything it takes to give you a clean, safe building. The interior is your baby. Send all the bills to me and I'll pay them from an account we will set up as line of credit in your name…"

For the next thirty minutes, Dil rattled off a list of what he would do and the things for which Karen would be responsible. When she brought up the cottage, he simply said, "I'll be leasing you the entire property, which includes any buildings associated with it. If you choose to live in the cottage, that's up to you. Again, I'll do what's necessary to make it a safe, livable dwelling."

Margo sat listening without too much comment and when they left, she was shaking her head as she looked at Karen. "Do you have any idea what a great deal you just made in there…or more truthfully, what a great deal you were given?"

"I…I think so. I just haven't been able to wrap my brain around the idea of a million dollar line of credit."

"But he's personally backing it. It's not the bank's money you'll be using, it's his personal holdings. Did you sign any papers? No. And you won't until you sign the lease next week. At that point, you will be responsible for payments only after the diner is open for business. If you get cold feet the day before opening, and walk away, he foots the bill. Of course that's not going to happen. He sees in you what I see in you. Determination, a will to succeed, and of course, honesty.

"Meanwhile, you'll be able to live in the cottage basically rent free. He even covered that in the lease. You'll only be responsible for the utilities and what you spend to fix it up the way you want it...which you would have to do wherever you lived."

Karen's eyes began misting over, and she wasn't sure if it was Margo's words that brought it on, or a culmination of emotions stemming from exhaustion and trepidation – or all of the above. Catching the look on her face as they approached the car, Margo stopped and made Karen look at her. "Are you all right, Kiddo? You look a little green around the gills."

"It's really happening, isn't it?" Her words were little more than a whisper. Then she reached over and grabbed Margo in a firm hug. "You made this happen, Margo. How can I ever thank you?"

Suddenly, Margo's eyes puddled up as she warmly returned the hug.

"Just doing my job," she quipped, trying to keep her voice level. "But don't slight yourself on this, Karen. You did your homework. Dil's a business man, and you obviously impressed him."

On the return home, Karen wondered how much Margo's presence affected the *great deal*. There was something in the way Dil looked at Margo. Memories of the past? A longing? And then there was the way Margo watched him whenever he spoke. It was more than simple admiration for a good business man. She was certain it had more to do with the *man*. There were obviously still feelings between them.

"When are you going to at least tell me where the hell you are?"

Amy's irritated question from the night before had left Karen feeling a bit guilty, but she was determined not to reveal her whereabouts until she was certain that this was a permanent location. Now as she dialed her sister's number, she became slightly apprehensive as to what Amy's reaction might be. There was no way in the world Amy had ever heard of Farmers, Kentucky. Probably not even Morehead. Lexington...maybe.

"Thanks for your prayers...and your patience, Amy."

Karen didn't give her sister a chance to say anything before she began telling her about what she was about to do; how she felt certain that Granny had guided her here, and that she was beyond excited and scared to death at the same time.

Ronnie, who had been reading the newspaper when the phone rang, watched his wife's face as she sat listening. He wasn't certain whether her slack jawed expression was merely stunned silence or horror at what she was hearing. Listening to only her side of the conversation made it all the more confusing.

"What can I say, Karen? I'm happy for you…I think. Actually, I can't think right now. So this is a permanent move. I guess I just thought you needed to get away to clear your head. I always assumed you'd come back once the divorce was final."

By the time she hung up the phone twenty minutes later, Ronnie was dying of curiosity, but maintained his composure as he asked, "What was all that about? You had a weird look on your face the entire time you were on the phone!"

When Amy finished telling him everything Karen had told her, he imagined he wore a similar look on his face.

"She is seriously thinking about opening a restaurant?"

"A diner."

"Whatever! On her own?"

"I think that's what I just told you."

"But how? Where did she get the money?"

"The guy who owns the property is backing her. Didn't I say that?"

"Well, yeah…but to get that kind of backing, I'd think you have to have a little up front money."

For the first time, Amy smiled as she spoke. "Or an honest face…and a lot of help from Granny Pickles and The Man upstairs."

Chapter 13

On Saturday morning, Mason called to say that there would be a cleaning crew at the Diner bright and early Monday morning. Karen's plans for the day were to take another look at the cottage. As she drove up to the front of the diner, the sign for Simon's church caught her eye. It had been over three weeks since she left Portland and she had been in Farmers for two weeks. During that time she had done a lot of praying while putting together her plans for the diner, but had yet to attend Simon's little church. It struck her that neither Simon nor Margo had pressed the issue. Would they be shocked if she showed up tomorrow? She wasn't even certain what time the services started, so decided to check out the church sign.

Returning to the diner, she was surprised to see a dark blue Mercedes parked out front, and then she spotted Dil coming around the side.

"Well good morning, Mr. Krus. I certainly didn't expect to see you here."

"I was just getting ready to call you," he said, smiling as he approached. "I wasn't sure if you or Margo had the keys. I wanted to get a first hand look at the mess in there before the cleaning crew got here. From what I saw through the window, they'll have their work cut out for them."

"I hope Mason warned them," she said. "I'd hate for them to show up on Monday and decide they didn't want to contend with it."

Dil laughed at Karen's worried look. "I don't think that will be a problem. These people are equipped to deal with hazardous waste. They'll be wearing safety masks, and if you go in while they're cleaning, I'll expect you to wear one as well."

"You'll get no argument from me. I held a handkerchief over my nose and mouth the entire time I was in there before. I took the pictures from the doorway, so you really got a limited view of the mess. You may want to reconsider going in now."

"Not to worry. I came prepared."

Walking over to his car, he reached in and pulled out two little paper masks like her dad wore when he was in his woodworking shop. Then he gave each of them a shot of a breath spray.

"Probably won't eliminate the odor, but might make it a little more tolerable," he said, handing one of the masks to Karen.

After spending about fifteen minutes walking through the diner in silence, Dil finally spoke. "I've seen enough of this. I'd like to take a look at the cottage if you think we can get in there."

"Actually, that's what I came to look at and I came prepared."

It was Karen's turn to head for her car, where she pulled out a small step ladder like the one Simon had provided the first time she viewed the property.

A melancholy smile crossed Dil's face as he entered the cottage. Karen thought she detected a slight mist in his eyes as well.

"Good memories in here," he mused, as his hand ran affectionately across the faded wallpaper. "I helped my dad put up this paper when I was around twelve. Before I was old enough to help in the diner, I spent many days in here. Paulie, my best friend back then, and I would spend our summer days playing in the creek and woods out back. At lunch time we'd go to the back door of the diner and Ma would hand us plates of whatever special she had prepared for the day. Sometimes the specials would sell out before we got there, so she'd give us hamburgers or tuna salad sandwiches. When it was raining, we'd run back to the cottage and sit at that little table over there; but if it was sunny, we'd head for the creek and sit on the bank while we ate."

Karen listened in silence, not wanting to interfere with his musings. When he turned toward her, his face wore a melancholy smile as he said, "Sorry, I didn't mean to ramble. I'm sure you could care less about my childhood memories."

"That's where you'd be wrong," she replied. "I had a wonderful relationship with my grandmother as well. As a matter of fact, she's the one who led me here."

When Dil cocked his head to the side and smiled, Karen could easily envision the young man who had once captured Margo's heart...as well as seeing the attractive gentleman who could easily do it again.

"Talking about food made me hungry," he added, his face brightening. It's probably a little early for lunch, but I never eat much for breakfast. There's a little place up the road that serves great hamburgers...and if you're not that hungry, they have wonderful soft serve ice cream."

"Actually, I'm a light breakfast eater myself," Karen replied, her mouth watering at the thought of a big juicy hamburger. "Sounds great to me!"

While waiting for their food to arrive, Karen opened the conversation by telling Dil about Granny Pickles and how she came to determine that Granny had led her to the diner. She didn't elaborate on her relationship with Chase, just said she needed to make a new start after her soon to be ex-husband became involved with another woman. When she told him about her box of granny's recipes, she closed by saying, "I'm sure that box is as sacred to me as Ma's recipe book was to your father. I suppose if I ever lost it, I'd go a little crazy looking for it," she sighed.

Before he began speaking, he cast his eyes down as the creases in his forehead became deeper. When he lifted his head, his eyes were distant.

"I guess I always knew that my dad's relationship with Ma was a little out of the ordinary. I imagined it stemmed from the fact that Ma lost two other sons, so doted on Dad. He, in turn, felt over protective of her, especially after Gramps died. Mom often accused him of caring more for Ma than he did for her. He never denied it. I suppose I shouldn't be so shocked that losing the recipe book impacted him that hard. He changed after Ma's death. Losing the recipe book was probably the proverbial straw that broke the camel's back. The last time I visited him after Mom's death, he was in the early stages of Alzheimer's. His most lucid memories were about Ma."

His eyes re-focused on Karen as a sardonic grin curled his mouth.

"I suppose everyone has moments in their lives that they regret, but I wasted over thirty years of mine making selfish, foolish and sometimes downright hurtful decisions."

Karen was about to ask if one of those decisions had to do with Margo, when the waitress appeared at the table with two burger baskets containing a plump hamburger surrounded by an exorbitant amount of French fries. She started to say that she didn't order the fries, when the girl obviously interpreted the look on her face and quickly said, "All our baskets come with fries unless you ask for a substitute, Ma'am."

"That's fine. I'll indulge myself," she smiled.

As soon as the waitress left, both she and Dil tore into their hamburgers like starving waifs, barely speaking until they were almost gone. Once their initial hunger was appeased, Karen decided to return to their previous conversation. By then, Dil had insisted that she "drop the Mr. Krus and just call me Dil."

"Thirty years of your life is a large chunk to regret, Dil. Surely there were some good times in there."

"I suppose there were. But it's like picking out good fruit from a basket that's mostly rotted. You're never quite sure if it's really good because it's been surrounded by rot."

Karen had eaten most of her burger and was slowly picking at the fries. She cocked her head and asked, "How do you decide that you've wasted that much of your life? Even the eight years I spent with my ex-husband included some good times. I prefer thinking of it as a learning experience."

Dil's smile was that same charming smile that she found irresistible. "Then I'm a mighty slow learner."

"I'd like to hear about it if you'd care to share."

"Maybe talking about it *would* help me put it in perspective."

"I'm all ears."

"I suppose it all began in high school with Paulie. You see, Paulie was… slow. These days they would probably diagnose him with a learning disability, but back then, they just called him retarded. I knew that wasn't really true. Paulie was smart as a whip. He just didn't process thoughts as quickly as most people do. You could ask him a question and he'd just stare at you for several minutes before he would answer. Then it would be in a slow cautious manner, as if he had to pull his words from some hidden part of his brain, one by one. Paulie lived next door to me and because we were friends since we could first walk, I understood him better than most. Consequently, I did the talking for both of us when we were around other boys.

"Despite the fact that Paulie was a terrible student, he kept getting advanced right along with the rest of the class; probably just so the teacher wouldn't have to deal with him for another year. The only class he really excelled in was shop. He could take apart an engine and reassemble it in no time. His woodworking projects were the best in the class.

"Anyway, I got involved in sports in high school and didn't have much time for Paulie. The boys who didn't know him, especially my teammates, teased him anytime he showed up at the practice field. I would tell them to leave him alone, but soon decided my popularity would be compromised if I maintained a relationship with him, so I avoided him.

"By the time Paulie and I graduated, the Vietnam War was going strong, and everyone was being drafted right out of high school. When Paulie was drafted, I was sure they wouldn't take him, but he was excited about going into the Army. The last time I saw him was the day he was leaving for basic training. He came by the house to say good-bye and his last words to me were, 'You're still my best friend, Dil. I understand.'"

The look on Dil's face was heartbreaking. Karen wanted to say something comforting, but he looked as if he might start crying if she broke into his thoughts. His voice had cracked with his last words, so clearing his throat, he began speaking again in a less solemn tone.

"I wasn't about to get drafted. My dad had lost two brothers to war, so I decided college was the better choice. My grades were mediocre at best, but because I had made the State All-Star football team, I was offered several football scholarships. I chose Boise State because it was the farthest from home. After four years of playing football, it took me two more years to get my degree in finance. Since Mom and Dad were supporting me as long as I continued my schooling, I spent a couple more years getting a masters in business administration and management.

"After graduation, I moved to Las Vegas where I put my knowledge to good use in sports gambling and shady business speculations. It was an up and down ride for almost twenty years. I was a high-roller and swingin' bachelor until I used up my inheritance from Granddad, then *borrowed* a large chunk of my parent's savings. Eventually, Dad cut me off.

"About that time, I met Patti. She was a gorgeous Vegas showgirl, fifteen years younger than me. Just my type, I thought! I got a job in the casino where she worked and for two years, we lived together in her little apartment. I'm not sure what made us decide we should get married, but we did."

The chuckle he emitted as he rolled his eyes, said more than his words.

"We walked out of the wedding chapel, looked at each other and simultaneously asked, 'what did we just do?' We laughed about it, went on a honeymoon to Lake Tahoe, came back and attempted to set up housekeeping. Patti was about as domestic as a wildcat and I knew nothing about a committed relationship. I found myself spending more and more time at the casino, gambling away my paycheck and dallying in flirtations with other women. I can honestly say I wasn't physically unfaithful to Patti, but that didn't lessen the rumors…or the hurt it caused Patti. When we were together, all we did was argue.

"We had bought a little house that she loved and I hated…or at least I hated what it represented. Responsibility. Not my bag, but I was supposedly the business expert, so I handled the household finances. When we received a foreclosure notice on the house because I wasn't making the payments, Patti kicked me out and sued for divorce. She was smart enough to know that I didn't have anything, so in lieu of alimony, her only stipulation was that she never had to see my sorry face again. After the divorce papers were signed, I collected my final paycheck and moved back to Kentucky, a broke and broken man. It was the first good decision I had made in over thirty years. Mom and Dad had been living in Frankfort ever since leaving Farmers. They took me back with open arms. Their only requirement while I was staying with them was that I find a job and accompany them to church on Sundays."

When Dil paused, his face relaxed for the first time since he began his story. Karen took the opportunity to say, "Well, you obviously turned your life around since then."

"I suppose…thanks to my dad. Through an acquaintance of his, I got a job at a small bank where I discovered I liked banking…and I was good at it. I started doing financial analysis for several clients and when I took over my Dad's portfolio, I got really lucky with a few investments that were more hunches than anything. Then I was offered an opportunity to get in on the ground floor of The City Bank of Winchester. Dad insisted on backing my half of the venture. He joked that it was my inheritance anyway, so if I blew it, I was the only loser.

"By then I had my own place, but after having avoided my parents for so many years, I found it really hard to leave Frankfort. Mom had always been frail and her health was declining. Two years after I left, she died of heart failure. I had no idea that she suffered from a heart condition since birth. After that, I visited Dad often, and when the Alzheimer's began, I wanted to bring him to Winchester to live with me. He insisted he couldn't leave Mom. Somehow, after all those years of believing that he never loved my mother enough, I found it comforting to know he felt that way. I hired a full time nurse to care for him. I would still go visit him every weekend until Janet, his nurse, asked me not to come so often. She said it would take her two days after my visits to get him calmed down.

"At first I was very hurt by this, but his doctor assured me that violence against loved ones was a common thing. His personal theory was that the closer you were to the patient, the harder it was for them to accept the fact that they somehow knew they should recognize you. Their anger stemmed from their inability to connect a face to a memory and was actually anger with themselves, but they would inevitably project it on the person who was causing their frustration. I would still go to see him as often as I could, I just wouldn't let him see me. I was there when he died, holding his hand."

Karen brushed at the tears that had begun trailing down her cheeks. She wanted to say something comforting, but couldn't find her voice, so reached across the table and patted Dil's hand. By then, the regular lunch crowd was beginning to drift in. The waitress had presented the check and was giving them an impatient look.

Dil looked around and said, "Guess we should make room for someone else. I'd like to discuss what you would like done with the cottage. I have a few ideas, but don't want to do anything that you don't approve. After all, you're the one who's going to live there."

Driving back to the diner, Karen asked Dil, "Whatever happened to your friend, Paulie?"

"I honestly don't know. The last I heard, he had been injured in Nam. I'll have to ask Margo the next time I see her. She probably knows."

Chapter 14

When Karen entered the church, she immediately realized she was way overdressed. Most of the women were wearing casual slacks or jeans. A few of the younger girls wore Bermuda length shorts. There wasn't a dress or skirt to be seen. She felt quite conspicuous in her long silk skirt and matching blouse.

Finding a seat three rows from the back, she hoped that Simon or Margo wouldn't notice her presence right away. No sooner had she settled in her seat when everyone rose, as a voice up front announced that the opening hymn would be "All Are Welcome" on page two twenty two. There were no books in the holder, but as soon as she stood, the young girl next to her held up her hymnal to share. Smiling, she mouthed "thanks," as the girl returned the smile, then continued to watch Karen from the corner of her eye. The hymn wasn't familiar to Karen, but by the second verse, she attempted to sing along in her soft soprano. The booming organ overpowered the voices in the beginning, but softened as more people joined in the singing.

After the hymn, Simon opened with a prayer. A strong feeling of reconnection came over Karen as she realized how much she missed being part of a prayerful community. The few times during her life with Chase when she had attended church, her mind was in such chaos trying to sort out everything she had to do, that she became lost in her thoughts. She ended up getting nothing from the service. It soon became more of a hassle than she could deal with to listen to Chase's list of "don't forget, we have to…you have to…" that preempted every exit. She finally just stopped going, using the open houses as her excuse to herself. Now she silently vowed that she wouldn't allow that to happen here.

Simon's sermon was excellent. Taking the bible reading and relating it to current issues, it became a guide on using the words of Jesus to deal with everyday life. Instead of standing at the pulpit he roamed around the church, up and down the aisles, touching children affectionately on the head, patting men on the shoulder, acknowledging the women with a nod and smiling warmly to everyone. His eyes met Karen in acknowledgement of her presence and she realized she was blushing. At the end of the final prayer and before singing the closing hymn, Simon asked if there were any visitors or newcomers. A few hands went up and reluctantly, Karen raised her hand as well.

"Let's give our guests and newcomers a warm welcome."

The congregation erupted in a loud applause, with several people around Karen turning to greet her. Overcome with emotion, her eyes welled up before she knew what was happening. Thank heaven the organ burst into the introduction to the closing hymn and everyone's attention reverted back to the hymnals.

Karen thought she could make a hasty retreat, but as she started to exit, a group of women, led by Margo, surrounded her. Margo began rattling off introductions and each woman in turn either took her hand warmly or grabbed her in an affectionate hug. Soon Simon joined the melee with a very lovely woman draped on his arm.

"Karen, this is Staci. I've been telling her about your project to re-open the diner."

So this is Simon's crossroads dilemma, Karen thought as she extended her hand in greeting.

"What he failed to tell me was that you were so…attractive," Staci whined, with a distinct Southern drawl. "I'm so pleased to meet you Karen."

About the same height as Karen, Staci Winthrop-Perkins had long honey blond hair, blue eyes and a model's figure. Dressed in casual slacks and a gauzy blouse, she made Karen think of a picture she has seen of Heidi Klum – just not as buxom. She offered her hand as she spoke, but the look she wore didn't match her warm words. All the while, she kept her other hand possessively hooked through Simon's arm.

Margo stepped forward saying, "Karen, I'm so delighted that you joined us this morning and I'm hoping you'll join us for brunch at the house. I promise not to talk business."

"Only if you'll let me help."

"Not a chance. Everything's ready. I'll just have to cook my casserole off while we sip on mimosas. Ride over with me, and then Simon can drive you back to pick up your car afterward."

Turning to Simon Margo said, "I assume you'll be riding with Staci to the house."

"Uh, well…yes, I can do that."

Staci was glaring at both Margo and Karen with an indiscernible look that made her face look harsh. Irritation? Or was it jealousy? Karen mused. Either way, it was certainly uncalled for and Karen decided that she didn't care too much for Staci Perkins.

As they were buckling their seat belts, Karen said, "Dil came by yesterday." Then she watched closely to see what Margo's reaction would be. "He wanted to take a look at the cottage and go over some ideas he had for fixing it up." Sure enough, Margo's eyes lit up at the mention of his name.

"Oh, I'm sorry I missed him. What time was he there?"

"Around ten. I knew you said you would be with that couple from Atlanta all morning or I would have called you. We had lunch together. He's really a great guy despite his misspent youth," she concluded, with an impish grin.

"He really wasn't all that bad. Being a jock, riding a motorcycle and having all the girls in school drooling over him, he was no worse than any other boy in that circle," Margo defended. "Better than most, really."

"How's that?"

"Well, he had this friend named Paulie..."

"He told me about Paulie. Dil didn't consider himself much of a friend to Paulie in high school. It was one of his first regrets."

"Really? Now that surprises me. I know he didn't have much time to spend with Paulie because of his involvement in sports, but no one got by with harassing Paulie if Dil was around. When Paulie got drafted, Dil sent his Dad down to the draft board to try to get a deferment for him. Sadly, at that time so many young men were trying to avoid the draft, making every excuse imaginable to get out of it, that the board didn't accept that he was a bit slow when it came to expressing himself as a viable reason for deferment. Paulie had a keen mechanical mind and worked for Shane Canton at his garage. He was also the best shot in the county. Then to top it off, he was anxious to go."

"Do you know where he is now? Dil said he didn't know what happened to him after his return."

"Oh Paulie's around. He still lives with his mother, Miriam, in the same house next door to Dil's old house. He had only been gone for a little over a year when he was shipped home with an injury to his head. Miriam told me, it took three operations to remove the shrapnel that was embedded in his skull. Aside from the fact that there was some brain damage, the experience was quite traumatic for him and she believes he often lives in his memories of the war. It's really sad."

"Do you know what happened?"

"When Miriam was at Bethesda where Paulie was being treated, one of the guys from his unit who had lost both his legs in the same raid told her that he and Paulie were on night guard duty. When the Viet Cong attacked, they bombarded the entire camp with grenades before rushing in with automatic weapons and killing anything that moved. Both he and Paulie were most likely assumed dead or they probably would have filled them with bullets despite their injuries. Paulie blamed himself for the twenty something men that were killed in the raid. He really didn't remember what happened, and thinks he fell asleep on his watch. Now Miriam says he can't sleep at night. The folks around here started calling him Possum because he roams the neighborhood and woods all night, sleeps for a few hours at daylight, works at Shane's garage 'til suppertime, then starts his night watch again."

Pulling into the drive as Simon and Staci were emerging from Staci's car, Margo concluded by saying, "Simon has talked to him a couple of times when his car was in the garage. He has a very high opinion of him…but then Simon sees only the best in everyone."

Her eyes were fixed on Staci as she spoke and the grimace on her face led Karen to believe that perhaps Margo shared her less than favorable opinion of the woman.

While the foursome waited for the casserole to bake, Staci attempted to dominate the conversation. She had recently returned from a cruise to Spain with several friends. She went into excessive detail about their many stops, the lavish meals they ate and the *highly professional* onboard entertainment. Karen got a distinct feeling that she was trying to impress them…or at least her, with this worldly knowledge.

Margo looked bored, Simon looked impatient and Karen feigned interest, almost feeling sorry for her since every time Staci paused, either Simon or Margo would ask Karen a question about her family or her plans for the diner. When Karen spoke, Staci would sit back in her chair, her legs crossed with her dangling foot in constant motion. Everyone seemed relieved when the timer for the casserole went off.

"That was wonderful, Margo. I want that recipe for sure," Karen beamed. "You absolutely have to let me help with the clean-up though. I'm afraid I over indulged and if I don't move around a bit, I'm going to turn into a slab of lard right here in this chair."

While Margo and Simon laughed at Karen's vivid remark, Staci's face held a look of disgust.

Realizing that her comment might have seemed rather unrefined, Karen blushed, saying, "Sorry. My granny used to say that to my sister and me to get us moving on clean-up detail. It was especially effective when we were teenagers and conscious of our weight."

Margo and Simon laughed once again and Staci managed a stiff smile.

"I'll gladly accept the help and thank you," Margo said, pushing her chair back.

Then turning her attention to Simon, she asked if he and Staci had any plans for the afternoon.

"Not really. Did you have something in mind?" Simon asked without consulting Staci.

"I just thought it would be a lovely day to take Karen out on the houseboat. She hasn't had much of a chance to see our beautiful scenery. We could pack some sandwiches and drinks for this afternoon…maybe even do a little fishing."

"Karen is hardly dressed for that kind of outing," Staci smugly remarked.

"Oh, but it sounds wonderful. I can take a quick run back to the motel and change as soon as we finish the dishes," Karen replied enthusiastically.

"Of course you can. Simon can run you back by the church to pick up your car while Staci and I prepare the sandwiches. By the time you return, we'll have the car packed and ready to go."

"Actually, I'm going to have to pass," Staci injected. "My parents are expecting me for an early dinner and I was hoping that you would join us, Simon."

Her eyes fairly fluttered as she looked pleadingly at Simon.

"Not today Staci. I'm not about to give up an opportunity to get out on the houseboat. Can't you call your folks and tell them you won't be there?"

"I would never do that. Unlike you, I don't see my parents every day, Simon. I could never disappoint them." There was a controlled anger behind her words as she walked to the table that held her purse.

"I'll walk you to your car," Simon said, not sounding properly disappointed.

Karen was at the sink watching as Simon held the car door for Staci. Staci looked up and, spotting Karen through the window, she pulled an unsuspecting Simon to her and proceeded to kiss him soundly. Pulling back abruptly, Simon asked, "What was that about?"

"Oh Simon, how can you ask such a question. You have to know how I feel about you. I just hope you aren't becoming infatuated with that…*girl*. She's much too… coarse to make a proper minister's wife."

Instead of dignifying her comment by defending Karen, Simon simply said, "Good-bye Staci. Enjoy your evening with your parents." Then he turned and walked back to the house without closing the door for her.

Karen didn't realize that Margo was also watching the scene outside over her shoulder.

"Thank you, Lord," she sighed. "I was so afraid that Simon would try to talk her into changing her mind. Maybe there's hope for him yet."

Karen turned around, shocked at Margo's words.

"I thought you liked her."

"There was a time…and I would certainly never say anything to Simon. He has the right to make his own choices."

The front door slammed, ending the conversation. Simon came into the kitchen to say he was going to get the ice chest from the garage and fill it with drinks. He sounded irritated.

Karen felt like Margo was going to say more, but wasn't sure if she should pry, so continued wiping the counter while Margo finished loading the dishwasher. She almost jumped when Margo began speaking again.

"Staci was a sophomore when her parents moved here from Florida. They are both professors at Morehead State. She was this shy, gangly little wisp of a thing. Pretty as a picture and at the time, unaware of it. My Ralph adored her and both the girls treated her like another sister. Over the next two years she developed into a lovely young girl physically, but as she became more aware of her looks, she became quite self-centered. Both the girls saw it, but Simon, and Ralph as well, seemed to be blind to the changes in her personality. I tended to side with the guys thinking the girls were a little jealous of all the attention she got from boys…including *their* boyfriends.

"It was the Christmas when Simon proposed that I decided the girls were right. He was so excited. He wanted the proposal to be unique, so he had the girls help him wrap this huge box which contained a smaller box which contained a smaller box…you get the picture. Each box was beautifully wrapped, right down to the last box which contained a brick with a note on it. It said, 'This is the first brick for our future home together. I love you Staci and want you to be my wife.'

"Staci had giggled all the while she was opening each box. When she got down to the brick, she just stared at it with this incredulous look on her face as she read the note. Then she turned to Simon and said, 'What kind of a joke is this, Simon? I told my parents you were giving me an engagement ring. How am I going to explain this to them?' Then she burst into tears.

"Poor Simon was devastated and for a moment, I thought Sandy was going to pick up the brick and throw it at Staci. She was only fourteen, adored her brother and thought his proposal was the most romantic thing she had ever witnessed. Belinda just left the room to keep from saying anything.

"Of course Simon had a ring; he had just planned on giving it to her when they went to her parent's house later. When he pulled the ring box out of his suit pocket, she at least had the courtesy to blush.

"She never really apologized for her outburst...at least not in front of us. Later she said it was a *sweet gesture*, but he should have had the ring in the box with the brick so she wouldn't have been quite so shocked."

Karen had to bite her tongue to keep from blurting out, *what a bitch*. Margo had been pulling the sandwich makings from the refrigerator as she talked. She paused, a puzzled look on her face, then said more to herself than to Karen, "Now where did I put that Swiss cheese I just bought?"

"Is that it on the counter?"

"Yeeesss!" Her voice indicated she was disgusted with herself.

"I don't know why I let that girl get to me."

Karen walked over and put a comforting arm around her saying, "Surely you've forgiven her for that by now. That had to have happened some time ago and if Simon still loves her..."

"I wish that were the only thing! She's played Simon for so many years, keeping him in a complete state of confusion. I don't think he has a clue as to what he really feels. I try not to pry and I've bent over backwards to hide my feelings from him, but I swear, it tires me out...she tires me out!"

Margo was close to tears, so Karen decided it was time to change the subject.

"If you'll tell me where you keep the bread, we can get started on these sandwiches. I'm really anxious to get to the houseboat."

Margo smiled, turned and gave Karen a hug. "Didn't mean to unload on you, Kiddo. Why don't you find out what's keeping Simon. I'll take care of the sandwiches while you go back to the hotel to get changed."

Karen found Simon in the garage, sitting on an ice chest, deep in thought.

"I thought you were getting the drinks ready, Mr. Lazy. No time for day dreaming."

He looked up, smiled that smile that made Karen's breath catch, tapped the chest and said, "All ready to go. I was just having a chat with The Man Upstairs. We have these impromptu sessions quite often."

"Sorry I disturbed you. I was just looking for a ride back to my car."

"Oh, right. Clothes change...but I have to say, what you're wearing is lovely. It's so nice to see someone dress up for church."

"Why thank you. However, I hardly think it's appropriate for an outing on the lake."

"By the way, did Mom mention a swim suit?"

"She didn't, but it doesn't matter. I don't have one I can get to. Most of my clothes are in the boxes that I put in storage with the rest of my things."

"Not to worry. Mom always has extra swim suits for when the girls visit. You look to be about the same size as Belinda. I'm sure she has one that will fit you."

The rest of the day was more fun and relaxation than Karen had experienced in years. The swimsuit that Margo gave her was brand new. A one piece black suit with cutouts at the waist, she had put it on at the house, then wore her shorts and tank top over it.

"I bought it for Belinda, but she can't wear it now that she's pregnant and by next year, she'll probably want a newer style. You might as well keep it if you like it."

Simon let out an appreciative wolf whistle when he first saw her in it. *That alone would make me like it*, she thought.

Chapter 15

The cleaning crew arrived at seven on Monday morning, ready to work. Karen met them with the keys, put on one of the masks they handed to her and did a walk through with the foreman. A heavy-set man of around fifty, Robbie was extremely patient with Karen as she pointed out fixtures that she hoped could be salvaged, and numerous decorative items that she would possibly use. Most were old pictures of the saw mill that had formerly occupied the corner. She definitely wanted the old cash register and there was a section of what must have been the sign for the 'Krus Mill' hanging over the doorway.

In her earlier visits she had never ventured into the restrooms, mainly because one of the overturned booths was blocking the entry. Robbie pushed the booth aside and she was delighted with what she found. The ladies room contained an ornate antique mirror over a wooden cabinet with an inset basin that had been plumbed. Everything else, from the paper holder to the water closet, appeared to be antique.

"Everything in here, if possible," she said enthusiastically.

The men's bathroom was equally well preserved and delightfully decorated. Without her saying anything, Robbie asked, "Same here?"

"Definitely."

She was standing outside with Robbie, trying to decide how or where they would store the items she wanted to keep until they were ready for reinstallation, when a truck pulled in. Lettering on the door proclaimed, Kern Construction – Kentucky's Finest Remodeling and New Construction Experts.

Karen looked at Robbie puzzled. "Is this part of your crew?"

"No Ma'am," he replied firmly.

The two men who emerged from the vehicle had to be father and son. They were about the same height with sandy hair, similar body build and near identical facial features. The older one was slightly heavier, with a serious face that was all business. The younger one looked like trouble waiting to happen. He had the roguish look of a fair haired Clark Gable and walked with the same arrogant swagger.

Karen, in a pair of ragged loose-fitting jeans she had borrowed from Margo, a long sleeve cotton shirt, work gloves; again from Margo – and her rattiest sneakers, had come dressed for trudging through the nasty diner. Her hair was tied back with a kerchief and despite the early hour, damp tendrils clung to her face. Seemingly oblivious to her appearance, the young man approached her with a look that made her blush.

Holding out his hand, he said, "You must be Ms Christian. I'm Toby Kern and this is my dad, Martin. Mr. Krus asked us to come by and take a look at the cottage. He wants us to give him an estimate on making it livable."

Karen was fumbling with the gloves and finally managed to free one hand to accept his handshake.

"I…I am…Ms Christian…Karen, that is. We…a…I didn't expect anyone other than the clean up crew this morning."

"Pleased to meet you, Karen," he said, obviously enjoying her flustered response. Then taking her hand in both of his and holding it, he continued. "Mr. Krus was anxious to get the work done on the cottage. He said it would be much more convenient for you to be close by for the construction."

Karen pulled her hand free and extended it to Martin, who had been introducing himself to Robbie.

"Dil said you were a pretty little thing. I suppose I'll have to spend most of my time keepin' Toby at bay if you're gonna' be hangin' around."

Karen's blush grew deeper and she thanked heaven she had enough sun from yesterday to disguise her bright color.

"Come on Dad, I'm not that bad. You're the one who taught me to appreciate beauty."

He had the kind of smile that Karen had always considered dangerous. But his pale blue eyes invited trust, despite their mischievous glint, so she decided she would proceed with caution where Toby Kern was concerned.

Before going to the cottage, Martin went back to the truck and picked up a clipboard. Karen already had the ladder in place and Toby climbed up first, then held out his hand to help her. She didn't really need his help, but accepted the hand rather than make an issue of it.

Without saying a word, he pulled a tape measure from his tool belt and began measuring the overall size.

"Thirty by eighteen," he yelled down to his dad. Less six by twelve for the bathroom and closet. Lower cabinets, standard depth by six feet on north… same depth by four feet on west."

"Pretty nice cabinets," he said, turning to Karen. We could refinish these if you like the oak or put in new ones if you prefer."

"I like the oak. From what I can tell, they look well made. I would like tile for the counter tops, though."

"No you wouldn't," he replied with authority.

When he saw the look on Karen's face, he gave her that crooked little smile, bowed his head and said, "What I meant to say is that I don't recommend it. It looks good and wears well, but it's a bitch to keep clean. At least that's what I've heard from all my customers who have it."

It was Karen's turn to smile. There was actually a slight blush on his face as he spoke.

"Do you have any recommendations?"

"Corian…or there's a new product called Silestone Quartz that my customers seem to really like.

"Sounds expensive."

"Mr. Krus said not to spare expense. He knows my dad and knows that we won't take advantage of him. I can bring you some samples to look at and you can decide then. What kind of flooring are you considering?"

"I honestly haven't had time to consider much of anything. Do you have any recommendations there?"

Karen started when he suddenly jumped up and down a couple of times. He was standing in the center of the room and moved to several different spots, repeating his jumps.

"Good and solid," he said approvingly, and then walked to the corner where the linoleum was curled back and pulled it away from the floor. It tore away easily to reveal wide, sturdy planks beneath.

"Wow, you don't see this often. That's a helluva a sub floor."

Karen walked over and looked at the object of Toby's admiration.

"Can it be sanded down and refinished? I love hardwood floors."

"Unfortunately, that's not a flooring grade plank, but we can definitely put a hardwood floor over it."

Karen was starting to get excited, thinking of what a lovely little cottage it would be with oak floors and cabinets, new countertops…

Her thoughts were interrupted by a voice from the doorway.

"How's it goin' in there," Martin called.

"Come on in Dad. I want you to look at these cabinets."

The elder Kern took the final step into the room and walked over to the cabinets. Running his hand across the upper doors, he opened the end one and closely examined the inside. His face looked positively reverent as he touched the lower corner. Toby stood by with a questioning look in his eyes.

"Yup. This is definitely Pop's work."

Calling Toby over to where he stood, Martin said, "See that little acorn carved in the corner. That was his mark. I knew he had done the cabinets at Dil's folks' house, but I had no idea he did these. He didn't normally do jobs this small."

Toby gave his dad a slap on the back as he said, "Guess Grams was right. He *was* sweet on Ma."

The two men laughed identical laughs and Karen felt like she was in intruder. She must have had an odd look on her face when Toby turned around.

"Don't worry, Karen, we don't charge by the hour for estimates."

"Dil told us we had to have it ready for you to move in within a month," Martin said as they were leaving. "You won't have time for indecision with your choices on the flooring and countertops. You also need to decide how you want the walls finished. I was thinking that if we put a little open divider just inside the door, it would give the illusion of a separate room and still keep the feel of a large open area. That way you won't have to use a single color throughout. I'll have Beverly, our interior designer, give you a call and set up an appointment to come in and look at samples. Appliances and fixtures too."

"But shouldn't Dil have a say in those selections? After all, it's his property."

"Dil doesn't have time for those kinds of things and you're the one who's goin' to live there. It's been nice meetin' you Karen. I'm sure we'll be seein' a lot of each other over a good many months to come."

It was almost noon when Martin and Toby left with numerous sheets of notes, some rough drawings and a little piece of Karen's heart. During the course of their time together, she learned that Martin had suffered a stroke the prior year. He had pretty much turned the business over to Toby, acting, "only as Toby's technical advisor," he had grumbled; "not that he listens to me half the time," he added with a smirk, "but on occasion I get in my two cents worth."

Toby had stood by with a silly grin on his face as his dad spoke. When Martin finished, he turned to Karen with a wink saying, "Now that was a lot more than two cents worth, Dad. I suppose you'll expect me to pay you overtime."

Karen was eager to tell Margo everything they were going to do with the cottage. She also wanted to call Dil and thank him for being so generous. He had not only told the Kerns to use top quality on everything, but had insisted on adding a wrap-around porch that would connect to a full deck on the back.

They would also add a door that opened to the deck. New vinyl siding, double pane windows, new appliances and fixtures in the kitchen and bathroom, and of course, a modern HVAC system were all in the plan.

Chapter 16

When she called Dil, he laughed at her enthusiasm and assured her that he was simply looking out for his own interests. He considered it an investment in the diner.

"If you're comfortable in the cottage, you may be a little more reluctant to run if the diner proves to be more than you bargained for."

"No chance of that," she assured him. "I only hope it will prove to be a sound investment for you."

"Well I have a good feeling about that." He hesitated before adding, "I really owe you a debt of gratitude. You've reconnected me to my family...and to friends from my past."

Karen was pretty sure she knew which *friend* in particular to whom he was referring.

No sooner had she hung up the phone, when there was a knock on the door. Simon stood there holding the tank top she had worn the day before. After her swim, she had slipped her shorts back on over her swimsuit and put the tank top in Margo's beach bag. By the time they got back to the house, she had forgotten all about it.

"You really didn't have to make a trip up here for this, Simon. I could have picked it up tomorrow if you had just phoned."

"Don't worry," he smiled smugly, "This was just my excuse to drop by."

"Why do you need an excuse to drop by?"

"In case you haven't noticed, this is a hotel...and that's a member of my congregation at the front desk."

"Then you'd better leave the door open. Frieda tends to wander around when things are slow. What's the real purpose of your visit, Simon?"

"I needed company. This is Mom's night to host Bunko at the house. I usually stay locked up in my office once the ladies arrive, but I just wasn't inspired to work on...my sermon. Would you like to join me for dinner? Maybe a movie afterward? I've wanted to see Cinderella Man and it's playing in Mt. Sterling."

"A movie! Wow! I haven't been to a movie in...ages. I think the last one I saw was a Disney flick with my niece. I take it Cinderella Man isn't about a prince and a glass loafer."

Simon threw back his head and laughed.

"Clever! And no. It's a true story about a boxer, and it's had great reviews. Russell Crowe and Renee Zelweger."

"Russell Crowe. 'Nuff said," she sighed like a schoolgirl, then added, "I like Renee Zelweger too."

Picking up her purse, she paused thoughtfully, asking, "Why didn't you call Staci? I got the feeling she was a little perturbed with you yesterday and this might have smoothed her ruffled feathers."

The sardonic "humph" emitted by Simon took Karen by surprise.

"I wish it was that easy."

His voice was low and distant, with a note of sadness that made Karen want to cradle him to her like a child. Restraining her impulse, she cheerily said, "So what fine dining establishment did you have in mind?"

His face brightened immediately as he replied, "It's a surprise."

The *surprise* turned out to be a little hole in the wall family restaurant that boasted "The Colonel took lessons from Grandma." It truly was wonderful fried chicken.

"I thought you might appreciate a restaurant inspired by a Grandma."

"I love it. It's a different atmosphere than a diner, but this type of food is what I want for the Krossroads. I've been thinking that I'd like to advertise for local family recipes. Maybe even have a contest, with the winning recipes featured on the menu. Of course, I'll credit the recipe to the person who submits it. What do you think?"

"I think it's a great idea. Honestly, every time we have a pot luck at the church, it's like a competition among all our great cooks. Whose dish is going to get the most compliments? Mom is as competitive as anyone. She doesn't think I notice how she checks everyone else's dishes at the end to see who has the most left over."

Karen laughed as Simon, holding his head perfectly still, lids lowered, allowed his eyes to roam around the table in what had to be an imitation of his mother.

"You're awful, Simon. Such disrespect from a man of the cloth."

His face broke into a broad grin, without a trace of remorse present.

"What time does our movie start?" she hurriedly asked, her heart racing at the sight of that gorgeous smile.

"Not for another forty-five minutes. We have time for a cup of coffee and some conversation."

"I hate to tie up this booth that long."

"Then we'll head on over to the theater. They have a little coffee area in the lobby."

Sitting in the car, Karen couldn't contain her curiosity any longer. Cautiously, she began, "Simon, if I'm being too nosey, please just say so, but I'm curious as to what you meant earlier when you said it wasn't that easy to smooth over Staci's ruffled feathers. Does she think there's something going on between you and me? Because if that's the case, us being together tonight isn't going to make it any easier. Or did you plan on keeping this from her?"

Simon's shoulders slumped and his head practically dropped to his chest.

"I don't know. I don't know anything anymore when it comes to Staci." Lifting his head he turned to Karen.

"I feel guilty burdening you with my woes. You have enough of your own concerns without me adding mine to your load."

"Simon," she began patiently, "I'm the one who brought it up. You and your mother have been so good to me. Right now, you're the only friends I have and I've never believed in one-sided friendships. The least I can do is listen to your woes."

Simon gave her a grateful smile and started the car.

"There are so few people I can talk to about Staci…about our relationship. All my other friends have known us as a couple for so long, that it's hard to know if anything I say might get back to her. I thought of talking to Brian, my friend that's a priest, but that poor man is run ragged. I don't want the little time we have together to be a counseling session for him.

"But you…you're so easy to talk to. That first day we met, I felt completely comfortable with you. Or maybe the proper word is safe. I didn't get the feeling that you were judging me or Staci. But then, how could you, you didn't know either of us."

"But I do know both of you now. Not that well, but I know you enough to form opinions…which I will keep to myself as long as you don't ask for them."

Seating themselves at a table in the empty lobby, coffee in hand, Simon looked around. "Monday night movie goers are few and far between. I have a feeling we might have the theater to ourselves."

The complex had six screens and the parking lot indicated that there weren't many spectators for the seven o'clock showings.

"Well at least we'll have privacy for our conversation." he concluded.

Karen didn't say anything, simply looked at him with raised eyebrows.

"Aaah, where to begin?" He sighed deeply before continuing.

"Needless to say, I just skimmed over my relationship with Staci that first time we met, but Staci's a complicated person. I've spent ten plus years trying to figure her out and pretty much came to the conclusion that, despite what everyone considers as conceit on her part, she's really a very insecure woman. I know I love her, but I'm not quite certain if it's the kind of love on which a marriage can be built. She's been hurt so many times – probably by me as much as anyone."

"How can you say that Simon?" Karen interrupted, despite vowing to herself to keep her mouth shut and just listen. "From everything you've told me, she's the one who keeps walking away from the relationship."

"Because I keep disappointing her."

"How? By being true to yourself? I know what it means to spend a large chunk of your life being someone else because that's what you feel is expected of you…and I don't think that's how real love works. Yes there are compromises that you make, but they have to come from both people involved, not just one."

"But there has to be honesty too. Don't you agree?"

"Of course. But I can't imagine you being dishonest with anyone."

"Then you give me too much credit. I was taught that failure to share a truth is the same as lying."

"I'm not sure I follow you."

"It would be like you representing yourself as a single, available woman, when in fact you aren't single or available at this time. If a man were to ask you out and you failed to tell him that you are in the process of a divorce that is not yet final, it would be the equivalent of a lie. Don't you agree?"

"Well, yes, but I still don't understand what this has to do with yours and Staci's relationship…unless you have a wife hidden somewhere?"

Simon emitted a low laugh that held no humor before he looked into Karen's eyes with an uncertain expression on his face. Taking a deep breath, he obviously decided to go forward with his confession.

"Are you familiar with the Jesse and The Jungle Angel books for children?"

"I love those books. I used to read them to Amy's kids every night. My niece has a stuffed owl she named Donato after Jesse's parrot. When…wait a minute. Are you trying to change the subject on me?"

Instead of answering her question, he asked another of his own.

"Do you recall the name of the author?"

She closed her eyes as if trying to picture the books, and then replied, "I believe it was something like C.S. Lewis, but not him, some other name with initials."

"Same initials, but reversed. Try S.C. Ford – as in Simon Craw-ford."

"You! S.C. Ford is you. But why Simon? Why would you be ashamed of writing children's books? Especially when they are so wonderful."

"It's not a matter of shame, Karen. It's a matter of privacy. I wrote the first one shortly after I came back from South America. The kids there, and especially a little boy named Jesse, were my inspiration. Jesse had only one leg, lived in a garbage dump and had the most upbeat, joyful attitude of anyone I had ever witnessed. When I first met him, he had a crutch that he had made for himself from a piece of wood and a discarded bicycle seat. He was twelve years old, but looked more like eight. He considered himself the guardian of several other homeless kids that lived in the dump with him. When I discovered him and his little band of ragamuffins, it took almost three months to convince them to come to the mission shelter for help. There was a young Methodist couple at the mission who fell in love with him… well, actually, everyone did. If Ken and Lizzie Matheson hadn't adopted him before I left, I vowed I would.

"After I wrote the first story, Mom convinced me I should get it published. I made it clear that any profits from the book should go to the mission and she was the one who suggested I use a fictitious name, since I didn't want any notoriety.

"When it became such a big success, the publisher asked me to write another. It was during the time when Dad got sick and Mom was facing some astronomical doctor and hospital bills. So I signed a contract for ten books, got enough of an advance to help out my parents and since then have been sending half of the profits to the mission.

"After Dad died and I reconnected with Staci, I was all set to tell her about S.C. Ford. I was certain that having a substantial savings account and an income other than what I earn as a pastor, would entice her to marry me. The day I planned on springing my surprise was the day she came in all excited about the job in Atlanta.

"I had a copy of the first Jesse book on my desk and as she sat down, she picked it up, looked at the cover with disgust and asked, 'Who writes this tripe? I read this to my cousin's little boy and it is positively nauseating. An Angel embodied by a parrot, and poor children living happily in a jungle infested with dangerous animals. Really, Simon, I hope you don't promote this kind of fantasy to your congregation.' I don't think I could have been more hurt had she slapped me across the face. I became totally defensive, so when she proposed the job in Atlanta, I didn't even consider it. And I've never told her that I am S.C. Ford. Lying through omission."

Karen sat there stunned. She couldn't have found words even if she could have found her voice. The ones that passed through her mind, she wouldn't dare say out loud. Something was obviously showing on her face. Simon looked at her, distress dimming his beautiful green eyes.

"I'm so sorry, Karen. I shouldn't be burdening you with this."

People were starting to line up at the ticket counter and several couples had sat down at nearby tables.

"That's what friends are for, Simon. I just wish I had some wise advice to offer…something to ease your anguish."

"Why don't we head on in to the theater? I feel better just having shared with a friend. Thanks."

Pushing back his chair, he stood, gracing Karen with his magnificent smile. "As far as giving me any advice, your earlier thoughts on being true to yourself are food for thought. Right now I'm ready to put all thoughts on hold and get lost in a movie."

Chapter 17

Driving to the diner the following morning, Karen was determined to put her musings of the night before on hold and concentrate on what she hoped to accomplish today. Despite her resolve, her mind kept returning to the movie – and subsequently, to her conversation with Simon. She felt that the movie's love story was as inspiring as Jim Braddock's determination to provide a good life for his family in the only way he knew. The fact that his wife set aside her personal fears to support him made her think, *that's how love is supposed to be.*

Arriving at the diner, she saw that the cleaning crew was dressed in special attire for handling hazardous materials. They had determined the day before that the ceiling tiles, as well as the insulation, contained asbestos. Special dumpsters for disposing of the toxic waste were located just outside the back door. Rounding the corner of the diner, she heard loud angry voices coming from the back.

"How the hell am I supposed to start work in the cottage with all this crap in here?"

"That's where the lady told us to put it last night. That crap is what she wants to reuse. We couldn't leave it out in the open to get stolen or damaged. You'll just have to take it up with her, Kern!"

"What's the problem here, gentlemen?" Karen asked, knowing perfectly well what the problem was, but hoping to calm the two men down.

Toby's red face relaxed as he looked down from the door of the cottage. Robbie still held a look of contempt, his eyes focused on Toby as he spoke.

"Good! You're here. Will you kindly let this hothead know that you asked us to put the pieces in the cottage?"

Karen wasn't sure if Toby's red face was left over anger or if he was now blushing. Either way, it made his eyes fairly glow. They reminded her of her mother's big gray tabby – when he was ready to pounce on something.

"I'm sorry, Toby. I didn't realize you would be here so early this morning. I have a portable storage unit being delivered today. Meanwhile, we can just move the things outside until it arrives."

Now she was certain he was blushing as he looked down and muttered, "Fine. I'll have my men…"

Robbie cut him off. "We'll take care of it. We're the ones who put it there."

"Or we could all work together and have it out in no time," Karen cheerfully volunteered.

"Whatever!" Toby mumbled.

The set of temporary steps leading up to the door made the task much easier than it had been the day before. Within twenty minutes, both crews were back at their individual tasks, while Karen considered the different pieces scattered on the ground. She had to determine what exactly would need to be done with each to render it useful. She was studying the little vanity cabinet from the ladies room when Toby approached.

"Sorry about the little altercation. I have a habit of setting goals for my men each day and I expect them to be met. I was just thrown by the unforeseen."

"Don't you think it's Robbie you need to apologize to?"

"Already done. He's a pretty decent guy. Reminded me that there's probably asbestos in the cottage as well, and volunteered to let us use the suits and containers to clear it out. I wasn't originally planning on redoing the walls, but we really do need to pull out any insulation in them. It'll actually work better for rewiring and setting up the HVAC."

"Sounds like you might be better off just tearing down the entire cottage and starting from scratch."

"No way! It's actually very well built."

"That's good to know," she said, turning back to her inspection of the vanity. He was looking at her with those cat eyes, as if studying his prey, and she was beginning to feel uncomfortable.

"Was there something else you needed?" She finally asked, not turning to look at him.

"Huh…oh yeah. If you're free this afternoon, I'd like for you to run over to Mt. Sterling and look at the flooring and countertop samples. Fixtures, too. Bev will be able to help you with paint and wall coverings as well."

"Actually, as soon as the storage unit gets here, I'm free."

Beverly was a delightful, slightly overweight woman, who had to be around the same age as Karen. Bright red hair topped a lightly freckled face that featured deep set brown eyes and a full mouth, giving her a naive school girl appearance. This was immediately dispelled by her completely professional demeanor.

After more than three hours of going over hundreds of samples of everything from paint to lighting fixtures, Karen was dizzy. "I've got to be taking up way too much of your time," she protested.

"Toby gave me implicit instructions to give you as much time as you needed today. What you have to understand about Toby is, once you make a selection, there's no turning back."

"A no nonsense kinda guy, huh?"

"Just like his dad. If they weren't so good at what they do, they'd probably run away most of their business. When they build a custom home, if the owners try to change anything they've already approved, they quote an outrageous price for the change. If, as Martin says, 'they're stupid enough to pay for it, I'm smart enough to take their money.'"

Karen laughed at Bev's gruff imitation of Martin.

"Well I'm certainly not going to have Dil paying for my mistakes. If my choices don't turn out like I picture them, I'll learn to live with it."

Driving back to Farmers, Karen felt really good about her selections. She began imagining the finished cottage and her heart raced with excitement. My own place! She thought, and then giggled aloud. She was still feeling giddy when she opened the door to her room to hear the phone ringing insistently. "I'm coming, I'm coming," she said, fumbling with the samples she had taken home to share with Margo.

"Hey, Kiddo. How'd your date with Simon go?"

Shocked at Margo's question, she stuttered, "Uh...it...it wasn't really a date, Margo."

Before Karen could continue, Margo burst into laughter.

"I know, I know," she said, "Simon told me about it. He really appreciates having someone he can talk to. I also know it can't be me. I'm not an impartial listener."

"So did you call just to give me grief or is there some other reason?" Karen teased.

"I was hoping I could catch you before you ate. Simon is with his men's bible study group this evening. They always go out for pizza afterward, so I'm flyin' solo tonight and wanted some company. Are you up to it?"

"Sound's good, but why don't you let me pick something up so you won't have to cook."

"Too late. It's nothing fancy…just a chicken casserole and salad. And for dessert, a huge helping of girl talk and wine."

"I would have thought you had your fill of girl talk with your bunko buddies."

"We don't talk. We gossip. It's *so* not the same thing."

"What time?"

"As soon as you can get here."

Hanging up the phone, Karen was smiling from ear to ear. Margo sounded as keyed up as she had been on her drive home from Mt. Sterling. Something was going on and she couldn't wait to know what it was. Checking herself in the mirror, she decided that the Capri's and t-shirt she was wearing would be fine. A quick brush through her hair, a touch of lip gloss and she would be ready. Just as she was picking up her purse, the phone rang again.

"Karen…this is Toby."

"Oh, hi Toby. What can I do for you?"

"I was just wondering if you had dinner plans."

"Actually, I was just headed out the door for Margo's."

"Well I could meet you there. Where is it?"

Laughing, she replied, "Margo Crawford's house. She's my real estate agent and we've become friends. Was there something we need to discuss?"

The silence at the other end of the line had Karen imagining Toby's face glowing red.

"It can wait 'til tomorrow. Enjoy your evening."

Click!

Karen stared at the receiver, shook her head and carefully returned it to the cradle.

What was that about?

The chicken and broccoli casserole was quite scrumptious. It was similar to one she made using Granny's recipe. When she said as much to Margo, her response was a quirky smile, followed by, "Straight from the Campbell's soup label."

"No way," Karen said, "I've made that one before and this tasted different."

"You caught me. I added some fresh herbs and Vidalia's to my rice."

Finishing up the dishes, the two women retired to the living room with the remainder of the bottle of Pinot Grigio that had accompanied the dinner. They had no sooner settled on the couch, than Margo blurted out, "Dil asked me to dinner on Saturday."

Karen tried to subdue her laughter. "So…what took him so long?"

"What do you mean? Did he say something to you?"

"Not verbally…but, my gosh Margo, how could you miss the way he's been drinking you in with his eyes ever since that first day we met with him?"

The already rosy color on Margo's face, probably a result of two glasses of wine, became a deep scarlet. Karen thought it was positively adorable and wanted to reach over and give her a hug.

Shifting uncomfortably on the couch, Margo spoke with a frustrated moan, "I don't know how to date any more! It's been forty years since I've been with any man other than Ralph. Oh, God, I don't even know what I'm saying. I mean, how do dates work these days? From everything you see in the movies, things usually go from the restaurant to the bedroom. Dil is so much worldlier than I am. Is that what he'll expect?"

Karen was biting her lip so hard to keep from bursting into laughter that she was certain she had drawn blood. What she wasn't certain of, was if Margo's question was rhetorical or if she expected an answer. Until then, Margo hadn't looked at Karen while she spoke, but her eyes refocused on her and they undoubtedly expected an answer.

"First of all, I think Dil has much too much respect for you to expect such a thing – but more important, why did you accept if you had those kind of doubts about his character?"

"I haven't accepted…yet."

"Yet?"

"I said I'd get back to him. I told him that my girls might be coming to visit this weekend."

"Well that's great. Maybe you could invite him to join you here…"

"I lied. They aren't coming until next week."

"Hmmm. Not a good way to start a relationship."

"Oh, I know. It just took me off guard when he called. I needed time to think about it."

"Then why didn't you just tell him that?"

"I didn't want to have to refuse him. I mean, if I thought about it and decided against it…"

"For Pete's sake, Margo, why don't you just admit that you're as attracted to him as he is to you? You know you want to go."

"I suppose you're right," she confessed, "but I also have to consider the fact that he is a client. I would never want to do anything that could jeopardize his business relationship with you."

"Again, Margo, I don't think you're giving him credit for being the gentleman he is. I had a chance to get to know him a little better last weekend, and I have to say, I admire him even more. I say, give him a chance."

"If I say yes, I'll be calling on you for further advice...and to handle any concerns from my son."

"You don't think Simon will approve of this relationship?"

"Let's not jump the gun. It's hardly a relationship at this point. But to answer your question, he'll be supportive as long as he approves of Dil."

"Does he know that you knew him from high school?"

"I've probably mentioned it. I just can't remember if I ever told him that we had once dated."

Karen was about to ask why that would make a difference when the sound of a car door slamming made both women look toward the front window. Simon was approaching the door as Margo looked at her watch.

"You're home early," she said as soon as the door opened. "Is anything wrong?"

"No. A couple of the guys were no-shows, so the discussion didn't go nearly so long as usual. Hi, Karen. This is a pleasant surprise."

Karen couldn't help but notice that his face looked haggard. Had he spent a sleepless night after their conversation of the night before? The drive home after the movie had been relatively quiet. What little was said had to do with the movie. When he dropped her off, she assured him that he didn't need to walk her to her door. He posted no arguments and simply said, "Thanks for the company," to which she replied, "Thank you for a wonderful meal and a most pleasant evening." She wasn't certain if her words even registered with him since he appeared to be miles away as she closed the car door.

"I asked Karen to keep me company. You know how much I hate eating alone."

"I probably would have enjoyed your casserole more than the pizza, tonight. I know I would have preferred the company."

His tentative smile at the two women looked forced, causing Margo to wonder what may have happened with his men's group to warrant that remark. He usually thoroughly enjoyed his evenings with the guys.

"Are you okay, Simon? You don't look well," she tested.

"It's nothing that a good night's sleep won't cure. I'll leave you two ladies to your wine and girl talk."

Karen picked up her wine glass and downed the last sip, saying, "Actually, I need to run. I'm meeting the contractor early tomorrow morning to finalize some plans for the cottage."

"Now I feel like I've chased you off."

"Not at all," Karen reassured him. "I'll call you tomorrow evening, Margo."

She reached over and gave Margo a hug, grabbed her purse and brushed past Simon with a quick, "Get some rest. You look tired."

Driving back to the motel, her mind bounced back and forth between Margo's dilemma and Simon's ragged appearance. If the source of his anguish was Staci, why didn't he just drop her? From everything he and Margo had told her, she had brought him nothing but grief. Did Simon really love her that deeply? *Why do I care?*

"Because I care for Simon and Margo and want them to be happy," she said aloud.

Between the two of them and Dil, they had sort of become her family in this new life she was establishing. Of course their happiness was important to her.

Thinking about family, she realized she hadn't called Amy or her parents in two days. She was anxious to share everything that was happening with Amy, but it was getting harder to keep her parents in the dark as to where she was and what she was doing. She had determined that once she had the signed divorce papers in hand, she would tell them everything.

Chapter 18

"I said yes and he wants to take me to some fancy place in Lexington. I'll need your help on choosing something to wear."

Margo sounded like a teenager preparing for her first date. She had come by the site and offered to take Karen to lunch. Her arrival coincided with Toby's appearance in the storage unit, and Karen had the feeling he was getting ready to ask her to lunch as well. She introduced him to Margo as Dil's contractor and it was easy to see that Margo was taken in by his roguish good looks. On the drive to Morehead, she commented on the way he looked at Karen.

"Talk about drinking someone in with their eyes," she teased.

"I don't take it personally," Karen assured her. "I have a feeling he looks that way at every woman he meets."

During their lunch, Karen agreed to come by the house and look over Margo's wardrobe.

"Everything I have is strictly business wear or far too casual. I have a couple of cocktail dresses that I wore when Ralph and I went on a cruise, but they're probably too dressy and definitely outdated. I may have to buy something new, which seems a little frivolous, but I haven't been to Lexington for an evening out in ages – and certainly not to a fancy restaurant."

"Well if we don't find anything in your closet, I'll go shopping with you. Where do you usually buy your clothes?"

"Mostly from Chadwick's mail order catalog. I hate shopping for clothes, but there's no time for mail orders. We'll most likely have to drive to Lexington to find anything."

"That's fine with me. I've wanted to check out Lexington. I'm sure I'll have to be going there fairly often when I start buying supplies for the restaurant."

"Maybe I can get Sandy to join us for lunch. She works in the City Planning offices so may not be able to get away. Of course you'll be meeting both my girls over the fourth of July. They always come here for a few days of boating and fireworks. I'm anxious for you to meet them. You will be joining us for the holiday, won't you? Simon was supposed to ask you about it."

"He didn't mention it, and I'd love to join you. I'm anxious to meet your daughters as well."

Karen hesitated before asking, "Will Staci be joining us?"

"No, thank God. She'll be in Cancun with her parents. They have a time-share or something there, and go every year at this time."

"Simon doesn't go with them?"

"She's never invited him. It's *her family time with her parents*. Actually, I think Simon is relieved. From the little she shares about their time there, they don't really do much more than sit around on the beach and drink. Simon would never admit that he'd rather Staci wasn't around when his sisters are here. He doesn't get to enjoy them if she is because she demands every ounce of his attention. It's almost as if she resents the close relationship they have."

"How do the girls feel toward her?"

"Pretty much the same as me. They love Simon too much to ever do or say anything to hurt him. As long as Staci is a part of his life, they'll do anything and everything to accept and love her. If he ends up marrying her, we'll all do everything in our power to support that choice."

Karen immediately remembered how Amy had withheld her true feelings toward Chase all those years. Smiling sadly at Margo, she said, "Yes. That's what families do."

On the drive to Lexington, they talked about business. Karen wanted to share the things Dil had told her about his past, but realized it was something he needed to tell Margo himself. They avoided talking about Simon, which always led to including Staci in the conversation. Neither of them wanted to rehash that topic.

"Did you get in touch with Sandy?" Karen asked as they pulled in the parking lot of the Lexington Mall.

"Yes, but she won't be able to join us. She has a lunch meeting with one of the City Planners and couldn't reschedule this late. I think she was as disappointed as I was. She's anxious to meet you."

"You've talked about me to your girls?"

"Of course. You're a part of my life now. I think our relationship has gone beyond a business association. I would certainly never dream of asking any other client to go shopping with me for a date dress."

Margo was smiling playfully as she spoke. It reminded Karen of how she and Amy bantered when they were together.

Their first stop was Macys, where, after trying on numerous outfits, they found a beautiful two piece navy ensemble adorned with a trace of beading on the top. It was elegant and tasteful; dressy, but not formal. The price tag, however, was over two hundred dollars and as perfect as it was, Margo started to replace it on the rack when a saleswoman approached.

"I was just getting ready to move these over to the sales rack. They're forty percent off and I have some early bird coupons up front that will give you an additional fifteen percent."

Before Margo said anything, Karen blurted out, "She'll take it."

"You sound just like one of my daughters," Margo said with mock disgust. "They are constantly reminding me that it's okay to spend a little money on myself – but old habits are hard to break."

"I'm sorry. That was presumptuous of me, but it looked so perfect on you."

"You're right. It is perfect. Now we have to find some equally stylish shoes. All of mine are far too sensible."

They spent another hour looking for shoes and accessories, had a delightful lunch at a small bistro restaurant and then headed back to Farmers.

It was three in the afternoon when Karen stopped by the diner to find that the clean-up was completed. Robbie's crew was gone, but there were several trucks bearing the Kern's Construction logo parked in the back.

Little more than skeletal remains were left inside the diner. Karen's imagination immediately took over as she pictured the new counter, booths and tables throughout, and local memorabilia adorning the walls. Amy had suggested that she check out the county libraries for copies of old pictures that could be placed in antique frames. Margo said there was a large antique mall just a short distance away in an old schoolhouse.

Wishing that Amy was here to help her with the decorating, she decided that she would ask her to come down for a few weeks when her kids went to spend their month at Ronnie's parents' farm. She was sure that Ronnie wouldn't mind after all the hunting and fishing trips he took with his brothers. He might even want to come along once she told him that Cave Run was such a great fishing lake. Walking back into the kitchen area, she was pleased to see that the smoker had been thoroughly cleaned. Even the inside racks appeared to be in good shape. Carefully, she reached in and lifted the lower pan, revealing the area where logs were fed into the smoker from an outside door. She recalled seeing the metal door at the back of the diner, but hadn't connected it to the smoker.

Dil had told her that his father designed the smoker himself and had it custom built. She liked the idea that the wood could be kept outside, remembering how she had once picked up a log to feed the smoker at Handi's, only to have some kind of spider jump on her arm. She totally freaked. It had been very entertaining to the kitchen staff, but after that, she never handled a log again and was certain that she didn't want spiders inside her kitchen.

Voices from outside drew her attention to the back door just as Toby stepped inside.

"I thought that was your tank parked out front," he said, flashing that dangerous Clark Gable smile of his.

"What do you have against my car?" she shot back. "Big Betsy has been a good and faithful companion for almost five years."

His laugh was as enticing as his smile.

"Someone like you should be driving a flashy little sports car. A convertible with the top down and your wild curls dancing around your face."

He walked over and fingered one of the curls that had escaped from the French braid – one of the few ways she could contain her wild mane.

"If you're flirting with me, Toby, I should warn you, I'm still a married woman. My divorce won't be final for several months."

He didn't back off, but dropped his hand saying, "Dil said you were in the process of a divorce…up in Oregon, was it?"

"That's right. What else did he tell you about me?"

"That's pretty much it. But just so you know, I'm single and currently not seeing anyone special. Since we'll be spending a lot of time together, I'd like to get to know you better."

"Well, that's straight forward enough," she said, not hiding her surprise. "But just so you know, I intend to put my full attention toward getting this diner up and running and have no intention of getting involved with any man for a good, long time."

"We'll see," he smiled, with much too much confidence, then abruptly added, "I have some plans drawn up that I want you to look over. I'm thinking we can enlarge the bathrooms a bit without cutting the dining area if we come to about here in the kitchen."

He walked over and stood just beyond the back door, all business again.

"Then, we can add a dry storage area with a walk-in freezer/refrigerator out back, so you won't lose any of the kitchen's working area."

Sitting down on his heels, he laid out a set of blueprints on the floor. Karen squatted down next to him and studied the plans as he continued describing them to her.

"I like it," she said. "I take it these are reach-in boxes along this wall?"

"Right. And your dishwashing area is here, next to the bathroom wall."

After walking through the blueprints, Karen's enthusiasm was building and by the time they stepped out front, she was beyond excited.

"It's really happening. I'm actually going to have my own diner. Who drew up these plans? They are positively perfect," she praised.

This time, Toby's smile was pure pride.

"I studied architecture and design, along with construction engineering. This is my first commercial kitchen, but I've done enough custom kitchens to know what it means to have everything accessible. I'm glad you like it."

They spent another twenty minutes discussing the parking lot and landscape plans. When Toby mentioned that Dil said there had been an outdoor seating pavilion for summertime overflow, Karen thought she might burst with excitement.

"It really gets that busy in the summer time?"

"From what I hear, yes. I'm usually too busy in the summer to partake of all the leisure activities on the lake. I prefer spending my free time on the golf course. Do you golf?"

"Not really," she replied, thinking about how she had tried it a couple of times with Chase, only to be declared the world's most uncoordinated golfer.

"Good."

His reply rather stunned her.

"Why good?" she inquired, feeling somehow offended.

"Women don't belong on golf courses," he declared firmly, "Unless they're professionals – none of which we have around here."

"You realize that remark sounds totally chauvinistic."

"Guilty as charged. I was raised to believe that women are equal to men in all things, but each should have their own areas of independence. Mine is the golf course. I'll take a woman to any spectator sport that she cares to attend – hell, I'd even take her fishing if she really enjoys it."

"How very magnanimous of you," Karen sarcastically mumbled.

Toby didn't even flinch. Just smiled, saying, "I think so."

Karen had to smile as well, wondering how serious he really was. She halfway believed he was just trying to get a defensive reaction from her. She opted not to give him that satisfaction. Changing the subject, she asked, "Can I take a look at what's happening in the cottage?"

"Nope. You are forbidden anywhere near the cottage until it's ready for occupancy."

"You're kidding. But what…"

"But nothing. You've selected everything you have any say about. I don't want you in there changing your mind and telling me how to do my job. That's Bev's role."

He was smiling, but she knew he wasn't kidding.

"So how long before I'll be able to view my future home?"

"We should be done in about two weeks, barring no hold-ups on supplies."

"Really? That soon. I'd better get busy finding furniture."

"Whatever keeps you out of my hair."

This time, she knew he was teasing her.

Chapter 19

Simon still appeared a bit haggard at the Sunday services, but Margo fairly glowed. Karen caught a glimpse of her as Margo seated herself in the front row next to Staci.

Having spent the past several days haunting furniture stores and department stores in Morehead and Mt. Sterling, she had hoped that Margo would call to tell her about the date. From the look on her face, she guessed that it went well.

Simon had chosen 1 Corinthians, Chapter 13 for the reading and his sermon theme. As he emphasized the qualities of love, Karen had to wonder if this was a personal plea to Staci, who appeared positively bored. From two rows back, Karen couldn't see her face, but the way she kept looking up at the ceiling, apparently shifting her crossed legs from one to the other, turning and leaning forward with each shift, it was obvious that she wasn't listening.

What a fool you are, Staci Perkins, Karen thought, then realized she was so distracted by Staci that she was missing much of the sermon herself. Shaking off her harsh thoughts, she turned to see Simon looking in her direction. His hand rested affectionately on the head of a small boy.

"...as a child loves. Completely. Unconditionally. Without reservation. Trusting that they will be loved in return. The way Jesus loved."

Giving the boy's already unruly hair an affectionate tousle, he returned to the front of the church saying, "Let us pray."

As always, Simon stood outside the door, shaking hands and speaking to each person as they exited. Karen waited inside until Margo got up to leave. Slipping her arm through Margo's as she passed, she said nothing as she gave her a questioning look. Margo's response was a rosy blush, followed by a gentle poke in Karen's ribs with her elbow.

"You do know that you're glowing."

"Shuuu! Someone might hear you."

Karen lowered her voice to a barely audible whisper. "You do know that you're glowing," she repeated.

Another poke in the ribs, this one not quite so gentle.

By then, no one else was in the church, so Karen spoke in a normal voice as they stopped walking.

"I really hoped you would call me yesterday. You must know I'm dying to know how your date went."

"I didn't get home until late yesterday afternoon…and before you let your imagination run away, it wasn't like that!"

"I didn't say a word," Karen protested with feigned offense.

Margo's face turned soft and dreamy as she began. "You were right, you know. Dil is a perfect gentleman."

"So are you going to tell me what happened?"

Margo was blushing again, but more in delight than embarrassment.

"Well, first of all, the dinner was fabulous. I don't even want to think about how much it cost. I have a feeling the bottle of wine alone was more than a month's groceries for Simon and me. It was still early when we finished dinner and he asked if I would like to see his home. It's actually a horse farm, just this side of Lexington. He has about a half dozen thoroughbred horses that he raises as a hobby and for personal use. One was sired by a Derby winner, but he has no interest in training them for racing.

"One of the reasons I agreed to go to the house was because he assured me we would not be alone. He has a live-in housekeeper that he calls 'Mama Sanchez.' She is an adorable little Hispanic woman, probably younger than Dil, but she definitely acts like a mother to him. She has three grown children, two in college and one married son who lives in Des Moines.

"After Dil gave me a tour of the property in his golf cart, we sat on the patio overlooking his pool, drank wine, and talked for hours. He told me about his conversation with you last week. I just want you to know that he's much harder on himself than he deserves to be. Regardless of his past, he's become a hard-working, responsible man and shouldn't dwell on the past. When I said as much to him, he thanked me. He is so sweet, and incredibly humble.

"Anyway…back to the subject. We had no idea how long we sat there catching up on way too many years, until Gloria…Mama Sanchez…came out to ask if *Mr. Dil* would like for her to prepare one of the guest rooms for his *lady friend*.

"I couldn't see having him drive all the way here and back at that late hour, but I certainly hadn't packed an overnight bag. I was debating about what to do, when Gloria said she had some clothes that her daughter left the last time she had visited. She was sure they would fit me. I got to wondering how often Dil had 'lady friends' spend the night, as Gloria led me up to a beautifully decorated, very feminine bedroom.

"She must have read my mind, because she said, 'You are Mr. Dil's first lady to bring to his home. You must be most especial.'"

Margo's face was radiant. She emitted a soft sigh, pausing only briefly before continuing.

"I can't believe how well I slept. When I awoke the next morning, a pair of cropped khakis and a lovely blouse were laid out on a chair. Gloria was right about the fit, but the look was much too young for me. The canvas sandals were about a half size smaller than I wear, but weren't a bad fit. I was a little dubious as to my appearance, but I have to say, I felt twenty years younger when I walked down to join Dil for breakfast. His smile when he saw me almost made my knees buckle.

"Now I have to tell you that I haven't been horseback riding since I was a teenager, but Dil insisted that we go for a ride before he took me home. I absolutely loved it. He invited me back next week and when I told him the girls would definitely be here for the Fourth of July weekend, he said we should all come. You too. He mentioned you specifically, so you can't say no."

"It sounds wonderful. I love riding. It's something that Amy and I used to do regularly before we both got married. I think she still rides when she visits her in-laws' farm."

"Trust me…it's like riding a bicycle. Once you're in the saddle, it all comes back. We even had a bit of a race on our way back to the stables. I won, but only because I took off before I informed Dil that it was a race. We were both laughing like a couple of kids. When he lifted me off my horse, he gave me the sweetest kiss. Then he apologized for taking advantage of 'my vulnerable position.' Can you imagine? I thought that kind of chivalry died long ago."

"Well I hope you grabbed him and laid a hot wet one on him," Karen said, forgetting that she was talking to a fifty-six year old widow…in a church. When Margo's face turned bright red, Karen quickly added, "Oh Margo, I'm so sorry. That was…"

Margo started giggling, her face still flushed with color.

"But that's exactly what I did. I mean…maybe not quite the kind of kiss you described, but I definitely kissed him back."

Karen couldn't determine if the deep sigh Margo emitted was a result of remembering the kiss or some kind of regret for her actions. The look she now wore was one of confusion.

"Seriously, Karen, do you think it's possible to find two perfect men in one lifetime? I honestly never considered getting involved with another man after Ralph died. I'm happy with my life, but…"

"Margo, do you ever read magazines or listen to current health reports. Don't you know that sixty is the new forty…or something like that. We are way past the time when women believed they were old at your age. In truth, you are in the prime of your life. I would wager any amount of money that Simon, and your girls as well, would be delighted if you found someone to love again."

As if on cue, Simon appeared in the doorway.

"No gossiping in the Lord's house, Ladies," he admonished as he walked down the aisle toward them.

"Simon Crawford, since when do you accuse your own mother of such a heinous thing as gossip?" Margo inquired indignantly.

Simon simply smiled at his mother saying, "Actually, I need to close things up here." Then turning to Karen he asked, "Will you be joining us for brunch?"

Margo didn't give her a chance to answer.

"Of course she will," Margo replied. "We have to talk about our plans for next weekend. Will Staci be joining us as well?"

"No. She has to finish her packing. They fly out tonight for Miami, then on to Cancun tomorrow morning. I'm going to join them for an early dinner, then drive them to the airport. Everett's car is in the shop and there's no way they can fit the three of them plus all the luggage in Mona's little Audi or Staci's Miata."

Karen had already decided that, despite her feelings toward Staci, she would join Margo and the girls in their support of Simon's choice. She attempted a sincere tone as she said, "It's too bad that she won't be able to join us."

Margo gave her an approving smile.

Brunch was Blueberry pancakes, country ham, scrambled eggs, fresh squeezed orange juice and fresh fruit. Karen fairly groaned as she got up from the table.

"Pastor Crawford, I do believe I need to confess to indulging in the sin of gluttony," she sighed.

"You'll have to talk to the Lord about it, Sister Karen, since this weak mortal is equally sinful."

Margo smiled with satisfaction, enjoying their lighthearted exchange.

"I vote we allow the cook to sit and rest while we tend to the clean-up," Simon volunteered, as he picked up his plate.

"Seconded and passed. No arguments. Go put your feet up and relax. Would you like some more coffee? I'll bring it to you," Karen added as she playfully pushed Margo in the direction of the living room.

"I'm not about to argue with that offer," Margo sighed, heading for the recliner.

While cleaning the kitchen, Simon and Karen talked about the progress at the Diner and the upcoming Fourth of July weekend; and bantered about the proper way to load a dishwasher. Margo listened more to the hum of their voices and the occasional laughter than to what actual words were spoken, and was soon lulled to sleep.

"I'm not sure if any of the equipment from the Morehead Café will fit into the plans that Toby showed me yesterday. According to him, Dil wants me to have all new equipment. Toby said they have a contractor who does custom fixtures for restaurants and he would get me a good price on whatever I wanted."

"I have to agree that starting with new equipment sounds like the better idea. When you're dealing with refrigeration and stoves, you could be buying someone else's problems."

"I agree with that on everything except the grill. It takes a long time to season a grill properly. The grill from the café is small, so I'll have to go to a used equipment dealer for a seasoned grill. Everything below it can be new. Toby said he would see what he could find."

"Don't they have pre-seasoned grills on the new equipment these days? I think I heard someone say that one time."

"It's not exactly the same. There's something about a grill that's been seasoned by actual food. If the grill is properly cleaned each day, it develops a certain smoothness that prevents sticking and somehow enhances the flavors of the items you cook. That might sound silly, but it's true. Ask any good grill cook."

"I'll take your word for it since the only grill I cook on is the Weber. I know nothing about such things."

"Time to change the subject," Karen said as she glanced into the living room to see Margo's eyes closed. A gentle nasal snore resounded from that direction, but she wasn't sure if it came from Margo or the large Calico cat that was curled up on her stomach.

Following her eyes, Simon smiled, saying, "She's sleeping. Princess will only climb on your lap if you're asleep." Then cocking his head, his smile changed to a quirky grin. "I have a feeling that the new subject is going to be Dil Krus."

"So-o-o-o, what do you think of him?"

"I just met him Friday night for about five minutes. Hardly enough time to form a lasting opinion."

"Okay, just first impressions."

"Good. I liked the way he looked at Mom. Not leering, but…appreciatively. He has an air of confidence about him without being arrogant."

"Very good read. I think you'll like him even more as you get to know him."

"I should have a chance for that this weekend, since he'll be joining us on the houseboat and then we'll be spending a day with him at his horse farm."

A loud "me-e-o-ow," followed by a thump alerted them to a now awake Margo.

"Did I hear something about Dil's horse farm?"

Margo's groggy question came just as Simon had pushed the start button on the dishwasher.

Over the next few hours, they talked about the plans for the upcoming weekend. Karen insisted that she would prepare dinner for everyone on their day of arrival.

"The girls should both be here by five on Friday and I expect to be home no later than four. Dil might not get here until closer to six, so would eating at seven be too late for you, Karen?"

"Not at all. I'll have some snacks and hors d'oeuvres to hold us over 'til then. Everything will be prepared and I'll just have to work on a few last minute items, so should be able to join everyone for most of the evening."

"And you're still not going to tell us what your menu is." Simon teased.

"No. That's why everyone has to stay in the sunroom while I'm in the kitchen."

The kitchen, dining room and living room were all open, so Margo had suggested the sunroom would be the best place to gather. Karen made it clear that she wanted the meal to be a surprise. She had already asked if anyone had any qualms about trying new things, in case none of them had eaten wild rice or Cornish game hens before. Both Margo and Simon assured her they were certain that whatever she prepared would be "enjoyed by all."

The plans for the rest of the weekend consisted of spending Saturday on the houseboat; then after church on Sunday, they would all head to Dil's for brunch; an afternoon of horseback riding and lounging around the pool; followed by an evening barbeque and fireworks. Everyone would spend the night and then head back to Farmers in time for the annual Fourth of July picnic at the church.

Karen was beyond excited about the upcoming weekend. Her thoughts went back to last year's Fourth of July when Amy and Ronnie had invited her and Chase to join them at Ronnie's parents' farm for an old fashioned family celebration. She could almost hear Amy's enthusiastic invitation.

"Mom and Dad are coming and Ronnie promised lots of food, lots of games, lots of children and more fireworks than the White House display."

However, without discussing it with her, Chase had already invited two couples from his office and an *important client* over for dinner, quashing any chance of a real family day. With his familiar charm, he cooed in Karen's ear, "You know how much I love to show off what a wonderful cook my wife is."

Of course, she relented; so on the Fourth, while the men golfed, the women sat around discussing trivial topics as they *watched* Karen prepare both lunch and dinner.

It was late afternoon by the time Karen got back to her room. She immediately called Amy to find out what she and Ronnie had decided about coming to visit. The boys usually went to their grandparents in mid July and she hoped they would come soon afterward. If Toby held to his schedule, she should be in the cottage by then. She wasn't certain how far along the Diner would be, but felt confident that with Amy's eye for décor, she would be able to give her lots of ideas. Meanwhile they could shop together for antiques and decorating items for both the diner and the cottage.

"How does the last week of July sound?" Amy asked, not hiding the excitement in her voice. "Do you think you could handle us for about ten days?"

"Oh Amy, that sounds wonderful. I take it when you said *us*, that means Ronnie will be coming as well."

"I think he's as anxious as I am to see what's there that has enticed my little sister to move to the middle of nowhere. At least that's what he says to me. Actually, I think it's the fishing at Cave Run Lake that has him counting the days. He's been on the computer checking out everything about the area."

"Well tell him he doesn't have to worry about bringing fishing gear. Simon has more than enough for all of us if we get our fill of shopping and just want to relax."

"Simon? Who exactly is Simon?" Amy taunted.

"C'mon Amy, I've mentioned Simon before...haven't I?"

They were on the phone for another thirty minutes while Karen talked about Margo, Simon, and Dil. She explained how Simon was seriously involved with a woman he had known since he was seventeen. Without giving too many details, nor expressing her own feelings about Staci, she made it clear that Simon was a good friend, as well as pastor at the little church she was now attending. By the time they said their good-byes, Karen's elation had faded to a confused melancholy and she wasn't sure where it came from. With a concerted effort, she shook off her negative feelings and began planning the shopping list for next Friday's dinner.

Ronnie walked in the kitchen just as Amy hung up the phone. The scowl on her face was a bit confusing to him. He knew she had been talking to Karen about their upcoming visit and expected her to be fairly dancing with excitement by the end of their conversation.

"What's up?" he tested, "Something awry regarding our trip?"

"Oh no!" she immediately replied, replacing the scowl with a forced smile.

Ronnie cocked his head, raising one eyebrow. He didn't have to say a word.

Amy waved her hand in a dismissive gesture while shaking her head.

"It's nothing. I hope. My big sisterly instincts are messing with my brain and I sense that Karen is falling for someone she can't have. I just worry that she may be setting herself up for another heartache."

Chapter 20

Several trucks and a Lowe's delivery van were parked to the side of the Diner and a blast of country music vibrated through the air. The door to the diner was open, so Karen peeked in to see Toby walking around the kitchen area, marking each stud with a green marker. He was obviously unaware of her presence, so she stepped just inside the door and watched him as he ran his hand along each stud, then made a note on a clipboard and wrote either RP or RF. Sometimes he added a slash, an E and a number next to the RP.

It was early morning, but the sun was already promising a scorcher. Toby's t-shirt was soaked in sweat and his muscular arms glistened with moisture. As Karen openly stared at him, she asked herself, *why am I not more attracted to this man? Certainly his physical resemblances to Chase aren't keeping me from seeing him as an individual? He's obviously interested in me and there would be no harm in accepting one of his invitations to lunch or dinner.*

She was so engrossed in her thoughts that she hadn't noticed him look over his shoulder, catching her study of him. When he said, "Good morning," displaying that lopsided grin, she instantly blushed.

"Uh…good morning. I was just wondering what you were doing," she mumbled, knowing perfectly well that he wasn't buying it. But it did provide a good diversion. *Ah yes!* She thought, *ask a man about his work and it will distract him every time.*

Toby immediately began explaining that the markings were to identify the studs for either replacement or reinforcement. The additional markings were for electrical wiring studs for either 110 or 220 connections. Walking over to a table in the middle of the kitchen, he unrolled a set of plans containing the schematics for the electrical wiring. After talking nonstop for several minutes, he suddenly lifted his head and announced, "By the way, I think I found a good used grill for you. It's a seventy-two inch custom commercial grill. It's split into two separate surfaces. Two thirds flat and one third ribbed. Both the grill and the under works are practically new, but it was heavily used for just over a year. I can get it for less than half the original cost."

"Why would someone be selling a good grill if it's just a year old?"

"Sort of a sad story."

"I don't want to keep you from your work, but I'd like to hear it."

Looking at his watch, Toby said, "I'm about ready for a coffee break. Would you like to join me? I have a full thermos and extra cups."

"Are you sure I'm not keeping you from your schedule," she teased.

"Let me worry about that," he shot back, displaying that grin again. Then pouring them each a cup of coffee, he began his story.

"About two years ago, Curtis Long, a sixty-eight-year-old widower, got bored with retirement and being alone, so he opened a little eatery he called the Wildcat Grill, just outside the KU campus. It was about one fourth the size of this diner and the only equipment he had was a couple of refrigeration units, four deep fryers and this grill. His entire menu consisted of hamburgers, a few other grilled sandwiches, onion rings, French fries, canned soft drinks, chips and Twinkies. The place was always packed, but he turned out the orders faster than any fast food restaurant in town. He also kept the prices affordable for the students. Too low. The fact was, he just loved being around the kids and wasn't interested in making money.

"When he had a heart attack and died, his two sons thought they were going to inherit a large bank account along with a little gold mine grill operation. One of them even considered taking over the Grill. That's when they discovered that he had refinanced his house to buy the equipment and keep the business in operation. The Grill had been losing money steadily since it first opened, so they just sold everything to pay off his debts."

"How do you know all this?" Karen inquired.

"Curtis Long was my mother's cousin. She's the one who put me on to the grill. I have a business card for the guy who bought it. If you'd like to take a run over to Lexington to look at it, he said he would hold it until he heard from me."

Karen was reaching for the card when one of Toby's men stepped through the back door, his hands cupped around what she took to be a baby bird since she could see nothing but a small tuft of gray showing above his cupped hands.

"Look what I found under the cottage," he said, his gentle voice contrasting his large burly appearance.

Toby gave him a hard look, obviously resenting the interruption.

Karen's hands automatically went out to take the tiny creature and she was beyond surprised to see that it was the tiniest kitten she had ever seen.

"Oh my goodness," she exclaimed. "Are there others?"

"Just the one. We crawled all over under the cottage and couldn't find anything else."

Toby, still wearing a scowl, said, "Its mother probably moved the rest of the litter and deserted this one because it's so scrawny. They'll do that you know. Discard a weak one in favor of saving the stronger ones."

It was Karen's turn to scowl, giving Toby an intense glare.

"Hey, I don't write the rules of nature," he protested.

Karen was holding it in one hand as she gently stroked it. Tiny as it was, it was softly purring with the attention.

"I'm going to take it to a vet to see what I can do for it. Poor little baby."

Toby rolled his eyes. "What a waste of money. It'll probably be dead by tomorrow."

Ignoring his remark, Karen went directly to her car, pulled out her cell phone and dialed Margo.

Two hours later, Karen was walking out of Wal-Mart, loaded down with pet supplies, kitten formula and a tiny bottle. The vet had pronounced the kitten reasonably healthy, considering its size, and judged it to be maybe two weeks old. Probably a female, although it was too small for him to make a definite call in that department. His reaction, as well as the receptionist's at first seeing the kitten, was the same as Karen's. Later, Margo and Simon would echo the same phrase. On her way back to her room, Karen spoke aloud to the kitten. "Oh-my-goodness," she cooed to the tiny creature curled up on a hand towel stuffed in the top of her purse, "That's what I'll name you. You are the most precious little thing I've ever seen."

Frieda's reaction when she saw Karen walking into the motel with a bag of cat litter sticking out of the top of one of her shopping bags, was to immediately inform her that animal's weren't allowed.

Karen held her purse up so Frieda could see the kitten, and then watched her visibly melt.

"I don't think that even qualifies as an animal. Wherever did you find it?"

Relieving Karen of one of the bags, Frieda followed her to the room, helped her set up a place in the bathroom for the kitten and assured Karen that if she had to leave it for any length of time, she would be glad to check on it for her.

For the next few days, the kitten slept most of the time. Karen had not been able to get it to drink from the bottle, but found that it would lap up the formula from a small dish. She crumbled little bits of Kitten Chow into the formula as the vet had suggested and Goodness would eat that as well. Karen never left her alone and had a box in the car that she carried with her wherever she went.

Chapter 21

On Friday, Karen arrived at Margo's house around ten in the morning just as Simon was on his way out the door. He was headed to the houseboat to stock it with food and refreshments. Afterward, he was meeting Sandy and her husband, Rick, at the dock to put their ski boat in the water.

"Rick's not too keen on pulling the boat up our hill, then getting it turned around," he explained. "We have enough space in the houseboat slip to tie it alongside. They just got the boat last year and it's a beauty. Do you ski?"

Karen emitted a low laugh and confessed that the numerous times she attempted water skiing, she started out in a squat, followed by a three point splash of about forty feet, and then a crash landing as soon as she tried to straighten her legs.

"It's rather embarrassing to watch your sister, as well as your nieces and nephews, aged five through eight, breeze around on skis like professionals when I was the supposed *athletic* one in our family."

"But you'll give it a try, won't you? If not the skis, then the boogie board, maybe? You kneel on that and it's a real blast."

"No promises. I'll have to see others on it before I make a commitment."

"Fair enough."

With a smile and wave of his hand he headed for his car as Karen watched from the doorway. Sighing deeply, she stepped inside and began her preparations. Goodness lay in her box under a dining room window, enjoying a nap while Karen spent the next five hours in constant motion.

Belinda and Adam arrived at almost the same time as Margo. Shortly afterward, Simon, Sandy and Rick pulled in. Karen had several trays of snacks prepared and when introductions were complete and everyone was seated in the sunroom, Karen informed them that she had the makings for frozen margaritas ready to mix. Everyone except Belinda said they would have one.

"Would you like a virgin margarita, Belinda? I have a recipe that's made with pomegranate herbal tea. It's quite tasty."

"That sounds wonderful," she replied, "if it's not too much trouble."

"Not at all," Karen replied, heading for the kitchen.

As soon as she left the room, both Sandy and Belinda looked at Simon.

"What a doll," Sandy said, her eyes staying focused on her brother.

"No arguments here, Sis. Just wait 'til you taste her cooking."

When Dil arrived just before six, Karen brought out a fresh tray of hors d'oeuvres and drinks, instructing everyone to "save room for dinner." At exactly seven, she appeared at the door again and announced "dinner is served."

Everyone loved the salad and Sandy, who thought she didn't like blue cheese dressing, raved about Karen's blue cheese vinaigrette. "This is so-o-o good. Why didn't anyone ever tell me that blue cheese dressing was this yummy?"

The rest of the meal garnered equal praise and when Karen mentioned dessert, there was a collective moan from everyone at the table.

"Are you kidding?" Adam asked the question that everyone was thinking. "If I ate anything else right now, someone would have to carry me upstairs and pour me into a bed."

"Just out of curiosity," Dil inquired, "What is dessert?"

"In honor of the Fourth of July, I made Granny's All American apple pie with homemade vanilla bean ice cream."

Again there was a collective moan and this time it was Rick who spoke up.

"I don't know about anyone else, but I'm not going to miss out on that! Give me about an hour or so to digest my dinner and I'll be ready."

"How about we let the cook rest while we clean up the dishes." Simon said, eyeing his two brothers-in-law, "Let the girls have a little gossip session and get better acquainted with Karen."

"I'm in," Dil said. "I need to move around for a while."

Karen started to object, but was promptly led from the table by Margo.

Saturday was a perfect day for the lake. The temperatures were supposed to climb into the low nineties, but a gentle breeze across the lake made it feel much cooler. After watching everyone but Karen and Belinda take a turn at skiing, they switched to the boogie board and with a little bit of coaxing, Karen tried it. She absolutely loved it. After two wide loops around the houseboat, she glided in like a pro, eliciting loud whoops and applause from everyone.

By the time they finished lunch, everyone was ready to just lay around for some leisurely sunning and an occasional dip in the lake.

Karen was lounging on the upper deck with Sandy and Margo while Belinda and Goodness were in the cabin napping. The four men were all congregated on the lower front deck discussing the best fishing spots to check out next week.

Margo had slathered herself with sunscreen and by the time she lay back on the chaise lounge, her eyelids became heavy. Soon she was sound asleep, giving Sandy the opportunity to do a little snooping.

Keeping her voice low, she turned to Karen and abruptly asked, "So Karen, what do you think of my brother?"

Karen couldn't help but smile at Sandy's straightforward approach and measured her response carefully.

"I think he's wonderful. He's a caring and compassionate minister to his congregation, a really terrific preacher and a dear friend."

"You didn't mention that he's not hard on the eyes, either," Sandy snickered.

Karen rolled her eyes and shook her head. "Look, Sandy – I'm not going to say that I'm not attracted to him. I'd have to be blind and heartless not to be. The fact is, I'm not the kind of person who would attempt to come between anyone who is in a meaningful relationship – especially considering my own *recent* personal experience. I have no doubt that Simon loves Staci, so I'll be content to have him as a friend. Besides, I have too much going on in my life right now to even consider *any* serious relationship of that nature."

There was visible disappointment on Sandy's face as she muttered, "My brother is such a good man. He deserves someone better than Staci Perkins. I just don't see how he can think of her as the same girl he knew when they first started dating." Sandy paused, breathing a heavy sigh, then added, "You're right though about him loving her – it's whether she really loves him that I question."

Karen desperately wanted to change the subject. The awkward silence that lay between them was interrupted by the roar of a small cabin cruiser pulling up alongside the houseboat. The helm was high enough to see the upper deck of the houseboat and a familiar voice yelled out, "Hey there Boss Lady, you interested in a ride on a *real* boat?"

Toby had never referred to her as the *boss*, and from the slight slur in his voice, she suspected he and his friends on board had all had a few too many beers.

Sandy sat up as Karen made her way to the rail to be greeted with numerous wolf whistles and cat calls. Maintaining a composure she didn't feel, she yelled back, "I thought you didn't do the lake thing, Toby."

"The golf course was too crowded to enjoy, so I thought this was a decent alternative. So, can I talk you into a ride?"

"Not today. We've been out here all day and are just about to head for home. Maybe some other time."

Sandy stood up and walked over to stand beside Karen. Ignoring Karen's refusal, Toby yelled, "You too, sweetheart. You look like a girl that enjoys a fast ride."

"But only with me," a deep threatening voice sounded from the lower deck.

Looking down at the six-foot-six hulk standing on the lower deck, Toby immediately recognized Rick Hanson, a former star forward for the Kentucky Wildcats basketball team.

"Hey, you're Rick Hanson. Didn't mean to offend, Rick, Ole Buddy."

"No offense taken Toby, Ole Buddy, but this is a private party and I'd appreciate it if you and your friends would take your celebration elsewhere."

The stricken look on Toby's face was almost comical. Karen had to turn her back to him in order to keep from openly laughing.

By this time, Simon, Adam and Dil had made their way to the upper deck, Margo was standing and Belinda was at the bottom of the steps holding Goodness, debating on whether she wanted to attempt a climb to the top.

When Toby spotted Dil, his face glowed a bright crimson and he sped away before Dil had a chance to acknowledge him.

"Who was that?" Sandy asked, poking Karen in the ribs with her elbow. "Despite his obnoxious behavior, he's quite a hunk."

"And he knows it," was Karen's only reply.

Back at the house, everyone teased Karen about her admirer and made fun of Rick for alienating an obvious fan. After dealing good naturedly with the harassment for several minutes, Rick turned to Karen saying, "Would you like to join me out on the deck, away from these clowns?"

"I would love to Mr. Hanson," Karen smugly replied, hooking her arm through his as they made a haughty exit, leaving the roar of laughter behind them.

"You said that Toby was the foreman for the work on your Diner?" Rick asked.

"Actually, he and his dad own the construction company that's doing the work. He's really a pretty nice guy. Just a little, shall we say, over-confident when it comes to women."

"Well you heard my wife's reaction to him. I suppose he has a right to be a little cocky."

"I guess," she reluctantly concurred. "There's always hope for those kind of guys – just look at Dil. He was a football star when he was in high school and according to Margo, had all the girls after him. He realizes he was quite arrogant back then, but Margo didn't think so."

"Margo knew Dil from high school?" Rick asked, obviously surprised by this revelation.

"Uh…well, yes…he was…uh…a couple of grades higher than her…"

"They dated, didn't they?" Rick interrupted, "I knew there had to be more to this relationship than a chance meeting just a few weeks ago. Margo just isn't the kind of woman who takes up with a man that quickly."

"Oh, Rick," Karen pleaded, "Please don't say anything to anyone else. It's Margo's place to share that information with her children. I don't think it was anything serious back then and I don't know if it will go anywhere now. I have a feeling that she wouldn't want Simon or the girls to think that it was even remotely possible that she loved anyone other than their father. Or more importantly, that she carried any kind of torch for another man while they were married. I really don't think that's the case."

"Hey – don't get upset Karen. It won't be easy, but I can keep a confidence. Sandy will want to know everything we talked about out here, so we better get on a different subject so I'll at least have something to tell her."

Karen's features relaxed again and she quickly said, "So your real opinion of my re-opening the Krossroads Diner."

The remainder of the weekend was more fun than Karen had had in years. Dil stayed at the motel on Saturday night so he could go to church with everyone on Sunday. Simon preached on freedom and the responsibilities of protecting that freedom for all people. His words were thought-provoking and timely on this Independence Day weekend.

Karen sat with the family, and her heart overflowed with the feelings of love that surrounded her. After church, she went back to the room to pick up Goodness, having left her alone for the first time. She rode with Dil and Margo to the farm and throughout the ride, Dil praised Simon's preaching and quoted him numerous times. Sitting in the back seat behind Dil, Karen could clearly see the glow of pride on Margo's face.

By Monday evening, Karen was emotionally exhilarated and physically exhausted. When she and Goodness got back to her room, she was too tired to call Amy. Beside, she reasoned, with the time difference they were probably still at the farm.

Chapter 22

For the next three days, Karen avoided going by the Diner. Except for a quick trip to Lexington to look at the grill, most of her time was spent with Sandy and Belinda while the men were out fishing. The grill turned out to be perfect.

They gathered at Margo's on Thursday for a fish fry and since they would all be leaving early Friday morning, Karen said her good-bys then.

Stepping into the diner the following morning, she was amazed at the progress that had been made. The bathrooms were framed out and metal studs replaced a large number of the old wooden 2x4's throughout the kitchen. The electrician was running wiring and the hole in the floor that was necessary to replace some of the main lines leading to the sewer was filled in and roped off – obviously not yet dry.

Toby was nowhere in sight, although his truck was parked out front. Recognizing one of the crew working on the drywall around the bathroom frames, Karen approached him to ask if Toby was around.

"He's in the cottage, Ms Christian," he politely replied. They're putting in the flooring this mornin' and he's overseeing the work. Would you like for me to go get him for you?"

"I don't want to keep you from your work."

"That's okay, Ma'am, I'm sure he would want to see you."

Stepping out the back door of the diner, her heart raced as she looked at the cottage. The new cream colored vinyl siding and deep brown window shutters completely changed the look of the cottage. The front porch looked like wood, but Toby said it was actually plastic. It was the same brown as the shutters. A bricklayer was building what Karen assumed would be planters along the foundation beneath the front porch.

When Toby stepped through the door of the cottage, he wore a tentative look on his face.

"Hi Toby," Karen greeted him, her face glowing with excitement. "This looks amazing."

Toby released an audible sigh of relief as he realized that Saturday's incident had obviously slipped Karen's mind at the moment.

"Glad you're pleased," he said. "Think you'll be ready to move in by the first part of next week?"

"Really? That soon? Oh Toby, that would be awesome."

He had reached the bottom of the steps and Karen resisted the urge to run over and throw her arms around him.

"Once the flooring is completed, we just have a couple of finishing touches inside. The landscaping won't be done until after we've completed the parking lot. We'll put in a temporary walkway between the cottage and the diner in the meantime. It's liable to get pretty messy back here once we start building the addition. We haven't had much rain lately, but when it does rain, this back will be a regular mud hole."

Karen's heart was still racing with excitement as Toby approached and she couldn't stop smiling. Toby's face turned somber, his voice humble with his next words.

"Look Karen, I want to apologize for my behavior on Saturday. I really didn't mean to intrude on your outing with your friends."

His head drooped down as he added, "I can't say running into you was accidental, but I certainly hadn't planned on being half lit by the time we found you. Can you forgive me?"

This humble, penitent Toby was very different from the Toby she thought she knew.

"Apology accepted. All is forgiven and forgotten."

She held out her hand, which he took in both of his, saying, "Thanks. Now you have to let me take you to dinner and prove that I really can be a gentleman." The crooked little smile was back.

"Okay," she replied, not quite sure if she had just been manipulated. "As soon as you let me see the inside of my future home." *Two can play that game.*

"Tomorrow then. It'll be too late for you to make any changes," he teased. "And tomorrow night, I'll take you to Lexington to celebrate your new home."

Karen felt tears welling in her eyes as she stared at the interior of the cottage. It was beautiful. It looked larger than she remembered – and she loved the little divider just inside the door. It would give her a place to display her family pictures and the few knick-knacks that she had taken with her. As a surprise, Toby had added a little wine rack at the end of the kitchen counter and had built-in bookshelves in the bedroom area. This time, Karen didn't even try to resist the urge to throw her arms around Toby crying, "I love it," as she gave him a quick smack on the cheek.

Taken totally off guard, Toby quickly recovered, wrapped his arms around Karen and smugly said, "I aim to please."

Hastily disengaging herself, Karen walked over to look at the bathroom and small walk in closet.

"It's all perfect," she said, wiping at a tear that threatened to escape.

Not really understanding Karen's emotions, Toby said, "You act like you never had your own place before. Didn't you and your ex…"

Before he could finish his question, Karen cut him off.

"Of course…but it wasn't the house I wanted. This," she said spinning around with her arms outstretched, "is more *me*. Cozy, homey and unpretentious."

Looking around, Toby began nodding his head in agreement. "The only thing missing is a fireplace. Why didn't I think of that? We could have easily added it on that west wall."

"This is far more than I ever imagined," she quickly replied. "Besides, I certainly wouldn't want Dil to have to put more into this remodel than necessary – and it's not like I'm going to have long leisurely evenings in here to enjoy a fireplace."

Karen's bed was being delivered to the cottage on Monday and she would spend the day unpacking the boxes from storage, as well as the many purchases she had made over the past few weeks.

Her dinner with Toby (she refused to call it a date), was surprisingly pleasant. She wasn't certain if he was on his good behavior to impress her, or if this was the real Toby. When he dropped her off at the motel, he escorted her to the back entrance where she gave him a sisterly kiss on the cheek and thanked him for a wonderful evening. He looked at her with longing, but backed away saying, "I enjoyed it. You're great company, Karen." Then he turned and walked back to his car.

On Sunday after church, Karen took Margo and Simon over to the cottage. Toby had given her the key so she could start moving in right away. They were both amazed at the transformation and listened attentively as Karen described her planned décor, enthusiastically adding, "I'm more anxious than ever to have Amy here to help me with wall decorations and accessories."

"Do you know how long before the Diner will be completed?" Margo asked as they were leaving.

"Toby said they promised Dil it would be completed by mid-September at the latest."

"That's just a little over two months away. Have you thought about your staff?"

"Only what positions I will need to fill. Should I start advertising for help this soon? I figure it will probably take a month to get the kitchen and grill stations organized the way I want them. We'll also have to stock the shelves and get the menu lined up and tested."

"So you'll need your staff on hand for that, right?"

"A good portion of them, yes."

"Well before you run any ads, let me do a little checking around. I know several people who live around here that would love to have work closer to home. Make me a list of what positions will be available."

Simon had been silent during this exchange between Karen and Margo. He cleared his throat to draw their attention to him, and then said, "I might have a lead on a top notch grill man for you."

"Oh Simon, that would be wonderful. I consider that the most important role to fill."

"Is it someone I know?" Margo asked.

"Actually, other than having met him once, I don't know him. It's someone Father Brian introduced to me and I think he's the one you need to talk to. I'll be seeing Brian on Wednesday and could set up a time for you to meet with him if you like."

"Well...yes, that would be fine Simon. Meanwhile, I'll get that list for you, Margo, and we can get together at your convenience."

"Are you still going to run that ad requesting local recipes?" Simon asked.

"I'd almost forgotten about that. Thanks for reminding me. I'll do that first thing tomorrow."

Chapter 23

By the time Karen returned to the motel on Monday evening, she was completely exhausted. As she came through the back door with Goodness in her carrier and a take out bag from Sonic balanced on top, Frieda met her holding her mail.

"I had to sign for this letter. It looks like some kind of legal papers. It's from a lawyer...in Portland, Oregon."

Somehow, Karen had assumed that everyone knew she was in the process of a divorce, and Frieda stood there with this look on her face like Karen owed her an explanation.

"Thanks, Frieda. I've been expecting this," she said, taking the envelope and proceeding to her room. She was too tired to deal with explaining her life to Frieda.

Once in her room, she took Goodness from the carrier and held her in her lap as she opened the envelope. *Why does this hurt so much?* Karen wiped the tears that streamed down her face. She hadn't thought she would be this affected by the Final Decree of Divorce. *It's not like it was unexpected. Something about the word "Final." Six years of my life cast aside as if they had never happened. And it was* final! Forgetting her earlier hunger, she curled up in a fetal position on the bed and cried herself to sleep with Goodness nestled in the curve of her stomach.

The clock read ten thirty when Karen was awakened by the phone ringing.

"Karen, you haven't called me in three days. Is everything alright?"

"Hi Amy," a sluggish voice replied. "Everything's fine. I've just been busy. I was going to call you this evening, but I fell asleep when..."

Amy didn't miss the crack in her voice as she stopped mid-sentence.

"Something *is* wrong."

Karen choked back a sob, took a deep breath and finally said, "I got the final divorce papers today. My God, Amy, I didn't expect it to hit me so hard."

"Oh Honey," Amy's sympathetic voice proclaimed, "Of course it affected you. I've known women who were in much worse marriages than yours that went into a depression after their divorces. But they weren't as strong as you. They had put their lives on hold while they waited. You began looking toward the future, and that's the way it should be."

Amy paused, and when Karen didn't say anything, she continued talking. "I wish I was there with you right now, Sweetie. We could sip on wine, exchange a little trash talk about your ex; laugh a little, cry a little…"

"And let the clouds roll by a little," Karen sang in a weak little voice.

"Now that's my sassy little sister," Amy laughed.

They talked for another fifteen minutes and by the time Karen hung up, she felt much better, despite the ache that still clutched at her heart.

On Tuesday night, Karen slept in her own bed at the cottage. The rest of her furniture was due to arrive on Wednesday and her phone, satellite dish and DSL hook-up were all being installed. Simon dropped by in the afternoon amidst all the hubbub, to say that Father Brian could meet with Karen on Thursday afternoon and they could use his church office for the meeting if she liked.

"Your confessional? Does this mean he wants to keep it short and to the point? She teased.

"Would you rather meet at my home office? I can disappear for as long as…"

"Don't be silly – I'm joking. Your office will be fine and you are welcome to be a part of the meeting."

"I might just do that."

Father Brian was older than Karen had imagined. She'd pictured him closer to Simon's age, but he had to be at least ten years older. He was a slight man, shorter than Karen, with dark hair, deep blue eyes and an open face that invited trust. Karen liked him immediately.

"I've heard a lot about you Karen," he said, clasping her hand in a warm handshake. "It looks like your project across the street is coming along quite nicely."

"I think that's why we're here, Father. I'll need to have my staff in place within a couple of months and I consider the person on the grill to be a key employee. So tell me about this *top-notch candidate* you have in mind."

"His name is Willie McKay. At this time he is an inmate at the Eastern Kentucky Correction Complex in West Liberty. He's scheduled for early release next month. One of the conditions of his release is that he has gainful employment."

Karen's reaction to this information was to immediately turn to Simon with a stunned look on her face. Before she could speak, Simon said, "You need to hear the story behind Willie's conviction before you make any judgments about his character, Karen. I assure you that Willie McKay is one of the most decent men I have ever met."

Turning back to meet Father Brian's compassionate eyes, she said, "Please tell me Father."

"Seven years ago, Willie was a grill cook at one of Atlanta's busiest restaurants."

Father Brian paused and gave Karen a wry grin.

"Before I go into further detail, I need to explain Willie's…appearance. He is a very large, very good-looking black man. Six-foot-seven, with shoulders as broad as mine and Simon's combined, and about a thirty inch waist. He's all muscle and looks more powerful than most professional football players. But I assure you, Ms Christian, he's the gentlest man you will ever encounter. Other than cooking, his greatest passions are his wife Natalie, their two daughters and oil painting, at which he's actually quite good.

"That's why it's hard for me to believe that he was guilty of the crime for which he was convicted. I've spoken to the lawyer who defended him, and he is convinced that what happened to Willie was a set-up. The story he told me goes like this.

"Willie had been at the Uptown Grill for almost five years – ever since he completed a tour of duty in the Marines. Everyone at the grill thought the world of Willie and there was a degree of familiarity among the employees that included Willie referring to the waitresses as 'sugar,' 'sweetheart,' and other pet names. They had pet names for him as well and it was just a part of their routine for him to yell out, 'hey sugar,' when calling out for them to pick up an order. You get the idea."

Karen smiled, remembering the same kind of camaraderie at Handi's.

"Anyway," he continued, "Late one night three white men, who were not regulars, came in to eat. They were seated at the counter and took offense to Willie referring to their *white* waitress as *darlin'*. Ella was a twenty-year-old student at Emory – blond, pretty, and a real flirt with the customers. One of the men had been trying to get her to agree to meet him after she got off work. When Willie called her darlin', he said, 'Hey Nigger, she ain't your darlin'. Apologize to the lady.'

"Ella immediately started to defend Willie, which garnered a crude remark from the man, after which he paid his check, and then he and his buddies left.

"Willie lived about a mile or so from the Grill and walked to and from work. Every night after work, he would stop by a little bar, a few doors down from the grill, to have *a* beer before beginning his trek home. Probably, because of his size and color, drunks, especially large redneck drunks, had a tendency to try to get him riled. He would ignore them – have his beer and leave – never allowing it to turn into any kind of altercation.

"That night, the three men from the grill waited for him to get off work and followed him to the bar. They sat down next to Willie and began goading him. As always, he didn't say a word, just drank his beer, then got up to leave. Unfortunately he had to make a stop at the restroom before leaving and the men followed him.

"Willie said that he was washing his hands when the three men came up behind him. They said they wanted him to come with them to the back alley so they could give him a few lessons on respect for white women. Willie tried to explain that the way he spoke to the waitresses was not meant to be disrespectful. He didn't want any trouble and all he wanted right now was to get home to his family. He said he was trying to sound friendly and stay calm and even offered to show them a picture of his wife and girls. When he started to reach in his back pocket for his wallet, one of them pulled out a gun. Willie immediately lifted his hands, but when he heard the man cock the gun, his Marine training kicked in and he reached out to slap the gun away. He heard a shot, and then everything went black.

"When he woke up, he was in the hospital. Natalie was there and she told him he was in a prison ward and had been unconscious for two days. He had a pretty nasty concussion from having been struck from behind with the lid from a toilet tank.

"When the police asked him what happened, he told them everything he remembered up to trying to slap the gun away. That's when they informed him that the *two* surviving men told the story a little differently and he was being charged with unlawful possession of a firearm and murder. His were the only prints on the gun, a man was dead and two eye witnesses identified Willie as the shooter.

"The two *witnesses* later admitted that they had followed Willie into the restroom to get him to apologize 'for being disrespectful to a young waitress earlier that evening.' They said he got all defensive and pulled a gun. When one of them tried to wrestle the gun from him, he pulled the trigger, killing one of the other men. Meanwhile, the third man managed to get the lid off the toilet tank and knock him out 'before he could shoot anyone else.'

"The charge was dropped to involuntary manslaughter, but despite the numerous character witnesses, including the waitress involved, he was found guilty. With the additional charge of illegal possession of an unregistered gun, he was sentenced to a total of twelve years.

"When he was transferred here after two years, his wife moved to Morehead to be closer to him. She's a surgical nurse and has been working at St. Claire's ever since she got here. Natalie is a lovely woman and Willie's daughters, Cassie and Jamie, are beautiful, bright little girls. Willie's been a trustee, working in the kitchen, ever since he got here. The warden has nothing but praise for him."

Father Brian looked questioningly at Karen, saying, "So – what do you think."

Perhaps it was Karen's memory of her time at Handi's that prompted her to share Father Brian's belief that Willie may have been falsely convicted. George Handi was a very large black man as well, although his largeness was in his girth, not his height. She had loved him dearly – as did everyone who worked for him.

"Would it be possible for me to meet him before I make a commitment?"

"Of course. I'll set it up with Warden Jakes. When would you want to go?"

"The sooner the better."

"I have mass at the prison on Monday morning. Would that work for you?"

Simon spoke up, saying, "I'll be glad to drive you over if you like. It's a bit of a trek."

"That would be great. I've...I've never been to a prison and I definitely wouldn't want to go alone."

Chapter 24

Karen spent the next few days setting up work schedules and defining positions to fill the schedules. She had insisted that Sunday morning brunch would be at her new home and was delighted that Dil was at church and agreed to join them. They all arrived bearing housewarming gifts. Karen was both delighted and touched by the gesture.

When Simon had to leave early to pick up Staci and her parents at the airport, Karen took the opportunity to ask Margo a question that had been on her mind ever since Staci had left three weeks ago.

"If I'm not being too nosey, Margo, I've been wondering where Staci works that she can get this much time off. She said her cruise was almost three weeks and now three weeks in Cancun…"

Margo's sardonic, *humph*, stopped Karen before she finished her sentence.

"Staci Perkins work! That's a laugh. Other than the year she spent as a receptionist in her ex-husband's office, I doubt she has ever lifted a finger for anything other than to have it manicured."

Karen was totally taken aback by Margo's scornful words. Especially in front of Dil, who was looking at her with a numb expression covering his face. With a startled awareness of how bitter she had sounded, Margo blushed profusely and began apologizing.

"I'm sorry. That was uncalled for. In answer to your question, Karen, Staci receives alimony from her ex-husband and I'm guessing that her parents, and probably her grandmother, provide her some support as well. They all dote on her. Everett and Mona were more than happy when she returned to Morehead. As close as Cincinnati is, they were devastated by Dr. Perkins' decision to move there."

Dil had taken Margo's hand and was looking intently at Karen as the two women conversed. Once Karen noticed the look on his face as he watched her, she became slightly uncomfortable. She wanted to say, *don't look at me like that. Of course I'm curious about Simon's girlfriend. He's my friend and I care for him.* Instead, she decided to redirect the conversation.

"Have you told Dil about my interview tomorrow, Margo?"

Before Margo could say anything, Dil answered, "As a matter of fact, Simon has told me all about Willie McKay and I'm looking forward to hearing your impression of him."

"That reminds me, Karen," Margo said, "When can we get together to talk about my recommendations for the other positions? I have four super candidates that I know are interested, and a couple of other people that I can suggest, depending on your needs."

"I know tomorrow evening is out because of your bunko group, so how about Tuesday night?"

"Done! Dinner at seven. That should give us ample time to talk while Simon is with his men's group. Meanwhile, we need to get going. We're hoping to catch an early movie before Dil heads back to Winchester. Would you like to join us?"

"No way! I still have to complete my schedules and I have at least a million other things to get done before Amy and Ronnie arrive next week."

Margo smiled, knowing perfectly well that Karen's response had nothing to do with anything other than the fact that she would never consider interfering with her time with Dil.

It was almost six o'clock when Karen hung up the phone after reconfirming, *for the fifth time*, Amy and Ronnie's flight schedule. She started when there was a light knock at her door. Peeking through the shutters, she was surprised to see Toby standing on the front porch with a bag of groceries and a bottle of wine. His quirky little lopsided grin greeted her as she opened the door.

Handing her the bottle of wine, he said, "I was in the neighborhood and thought I'd drop by with a little housewarming gift."

"And the bag of groceries," she inquired, "is that part of the gift as well?"

"Actually, these are bribes. The gift is in the truck," he said, as he handed her the grocery bag and headed back to his vehicle.

Karen watched in stunned silence as he pulled a large gift wrapped box from the truck.

"What on earth have you done, Toby Kern? This is…too much! That box won't even fit through this door."

"I'll take it around to the back and you can open it on the deck."

The sheepish grin he wore had Karen's curiosity more than aroused. After placing the groceries and wine on the counter, she opened the sliding doors just as Toby sat the box on her new glass topped patio table.

"Go ahead. Open it," he demanded, standing there looking like a kid on Christmas day.

The large domed Weber grill was exactly what she had wanted for the deck.

"Oh, Toby!" she cried, as she gently ran her hand over the smooth enameled surface. "How did you know? It's perfect." Then turning to him she threw her arms around his neck and gave him a quick kiss and hug.

Wrapping his arms around her, he held her in a fast embrace, saying, "Glad you like it."

He stood there enjoying the feel of her in his arms, until she pushed away to look him in the face.

"I take it you're expecting to put this to use right away?"

"Guilty as charged. Please tell me you don't have any other plans."

"I plan on unloading those groceries to see what delights you have in store while you put this marvelous piece of equipment together. I'll do all the inside preparations if you'll do the outdoor chores."

"Exactly what I had in mind!" Toby was beaming as he spoke. "I'll get the charcoal and a few tools from the truck while you check out the groceries. I think I have everything covered."

Thirty minutes later they sat on lounge chairs on the deck, sipping on cold beer while the charcoal heated. Karen had salads prepared in the refrigerator, potatoes baking in the oven and the onions and mushrooms ready for sautéing once the steaks were on the grill. The wine was *breathing* on the counter and the table was set. Toby had even thought to bring a small container of sour cream, chives and real bacon bits.

Something tells me he's done this before, Karen thought as she leaned back in the lounge chair, enjoying the fresh air. The temperature was in the mid eighties, but a gentle breeze combined with the dry air and the shade of the house made the deck feel much cooler. She breathed a contented sigh as she turned to Toby saying, "This is nice."

Toby reached over and caught her hand. "I'm glad it pleases you Karen. I know I should have called first – to make sure you didn't have other plans – but then I figured you were worth taking the chance."

Oh Toby, I do want your friendship and I hope you aren't trying to push this beyond what I'm capable of at this time, Karen thought.

After letting her hand rest in his for a brief period, she gently pulled it away, swatting the air to chase away an imaginary insect.

"I think I'll go check on the potatoes. I'm not used to this new oven yet and don't want them to overcook."

As she arose, she looked at Toby and thought she saw a hunger there that had nothing to do with food. *Please God, don't let him expect more than I can give.*

Despite her earlier discomfort, the remainder of the evening went well. Over dinner Toby entertained her with tales of his college years, his golfing mishaps, and his dog, Buster. When they moved to the living room after she had cleared the dishes, she picked up Goodness and nuzzled her nose in the kitten's soft fur. Since Toby sat on the couch; Karen took a seat in a chair with the coffee table between them.

"You can sit next to me, Karen. I promise I won't bite."

"I wasn't sure you would want to be that close to the kitten." *Lame!*

"I'm surprised at how much she's grown. I really didn't think she had a chance, but she's still little more than a tasty snack for Buster."

No denial. He's probably afraid of her. Karen's scowl at his comment was rewarded with an impish grin. Returning her attention to the kitten, she said, "Granny always said you could love a sick animal back to health."

She had hoped that the mention of her granny would redirect the conversation – maybe even get him to ask some questions about her family. Instead, after a short pause, he went in a totally different direction.

"The electrical installation for the diner should be finished tomorrow and the plumbing is almost done as well. Then all we have to do is complete the addition for the walk-ins and the storage area and we'll be able to start installing the fixtures and equipment."

"That's wonderful, Toby. Does this mean you'll be ahead of schedule?"

"As long as the weather cooperates – yeah."

For the first time in the evening, there was an uncomfortable pause. Karen was about to offer Toby some coffee and dessert – she had some of the fruit tart left from this morning's brunch – when he suddenly stood up.

"Speaking of schedules, I should probably head out. I want to get an early start tomorrow."

He started for the door as Karen stood. Placing Goodness on the floor, she said, "I have a busy day tomorrow as well. I really do appreciate the gift, Toby – and the meal. Next time, I'll provide the food."

Toby suddenly stopped and turned, almost causing Karen to run into him. Grabbing her by the shoulders, he kissed her firmly, then wrapping his arms around her spoke into her hair.

"I hope there'll be a lot of next times, Karen." He released her as abruptly as he had grabbed her, turned, and walked out the door before she could say anything.

Chapter 25

On Monday morning, Karen was shutting down her computer just as Simon's knock sounded on the front door. When she opened it, he asked in what he considered a menacing tone, "Well are you ready to go to prison, Ms Christian?"

"Very funny, Simon! You sound about as intimidating as Goodness when she hisses at Princess."

"Thanks," he laughed, "that really does wonders for my male ego."

They were both laughing as they headed for Simon's car and Karen caught a glimpse of Toby in the doorway of the diner, glaring critically at them. *Now that's intimidating,* she thought as Simon held the car door for her.

"So how was Staci's vacation?" Karen asked, as soon as they were driving away from the diner.

"Don't know," was Simon's surprising reply.

When Karen looked over at him, her mouth agape, he added, "She wasn't with her parents yesterday. She decided to stay with her grandmother in Boca Raton for a while."

"She didn't call you ahead of time to let you know?"

"It wouldn't have mattered. I had to pick up her parents anyway. They were probably afraid that if I knew Staci wasn't going to be with them, I wouldn't have come – which is of course ridiculous. Mona said Staci would be calling me this evening."

Karen couldn't decide if his tone was disappointment or anger. If it were her, it would definitely be the latter.

They sat in silence for several minutes before Simon spoke again.

"Do you mind if I ask what exactly you will be looking for in this interview? I get the feeling you have some reservations – not that I blame you," he quickly added, "it's not like you've been presented with a glowing resume."

"I'm really not questioning his qualifications. I'm sure if he spent five years at a busy diner in Atlanta, he's more than capable of handling my little diner in Farmers." She paused as if measuring her thoughts before she began speaking again.

"My biggest concern is his attitude. I can't imagine that there isn't a degree of bitterness at what appears to be a gross miscarriage of justice. I'm guessing that a large portion of my business will be travelers and tourists, many of whom will be hunters and fishermen. There's bound to be some of the same type of – shall we say, *troublemakers* – as those who caused all of this to happen. If Willie were to react to some bigoted remark or threat by such characters, who knows what might occur. I don't want to place my staff or my customers in a situation that could be dangerous or threatening to them."

"But don't you think that Willie will be all the more cautious *because* of his experience?"

"That's just it. If he constantly feels that he has to be aware of his every word – his every action – then he won't be able to maintain the kind of camaraderie with the rest of the staff and the customers that he had at the Atlanta diner. I worked at a diner long enough to know that your repeat business comes from people who enjoy not just good food, but a homey atmosphere. They just like being there. That's what diners are about. Friendly people, who know your name, know the things you like and don't like; who aren't afraid to playfully harass you a little if you come in grumpy; or to talk you out of a down mood. I worked mostly in the kitchen at Handi's, but I knew all the regulars and they knew me. Handi made sure of that. Anytime we weren't busy, he would send us out to the dining area to talk to customers. We never asked if the food was okay, we asked if they were enjoying their meal. That covered not only the food, but the overall dining experience. I don't want a grill cook who's afraid to face the customers; to walk out from behind the counter and meet people. I don't want a machine just turning out orders."

Karen turned to Simon, her golden eyes filled with passion. "Do you know what I'm saying?"

"Wow. And I always thought it was just about the food – but you're right. I've been to those kinds of places and definitely return to them if I'm in the neighborhood." Then his face broke into a broad grin. "It's sort of like a friendly little church as opposed to one of those mega churches where you go in, fulfill what you feel is your duty, and leave – without knowing the person sitting next to you – afraid to get involved."

"Precisely! That's a perfect analogy. Imagine someone coming into your church, sitting there ignoring any friendly attempts to draw them into the spirit of the community. Not because that person was unfriendly by nature, but because they were afraid of saying or doing something that might offend."

Together they breathed a sigh of mutual understanding as they rode quietly for the next several minutes. When the conversation resumed, it was about the progress on the diner and her sister's upcoming visit.

Upon approaching the prison complex, Karen emitted a small gasp. The size of the facility was rather intimidating, but the overall appearance was quite impressive.

"This must be a new facility. I've never been inside one, but the ones I've seen from a distance aren't nearly as…nice? That's a strange word to use in conjunction with prison, isn't it?"

Simon laughed at Karen's observation and assured her that it really was a *nice* facility compared to many others he had visited.

The guard at the security area greeted Simon by name and assured him that Father Brian had everything set up for Karen's meeting with Willie. They would be meeting in the Warden's office since he had requested that he be present for the interview. Simon wasn't certain if this was standard procedure, but knew the warden had taken a special interest in seeing that Willie got his early release.

Even with Father Brian's description of Willie, Karen wasn't quite prepared for the reality of him. She immediately thought of the cartoon super heroes with the exaggerated broad shoulders and exceedingly small waists. Willie was just like that. Even the loose fitting prison garb didn't hide his muscular build or disguise the distinct V that separated his upper body from his lower body. Since she was already seated, she hoped he would sit down soon so she could stop craning her neck. It wasn't until she looked into his gentle face that she realized she had been holding her breath, which she now released.

Warden Jakes was a pleasant-looking man of medium build and height, but both he and Father Brian looked like a children standing next to Willie.

Father Brian began making the introductions – first to Warden Jakes, then to Willie. Both took her proffered hand in a warm shake and then seated themselves. Once seated, Karen looked directly at Willie and smiled. It was Warden Jakes who broke the silence.

"Ms Christian, before we begin this interview, I would like for you to read several letters that I have received from Willie's former boss and co-workers. While I know that the work Willie has done here isn't exactly the same, I personally would like to vouch for his excellent skills in the kitchen, his work ethic, and his attitude toward his fellow inmates. I have yet to find anyone who's taken the time to know Willie who doesn't regard him with respect. Even those who are perhaps envious, or just outright troublemakers, tend to stand down in his presence."

All the while the warden spoke, the smile covering the face of the big black man never wavered, although something in his eyes told Karen he was blushing profusely. In reality, she had pretty much made up her mind when the warden mentioned attitude — but she had to be certain that this positive attitude would carry over in the outside world. Taking the letters from the warden, Karen haltingly spoke. Her words were directed to Willie.

"I'll read these letters, but I honestly don't doubt your ability to do the job. My only concern is how this overall experience has affected you, Willie. How do you feel about having been locked up for all these years? Torn away from your family and friends."

Karen deliberately did not use the phrase "falsely accused," despite the fact that she now, more than ever, could not imagine this man being violent.

The smile never left Willie's face as he spoke.

"I gotta' be honest, Ms Christian. I was real mad at God and the world when all this first happened. It wasn't 'til I came here and met Father Brian that I really understood why this happened to me. Father Brian explained to me that God doesn't cause these things to happen, but he lets them happen for a reason. It took me a while to figure out that reason, and when I did, it made perfect sense."

Every one in the room sat fascinated by Willie's speech. His deep calm voice was mesmerizing, but it was his words that had them all spellbound.

"You see, Nattie…Natalie, my wife and I always talked about gettin' out of Atlanta and movin' to a nice small town to raise our girls. But we were stuck. I was working seven days a week and she was working almost as much as me. We had to pay a lot for daycare for our babies and couldn't afford but the one car that Nattie needed to get to her job. During most of that time we were payin' for a nursing home for my mama as well. We could have sent her to a State facility, but it was Nattie that insisted on keepin' her in a nice place close enough for us to visit.

"After Mama passed, we just couldn't seem to save any money. It seemed like every time we got ahead a little, something came up to wipe us out. Then this happened and here we are in this beautiful place in Kentucky. We never would have considered movin' to Kentucky, but it's where the Lord sent us.

"Nattie loves her job at the hospital. The girls are happy and doin' good in school. They're well-liked and accepted by everyone, so when I'm out of here and workin', we might even be able to afford to buy a house like we always wanted. Then Father Brian tells me about this possibility of a job at a place called the Krossroads Diner. Well I knew right then that this was the Lord tellin' me that he was given' me a chance to make a new start. Leave the past behind and take a new road. Why would I be anything but joyful about that?"

Four sets of eyes, all a little misty, stared in wonder at Willie, who seemed oblivious to how he had touched each of them.

Karen's words were slightly choked as she turned to the warden. "When will he be available, Warden?"

You wouldn't have thought that Willie's smile could get any broader, but with her words, it practically split his face.

Father Brian followed Karen and Simon out to the car. They had all walked from the warden's office to the vehicle in silence, each deep in their own thoughts about what had just transpired.

"You've done a wonderful thing, Karen," Father Brian said as he held the door for her. "Thank you...I know God will bless you for this."

The tears that had threatened earlier now came streaming down her face as she reached over to give the gentle priest a hug.

"I should be thanking you Father...and I've already been blessed," she replied, taking a deep breath to ward off her emotions. "What an amazing man! What a truly amazing man!"

Father Brian returned the hug, smiling happily as he closed the door.

Chapter 26

Once again, the return trip began in quiet reflection; both Karen and Simon lost in their own thoughts. When Simon finally spoke, his words were a shock to Karen.

"I'm thinking of taking a trip to South America. I have a close friend in Ashland who attended seminary with me, and he's filled in for me several times when I've had to travel. If he can get away for a few months to help me out, I'll probably leave at the end of August."

The tightening in Karen's chest was almost as painful as what she had felt when Chase had told her that Debbie was pregnant with his child. As much as she had tried to deny to herself that her feelings for Simon were nothing beyond friendship, there was no way to deny what she was feeling at this moment.

Simon didn't take his eyes from the winding mountain road, but she knew he was waiting for her to comment. It took several seconds to compose herself enough to ask, "Does this decision have to do with Staci?"

Still not turning to look at her, he replied, "Yes…and no."

He hesitated before giving an explanation of his ambiguous response.

"When I picked up Mona and Everett yesterday, I realized that I was – relieved – that Staci wasn't with them. I should have been disappointed, but all I could think of was that now I didn't have to face discussing our relationship. Ever since I talked to you about my not being totally honest with her, I've known that I had to get S.C. Ford out in the open. Not just because she has a right to know, but because I needed to know if it would make a difference in how she looked at our future."

"And if it did make a difference, what then?" Karen solemnly asked.

"I don't know. I honestly don't know. There's a part of me that feels that if money is that important to her, then she can't be right for me. Then there's the part of me that has loved her for all these years that says if money is that important to her, I should be willing to give her every thing she wants to make her happy. That's why I think being away from her will give *her* the chance to decide if it's me she really wants, and for me to sort out my own feelings..."

His voice trailed off as if he hadn't completed his thought, and Karen knew he had to stop talking before he broke down. She gave him a few minutes to clear his head before asking, "So that's the yes side. What's the no side to my question?" Her attempt to make her inquiry sound like friendly curiosity rather than some desperate hope that she might be part of the equation failed miserably.

Clearing his throat, Simon's voice was once again stable as he answered.

"My latest Jesse story is sorely lacking in inspiration. I think being down there, having a chance to reacquaint myself with Jesse and all the children at the orphanage, will provide the inspiration I need to finish this latest book. I have two more due to fulfill my contract and if this one is giving me such a difficult time, I can't imagine writing two more."

Karen nodded her understanding, not daring to say anything for fear her emotions would get the best of her. She turned her head to stare out the window and was soon caught up in the glorious landscape that surrounded them – along with her own thoughts. *Oh to have Willie's faith. To truly believe that even the worst of things happen for a reason!*

"Thank you for driving me to West Liberty, Simon. It really means a lot to me to know that I have the grill position covered."

"It was my pleasure," he said with complete sincerity. "I always enjoy being with you, Karen. It means a lot to *me* to have a friend who is such a good listener."

He had dropped her off at the front of the diner instead of driving around to the back as he had this morning. Stepping out of the car, she wasn't surprised to see Toby coming toward her as if he had been waiting for her arrival.

"Good afternoon, boss lady. I was hoping you'd show up before the restroom fixtures arrived. I need to check out a few details with you before we start the installation."

"I wish you wouldn't call me *boss lady*, Toby. It sounds so...bossy!"

The scowl he had been wearing as he approached immediately turned to a charming grin, with a touch of laughter behind it.

"Whatever you say, boss lady," he teased.

She gave him her most disgusted look and walked past him toward the diner. Catching up to her, he fell in step with her determined stride, and as they reached the door, he picked up the hard hat that he kept on a hook just for her and sat it on her head before she entered the building. Reaching up to adjust it to her head, she asked, "What can I possibly know about installing restroom fixtures?"

Twenty minutes later, she was in the cottage kitchen slicing up her leftover steak from the night before. Toby had lit up at her offer to make him a sandwich. The thick rib eye steak had been far more than she could handle at one sitting and as she piled the meat onto the two slices of bread laid out on the cutting board, she attempted to sort out the emotions that still lingered from this morning. Spreading a horseradish mayonnaise on the top slices, she began chastising herself for allowing this to happen. *You are not in love with anyone, Karen. You are just emotionally vulnerable at this point…and lonely.* It was the first time that she had admitted to herself that she really was lonely. She missed her family, her friends, and yes, she missed the feel of someone lying next to her at night. *Snap out of it girl! You're just in a lovesick funk and there's too much going on in your life to indulge in such nonsense.* Maybe Simon's leaving would be a good thing. She could concentrate fully on the diner and, who knows, she might even learn to care for Toby.

Suddenly a line from *The Little Mermaid*, her favorite Disney movie, flashed through her mind. "…*far better than any dream girl (guy) is one of flesh and blood, one warm and caring and right before your eyes.*" "And face it Karen," she said aloud to herself, "Simon's a dream and you're no beautiful princess." Lifting her head, she looked out the front window where Toby stood talking to his electrician. With a resolute smile, she cut the sandwiches in half, placed them on plates and pulled two Ale8's from the refrigerator.

"You ready for a bite of lunch, Toby?" She called as she stepped out her front door.

Sitting down on the porch steps, she watched his crew scatter, either to their trucks to fetch their sack lunch, or to the little bar-b-que place around the corner. She had set up a picnic table at the side of the diner and several workers soon gathered there.

"Mmmm! This is great! What's that sauce on it?" Toby had taken a huge bite out of the first half of his sandwich.

"I'm glad you like it. It's one of Granny's recipes," she said. "I'd tell you what's in it but then I'd have to shoot you."

Toby smirked and devoured the rest of his sandwich before Karen had finished her first half. She offered him her second half and he didn't hesitate accepting.

Chapter 27

"That would be Sherry," Margo said, pointing to Karen's list of needed employees with job descriptions next to them.

"Sherry practically ran the Morehead Diner before it closed. She worked the counter and ran the cash register, knew every customer by name – even those just traveling through. She'd give them a menu and say, 'I haven't seen you in here before. New to town or just visitin'?' By the time they left, they were on a first name basis. When the diner closed, she went to work as a kitchen supervisor for a cafeteria in a retirement community over in Olive Hill. It was around the same time that her son Brandon's wife up and left him with three little boys to care for. She and Brandon have side-by-side trailers just up the road in Salt Lick. Brandon's a school teacher at the Bath County middle school and has a real struggle managing his job and the boys. Sherry's always said she would love to work closer to home so she could be more help with the boys. I'm sure she'll jump at the chance to work at the Krossroads."

Margo's discourse, given in practically a single breath, left Karen's head spinning. Each name Margo suggested was presented in much the same manner. A name and qualifications followed by a brief family history. It was all Karen could do to keep from bursting into laughter at Margo's passion in selling these people as candidates for employment. With each name she would point at a position and begin with, "That would be..." and end by assuring Karen that the person would eagerly leave their present employment to join her staff.

When she finished with the last job on the list, Margo looked at Karen, who was biting her bottom lip. Recognizing the humorous glint in her eyes, she sheepishly muttered "You can go ahead and laugh now. Simon's always telling me that the reason I'm such a successful sales person is because I don't give my clients a chance to refuse."

Karen did exactly that as she reached over and pulled Margo into a firm bear hug.

"I'm really not laughing *at* you Margo. Do you have any idea how much easier you are making my life? Everyone you recommended sounds perfect. If you can let them know that I'll be hiring in about another month, I'll hold off advertising for help until I've spoken with each of them."

Pulling away, Karen's face grew serious.

"I've set up a tentative payroll budget and think I have a pretty good feel for what I can pay. I completely trust your judgment as far as skills and character goes, but I don't want anyone giving up sound employment if my pay scale won't meet their needs."

Driving back to the cottage, Karen was overwhelmed with emotion as she realized what a treasure she had found in Margo's friendship. She had purposely left before Simon's return, not quite sure if seeing him might throw her back into a *lovesick funk*.

"Now I can concentrate on getting ready for Amy's visit," she said, reaching over to stroke Goodness. "Amy's going to flip out over you and I'll probably have to hide you from her when she leaves – otherwise she just might pack you up and take you back with her."

Goodness was watching her as she spoke and when Karen stopped talking, she stretched and yawned, then curled up into a little ball.

Karen paced in front of the luggage carousels. Amy's flight was on the ground. Like most people, she hated the fact that you could no longer greet people at the gate. It seemed an eternity before any passengers came into view in the luggage area. As soon as she spotted Amy, she gave a little yelp and practically ran over several people as she raced to reach her sister. Amy dropped her carry-on bag and both women reached out to the other. Soon they were locked in a death grip hug, tears streaming down both their faces, while Ronnie stood by shaking his head and grinning from ear to ear.

"Lord, you'd think the two of you hadn't seen each other in twenty years. How about we take this love fest out of the way of traffic."

Reluctantly, they released their hold on each other and moved to a clearing next to a carousel. Ronnie sat down both his carry-on and Amy's retrieved bag, and held out his arms to Karen saying, "Do I get one of those, Little Sister?"

Swiping at her tear streaked face, she melted into Ronnie's strong arms.

"Thank you for coming Ronnie – and for bringing my sister to me. You know you're the greatest brother-in-law in the world."

"I'm not sure about that, but I'll take your word for it. As far as me bringing your sister, I think you have that a little backward."

"Oh yeah," Amy said, "Like I had to drag you."

Once they were in the car, Amy and Karen kept up a constant stream of chatter between Lexington and the motel. Karen had reserved the same room she had been in before moving to the cottage. When they entered, they were greeted by the staff like family. Frieda even came around the front of the desk and hugged all three of them.

"Friendly people!" Ronnie exclaimed, as Karen opened the door to their room, still not sure if he liked being grabbed in a bear hug by strange women. "Is everyone here like that?"

"Almost everyone." Karen replied, noting the dubious look on Ronnie's face. "Don't worry; I'll try to forewarn you about the huggers."

Amy laughed, giving Ronnie a gentle poke in the ribs. "Ignore him Karen – he really loves it." Then turning to her husband, she said in a sing-song baby voice, "Don't you worry Sweetie Pie, I won't let any of them whisk you away from me."

Watching her sister and brother-in-law's playful exchange, Karen released a gentle sigh of pure joy. *Oh how I've missed you two lovers. You are my hope that I can find what you have.*

Just as Karen predicted, it was love at first sight between Amy and Goodness. Even Ronnie, who *tolerated* Amy's three cats, couldn't resist the little ball of fur with the huge green eyes. Sitting on the couch with Goodness curled up in his lap, he mused, "If they would just stay this small, I could deal with them a whole lot better." His words fell on deaf ears as the two sisters were deep in conversation – Amy sitting at the counter and Karen putting the finishing touches on their dinner.

"I've missed your cooking, Little Sister. I can just imagine you in seventh heaven working in that big kitchen over there. When do you think you'll be up and running?"

"If Toby's able to stay on schedule, I'll be able to take occupancy by mid September. I'm looking at sometime in October to be open – hopefully for the beginning of deer hunting season. I understand it can get pretty busy in this area, and that should be a big boost to my opening. Everyone I talk to – especially the old timers who remember the original diner – says I'll be an instant success as long as I serve good food."

"No need to worry on that point. I don't think I've ever tasted anything you've cooked that wasn't yummy. You have a real knack for seasoning. Granny gave me a lot of her recipes and, honestly, they never taste nearly as good as when you prepare them."

Karen blushed at her sister's sweet compliment. "Don't sell yourself short, Amy. You're a wonderful cook." Then nodding her head toward the couch, she added, "Ronnie doesn't exactly look like he's been starving on your cooking."

"I heard that!" Ronnie injected. "Are you saying that I'm getting fat?"

"Of course not," Karen defended. "I'm merely saying you look… healthy."

Chapter 28

"Holy cow, Karen, he's gorgeous!" Amy whispered as they entered the little church the following morning.

Karen had just introduced her and Ronnie to Simon, Margo and Dil, who had all waited anxiously out front to meet Karen's sister and brother-in-law. Margo and Dil walked in ahead of the two sisters, and Ronnie was still outside talking to Simon about fishing.

"He's also taken – not that I have the time or inclination to get involved with anyone right now."

"Right," Amy cynically exclaimed, watching Karen's eyes as she added, "I didn't see a ring – or anyone clinging to his arm."

"She's out of town right now – and trust me, if she were here she'd be draped all over him – especially when I'm around."

Amy's eyes lit up. "Jealous of you, is she?"

"Probably of any single female that speaks to Simon. I'm just at the top of her list because I spend time with Margo. She, Simon, and now Dil, have sort of taken me under their wings. They're the closest thing to family that I have here…and that's really all there is to it, so let it rest Amy. Please."

Amy smiled smugly. *Oh, you've got it bad, Little Sister!*

It didn't help Karen's arguments against her having feelings for Simon, when Margo insisted that the three of them join them for brunch. Karen found herself watching Simon as he and Dil swapped fish stories with Ronnie. Inevitably, she would turn back to the women's conversation to find Amy watching *her* as her sister bragged to Margo about her three amazing children.

It was going on three in the afternoon by the time they returned to the cottage. While Ronnie napped, Karen and Amy discussed what could be done to the cottage to give it a homey air. Then, leaving Ronnie sprawled out on Karen's bed with Goodness curled up on his stomach; they headed to the diner and then to the storage unit to discuss what could be used from there.

Karen was showing her some of the old pictures she had rescued from the diner when a shadow appeared at the door. Thinking Ronnie had come to join them, Amy turned around, exclaiming in an excited voice, "Honey, you have to look at this. It's…"

The large man standing in the doorway, wearing snug blue jeans, a form fitting t-shirt and a roguish grin, said in a deep amused voice, "You must be Amy. You're a lot friendlier than your sister."

Amy realized her mouth was gaping open and immediately closed it. Blushing profusely, she turned to Karen, who burst into laughter.

"As you know, she's also blissfully married, Toby, so you can turn off the charm."

After proper introductions were made, they strolled back to the cottage to find Ronnie helping himself to a beer from the refrigerator.

"You must be 'Honey,'" Toby said, holding out his hand to Ronnie.

Ronnie's eyes went suspiciously to his wife as he returned the handshake and replied with a smirk, "That would be me, yes, but my *male* friends call me Ronnie."

Soon they were all out on the deck, enjoying drinks and the warm sunshine. While the men began a conversation on sports, Karen and Amy discussed their shopping plans for the upcoming week. Simon would be taking Ronnie out in his fishing boat and promised to keep him occupied until suppertime, which would be a barbeque on the back deck of the cottage. When Karen invited Toby to join them, he said he had another commitment. Karen wasn't sure if the real reason behind his refusal was that he still felt uncomfortable around Dil after the boat incident over the fourth. She didn't press the issue and said that maybe later in the week he would like to come to dinner. "Just the four of us," she emphasized. "I don't have room in my little cottage for more than that if I want to prepare an indoor meal."

"Bet I know what it's going to be," Amy smugly said.

"Our favorite?" Ronnie asked, hopefully.

"Cheez! You two are incorrigible. I can't even plan a simple surprise without you getting into my head. Now I'll *have* to make *your favorite*'"

"Mind if I ask what that might be?" Toby said, wanting to be a part of the repartee.

"Chicking potta," three voices said in unison.

"With diapers," Ronnie added, as they all burst into fits of laughter.

"I'm obviously missing out on some kind of family joke," Toby said, "Or are you testing my unsophisticated knowledge of fine dining?"

Karen immediately sobered as she explained the reason they were laughing.

"Chicken Piccata with capers is a real dish and it is Amy and Ronnie's favorite. About once a month I would go over to their house while Chase was out of town and prepare it for them. Unfortunately, it caters more to adult taste and my niece and nephews didn't care for it too much. As soon as they would see me walk through the door with a bag of groceries, Mindy would say, "Chicking potta is here." Then the boys would add, "With diapers.""

Toby gave a muffled chuckle, but wasn't sure if he might not agree with kids on this one. About the only way he really liked chicken was fried.

"So did you make them eat it anyway?" he inquired.

"No…at least not after they tried it. I prepare them their own special dish," Karen replied.

"Chicken fingers, I bet," Toby ventured.

"Oh no…much more exotic than that." Karen gave Amy and Ronnie a conspiratorial look and together they all roared, "Frank 'n Macdoodle."

Toby rolled his eyes and shook his head. "I can hardly wait to hear this one!"

It was Amy who began explaining how she began preparing frankfurters with macaroni and cheese for the kids when she knew Karen was coming over to prepare their dinner.

"It's always been their favorite meal. I insist on adding a vegetable and the only one they will all eat is peas and carrots. However, my dear sister has to get creative – even with their menu. Instead of the boxed macaroni and cheese I use, she makes her own recipe with a touch of green food coloring added. Then she plates it with a circle of the macaroni and cheese, topped with frankfurter bits forming the eyes, nose and mouth. Next she adds two ears made of peas and fresh carrot curls as hair. It was an instant hit with the kids. Keith, my oldest, dubbed it Frank 'n Macdoodle. Now I have to make it every time they have friends over."

"Sounds good. I think I'd prefer that."

"You aren't serious?" Karen asked. "You aren't even willing to try something new? Chicken Piccata is *not* that exotic."

"Aren't capers those things that they use pigs to find?"

"Those are *truffles* and they are way too expensive for diner food. Capers are the bud of a flower that grows in the Mediterranean. Chicken Picatta is an Italian dish."

"I grew up on plain ole' meat and vegetables. My mom isn't the greatest cook in the world, but she does okay with the simple things. I've learned to eat some ethnic foods when I eat out…Mexican, Chinese, and Italian…, but when it comes to fancy smancy dishes that have ingredients you can't grow on a farm, forget it."

"Well guess what, Toby? If you're going to hang around me, you're going to have to learn to try new things. I fully intend to use all my friends as guinea pigs for any recipes I'll be using in the diner. I'm going to make it my personal goal to introduce you to as many new dishes as possible. I don't know what you consider *fancy smancy*, but there's nothing wrong with adding flavor to plain dishes and presenting them in a way that has eye appeal."

It was Toby's turn to laugh at Karen's defensive outburst. With a devilish smirk, he said, "You're on boss lady. I'll be here to try your, what was it – chicking potta with diapers? Just name the day"

After a pleasant dinner of grilled hamburgers, Toby left shortly before Amy and Ronnie headed back to the motel.

"Wow, Karen. He's quite a hunk…and obviously very interested in you." Amy observed as soon as Toby was out of ear shot.

"That seems to be the general consensus…and he's well aware of women's attraction to him. As far as his interest in me, I just can't see him that way."

"What on earth is your problem, Girl? I know it hasn't been that long, but you really have to move on past Chase."

Karen cocked her head as she looked at her sister, then tentatively asked, "You didn't see any…similarities…between Toby and Chase? That same sort of arrogant confidence? He knows he's a *hunk*, and I think his major attraction to me is the fact that I didn't start throwing myself at him the minute we met. I have a feeling that if I got all gaga over him, he'd bed me and dump me. Conquest complete."

A sad look came over Amy's face.

"Oh Karen, I hope Chase hasn't ruined your ability to trust men. There really are some good ones out there. Maybe not as great as my Ronnie," she added, looking lovingly at her husband, "but good men worthy of…"

Karen cut her off as she reached over to give her a warm hug. "I know that, Amy. I'm just too tied up with the diner right now and still licking my wounds. There's no need for me to rush into a relationship. Who knows? I might be completely wrong about Toby. He really is fun to be around and I do enjoy his company. Maybe…in time…"

Chapter 29

Amy's visit went by much too fast. The two sisters spent endless hours haunting antique stores that ranged from elegant shops to consignment malls where much of the merchandise was little more than junk. However, some of their best finds were at those malls. Amy's knack for sorting out the unique from simply *old* – the treasures from the trash – astonished Karen. She would have completely overlooked most of the items that, when cleaned, polished and placed in an attractive background, turned out to be both interesting and eye-catching. Some of the picture frames were positively magnificent. Karen had a tendency to see the picture and overlook the frame.

Ronnie and Simon became fast friends and were out fishing or hiking every day. On the weekend, Karen and Amy joined them, along with Margo and Dil, on the houseboat for swimming, water skiing and soaking up sunshine. On the last Sunday of their visit, they went to Dil's after church for brunch and horseback riding. The weather had been particularly co-operative the entire ten days.

On the day they left, Simon offered to drive them to the airport so Karen wouldn't have to drive back at night alone. Since her evenings throughout Amy's visit had been split between Simon and Toby, she felt that she could deal with being alone with Simon for an hour or so without getting tangled up in her emotions. She had come to terms with the fact that he would be leaving for South America soon, which was probably for the best. She could concentrate on testing recipes; finding the pictures she wanted for the dozens of frames she and Amy had restored; and all of the other things she needed to accomplish before opening.

The work on the diner was progressing quickly, with the back addition having been completed this past week. Toby said they would be looking at blacktopping the parking lot by the end of the week if the weather held. The equipment delivery was set for Wednesday and installation would begin shortly after that.

Karen planned on interviewing all of Margo's recommended candidates this week, and Willie's parole hearing was coming up in just over a week. The more Karen thought about it, the more she realized how quickly the next few weeks would pass. Consequently, the ride home from the airport was spent with her excitedly relaying all these upcoming events to Simon, who listened attentively as he drove. His only comment came when they were almost home.

"You know, Karen, I'm really sorry that I'll be missing out on all the excitement of the opening. I hope you understand that I need to do this…to get my head back where it needs to be. I haven't been able to give myself fully to my pastoral duties or my writing for several months. This past week – being with Ronnie and just relaxing – has been good for me. Thanks for sharing your family with us."

"I should be thanking you…and your mother. You made them feel so welcome. Amy made a comment about how she can stop worrying about me now that she knows I have such wonderful people watching out for me. She understands that I'm not alone. I haven't been alone since that first day when you and your mother took me in. You've become my family here and that means the world to me."

Simon turned his head to Karen for a brief moment and in that moment Karen saw something in his eyes that was different. A kind of…*longing? But longing for what?* She didn't dare to imagine it was for her. Before her thoughts could get too carried away, Simon gave her another quick glance – this time he was smiling.

"You are family, Karen."

Karen's first interview was with Kathy Hansen, a slightly overweight, middle aged woman with ten years of experience. Divorced, with two teenagers, she lived in Polksville and was thrilled with the idea of finding a job so close to home. Karen, who had been a little apprehensive about the idea of interviewing, was immediately put to ease by Kathy's bubbly personality. She could easily see Kathy bouncing around the diner, chatting and joking with the customers. *Perfect!*

Kathy was being paid slightly over minimum wage for tipped personnel, but assured Karen that the money she would save on transportation to and from work would more than compensate for any difference in wages. The interview was pleasant, brief and resulted in an excited response to the offer of a job.

The remainder of the interviews went pretty much the same, the one exception being Darrell Mackenzie. He was applying for a job in the kitchen and said he was willing to do anything from dishwashing to working the grill. He had held numerous positions in various restaurants for the past sixteen years. Most recently, he had quit a good job in Grayson to work for a new restaurant in Morehead called Dora's. It lasted only about three months. The thought of a restaurant failing in that short a period scared Karen beyond words. Reluctantly, she asked if he knew why the restaurant failed.

Without hesitation, he replied, "The Clarkson's put way too much money into getting the restaurant up and running. By the time they opened the doors, they would have had to do twice the business they were capable of doing to keep up with the bills. They had enough traffic to start with, but their menu prices were too high and their food costs were much higher than they should have been – mostly because they had way too much waste. After two weeks, they were lucky if they took in enough to pay the rent. Very few people around here can afford twenty-five dollar steaks and nine dollar desserts. The cheapest item on the menu was a hamburger plate for eight ninety-five."

"Was the food good?" Karen asked.

"It was okay...but not worth the money they were asking. They used a lot of pre-cooked frozen entrees for everything but steaks, chops and burgers. Even used a frozen pre-breaded chicken and tried to pass it off as their own special recipe. Hell, it might as well have been a fast food place."

"Are you saying they didn't have anything that was home...er...cooked at the restaurant other than grill items? No soups; sauces; desserts?"

"All pre-packaged – cans, cartons and jars. I even offered to make chili – it's sort of my specialty – but Dora said that chili was a *diner food* and Dora's was for fine dining. My response was to ask her, what about hamburgers. She said their hamburger was a *gourmet burger*, made with ground sirloin, not some fast food patty. I guess the gourmet part was the blue cheese topping and arugala in place of regular lettuce."

Karen shook her head in disbelief.

"Well I hope you know that *everything* in my diner will be cooked and prepared in-house by yours truly. I have a wonderful chili recipe that my grandfather made. We'll have to have a chili cook-off to see if yours is better."

For the first time Darrell smiled, giving his otherwise somewhat homely face a pleasant, rather adorable, little boy look. "Does this mean I have the job?"

"I'm not sure what your exact job description will be – but yes. I've already hired a nighttime grill cook, so you'll probably have to start out as a dishwasher and utility person in the kitchen. Then if business warrants it, maybe I can move you to a full time prep position...sort of my assistant."

He hesitated a moment, his face turning serious again, then added, "I really need a job as soon as possible, Ms Christian. I've been living off my sister since Dora's closed. I'll do anything. I've even done some construction with my brother-in-law over the past couple of months and you'll need help getting set up before you open."

His face held a desperate hope that touched Karen deeply.

"I won't be able to put anyone to work in the diner for a couple more weeks, Darrell, but I'll definitely need all the people I hire to help with setting the place up and testing the menu. Meanwhile, I'll talk to Toby. He's the head of the construction crew and maybe he can put you to work until then."

For a minute, Karen thought Darrell was going to hug her, he was so excited. Instead, he reached for her hand and began pumping it vigorously.

"Thank you. Thank you *so* much. I won't disappoint you. I promise."

Karen had been conducting all the interviews in the cottage. Her final interview was Sherry, who had worked all day in Olive Hill and stopped in on her way home. The bright-eyed, smiling woman at her door hardly looked like someone who had just spent the last eight hours on her feet in a hot kitchen. It was after four and there had been a break between this interview and the last one, so Karen had taken the time to put together a pot roast dinner that was now simmering in the oven.

Sherry's opening greeting was, "Lord, you'd think the smell of food after a day in the kitchen would make a person lose their appetite, but whatever you got cookin' in here smells like heaven."

"You're welcome to join me. I have way more than one person can eat."

"That's a temptin' offer, Sweetie, but I gotta hurry home and fix dinner for my adorable little guys. Their daddy had to be at a plannin' meetin' this afternoon and the baby-sitter is just a teenager. About the only meal she's capable of puttin' together is peanut butter and jelly sandwiches."

The remainder of the *interview* consisted of Sherry doing about ninety-five percent of the talking. When it came down to a discussion on pay, Karen offered her full minimum wage since she would be in charge of the register as well as waiting on the counter customers. Sherry's only concern was the loss of medical benefits. This had been a big concern for Karen, and Margo gave her the name of the agent she dealt with, where Karen was able to find a reasonable small business policy. She intended sharing the cost with her employees and thus far, everyone seemed pleased with it. When she quoted the employee share to Sherry, her face scrunched up. Then, reaching in her purse, she pulled out a pen and small notepad. Without saying anything, she started writing some figures on the paper and after several minutes, looked up, smiled and said, "That'll work. I'll be savin' at least fifty dollars a month on gas plus I'll be makin' tips in addition to my hourly wage. I'm guessin' that will more than cover the difference in the insurance and my current salary – plus I'll have more time with my boys. Just let me know when you'll be needin' me."

Karen followed Sherry outside and watched as she drove off. Then she headed over to the diner to find Toby.

"What would you say to sharing a *plain* old dinner of pot roast with me?"

"I'd say that sounds great. What time."

"In about thirty minutes, if you'll be done by then."

"I was just about to send the guys on their way. Just a little cleaning up left for the day."

"Great! Would you like a cold beer first?"

"A girl after my own heart," Toby quickly replied with a flash of that lopsided Clark Gable grin. It was hard to deny its appeal.

They sat quietly on the back deck for several minutes after Toby had washed up and changed into the fresh t-shirt he always carried in his truck. Karen suspected he had some cologne in there as well, since he usually had a pleasant musky smell overlaying the faint smell of manly sweat.

Karen broke the silence by confessing to Toby that, "I have an ulterior motive for asking you to join me this evening."

"Uh oh! What kind of changes are you going to throw at me this late in the game?"

Thank heavens he didn't try to turn this into some kind of sexual innuendo, she thought, after realizing how her admission could have been misconstrued.

"No changes. Just a favor."

He eyed her suspiciously, and then said, "Go on."

She went on to explain Darrell's situation, his desperate plea for immediate employment, and his willingness to do anything.

"Actually, I'll be hiring some temporary help for the installation. I have other jobs for my skilled labor and just need a few strong backs for moving around the equipment and hauling off the trash. As long as he's not some pansy who can't lift a few pounds, I might be able to use him."

"He looked quite strong to me and he's been working some construction with his brother-in-law, so I'm sure he's used to hard labor."

"Have him come by tomorrow and I'll talk to him."

That settled, they proceeded to have a pleasant meal, which Toby praised as 'the best pot roast I've had ever had.'

"You have some different seasonings in there than what my mom uses. Will you be serving this on your menu?"

His enthusiasm pleased Karen and prompted a timid blush. He had admitted he enjoyed the Chicken Picatta last week, but when she said she would probably serve it as a *special* in the diner, he gave her a rather dubious look.

Toby left as soon as he had polished off two full servings of pot roast as well as a piece of cherry pie with ice cream for dessert. His quick kiss at the door was anything but passionate and Karen felt he was avoiding getting too close because of his imagined body odor. She couldn't help but laugh to herself as she watched him head out to the truck.

A few minutes later, she was on the phone with Darrell. She could feel his excitement as he thanked her again and again. His arrival at six thirty the following morning left no doubt in her mind that he would be a dependable, hard-working employee. Toby put him to work immediately and by the end of the day, jokingly asked Karen if she could find him about three more just like him.

Chapter 30

"She's here!"

The excited voice on the phone was Margo's. She had been in Covington for the last three days awaiting the arrival of her first grandchild.

"She is absolutely gorgeous...and perfect...with golden peach fuzz on her tiny beautifully shaped head and the biggest blue eyes you'll ever see. She looks just like Belinda. Just like her."

Karen chuckled at Margo's enthusiasm. After clearing her throat, she calmly said, "Settle down, Grandma. There's syrup gushing out of this end of the phone line." Then she added more seriously, "Congratulations! I trust everyone is doing well." She could picture Margo, beaming and bursting with pride.

"Yes, everyone's great. It was a smooth delivery, only three hours of hard labor. Oh Karen, I know this *sounds* like grandmotherly pride, but you'll see. She's the most beautiful baby I've ever seen. And so small. She weighs almost a full pound less than any of my babies did."

Hanging up the phone, Karen thought about calling Simon to congratulate him as well. She had been so busy with the restaurant over the past few weeks that she rarely saw him outside of church. More and more Margo was spending her free time with Dil. It was obvious that theirs was a romance in bloom. Any time spent with Simon included Margo *and* Dil. Dil had even driven Margo to Covington, stayed through the weekend and would be picking her up in another week or so. The last time Sandy had come to visit, she hinted at *wedding bells* in her mother's future. It was clear that all of Margo's children approved of the relationship. Margo had told them that she and Dil dated back in high school. All three had mentioned it at some point to Karen, and none of them seemed to feel it had anything to do with their current romance.

While she was still mulling over whether to call Simon or not, there was a knock on the door. Startled from her musings, she jumped at the sound.

"Hey pretty lady! Care to join me in a celebratory toast to my new niece? I've been informed that she's the most perfect, most beautiful baby that has ever blessed this planet."

Simon stood there holding a bottle of champagne, beaming like the proud uncle he obviously was, and wearing that magnificent smile that had mesmerized Karen from the first time she witnessed it.

"I believe I heard the same rumor from the same source – I just got off the phone with your mother. It definitely deserves a toast."

As she stepped aside to allow Simon to enter, Karen inadvertently looked out to see if Toby was watching. Fortunately, his truck was gone, so he was either called away to another job or on an errand. *Good! No jealous inquiries to face.*

Simon sat the champagne on the counter, and then walked over to Karen's computer.

"Mind if I do something here?"

"Not at all," she responded, her curiosity completely aroused.

He pulled a small slip of paper out of his pocket, went to the internet and began typing in an address. A few minutes later, there was a picture of a newborn baby on the screen. A pink cap covered the peach fuzz hair, but the big blue eyes stared in wonder at this new world in which she had been so abruptly tossed.

"Meet Caitlyn Denise Connor. Isn't she amazing?"

"Oh my gosh! Your mother's right. She is the most beautiful baby I've ever seen. Those eyes are incredible. She looks like a baby doll...almost too perfect."

Karen didn't think it was possible for Simon's chest to expand any further, but he almost burst the buttons right off his shirt. "Definitely worth toasting," she reiterated, feeling as proud as she had the first time she saw her own nephews and niece.

Once they had the champagne open and were settled on the couch with their glasses, they clinked the lips of the glasses together as they said in unison, "To Caitlyn Denise Connor." Still holding their glasses high, Simon added, "Thank you Lord for bringing her safely into this world. May her life be filled with love, health and joy."

"Hear, hear!" Karen said solemnly, as their eyes met.

Suddenly she knew that this was a bad idea. Averting her eyes from him, she took a sip of the champagne and tried to refocus her thoughts. Simon appeared to be having a similar reaction, so they sat in awkward silence for several seconds, each staring idly at their glasses.

"Not bad champagne," Simon finally said, picking up the bottle and studying the label.

"I'm not familiar with this label," Karen said, then added with a wry smile, "Not that I'm that well versed in champagne."

Why does this feel so awkward? That's when she realized that it was the first time she had been alone with Simon in the cottage. *Pull yourself together you stupid girl. This is Simon. Your friend, Simon!*

"So, how are preparations coming for your trip to South America?"

"I talked to Lenny in Ashland and he's very enthusiastic about coming here for the three or four months I'll be away. He's been an associate pastor at his church for too many years and thinks the only reason he hasn't been given his own church is because he's considered too liberal. He's looking forward to being somewhere that he can preach without his sermons being censored. Mom found a little rental house for them just on the edge of Morehead. Did I tell you he's married and has four children?"

"I believe you may have mentioned it. Will it be a problem for the children to get in school here, and then have to transfer back mid-year?"

"I don't think so. I sort of got the impression that they might stick around this area. Lenny has a Master's in social psychology and may look for a job outside his ministry. His wife, Gail, is a lab technician and could probably get a job at St. Clair's."

"And what about arrangements on the other end…in Brazil?"

"Actually, I had written to the Mathesons some time ago…when I first started having trouble with my latest book. I heard back from them a couple of weeks ago and they said I could stay at the new mission quarters for as long as I wanted. I haven't seen the new mission building and the last time I was there, the church was only half finished. They said Jesse was so excited at the possibility of a visit that he put off a trip to New York. He's considering becoming a Missionary Priest…or a doctor. Hasn't quite made up his mind yet. He has an amazing mind and an incomparable compassion, so would be wonderful as either."

"A priest?" Karen asked, not hiding her surprise. "I thought you said the Matheson's were Methodist."

"They are – but Jesse is Catholic – like the majority of the people in that area. Ken and Lizzie wouldn't dream of asking him to give up his natural parents' faith – the church in which he was baptized."

"I don't think you've ever told me what happened to Jesse's parents – or how he lost his leg."

For the first time Karen saw something akin to anger in Simon's eyes. She wished she hadn't asked the question. "Jesse never talks about it – not that he could remember that much – he was only five. It was Father Manuel who told me the story.

"Jesse was one of five children living in a small house in a poor neighborhood just outside the city of Sao Paulo. His father worked in the city and would often walk home rather than spend money on a bus that took him only half the distance anyway. One day he came upon what he realized was a drug deal. One of the dealers spotted him and chased him, but he managed to escape. Instead of going to the police, he went to Father Manuel and asked what he should do. Of course Father Manuel told him he must go to the police. He was able to identify several of the men from mug shots, but there had been at least two others that he couldn't identify. A few weeks later, a fire bomb was tossed into Jesse's house in the middle of the night. The only one who survived was Jesse – and only because he liked to sleep in a hammock in the back yard when it was hot, rather than in a bed with two of his brothers. The blast from the initial explosion hurled a large piece of glass along with other debris into the hammock and almost severed his leg. It had to be amputated just above the knee.

"Jesse was placed in the Catholic mission orphanage once he was out of the hospital. He was there for three years before a young couple wanted to adopt him. By then, he considered the orphanage his home and didn't want to leave his friends. The day he was to be sent home with the couple, he disappeared. It was reported to the police, but they never found him. After several months, it was assumed that he was either dead or had been picked up by someone dealing in human trafficking. Unfortunately, that's not uncommon in poor neighborhoods and Jesse was a beautiful child. He doesn't talk about how he survived or how he evaded the authorities. It was a total accident that I found him."

Up to this point, Simon's head had been lowered, his eyes focused on some distant place that held his protégé's painful memories. Now, a poignant smile came to his lips as he looked up at Karen, who was completely enthralled by his story.

"It was the day I received the engagement ring from Staci. I couldn't sleep that night, so decided to go to town. Truth be told, I was considering getting drunk. It was after midnight and I wasn't familiar enough with the city to know where – or even if – there were any bars open, but I took the mission jeep and headed toward the city. I was driving through a rather seedy part of town, so was driving faster than I should, when a child darted out in front of the car. I swerved to miss him and almost ran into a tree. When I looked back, the child was gone and all I saw was a large, open air dump. There was a fence around it and I didn't think the child had time to climb a fence and disappear in the dump by the time I looked around, so I drove slowly around for several minutes. I eventually gave up my search, thinking that the Lord had sent an angel to distract me from my intended destination. I headed back to the mission.

"The following morning, I told Ken about the events of the night and he said I probably did see a child. It wasn't uncommon for homeless children to haunt the local dumps, looking for everything from discarded clothing to food. I decided I was going to go back and check it out. For the next three nights, I would drive out, park the jeep in a cluster of trees next to the road, and watch the dump. On the third night, I must have dozed off for a moment, because I was startled by a rattling of the fence – and then I saw Jesse. I knew it wasn't the same child I had seen the other night. He hadn't had a crutch, and I was certain I had seen two legs. Jesse made his way across the road then disappeared in a wooded area. I wasn't about to follow him into the woods at night. Besides, I wanted to find the other child I had seen as well.

"The next day, I went to the dump, found the spot where the fence was loose, and began my search. Eventually, I found a sort of path through the rubbish. It led me to a shelter that was constructed from all kinds of trash – wooden crates, cardboard boxes, rusted car parts and heaven only knows what else. There were three children inside, including Jesse. I spoke enough Portuguese to communicate with Jesse that I would not report them to the authorities, but I hoped he would come to the mission for help. He asked if I was a priest. I explained who I was and when I said I was American, he began speaking to me in English. It surprised me that he was almost as fluent in English as he was in Portuguese.

"I knew I had to gain his trust before he would come to us for help, so I began visiting his little group every day. There were actually seven in all. Five boys and two girls – Jesse was the oldest, although he appeared to be about the same age as a couple of the other boys. I'd bring fresh fruit and vegetables, and sometimes a sweet treat. I told him where our mission was located and assured him he could come to us if he had a problem.

"It took almost two months to gain his trust enough that when the youngest girl – she was seven years old and their newest member – became quite ill. She had been with them for only three months and had become Jesse's – for lack of a better word – pet. Her name was Monica and she was a beautiful little girl. When I offered to take her to the mission hospital, Jesse insisted that he had to come along. I don't think he realized that the only mission hospital was the Catholic hospital next to the orphanage. We had a small clinic at our mission, but Monica was dehydrated and running a high temperature. I was pretty certain she needed more help than our little clinic could provide. When we passed the orphanage, I noticed a panicked look on his face, but said nothing. It passed when he realized we weren't turning into that drive.

"Monica was diagnosed with a severe case of intestinal parasites and the doctor recommended that all members of her household be tested and treated. It took a lot of persuasion from both me and the doctor to get Jesse to agree to let me bring all the children in for treatment.

"Doctor Padilha was close friends with Father Manuel and when he told him about the *band of ragamuffins* that I had brought to him, he mentioned that their obvious leader had only one leg. Father Manuel immediately thought of Jesse and came to me to ask if I knew all their names. When I mentioned Jesse's name, he got this amazed look on his face and said, 'Unbelievable.' That's when he told me Jesse's story, saying that he would be willing to wager his last bottle of Irish whisky that it was the same spirited boy who had run away from the orphanage four years ago.

"It was a hard sell, but Father Manuel and I eventually coerced Jesse into returning to the orphanage. I think he did it more for the other children than for himself. Eventually, the Matheson's adopted both Jesse and Monica. The other girl in the group, Sophia, and her brother Enrique were adopted by an American couple and now live in California. The last I heard from Father Manuel, Tiago, Emil and Carlos are still attending school. He calls them his three musketeers and says they are good students. They're all teenagers now, so not likely to be adopted."

Karen, who had been fascinated by Simon's story, emitted a deep sigh before saying, "Why do I feel like I should be crying?"

"Probably because you are imagining how horribly these children's lives began. But you should see them Karen. They are all happy, well-adjusted children – and I think a large portion of the credit goes to Jesse. He doesn't know the meaning of deprivation. His attitude is that he has always been blessed. I'm telling you, he's the most incredible kid I've ever met."

"And he's never shared with you how he survived after he ran away from the orphanage?"

"All he's ever told me is that he promised God that if He watched over him, he would be honest and never take from others. He says God sent him a very strong guardian angel, then he gives me this playful smile and that's it. End of story! In my books, I named his *guardian angel* parrot Donato. It means 'given by God.'"

Karen realized she had been completely at ease with Simon for over thirty minutes, listening to him talk – caught up in his story and feeling his passion for the young boy who inspired his writing. Taking another sip of her now warm champagne, she glanced at her watch and realized it was after four.

"Would you like to stay for dinner, Simon? I'm testing the first of the recipes that I received in response to the 'Calling all Good Cooks' ad. It's a fish stew recipe that sounds great."

"Tempting, but it's Tuesday – Bible study night. I'd back out except for the fact that this is my last meeting before I leave. I'm going to drive up to Covington next Monday, meet my niece, then fly out of Cincinnati International on Thursday. I'm leaving my car with Belinda while I'm gone. Can I get a rain check for say, Thursday or Friday?"

Karen tried to hide her disappointment with a forced smile that she imagined looked as fake as it felt. It wasn't just about tonight – she hadn't thought he would be leaving quite so soon.

"Either day…or both. I have at least a dozen other recipes that I'll be working on over the next week. Salmon fritters, Scotch broth, turkey pot pie and an Italian meat loaf that sounds really interesting."

"They all sound great. Surprise me…and let's make it Friday. Chances are I'll be helping Lenny and Gail move in on Thursday. I don't know how late that might keep me."

"I'm anxious to meet them. How would it be if I brought over supper for all of you?"

"I couldn't expect you to do that, Karen. It's liable to be a chaotic mess. We'll probably just order a pizza or something…"

"Simon, you didn't ask me to do anything. I volunteered. I make a pretty mean pizza if that's your choice."

"I'd prefer anything but pizza, since that's the standard bill of fare for tonight. If you insist on doing this, some sandwiches and chips will work fine. It's highly unlikely that Gail will have the dishes unpacked."

Simon stood, drawing Karen up with him. He pulled her into a warm hug as he spoke into her hair.

"You're a wonderful, generous person, Karen. I'm glad I have you for a friend."

There it is again. That awkward emotional upheaval. Friend, Karen. He said friend!

"Ditto, friend," was all she could choke out.

Chapter 31

Upon meeting Willie, Toby's reaction took Karen totally off guard. She had never considered Toby to be a bigot. He had several black men working for him and appeared to be as friendly with them as he was with all his workers. But when she introduced Willie to him, he stammered through the introduction and glared at Willie with an indiscernible look that Karen couldn't quite interpret. After the introductions were complete, Toby, somewhat reluctantly, put Willie to work uncrating equipment, and then followed Karen to the cottage.

"Where the hell did you find that behemoth? He looks like he could tear a man apart with one hand tied behind his back!"

Oh my gosh! He's intimidated by Willie's size. For the first time, Karen realized that every man that worked for Toby was at least two inches shorter than him. Toby didn't like looking *up* to his workers. *How funny!*

Karen held back the laughter that threatened to burst forth when she turned to Toby and attempted to sound serious as she said, "You're right. He probably could. But he won't. Just look at him as a gentle giant…and stand on a stool when you talk to him if you don't like straining your neck looking up at him."

She suspected the color flooding Toby's face was more embarrassment than anger at being exposed. He looked like he wanted to say something, paused, then burst into laughter.

"Busted!" he finally managed to say. "Damn, he's big. Seriously, Karen, a grill cook? He looks like he'd be more comfortable bench pressing the grill than standing over it."

Karen finally released her bottled laughter, and then sobered enough to quote her granny.

"'A person's strength is not determined by their size or their character by appearance'. Willie would be more likely to pick a flower than dismember a man."

"You mean he's…"

"Oh for heaven's sake, Toby. Can't a man be gentle without you male chauvinists classifying them as gay? Willie is married to a beautiful woman and has two equally beautiful daughters. He's been a grill cook for many years. You seem to think it's macho enough to stand over a little barbeque grill on the deck. Why would you think it any less manly to stand over a commercial grill in a diner?"

"I didn't say it wasn't a manly job. For cryin' out loud, Karen. Most grill cooks *are* men – they're just not seven feet tall and built like professional weight lifters."

"Six-foot-eight…and according to Father Brian, he can bench press over five hundred pounds. I have no idea how close to professional status that would be."

"Who's Father Brian?"

"A friend of Simon's. He's the one who…uh…found Willie."

When Toby started to say something else, Karen quickly cut him off.

"I really have to go Toby, and I'm sure you have things to do as well."

Rather than being upset by Karen's abrupt dismissal, Toby gave her a broad smile.

"So what's on the menu tonight?"

For the past two nights, Toby, Darrell and several other members of the crew had been Karen's *guinea pigs* for testing her recipes. Both the fish stew and turkey pot pie had been huge successes.

"Sorry to disappoint you, Toby, but I have other commitments for tonight and tomorrow. My test kitchen won't reopen until Monday."

"Now that's what I call a sandwich!" Lenny had just downed the second half of one of the huge, meat-packed hoagies that Karen had made for the adults and older children. For the younger ones she had made her special peanut butter and jelly sandwiches. There was also potato salad and chocolate chip cookies. Two year old Kitty ate only half of her sandwich before demanding a cookie, so Simon polished off the second half.

"That's not your standard peanut butter and grape jelly sandwich," he noted. "What's in this? I believe it could be addictive."

This comment prompted Lenny to snatch a bite of four year old Seth's sandwich, which evoked a harsh protest from the cherub faced toddler.

"Mine Daddy! Mine!"

"I have more, Sweetie," Karen soothed, offering Lenny a PB&J of his own. He took it without hesitation.

"Who needs chocolate chip cookies," Lenny said. "This is my dessert."

Simon had been right about the chaos. They were all seated on the floor of the dining room, enjoying their picnic dinner. The truck was mostly unpacked, but with the exception of the beds, all the furniture was still covered in packing wrap and scattered throughout the house. Boxes were stacked everywhere.

After their meal, Karen helped Gail locate the bedding so they could make up the beds. By nine they had the children bathed and tucked in. The exhausted crew settled down on the back deck with a bottle of wine that Karen supplied. She and Gail hit it off immediately. Gail was a tiny wisp of a woman, with strawberry blond hair framing a big-eyed, freckled pixie face. She looked more like a twelve year old than a thirty year old mother of four.

The children had already dubbed her 'Aunt Karen,' which pleased her to no end. Kitty had wrapped her arms around Karen's neck when she told her good night and on the way back downstairs, Karen said, "I might have to steal that one from you."

"Please do," was Gail's exhausted reply. "Any time…of course on a temporary basis. That one wears me out more than the other three put together. Leah tries to help, but she's only seven and Kitty can beat her down in five minutes."

Her words sounded just like Amy when she was tired. She put her arm around Gail's shoulders saying, "Maybe I'll come by tomorrow and take her off your hands for a few hours. She's not allergic to cats is she?"

"That would be wonderful. I could accomplish so much more with her not being underfoot. As far as being allergic to cats, you might want to keep the cat away from her…for its safety."

The following morning, Karen picked up Kitty *and* Seth at nine in the morning, saying she would bring them back by noon. "I'll try to have them sufficiently worn out by then so they'll sleep the rest of the afternoon."

"You are an absolute saint." Gail exclaimed, giving her new friend a hug.

Karen was surprised to see how much they had accomplished. "You must have been up half the night to get this much done."

"We had to push Simon out the door at eleven-thirty, and then Lenny and I collapsed into bed shortly thereafter. We were up and running at seven this morning. Lenny made it a priority to get the swing set put together by this afternoon. Hopefully that will keep the little ones occupied the rest of the day."

After rescuing Goodness from an enthusiastic greeting by Kitty, followed by a near strangling hug from Seth, Karen asked them if they would like to help her bake some cookies. This appeared to be an appealing distraction and they both settled on stools placed on either side of her to watch as she put together the dough. She bribed them into sitting *perfectly still* until she rolled out the dough, by promising them they could cut out the cookies, and after they were baked, they could decorate them. This had been one of Granny's tactics with her and Amy, and was the beginning of her love for cooking.

Her constant chatter as she added ingredients, explaining everything she did, kept them completely engrossed. By the time she rolled out the dough, both of them were beyond anxious to *help*.

Seth proved to be quite artistic with the decorating. Karen carefully guided Kitty's little hand while squeezing the different colored frostings she had spooned into baggies with a small corner snipped off. Since her only cookie cutters were Christmas themed she set aside the Santa, the tree and the reindeer, using only the star, the dove and the angel, and sticking to pastel colors for the frosting. She was having so much fun she hadn't realized how close it was to twelve.

"Goodness gracious, it's time for me to take you home," she said as she wiped the multi-colored frosting from the two adorable faces, giving each a peck on the nose as she finished.

"Can we take some cookies for Mommy and Daddy?" Seth asked, then thoughtfully added, "Leah and Max too."

"You can take *all* the cookies home, Sweetie. After all, you made them."

Seth's little chest puffed out as he added, "But you helped."

Chapter 32

It was after three by the time Karen got back to the cottage. Simon was supposed to come at six and she had dinner to prepare. She hoped Toby wasn't around when she returned and when she didn't see his truck, she stopped in the diner to see how much progress had been made.

"Wow!" she exclaimed, as she walked through the door. The entire grill area was in place as well as most of the kitchen equipment. The walk-ins, along with the booths, counter and stools wouldn't arrive until next week. Karen's heart raced as she made her way through the diner. Just as she reached the back door, Toby stepped inside.

"So what do you think, boss lady?"

As always, Toby's lopsided grin disarmed her a little…aside from the fact that she didn't want to get into any long discussions with him.

"It looks great, Toby. I get more excited every time I walk in here."

"Is this place the only thing that excites you, Karen?"

His voice was teasing, but his eyes focused directly on hers. He wanted an answer.

"As a matter of fact, it's the only thing I have time to get excited about."

"But you have time to baby-sit a couple of br…kids. Whose are they, anyway?"

"Not that it's any of your business, but they belong to our new minister. They just moved here from Ashland. Now if you'll excuse me, I have…a lot of things to do."

She had almost said "dinner to prepare." Heaven only knows what kind of interrogation that would elicit.

Toby stepped aside, but Karen could feel his eyes on her as she covered the distance between the diner and the cottage. *Oh Toby, if you were only less possessive…less Chase…it would be so much easier to learn to care for you.*

As always, cooking simultaneously relaxed and invigorated Karen. As she carefully frenched the rack of lamb – Simon's favorite – she sang along with her favorite Allison Krauss CD.

The mint flavored pepper jelly she had found wasn't nearly as good as Granny's, and she vowed she would make a large batch once she was in her diner kitchen.

She was running slightly behind schedule, but determined a glass of wine, or maybe a drink before dinner would give the lamb time to cook.

Maybe I'll get him drunk and throw myself at him. Forget about food, she devilishly thought, and then blushed at her own imaginings, knowing she just wasn't made that way. She had never considered herself to be prudish, but she had been raised to believe that sex wasn't a casual sport; nor was it a prelude to marriage. It was a sealing of the marriage bond. As of late, she wondered if the only reason Chase had married her was because he figured it was the only way to get her in bed. She had always believed they had a relatively good sex life, although it certainly wasn't the mind-blowing, earth-shaking experience described in some of the books she read. That, she had decided, was total fantasy.

Giving herself a mental slap in the face, she abruptly redirected her thoughts as the timer rang, signaling her crème brulee was done.

"As always, that was fantastic," Simon praised as he took his last sip of the Pinot Noir that had accompanied the meal. "I'll have to sit a while before I can tackle dessert."

One of the things she loved so much about her little cottage was the fact that a guest could sit in the living room area and still converse with her in the kitchen. Simon offered to help with the clean-up, but Karen immediately ordered him to sit.

"You'll just be in the way," she protested. "This is a definitely a one person kitchen."

As soon as Simon sat down, Goodness jumped up on his lap, her purr at full throttle.

"She's really grown," Simon said, scratching her head. "Did I ever tell you that Ken and Lizzie had a pair of puma cubs as pets when I was there the first time?"

"You're kidding. Don't they get huge…and dangerous?"

"They donated them to a zoo in Sao Paulo when they adopted Jesse and Monica. The cubs were about half grown by then and Lizzie was afraid they might hurt Monica. They were adorable…just a couple of overgrown kittens.

Jesse *loved* them and would get on the ground and tumble around with them all the time. But he understood their concern for Monica."

Simon's voice had trailed off as he finished speaking, his eyes focused on some distant place.

"You're anxious to be there, aren't you?"

"Huh? I'm sorry, I sort of drifted away for a minute," he replied, his head jolting up to meet Karen's gaze. "Yes...yes I am. As much as I love my life here, there's something so fulfilling in being part of a much larger world."

"I've never been anywhere beyond our continent. Prior to coming here, the farthest north was Whistler in British Columbia and the farthest south was Corpus Christi, Texas. Both were family vacations. I was sixteen when we went to Whistler and discovered that I wasn't a whole lot better at snow skiing than I am at water skiing." Karen realized that Simon was watching her as she spoke – wearing that breathtaking smile – so she quickly turned away. *Don't need to go there. Don't need to go there.*

A little later, after downing his dessert and coffee, Simon once again praised Karen's cooking and thanked her for preparing such a memorable meal.

"You'll be at the church dinner tomorrow, won't you?" he asked as he pushed away from the table.

"I'd better be since I signed up for Lasagna and promised your mom I'd cover her dessert item."

Simon had insisted that his mother should not make the two hour drive back home just to attend his farewell dinner. He knew she would have a difficult time leaving little Caitlyn so soon. He reasoned that he would be coming up there on Monday, so it wasn't like she wouldn't have an opportunity to see him before he left. Karen had completely agreed with Simon when Margo called about the dessert.

Looking down at his watch, Simon pushed back from the table and stood up. Karen knew the evening had come to an end. Despite a few rough moments for her, it had gone well. She loved being with Simon and once they immersed themselves in conversation, she could set aside her conflicted emotions and just enjoy his company.

He walked around the small table and pulled Karen to her feet. Wrapping her in a warm embrace, he spoke into her hair. "I'm going to miss you, you know." Then he gave her a squeeze, kissed the top of her head and turned toward the door saying, "Thanks again, for a wonderful meal."

And he was gone. There would be no more time alone with him before he left. Not tomorrow night. Certainly not on Sunday at church. The rest of his time would be spent packing for the trip and she knew he had accepted an invitation to dinner from Father Brian for Sunday night.

Wiping away the uncontrolled tears that were streaming down her face, she reached down and picked up Goodness, who had been brushing back and forth at her ankles.

"Back to the real world, Karen," she muttered, nuzzling her nose in soft gray fur.

Chapter 33

"Simon! What on earth are you doing here?"

Candace Treadway, Staci's grandmother, was a striking woman, who, at sixty-nine could have easily passed for her mid fifties. How much of her youth was cosmetically attained, Simon had no clue.

"Hello Candace. It's good to see you too."

The maid who had admitted Simon asked if Ms Treadway would like for her to bring refreshments for her guest. Without answering, Candace turned to Simon for a reply.

"No thank you, Bernice. I'm here to see Staci. Is she around?"

Bernice looked at Candace, who waved her off in dismissal, but not before the two women exchanged a peculiar look. Returning her attention to Simon, Candace spoke, obviously irritated by Simon's unannounced visit.

"Staci is…resting at the moment. I'd rather not disturb her."

Simon was about to protest that he was here for only a short while, when the sound of laughter from the back of the house caught his attention. Walking past Candace toward the direction of the laughter, he ignored her protest as he passed.

"You can't go back there, Simon. I'll get her…"

When he reached the open glass doors that led to the lanai, he halted abruptly as Blake Perkins spotted him. Following Blake's eyes, Staci looked back over her shoulder and almost choked on the drink she had just sipped.

"My God! Simon! What on earth are you doing here?"

"Popular question," Simon said, not hiding his own confusion. "I'm a little curious as to what Blake is doing here."

Blake shuffled his feet and gave Staci a sideways glance. Staci's eyes turned to Blake as if looking for him to answer. When neither spoke, Simon said, "I'm here to talk to you Staci…alone."

"You can say whatever you have to say in front of Blake. He knows everything about our history as a couple," She replied, her eyes never leaving Blake's.

Simon had to fight back an anger that threatened to destroy his determination to resolve his relationship with Staci once and for all. With a calm he didn't really feel, he said, "That's really odd, Staci, since I know *nothing* about your history with Blake, aside from the fact that you were once married."

The uncomfortable silence that followed Simon's statement was broken when Blake took the glass from Staci's hand, saying, "I think I'll go see if Candace finished that pitcher of margaritas. Can I get you something to drink, Simon?"

"Nothing for me, thank you."

Blake closed the door behind him.

"Why are *you* here, Staci? Why didn't you return home with your parents? Why is Blake with you? Are you two getting back together? When were you going to let me know?"

As he spoke, Simon moved to the front of the lounge and sat in a chair directly in front of Staci. She immediately pulled her knees up to her chest, crossing her arms over them – as if she was withdrawing from him.

"I'm here because Grandmother asked me to stay. She invited Blake. Honestly, Simon, I had no idea he was coming any more than I knew you were coming." Her face took on a hard look as she added. "Now it's your turn, Simon. Why are you here?"

"I'm on my way to South America. I plan on being there for three or four months and I wanted to clear the air between us before I left. I need to know if there is an *us* any more."

When he lifted his eyes to look at her, she turned away. Tears began forming at the corner of her eyes and her reply was almost inaudible.

"I'm not sure there ever was an *us* Simon. Our wants and needs are too different. You're perfectly content being a nobody, living in a nowhere town with your mother. I've never been a priority in your life. You are passionless and apathetic toward me. You say you love me, but you've never made love to me. When my life has been in turmoil, you console me with words instead of actions. The only reason I keep coming back to you is because I keep hoping you'll begin seeing me as a woman instead of the little girl you met in high school."

Her attack was more hurtful than her criticism of his Jesse books had been. Instinctively he sought to defend himself. He just wasn't sure where to begin. *Passionless! Apathetic!* Was he really those things? He said a silent prayer before he began speaking. *Please God, don't let this hurt turn to anger. Give me words that will heal, not further wound both our hearts.*

"Before I say anything in my defense, I want you to know that I'm sincerely sorry that you see me this way. I always thought we shared the same belief that sex was something reserved for the marriage bed. The first time we talked about marriage, I knew I wanted you more than anything – physically as well as emotionally. Being away from you made it easier to deal with my carnal desires, and when we were together, I fought to respect what I believed was a shared principle.

"Admittedly, I put my family ahead of you after Dad's death. Sandy was still in high school and Mom was lost without Dad. I should have made it clear to you that it wasn't merely the idea of moving away that prompted my refusal to consider the possibility of Atlanta. It was mostly the idea of deserting my family at that time. As far as seeing you as a woman; my God, Staci, all you should have to do is look in a mirror to see that you are a beautiful, desirable woman. I wouldn't be a man at all if I couldn't see that."

"I wish I could believe you Simon," she said coldly. "But I *have* looked in the mirror at myself and what I always saw was a flat-chested, stringy haired mouse. You never acted in any way to disprove that image."

Simon couldn't hide his shock at Staci's statement. She had always been thin, and the fact that she had small…that's when his eyes were drawn to her breasts. Her very obvious breasts. For the first time he realized that what he had at first thought was a long swim suit cover-up, was in fact a bathrobe.

"What have you done, Staci?"

"What I should have done years ago," was her curt reply.

"By why, Staci? Certainly not for me! I would never…"

"I did it for *me*, Simon. *For me!*"

No longer able to control his anger, Simon asked through gritted teeth, "And what exactly does Blake have to do with this? Is he the one who talked you into it?"

Staci's glare turned to a smug snarl as she replied, "Actually, it was Grandmother's suggestion. I was afraid of it, so she called Blake to reassure me that it was perfectly safe. In case you've forgotten, *he is a doctor*. He didn't hesitate in taking time off to come down here to be with me."

Simon was at a loss for words. For several minutes he sat with his elbows on his knees, head resting in his hands before he spoke. Lifting his head, he stared hard at Staci, his voice dull with defeat.

"I don't think I know you anymore, Staci. I wonder if I ever knew you. You've always been so evasive when I asked you anything personal. I don't even know why you and Blake got divorced. The most you ever said was that it didn't work out. I've always accepted your inept answers because I felt it was too painful for you to talk about. Now I know that you never trusted me with the truth."

The misery in his voice didn't escape Staci, but she had no response. She simply stared back at him, her face a mask of indifference.

"I have one last question for you, Staci, and then I'll leave."

She gave him a, *whatever* look, drumming her fingers on the sides of her knees.

"If I had an income outside of my church ministry – one that would allow me to provide for you in the manner to which you are accustomed – would that make a difference in how you felt about me?"

There was something close to contempt in her voice as she replied. "Oh Simon, why would you ask such a question? You don't and you can't, so my answer is completely irrelevant."

He stood for a minute, absorbing her response, then turned and began walking toward the side gate.

"Tell your grandmother I'll let myself out and I'm sorry to have bothered all of you."

Chapter 34

Karen stood in the doorway of the diner, her heart racing and tears welling in her eyes. It was done. She had hung the last of the wall decorations and everything was exactly as she had pictured it. Toby stood at the end of the counter watching her. They had finished the diner three days ahead of schedule. The landscaping and striping of the parking area would be complete by the end of the week and all the pots, pans and kitchen utensils were unpacked and ready for use.

"You look pleased," he said, not hiding his own pride in the finished product.

"Thank you Toby. You did a wonderful job. Now all *I* have to do is fill this place with customers every day and I might be able to keep it."

"Are you kidding me?" He teased, patting his stomach. "If you keep putting out the kind of food you've been feeding me for the past weeks, I'll be building on an addition by next year. I think I've put on at least ten pounds."

Obviously pleased by his praise, she sighed deeply before saying, "I don't want any more than what I have right here. I'm not in this to become rich and I certainly don't want more than I can handle on my own. It's frightening enough to be responsible for the employees I already have. I'm still working on schedules that will give them at least one day a week off, so I have several more openings to fill."

"I'll be more than happy to work double shifts seven days a week," Darrell said as he stepped out of the kitchen.

"You say that now, but you'd burn out in a month." Karen shot back. "I want you around for much longer than that."

Over the past month, Karen had received almost two hundred recipes from local housewives and even a few from some men. Not surprisingly, about half of the men's were for chili. These she had shown to Darrell and he agreed that some might be worth trying, but was still confident his recipe would win out over all of them.

Sorting through the other recipes proved to be a real challenge. It was easy to determine those that weren't cost effective and those that were too complicated, but the ones she had tested in small quantities had all been quite good. The trick would be to maintain the integrity of the dish when making it in large quantities. Simply multiplying the ingredients didn't always produce the same taste. She had learned this the hard way when she shared an Irish stew recipe of Granny's with Handi. He had loved the stew when she brought him a sample, but when he let her make up a large batch for a lunch special, some seasonings were overpowering, while others were barely discernable. The result had to be reworked by Handi – considerably – to produce a final product that was close to the original recipe, but not nearly as tasty. She was surprised when he said they would be making it again, but this time, he stood next to her and explained which flavors would fade in such a large quantities and which would be too intense.

"A lot of it has to do with the cooking time it takes for larger batches," he explained. "Sometimes, it is simply a matter of when to add the seasonings. The more subtle flavors should be added closer to the end." It was good advice and she had a strong sense of taste so eventually was able to reproduce Granny's stew to near perfection.

"So Darrell, Are you ready to start testing recipes?"

"Ready, willing and able. I've checked out all the stoves and ovens. That's a hell'u'va smoker you have in there. We'll be able to put out some awesome smoked barbeque – or any other smoked items you decide to serve."

Darrell had been a regular member of the recipe taste-testing at the cottage over the last weeks – along with Toby, several of his crew and Willie on the days when they worked late.

Karen had discovered that Darrell knew how to butcher a side of beef, something that would save them a lot of money in the end. She had already determined that he would be of far greater value to her working full time in the prep area. Wayne, the young man she had hired as a daytime busboy, assured her he could handle the dishwasher and the bussing without a problem. She hoped she would be able to find equally cooperative people for the evening shift and relief positions.

When she had gone to Dil with her final anticipated payroll figures, she was more nervous than she had been at their first meeting.

"I can't honestly guarantee that we will have enough business to support this much payroll, and I can probably tone it down once I have a better idea of what our volume will be, but I know that opening a restaurant understaffed can seal it's doom from the start."

Karen's nervous defense of her payroll numbers brought a smile to Dil's face, followed by a reflective sigh.

"Unfortunately, Karen, I didn't pay much attention to the diner when I was growing up. All I saw was long hours of hard work and more responsibility than I ever wanted to deal with. I'm going to trust your judgment on this. The closer the reopening of the Krossroads comes to being a reality, the more I realize that you are very much like my grandmother. Ma had a passion that I never understood, and my dad supported it. Looking back, I realize he never really shared her passion. If he had, the diner would never have died with Ma."

He looked hard at Karen, as if studying something beyond her mere appearance before he continued.

"You, Young Lady, have given me far more than any amount of money can buy. You've brought me back to my roots, and more importantly, you have reconnected me to the love of my life. I don't want you to be concerned with money. I want you to concentrate on providing good food at an affordable price, served in a friendly atmosphere and in a timely manner. If this is what it takes to do that, you have my full support. Everything you've done; everything you have shown me thus far – the menu, the food costs, the overhead figures, the advertising budget and even the projected customer volume – are all realistic. I have a feeling that the biggest difference will come in your estimates on volume."

He paused, a sly grin twitching the edges of his mouth. "I've added one item to the advertising, but it won't affect your budget. I've rented a two sided billboard on Interstate sixty-four at the Sharkey exit. It's my opening gift to you and it goes up on October tenth. Think you'll be able to open the doors by then?"

Karen couldn't stop the tears of gratitude from flowing. When she stood up and walked around the desk, Dil met her with open arms.

"Margo's a lucky woman, Dil. Even luckier than I am to have found the Krossroads and such a wonderful benefactor."

Chapter 35

"Good night Karen. See you tomorrow."

Willie was the last member of the crew to leave after the clean-up. Karen beamed as she thought about all the wonderful compliments and the smoothness in which the entire evening had progressed. Yes, all of the guests had received a free meal, but they had also cleaned their plates, exchanged tastes of each other's menu selections and appeared to thoroughly enjoy the entire evening. The dining room had been filled with lively chatter, laughter and camaraderie. Even the children had cleaned their plates, although Karen suspected that several had help from curious parents. Her Frank 'n Macdoodle platter had been a huge success, especially with the boys. The only person remaining in the diner was Toby, who sat at a booth watching as Karen locked the front door.

"For someone who's been on the go since five o'clock this morning, you look great."

Karen looked at her watch and realized that it was actually early. Nine twenty-five. Their two seatings had started at five-thirty, with the second at seven. Everyone was aware that there were still a lot of preparations ahead for the grand opening on Saturday, so no one lingered after their meals. The waitresses had handled the guests with ease, all showing a high level of professionalism combined with friendly familiarity. Consequently they were rewarded with generous tips. They had shared a liberal amount with the busboys and even offered Willie a share. To their surprise, he refused, smiling broadly and saying, "You ladies earned that for your good service. I'm just happy gettin' paid for doin' what I love."

After Willie's departure, Toby followed Karen to the cottage. As they reached the door, she turned to him.

"I still have a lot to do to get ready for tomorrow, Toby. It would probably be best if…"

Toby reached over and pulled her into his arms.

"I'm crazy about you, Karen. You've got to know that. We no longer have a working relationship to consider, so you can't use that as an excuse. I want to be more than friends. Don't you think we should…celebrate?"

Karen froze in his arms. She was fairly certain about what he had in mind as a way of *celebration*. Pushing away, she said, "Oh Toby, I wish you wouldn't press the issue right now. I can't possibly think of anything but the diner at this time."

His response sounded more angry than disappointed. "So when, Karen? Or am I just spinning my wheels? Do you have any feelings for me at all?"

"Of course I do. You've been a great friend and an excellent contractor. You did a wonderful job in turning the Krossroads from a dump into my beautiful diner. I enjoy being with you, but it's been less than six months since my life was turned upside down. I'm just now starting to feel that my feet are back under me." There was a pained look on her face as she continued. "I really can't consider anything beyond friendship until I'm established, not only in my business, but in my personal life as well. I'm just asking for your patience."

He stood there staring at her, his obstinate posture speaking much louder than his words. "Well be sure and let me know when you're ready for a more personal relationship. I'll be waiting with baited breath."

The sound of his boots stomping down the steps made Karen cringe. Had she just dodged a bullet…or hurt someone who truly cared for her? These feelings were *not* how she wanted to end what had been an otherwise perfect day.

Tomorrow would be the first actual business day. A full day that would begin at four-thirty a.m. and most likely end after eleven p.m. Hoping to get a good night's sleep for her early start, she took a shower, two PM Tylenol, set the alarm for four-thirty and crawled into bed – but sleep evaded her. After tossing and turning between brief periods of dozing, her mind a jumble of sorting out her emotions as well as tomorrow's activities, she sat up, disturbing a sleeping Goodness who voiced her displeasure with a startled "r-reooow."

"Sorry, baby," she murmured, scratching the kitten's head. Ten minutes later she was headed over to the diner. *The best antidote for insomnia is to be productive. I'll get a head start on the pies for tomorrow…today…whatever!*

The air was crisp and the bright moonlight, combined with the stillness of her surroundings as she stepped out the door, overcame Karen. A feeling of peace settled within her as she walked the distance between the cottage and the diner. When she heard a crackling of leaves in the woods, she smiled, imagining a deer making its way to the creek. She had seen them often through her kitchen window, drinking at the creek or grazing in the grass that grew along the shore. Opening the back door to the diner, she switched on the lights and her heart did a little dance. *Thank you God for all this...and thank you Granny, for leading me here.* Donning an apron over her sweater and jeans, she turned on the oven and set about pulling out the necessary utensils and ingredients for her pies. As she worked, she hummed and occasionally broke into the verse of a song, tapping the stainless steel work surface with whatever utensil was in her hand. Placing lemon filling on a burner, she turned around to begin rolling out the balls of crust that she had prepared earlier in the day. A shuffling sound brought her attention to the door, and emitting a loud gasp, she dropped the spoon she held in her hand and froze.

Standing just inside the door was a man. A man she had never seen before. He wore a faded army coat over neatly pressed kakis, and appeared to be as shocked by her presence as she was by his. Tall and slightly built, with sandy colored hair streaked with gray, he appeared to be between fifty and sixty.

"You...you ain't Ma." he stated accusingly, his words coming in slow articulate bursts.

She wanted to scream, but what good would it do? The closest house to the diner was at least a quarter mile away. When she opened her mouth, nothing came out.

"Why are you cookin' in Ma's kitchen?" the stranger asked. "Ma wouldn't like that."

Finding her voice at last, Karen's quivering voice asked, "Who...who are you?"

"I'm Paulie Kendrick. I'm Ma's night watchman. When she's not here, I'm in charge of..." He stopped, a confused look covering his face.

"You're in charge of what, Paulie?"

Each time he spoke, there was a pause before the words found their way out of his mouth.

"Of protectin' Ma's things. That's what. And she wouldn't like no one to be cookin' in her kitchen."

Suddenly it dawned on Karen. This was "Possum," Dil's childhood neighbor and friend. The man she would supposedly never see. But of course, it was nighttime, so he was *making his rounds*. What she wasn't sure of was how to put him at ease. Was he a danger to her? He didn't appear to have any kind of weapon on him...just the small flashlight he held in his hand.

"Well Paulie, my name is Karen and this is my kitchen now. Ma's grandson...your friend Dil...said I could use it." She hesitated before continuing as she watched his confused look grow deeper. He looked as if he was trying to remember something. Cautiously, she continued. "You…you do know that Ma is…gone."

His expression instantly went from confusion to pain. He looked as if he were going to cry and Karen's heart lurched at the sight of this man/child who was trying to grasp an awful reality.

"I shouda' took better care of her. I fell asleep on my watch…again."

Obviously confusing his past life as a soldier with the present, he crumpled to the floor sobbing. Then grasping his knees, he rocked back and forth on the balls of his feet.

Karen couldn't bear it. She walked over, stooped down beside him and put an arm around him, consoling him as a mother would a child.

"Oh no, Paulie. It wasn't anyone's fault. Ma was an old woman and God called her home. That's all. You took good care of her…and you've watched over her diner for all these years, haven't you?"

"I promised her I would. I'm her night watchman." His words came out in slow choked sobs.

When his shoulders stopped trembling and he seemed to settle down, Karen released him and stood up.

"You know Paulie, I'll need a night watchman now that I'm opening the diner again. Would you be my night watchman? I'd like that."

His mood changed as rapidly as a child's. His face brightening, he stood up and took a soldier's stance, lifting his hand in a military salute.

"Private First Class Paul Ewell Kendrick at your service, Ma'am."

The serious look on his face as he spoke changed to a bright smile when he took an *at ease* stance.

"Would you like for me to fire up the smoker? That was one of my jobs too, Miss Karen. You're pretty."

The last was said with the innocence of a first grader who was smitten with his teacher. Karen looked into a pair of clear blue, guileless eyes that held something familiar about them. *Oh Granny, I think I'm in love!*

"I won't need the smoker fired up until morning, Paulie, but you could help me make my pies. Think you can stir the filling while I make the pie crusts?"

"I help my mama when she cooks. I'm good at stirring."

Minutes later, Paulie was concentrating on his task as Karen began rolling out the balls of chilled dough. They worked in silence, each seemingly concentrating on their individual tasks, when in fact Karen was trying to remember everything Margo and Dil had told her about Paulie and the diner. When she remembered the story of the mysterious light in the diner, she began to wonder.

"Paulie, did you ever see a light in the diner after it was boarded up? Some people thought there was a ghost inside."

After a long pause, Paulie turned his head just enough for Karen to detect a little upward quirk at the edge of his mouth. "There's no such thing as ghosts, Miss Karen. That was just me makin' my rounds."

"But how did you get inside the diner, Paulie. It was locked up tight and all the windows were boarded up. Did you have a key to the padlocks?"

"The key Ma gave me didn't work anymore…so I climbed in through the smoker."

Of course! Karen thought. The bottom shelf of the smoker had been removable – and with Paulie's slight build, he could easily maneuver himself through the door where the logs were fed to the smoker. *Margo's going to flip when she hears this!*

Chapter 36

The first customers through the door on opening day were Dil and Margo. It was actually ten minutes before they were officially open, but Karen unlocked the door for them, anxious to tell Dil about Paulie's appearance.

"I had no idea he was still making his rounds. Margo told me about his nighttime wanderings. I've been meaning to get over to his house and talk to Miriam." Dil paused before he added in a somber tone, "I'm not sure Paulie will remember me after I've neglected him for so long."

Margo reached over and patted his hand. It was obvious that he was stricken with guilt over what he considered abandonment of his childhood friend.

"If you stick around for about an hour, you'll get a chance to see for yourself. He's promised he would come and fire up the smoker for me at seven. He insisted it was his job and I didn't have the heart to refuse him. I'll be curious to see if he actually shows up. He was here until after two."

"As long as we aren't tying up a booth you'll need for other customers."

"Anxious to start getting a return on your investment, are you?" Karen teased.

Dil watched as Karen headed back to the kitchen. Turning to Margo, he smiled, rotating his hand to grasp hers.

"When was the last time you saw Miriam? She has to have been retired for quite a while by now."

"Actually, she was active in the bank until she turned eighty and is still on the board of directors. From what I understand, over the years she has transferred a major portion of her interest in the bank to numerous employees who have worked there for over thirty years. Rumor has it that a large national bank is looking to buy it. It's the last of the small independent banks in this area and there are a lot of farmers and local businesses that won't take kindly to that."

Dil remained quiet for several minutes, as if he was hashing over Margo's information. Then his face took on a pensive look and a slow smile returned to his lips.

"Did I ever tell you that I had a major crush on Miriam when I was about twelve? She was like a second mother to me – much the same way my mother was to Paulie – but Miriam was much more affectionate. I used to pretend I was sad or upset about something and I'd make up some line like, 'I wish Dad could take me and Paulie fishing tomorrow,' or some other lame statement involving one or both of my parents. She would always wrap me in her arms, kiss the top of my head and defend my parents against whatever my imaginary complaint might be. Meanwhile, I would sit there basking in the feel of her arms around me."

Emitting a wistful sigh at this childhood memory, he added, "Now I barely remember what Miriam looks like. My childhood vision of her was sort of Deborah Kerr, but I have a feeling that was a little delusional because of my crush."

Margo cocked her head, trying to picture Miriam. It had been quite a while since she had seen her, but she knew she still had the same look about her as when she came to all of Dil's football games back in the sixties. Of course, she realized, there was a big difference in actually watching a person age as opposed to seeing them after forty years. While Margo certainly never considered her as beautiful as Deborah Kerr, she could see the connection – the red hair, the aristocratic facial features and stately bearing. Her hair was totally white now, but she still walked with the grace and stride of a much younger woman.

With an impish grin, she asked, "Are you telling me I have competition?"

Squeezing her hand, he whispered, "You never had any competition. Never!"

As soon as Paulie arrived, Karen began pushing him toward the dining area. When they were a few feet from the door, Paulie froze in his tracks, almost causing Karen to collide into his back.

"I can't go out there, Miss Karen. Mr. Cliff says I…distract the customers."

Paulie's objection was more of a statement than an excuse as he backed away from the door.

"Now Paulie, you know that Mr. Cliff is not here any more. We talked about that last night. I'm in charge and I say you can. There's someone in the dining room that is very anxious to see you. I promised him that I would bring you out as soon as you arrived.

"But I need to…"

"There's plenty of time to get the smoker going. I think you'll want to see who's waiting."

Reluctantly, Paulie allowed Karen to guide him through the door. As soon as he entered the dining area, his eyes began scanning the booths, and then chanced a glimpse at the grill. No one seemed to take particular notice of him. Dottie, the breakfast cook at the grill, was far too busy filling orders to even look their way. Paulie appeared to relax a bit as Karen stopped at Dil's booth.

"Hi Paulie. Remember me?"

Karen had already adjusted to the pauses that preceded any words spoken by Paulie, but now was holding her breath.

"Hi Dil. I always remember you. You're my best friend."

It was easy to see that Dil was fighting tears that immediately welled in his eyes. Standing, he reached out and embraced his childhood companion – who still considered him to be his *best friend*.

Several people looked up from their meals to watch the touching reunion. Most of the early morning customers were business men and women who had come to check out the diner. Many knew Margo, some were even acquainted with Paulie, but few knew who Dil was. They watched until Paulie settled into the booth next to Margo. It had taken several minutes for Dil to coax Paulie into joining them. Karen had to reassure him that there was plenty of time to fire up the smoker, after which she excused herself and headed back to the kitchen.

"You look great Paulie. You haven't changed all that much." Dil had regained his composure and a broad grin stretched across his face.

"You're old," Paulie said, in his honest, straight forward manner.

Dil and Margo both laughed, and then Dil remarked, "But not as old as you, Paulie. As I recall, you are several months older than I am."

A shy grin crossed Paulie's face.

"Oh yeah! I am. I must look old too. It's been a long time, hasn't it Dil?"

When Paulie returned to the kitchen, he wore a huge smile that stayed with him for the remainder of the day.

Chapter 37

After their parting the night before the diner opened, Toby had obviously sulked for several weeks before showing up at the diner on a Wednesday night. Rather than apologize for storming off in a huff, he apologized for not getting by sooner. This was followed by a list of all the jobs that had him tied up over the last weeks.

"I understand," she said. "It's been pretty crazy for me, too."

He hesitated before asking, "Could I come by after you close? Just to talk. I promise."

Karen looked at her watch. It was seven-thirty. Wednesday was their slowest night and they only served grill items, soup, salad and sandwiches after eight on weeknights.

"Give me about forty-five minutes and I can slip away until closing. How does that sound?"

"Super!" he said, gracing her with that lopsided grin that could look either roguish or playful, depending on the way his eyes looked at you. Karen could imagine girls swooning over that smile – either version – and wondered why it only triggered suspicion in her.

The result of their ensuing conversation was that they each had very different definitions for what constituted a serious relationship. For Toby, it was exclusivity and sex. For Karen it was commitment, eventual marriage, and then sex.

"How do you know if the sex part is going to work out if you wait 'til after you're married?" Toby argued. "I know I wouldn't dream of marrying a woman if I wasn't sure we were compatible in bed. That's a pretty big deal in a marriage, isn't it?"

His words made her think of Chase. He had used almost those same words the first time he tried to get her to bed before they were married. Her response had been, "I was taught that if you truly love someone, the sex part comes naturally. I don't want to simply have sex with anyone. I want to make love to the man with whom I will spend the rest of my life." Her remark had resulted in Chase giving her an engagement ring the following week – and obviously making a commitment he wasn't prepared to honor.

Well she wasn't interested in marrying anyone right now and she was certain that Toby was years away from being able to make that kind of a commitment. She prayed her response would help him understand.

"I won't apologize for who I am, Toby, and I certainly won't apologize for sticking to my values. I truly cherish your friendship, but I'm not in this for a quick roll in the sack. If you want to get to know me better; if you think I'm worth spending time with on a strictly non-sexual basis, then who knows how I might feel in time. I enjoy your company and would love to get to know you better, but it has to be on my terms. If you can't do that, then..." Her voice trailed off as she swallowed the knot in her throat.

Toby sat there, head down, for several silent minutes, as if contemplating her words. When he eventually looked up, his eyes held disappointment – and perhaps a tinge of resignation. He reached over, took her hand, and then releasing a deep sigh, he finally spoke.

"I would never ask you to apologize for who you are Karen. I hope you believe that. I don't know many – make that any – other woman who would pack up and drive across the country on their own to start over." He gave her a half smile, chewing his bottom lip as he continued.

"I admit that in the beginning, I thought you would be an easy target. You know what they say about divorcees. It didn't take me long to realize you were more of a challenge – and there's nothing I love more than a challenge."

That grin again.

"I really do like you – a lot. But me and the idea of marriage – not gonna happen anytime soon. I'm a good six or seven years from thinking in that direction. By then you'll be married with four or five rug rats hanging on your apron."

Without releasing her hand, he stood, drawing her into an embrace. His kiss was sweet and filled with longing.

"I expect we'll probably see each other over the years. You've already hooked me on your cooking, so I'll be back to visit the diner for certain."

Resting her head on his shoulder, she attempted to control her trembling voice as she spoke. "I sincerely wish we had met at a different time, Toby. You're a great guy, and one day, I'm sure you're going to make some woman very, very happy."

With one last squeeze, he released her and headed out the door.

Chapter 38

As always, cooking was the way Karen dealt with her emotions. By the time she returned to the diner, Darrell had the kitchen cleaned and shined like new. Customers still occupied half the booths and a few late night regulars – that would be after eight in Farmers – sat at the counter chatting with Cricket Donovan, Sherry's replacement on Sunday and Wednesday. Cricket also worked the floor on other day and night shifts as needed.

Cricket – her real name was Christine – had been one of the few employees that wasn't on Margo's list. She had stopped by the diner shortly before they opened to ask if they had any jobs available, saying she drove by every day and when she heard there was a woman running the diner, she had to stop and ask.

"Back in Dayton, I was a waitress for over ten years. I'm afraid I can't give you any references 'cause my ex was also my boss. But I'm good and I like people. Ziggy was always gettin' on to me for bein' over friendly with the customers, but I was never flirtin' like he said. He was just one jealous bas…man."

Karen had smiled at her near slip and asked what brought her to this area.

"I was born and raised in Salt Lick. My momma died a couple of years back and Daddy knew I wasn't happy, so he asked me to come live with him. He's not in the best of health, so can't do much around the house, and he's used to the spotless house Momma kept. I don't particularly like workin' nights, but I make more money doin' cleanin' than I could as a waitress. I'm what they call an independent contractor, so I got no benefits. I been thinkin' I'd like to go back to school – get my GED and maybe even take some college courses in business accounting. I like workin' with numbers. Daddy says I'm a genius in math, 'cause I can look at a bunch of numbers and add 'em in my head faster than most people can usin' a calculator."

Listening to her nervous ramblings, Karen had thought of her first interview with Dil. If Margo hadn't been there to keep her focused, she would most likely have rambled in much the same way. Like Karen, Cricket had recently been divorced, and though she never said anything beyond her comment on her ex's jealousy, Karen sensed that there may have been some abuse involved. She based her assessment on Cricket's comment about how glad she was to find out the diner had a woman in charge…and the obvious scar on her left cheek, which wasn't completely hidden by her make-up.

Cricket was a pretty woman, with deep set almond shaped green eyes, a small perfect shaped nose, short black hair and an enchanting smile. Darrell almost tripped over himself the first time he met her and Karen sensed an immediate attraction between the two. But it was easy to see that Cricket had to get past her bad marriage before she would trust a man again. Without Karen saying anything to him, Darrell had sensed this, and proceeded with caution. He was a gentleman by nature and it became obvious that Cricket was warming up to him more each day.

"Are you alright, Karen?" Darrell asked as she returned to the kitchen. "You didn't have to come back 'til closing. I'm sure the crew can handle the front and I'll be glad to stay 'til then and take the deposit in for you. It's right on my way. I've already punched out so I'm on my own time."

"I'm fine, Darrell, and I appreciate the offer, but I'm in the mood to do a little baking," Karen replied, then added with a smirk, "You know you don't need an excuse to stay up front and visit with Cricket."

Darrell blushed as he always did when Karen referred to Cricket in any manner. He was completely smitten.

"As far as the deposit," she continued, "I'll leave that up to you and Gordie to decide. He says he doesn't mind going a little out of his way to make the deposit."

Gordie, their relief grill man, was a retired marine sergeant. He reminded Karen of Handi. Built like a potbelly stove, he was surprisingly agile and strong as an ox. Although he wasn't nearly as natural in handling the grill as Willie or Dottie, he was methodic and well-organized. He and Willie hit it off immediately, having both been ex marines.

As Karen began pulling out ingredients for her pies, she realized she was on the verge of a real *funk*. While her encounter with Toby on the night before the diner opened had felt like a break up, it didn't hurt as much as tonight's for real break up. Her body was on automatic as she began combining the ingredients for the pie crusts, but her mind began questioning her present emotional state.

Okay, KC – time for a reality check. You just turned away a really great guy because you said you weren't ready for a serious relationship. If you really feel that way, then why is it that the mere thought of Simon Crawford makes your heart take flight without regard to where it might land? If he were to walk through that door right now and proclaim his undying love for you, you would probably jump in the sack with him in a heartbeat – if that's what he wanted.

But then, Simon would never do that – and that could be the answer to why you allow yourself to have feelings for him. He's safe. He's in love with another woman. Even if it didn't work out for him and Staci, could I 'settle' for being his second choice? Probably! Ouch! There's that ubiquitous word that I swore off of... but somehow I could never consider being with Simon as settling.

Toby was honest enough to share his feelings about the kind of relationship he was looking for with you. Why couldn't you be honest enough with him to say that you were afraid of becoming involved with someone who reminded you too much of Chase? And who knows – Toby might be right about the sex aspect. Maybe if I had slept with Chase before we got married, we would have realized that we weren't right for each other. Maybe there really is such a thing as fireworks and earth-shaking passion. The kind you read about in books. It was certainly what I expected – what I wanted – and when it wasn't there, I simply wrote it off as a fantasy.

Face it! I knew next to nothing about sex when I married Chase. Mother explained the 'birds and the bees,' along with the fact that sex should be reserved for the marriage bed. But that was when I was still young enough to consider the whole idea 'icky.' Until Chase came along, I never dated anyone seriously enough to get to the point of anything beyond a little necking. Then on the night before my wedding, the proverbial Mother/Daughter talk consisted of her simply saying that I shouldn't expect too much on the first night – that it would get better.

'Better' had been that there was no longer actual pain involved, and that I could take pleasure in knowing I had pleased Chase. I never denied him. Not even on the days when I was sick or dog tired and wanted only to go to sleep. All he had to do was nuzzle my neck while caressing my breast, and I would set aside my exhaustion and open my arms to him.

But I never instigated sex. Oh, I would put on a sexy nightgown and try to make a romantic setting for him – especially after he had been gone for several days. How often was it Chase who protested at those times that he was too tired? And truth be told, I felt more relieved than disappointed.

Maybe I'm just one of those cold women who don't really like sex. Is that what I am?

As quickly as the thought crossed her mind, she thought about Simon. *No way, José!*

"...and the deposit's ready to go."

Karen hadn't realized she was so deep in her self analyzation that she failed to hear all of what Cricket's soft, childlike voice had said.

"I'm sorry, Cricket, I was daydreaming. What did you say?"

"Everything's cleaned and set up for morning. I have the deposit right here. Darrell said he was going to drop it off for Gordie, so Gordie's already gone. My cash report is in the change bag with the credit card receipts. Anything else we need to do before we leave?"

"I don't think so. I'll do my walk through after I lock up. If there's anything you forgot, the girls will take care of it in the morning. How'd we do?"

"Better than last week. We must have had half dozen big rigs parked in the overflow section."

"Dil's billboard is obviously doing its job," Karen said with enthusiasm.

"Actually, most of them said their buddies sent them."

"That's great! Word of mouth is the very best kind of advertising."

"I'll see you Friday morning."

Cricket disappeared behind the door, followed by Karen. After locking the front door and turning out the remainder of the lights, she picked up the receipts and headed back to the kitchen. Looking at her watch, she realized that she would have to stay another hour or more to see the pies baked. She had stacked today's mail on her desk in the house, so decided she would go to the cottage, check on Goodness and pick up the mail.

Chapter 39

Goodness was growing bigger by the day and could now jump up on the desk. This, she had obviously done, scattering the mail everywhere, including the floor. As Karen sat on the floor gathering the mail, Goodness began brushing back and forth along her leg, purring so loud it sounded like a motor running.

Karen began gently scolding the kitten. "You know you're a bad little girl, don't you." The purring became even louder and just as Karen reached down to pick up the kitten, she spotted a letter from Simon amidst the scattered mail.

Grabbing the envelope, she tore it open immediately, ignoring the remainder of the mess…and Goodness, who curled up on her lap.

Dear Karen,

First of all I want to say how sorry I am to have missed your grand opening. Mom said it was a huge success and that the diner is doing well. I must say I'm not surprised. Thinking about the wonderful meal we shared the Friday before I left, I can imagine what delights you are serving up to your customers.

I have been staying extremely busy since arriving. The new mission church is nearing completion and I have to admit that eight to ten hours of physical labor leaves me rather exhausted by the end of the day.

Jesse is working by my side every day, thus affording us the opportunity to visit. He's quite the talker and has given me numerous ideas for my books. I'll probably start spending more time with my writing after this week.

I wish you could see how beautiful it is here. There is an air of untouched wilderness that you can't find in the States. The last time I was in South America, I took a boat tour of the Amazon. Believe it or not, according to the tour guide, a group of natives that stood along the shore observing us were actual headhunters. Cannibals. I'm not sure if this was merely a con to make the tour more exciting, but I've heard that such people do exist here.

Beyond the beauty, the other side of the coin is the existence of severe poverty, which is more out in the open than I'm used to seeing. In the States, our Appalachian Mountain folk are considered to be the poorest Americans, but because they keep more to themselves, it isn't so obvious. Here they have entire communities called "favelas" that spring up alongside the affluent areas of Sao Paulo. The homes in these favelas are mostly shanties, with no sewer systems, running water or facilities for personal hygiene. Needless to say, illness and disease run rampant – and that's why the missions are so important. One of our buildings is a large bath house that provides showers and restrooms to the nearby villagers.

When I first began the Jesse Foundation, I thought the first building should be a church. It was Ken who reminded me that "cleanliness is next to Godliness." We can worship anywhere, but we can bathe only where there is clean water.

Enough on that subject.

I can't believe how much Jesse has grown. He's almost nineteen and with his new prosthesis, he walks with only the slightest of limps. Doctor Manuel says the limp will probably go away as he adjusts to his new (and hopefully permanent) limb.

Jesse remains an inspiration to me. He exudes an inner joy that is contagious; and an attitude that belies his tragic beginnings. His joy has rubbed off on Monica, who is now a beautiful and delightful teenager. Jesse still adores her and is very big brotherly toward her. If too many boys gather around Monica, he's right there. He's never unkind or threatening, but everyone here has too much respect for him to cross the line where his little sister is concerned. Monica sometimes pretends to be upset and tells him she doesn't need a "condutor," which means guard or protector. He just laughs and says, "Oh yes you do, little sister."

My eyes are starting to get heavy, so I'll close for now. I miss everyone back home and particularly enjoy getting mail. Please continue to write. I love your letters and truly appreciate your taking time from what must be a very hectic schedule to remember a friend.

Affectionately,

Simon

Karen started to read the letter over, and then realized she had pies baking in the diner kitchen. Ignoring the remainder of the scattered mail, she stood, dislodging a now comfortably sleeping Goodness who let out a loud "reow" in protest.

Picking up the distressed kitten, she kissed her on the nose. "Sorry baby. Mama's gotta' go rescue some pies."

Fumbling for the keyhole, Karen almost jumped out of her wits when Paulie appeared next to her.

"Is everything okay, Miss Karen?"

"Everything's fine, Paulie. I have some pies baking and need to get them out of the oven before they burn."

She realized her hands were shaking – probably a combination of the cold night air and Paulie's sudden appearance. Without her having to ask, Paulie took the keys and deftly unlocked the door.

"Isn't this a little early for your rounds, Paulie?"

"I got restless. I guess I'm just too excited about this comin' weekend"

"What's happening this weekend?"

"Dil asked Mama and me to come to dinner at his horse farm. I love horses. He said I could ride…" Paulie paused, as he was prone to do when he couldn't remember an exact word. Finally he said, "…a gray horse."

Karen suppressed a smile, not wanting Paulie to think she found his inability to recall certain words amusing.

"That would be Mountain Dulcimer. I've ridden her before and she's very gentle. She's a gray thoroughbred and got her name when she was still racing. Her previous owner gave her the name because he said she was so high strung. Dil believes she just didn't like the gates, or being crowded by other horses – but he says he kept the name because he thought she was as sweet as the music of a dulcimer."

Karen spoke slowly any time she was explaining something to Paulie. He usually grasped what was being said as long as you didn't rush your words. Everyone at the diner had learned to speak to him in this manner, without sounding like they were talking down to him. Paulie and Darrell had become *buddies*, and all the women thought he was "the sweetest thing since chocolate candy." Those had been Sherry's words and Karen suspected that she was a little infatuated with Paulie.

Paulie smiled that sweet smile that could melt butter. "That's the one. But Mama can't ride a horse. She's too old." The smile disappeared with his last words.

"But I'm sure she'll have a wonderful time anyway. Dil has a beautiful home. I know I could just sit on his patio and look out over the hills all day. Besides, your mother is as perky as most women who are much younger."

"Not so much anymore. She gets tired easy…and she doesn't see too good either…and sometimes she doesn't eat."

Not knowing how to respond to Paulie's observation, she decided to change the subject. Fortunately, the timer rang so she had a chance to gather her thoughts as she pulled the pies out of the oven.

It was almost midnight when Karen let herself back into the cottage. Paulie left shortly after she had given him a piece of a fresh baked peach pie. At least it had distracted him from the subject of his mother's aging. So what if she lost a couple of pieces of pie by cutting into it before the filling was cool enough to set. Paulie was worth a dozen pies and just seeing the smile on his face as he practically licked the plate, brightened her day.

In the cottage, she gathered up the remainder of the scattered mail, deciding it could wait until tomorrow. What she needed now was a hot shower, a glass of wine and sleep. At least, with the pies already baked, she wouldn't have to get up quite so early.

After a day of emotional upheaval, the shower felt soothing and relaxing. Afterward, bundled in pajamas and a thick bathrobe, she sat on the couch with a glass of wine. Clicking on the TV, she perused the guide for anything that looked remotely interesting. When nothing caught her attention, she turned the TV off and simply sat sipping her wine. *Bad move!* Within minutes, her emotions caught up with her and she wanted to bawl. *Pull yourself together, KC. You're just tired and feeling sorry for yourself.* For a moment, she had the urge to call Amy. Then remembering the last time she had called this late, she set that impulse aside. She was definitely not in the mood for another ten minute lecture on sleep deprivation and improper eating habits. It was true though. She had been going for over seven weeks on five to six hours of sleep at night, rarely taking the time to sit down to a normal meal. *That's what's wrong with me. I need to set aside some time off for myself. My staff is capable of handling the diner for at least one day without me.* With that decision made, she finished her wine, crawled in bed, and slept soundly for the remainder of the night.

The following day, with Darrell's help, she redid the schedule to allow herself the full day off on Sunday instead of just the few hours she reserved for church. They also decided that they would close on Thanksgiving, Christmas Eve and Christmas Day, agreeing that these were family times. Margo and Dil had already assumed that they would close for Thanksgiving and invited Karen to a "cook-free day of rest and relaxation" at Dil's. Paulie and Miriam would be coming as well.

On her first Sunday off, Karen *slept in* until seven. Feeling somewhat guilty, she had the urge to run over to the diner, but Darrell had threatened to put an inside bolt on the back door if she even stuck her head in at any time.

"You can come in the front door, *as a customer,* if you don't feel like cooking, but I had better not see your face in this kitchen for the entire day! I will take it as an insult and lack of trust in my ability to run the kitchen without you."

Envisioning his impish smile as he made his bold statement on Saturday night brought a smile to her face. It also allowed her to relax enough to take a leisurely shower and enjoy a cup of coffee while sitting at her own table. She was still receiving recipes from locals, and had even received a few from tourists. Since the *specials* menu included the names of the persons who submitted the recipes, visitors were always asking the waitresses if anyone could submit a recipe. Seeing the stack of submissions on her desk, she was tempted to look them over, but immediately dismissed the idea as business related. She had promised herself she would not do *anything* that was business related on her day off. Instead, she picked up Simon's letter. After reading it for the fourth time, she decided that she would write a long newsy letter to him instead of a brief note as in the past. Simon was being very generous in referring to them as letters.

By the time she finished the letter to Simon, it was time to head to church. Lenny's manner of preaching was very much like Simon's – thoughtful, uplifting and inspiring – tinged with just the right amount of humor to hold everyone's attention. Dil had become a regular attendee at the services. Karen always sat next to him and Margo on one side of the front row, while Gail and her four little ones occupied the other front row seat. Sometimes, Kitty would walk over to snuggle up next to Karen, and usually ended up asleep on her lap.

The other three children were always bright eyed and well behaved, seemingly enthralled by their father's words. Gail once told Karen that Max could repeat his father's sermons almost word for word, adding, "I think that one is going to follow in his father's footsteps."

Karen ended up spending the remainder of her day at Lenny and Gail's house. Dil had asked her to join them, but knowing that this was the day Miriam and Paulie would be there, she asked for a rain check and after they left, accepted Gail's invitation for an evening with the "Zoo Crew," a term she had coined for her four lively children. She couldn't have found a better distraction from thoughts of Toby, Simon or the diner.

Chapter 40

"Is that a letter from your sweetheart?" Jesse asked, his familiar smile both teasing and curious.

"Just a good friend," Simon replied, looking up from Karen's letter. He had been in Sao Paulo for over three months and still could not get used to the tall, handsome young man that stood before him. Jesse had been fifteen the last time he saw him and still rather small for his age. Now he stood eye to eye with Simon, his new, hopefully permanent, prosthesis allowing him to walk with what Ken called his "John Wayne swagger."

"For someone who is *just a friend*, your face shines when you read her letters."

Over the years, Jesse's mastery of the English language, like everything else about him; his intelligence, his ability to read people, and his natural zest for life – never ceased to amaze Simon.

"So did you come in here to harass me Mr. Nosey, or is there a purpose to this visit?"

Jesse smiled his slow easy smile, as he took a seat opposite Simon. Ignoring Simon's chiding, Jesse asked, "What is your *friend's* name?"

"Her name is Karen."

"And is she beautiful?"

"She's quite lovely – on the inside as well as the outside."

"So she is not the woman who breaks your heart so many times."

"And just what would you know about my broken-hearted affairs?"

"I hear Papa Ken telling Mama Lizzie that 'that woman has broken his heart again.' And then he says that you come here every time to clear your head. He says he hopes this is the last time you will have to make this trip for that purpose. He would like to once again see the young man who was filled with excitement about his future; the way he was when he first came to Sao Paulo. I don't think I have ever met that person."

Simon's mouth twitched with a suppressed grin. He tried to sound serious when he asked, "Do you always eavesdrop on your parents' conversations?"

With a shrug of his shoulders, Jesse replied, "Not always. But they sometimes forget I am still awake when they go to bed. If they leave their door open, I can hear them talking. When I first came to live with them, listening to the sound of their voices put me to sleep. I just never paid attention to what they were saying back then – and I usually don't even now. But I heard your name mentioned, so I listened."

"Remind me to warn your parents that their *private* conversations aren't always so private!"

Jesse threw back his head and laughed at Simon's serious tone. "I'll be sure to do that Senhor Simon. But they will not have to worry about that much longer. I was just talking to Father Manuel and he said that it would be good for me to go back to Kentucky with you. He said I should experience secular life before I made a decision to enter the priesthood and it would be much better for me to be where I knew someone. I think he believes you would be a good influence on me – keep me out of trouble."

His last remark gave Simon a good chuckle, knowing that Jesse was far more of an influence on him than he could ever imagine being on Jesse.

"I'd like that, Jesse. I know my mom would love meeting you – and depending on whether you decide to attend Morehead State or the University of Kentucky, you could stay with us either full time or during breaks. I'm sure you would have no problem getting accepted at either college."

"I have my passport and visa already. When can we go?"

"I promised my mother I would be home for Christmas, so I'm thinking maybe around mid-December. I also promised your folks I would stay for the dedication of the new church."

They visited for several minutes, discussing their travel plans. After Jesse left, Simon picked up Karen's letter and a wave of guilt passed over him. She had written him faithfully, at least once a week, while he had written her barely once a month. It seemed that every time he would sit down to write to her, his thoughts would go to Staci. He knew it was over and it hurt to realize that he could never make Staci happy. *Happy? How long had it been since either of us felt truly happy when we were together?* He remembered when just the sight of her made his heart do flip-flops, and he sensed that she felt the same. In the beginning she respected the fact that he was the son of a preacher and accepted that he wanted to follow in his father's footsteps. *When had it changed? When had they changed?* He knew it wasn't just Staci – he was different as well. More than anything, he wanted a wife, children, and a life that included his ministry.

Shaking his head, Simon redirected his thoughts to Karen's letter. He immediately decided that he would answer it right away. *It doesn't have to be long and newsy – I'll be home soon.*

Both exhausted and elated over the first month's report from her accountant, Karen sat at her desk in the cottage, sorting through the mail. When she spotted the letter from Simon, she set aside everything else and opened it immediately. His prior letters were always lengthy, filled with news about the mission and excitement over the progress he was making with ideas for the Jesse books. This time it was a single page and the closing paragraph set her heart racing with excitement.

The church will be completed in less than a month, and I will be headed home as soon as the dedication is celebrated. It's scheduled for December 11th so I should be arriving sometime around the 15th. I'm looking forward to seeing you and sampling some of the marvelous cuisine that Mom is constantly bragging about.

As always, he signed his letter, 'Affectionately, Simon.'

Karen usually read his letters several times, making certain she hadn't missed anything. Today she simply sat it down, and with a deep sigh, allowed herself to absorb his last sentence.

Simon is coming home and looking forward to seeing me. Did he maybe miss me or was that just a polite ending to his letter? What does it matter? *Simon is coming home.*

Chapter 41

"Mama's sick." Paulie announced as soon as he walked through the door. "She says it's nothin' but she don't look right."

"Have you called a doctor, Paulie?" Karen asked, her voice filled with concern.

"Mama said she was okay and I shouldn't worry. She wants to talk to Dil. Can you call Dil for me, Miss Karen?"

She started to ask why he didn't call Dil himself, but realized he was so distressed he probably wouldn't be able to make much sense on the phone.

"It's pretty early to call him right now, Paulie. Why don't you go back home and look after your mama and I'll call Dil as soon as I think he's awake."

"But who'll fire up the smoker?"

"Darrell will be here in a few minutes. I'm sure he can do it. You just go on back home and look after your mama. Okay?"

It was the Monday after Thanksgiving and Miriam had looked fine last Thursday. She hadn't eaten a lot, but as thin as she was, no one thought anything of it.

Paulie gave Karen a hesitant look. He was not one to shirk what he considered his responsibility. He was spending more and more time at the diner and Karen felt guilty that he refused to let her pay him. She had finally convinced him that he and his mother were entitled to free meals. After meeting Miriam and expressing her feelings about paying Paulie, they agreed on a regular schedule of meals, which included breakfast, lunch and dinner at least several times a week.

It wasn't quite five a.m. and Karen estimated it would be at least six before Dil would possibly be awake. She went back to the biscuits she had just patted out and tried to concentrate on the next task, but kept glancing up at the clock, her mind filled with concern for both Paulie and his mother. Paulie had brought Miriam into the diner regularly as agreed. For a woman of her age, she was sprite and alert – not that Karen knew her exact age, but figuring that Paulie was about the same age as Dil, she estimated Miriam had to be in her late seventies or early eighties.

"Dil, I hope I didn't wake you. It's Karen."
"Not at all. Is there a problem at the diner?"
"No! No! Everything's fine here…it's Miriam. She's evidently sick and Paulie said she's asked to see you. I was afraid I'd get busy once the diner opened and might forget to call, so I wanted to catch you before you went to work. I'm sure she didn't intend for you to come over immediately."
"I don't have any meetings scheduled this morning so I'll come right away. She may need to be taken to the hospital. Has she contacted her doctor?"
"According to Paulie, she says she doesn't need a doctor, but I'm worried. I'll feel much better once you've seen her."

Karen hung up the phone, knowing she would not be able to concentrate on her work until she had heard from Dil that everything was alright with Miriam.

Dil stood in the doorway taking in the familiar house that had been his second home so many years before. Little had changed – newer furniture and fresh paint – but the color scheme and general patterns on both furniture and drapes were as he remembered.

Paulie led Dil to Miriam's bedroom where she was propped against several pillows in a near sitting position. The sparkle that normally lit up her blue/gray eyes was dull and she looked as frail as his mother had in her last days. Upon seeing Dil, she forced her head off the pillows, asking Dil to help her sit up. Placing another pillow behind her back, he then took a seat in the chair next to the bed.

Miriam turned her head to Paulie, saying, "Would you get me a drink of water, Dear?"

As soon as Paulie left the room, she turned to Dil.

"I need to talk to you…alone. Do you think you can send Paulie on some kind of errand…maybe tell him he's needed at the diner? What I have to say to you may take a while, but it needs to be said."

Dil couldn't hide the puzzled look on his face as he mumbled, "Of course, Miriam. Take all the time you need."

When Paulie reappeared with the water, Dil asked him to step outside the room for a minute.

"But Mama…" Paulie protested.

"She'll be fine, Paulie. I need to ask you what she's eaten since she's been sick."

Dil was used to Paulie's way of mulling his words around in his head before he actually spoke, so was surprised by his quick response. He was obviously very concerned.

"She won't eat anything I make for her, Dil. She drank some tea yesterday, and that's all…and then she threw up."

"How long has she been in bed?"

Again he didn't hesitate before he spoke. "Since I came home from work yesterday. She was up in the morning, but when I got home, she was in bed. I poached her some eggs 'cause that's what she likes when she isn't feelin' good, but she didn't eat them."

Paulie's troubled face prompted Dil to pat him on the shoulder as he assured him that he would get her to eat before he left.

"You know how much she loves Karen's chicken and rice soup. Why don't you run over to the diner and get a bowl for her. I'll bet she won't say no to that."

Dil's reassuring smile as he spoke appeared to calm Paulie.

"You won't leave before I get back, will you? I don't want to leave Mama alone again. I should'a called Miss Karen this mornin' instead of goin' over there, but Mama was sleepin' and I wasn't gone very long."

"You did fine, Paulie…and I won't leave before you get back. I promise."

As soon as Paulie walked out the door, Dil called Karen and told her to keep Paulie there for as long as possible. He said he'd explain later.

"Thank you for coming, Dil," Miriam began, "But before I say what I have to say, I want you to understand that this isn't about money. This house is paid for and I have a trust fund set up for Paulie that has enough in it to care for him for the rest of his life. I hope you don't mind that I've named you executor for the trust. What this is really about is Paulie being alone; not physically, but emotionally. He's perfectly capable of caring for himself and this house. Since my parents and my mother's one sister are all gone, I'm the only family he's ever known. That's where you come in."

"I'm honored you would place that kind of trust in me, and you know I've always felt that Paulie was more than just a friend. But I really don't think you need to be concerned about him being alone for a long time. You'll probably out-live the both of us." He tried to sound lighthearted as he spoke, but the knot in his throat denied him that ruse.

"How I wish that were true," she sighed. "I have stomach cancer, Dil. My doctor confirmed it last week. I don't know how advanced it is yet, and he recommended further testing. If it requires surgery, as he suggested, there would probably be follow-up treatments. But at my age, I'm thinking I'd rather endure my current discomfort and remain lucid for what time I have left. Paulie gets frightened enough seeing me laid up with a cold…that's all this is you know…just a little bug. I'm not going to bite the dust quite yet, but I have to get my life in order…isn't that the term? That's what I need to talk about."

Dil let out the breath he had been holding. His hesitant smile encouraged Miriam to continue. She studied his face as she began.

"I always thought you looked more like your mother, Dil; but seeing you now, I think you have more of Cliff in you. You have his eyes and that square jaw that I always thought was so striking."

Dil noticed that as soon as she said his father's name, the stressed look on her face faded. It was as if years had dropped off her age and her eyes once again held the sparkle that he had always loved. Those same eyes seemed to drift to a far off place as she began speaking again.

"I think you know that your daddy and I grew up in these same houses as you and Paulie. We were best friends, too. Rather unusual for a boy and girl to be best buddies back in those days, but that's what we were…up until high school. That's when I decided I was in love with him. I was a year younger and knew he still thought of me only as a friend…maybe more like a little sister. The days of our romps in the woods, fishing excursions and Saturday movies were gone. I understood that his feelings for me were different than what I felt. I began flirting with all of his buddies, trying to make him jealous – but it didn't work. They all knew if they tried anything with me, they'd have to answer to him. He looked after me the same way you looked after Paulie.

"After high school, I went to live with my recently widowed Aunt Glenda in Cincinnati. While I was there I attended college and got a degree in Business Administration. I rarely came home, and when I did, I avoided your father once I learned that he was dating your mother and they were in a serious relationship. I fully intended to stay in Cincinnati after I got my degree, but Mom and Dad begged me to come home. Daddy wanted me to come to work at the bank with him. I agreed to spend the summer, but made no promises beyond that. I knew it would be too difficult for me to live next door to your parents once they were married.

"By then, Cliff was practically running the diner…he and Ma. I rarely saw him, but one night, about a week before the wedding, I noticed a light on in his house when there shouldn't have been anyone home. When I saw Cliff step out on the front porch, I wandered over, thinking he might be ill. He greeted me like he always did…with a bear hug and a quick kiss on the cheek. After he scolded me for not coming around the diner more often, I asked him why he wasn't there himself. He said Ma sent him home because his head wasn't in his work. She figured he was too caught up in his upcoming wedding to concentrate. He had burned several orders and undercooked another. I started teasing him about getting cold feet, and that's when he admitted that he was scared out of his wits.

"I'm probably the only person in the world that he would have admitted this to, but he said it wasn't exactly cold feet. Then he went on to say that he had never been with a woman; and he was pretty sure that Mavis was far more knowledgeable in *those matters*. He was certain that he would be a big disappointment to her."

Suddenly, Miriam turned her eyes away from Dil. Her old hands began nervously twisting the ribbon on her gown. After taking a deep breath, she continued.

"I volunteered to show him how to please a woman. He didn't want to have anything to do with my idea at first, but after I argued that if your mother *was* an experienced woman, then she would expect him to be equally experienced. Then I led him into the house and …I seduced him. Of course my ulterior motive was to make him see that he really loved me. In that, I failed miserably.

"A month later, I realized I was pregnant. I moved back to Cincinnati and with Aunt Glenda's help, concocted a story about having married my college sweetheart the day before he was shipped out somewhere in the Pacific. Aunt Glenda even gave me her wedding ring and I promised her I would name the baby after Uncle Paul. My parents were *very disappointed* in me for having kept such a secret from them. Even worse, was their belief that I had married someone outside our church…someone they had never even met. I had to maintain the integrity of my story, so I've used the last name of Kendrick for the past sixty years. I actually had dated a boy named Steve Kendrick who joined the navy, but I've never been married.

"When Daddy was killed in the car wreck that left Mama partially paralyzed, Paulie was almost two. I had already killed off my imaginary husband…a casualty of the war, poor thing."

A wry grin crossed her lips for a brief moment.

"We moved back here so I could care for Mama. You were several months younger than Paulie, but he was so small for his age; and with his being a little slow and all, everyone assumed you were older. It meant the world to me that you always looked after him."

When she finally lifted her eyes to Dil, his face was filled with emotion. Deep creases covered his forehead as he raised his eyes to hers and said, "Paulie's my brother. My actual brother. I have a brother." The last was said with an air of wonder and a winsome smile trembled on Dil's mouth. "I always thought of him as a brother, but I never imagined…."

Then he cocked his head to the side and studied Miriam's face before asking, "Did Dad ever know? Did he or Mom ever suspect?"

"Oh, heavens no! The only one who figured it out was Ma."

"Ma knew?"

"Ma was probably the most observant woman in the world. She knew how I felt about your father, so I doubt it was a surprise to her. One afternoon, Paulie and I were having a late lunch at the diner. It was one of the rare times when Cliff wasn't there. Ma came over to our booth, sat down and handed a picture to me. She asked if I knew that she had had a younger brother. He died when she was twelve. The boy in the picture looked to be about the same age as Paulie and their faces were identical; right down to the little birthmark on his left cheek. I must have had a shocked look on my face because she reached over and patted my hand, saying, 'This is the only picture of Eugene that I have. I've kept it in the back of my recipe book, so I doubt if Cliff or Mavis has ever seen it.' Then she handed the picture to me and walked away.

"I later asked if she wanted the picture back and she said she didn't need it any longer. She said she could never forget what Eugene looked like as long as Paulie was around."

Dil was still somewhat stunned by Miriam's story and uncertain as to what he should say. Surely she knew that he would have watched after Paulie even if they weren't brothers. Before he could say as much, Miriam added, "There's one other thing, Dil. I have something that belongs to you."

Reaching over to the table alongside the bed, Miriam picked up a small trinket box and removed a key, which she held out to him, saying, "This key opens that middle drawer at the top of the chest of drawers. I'll explain how and why I have it once you see what it is."

Dil stared in awe at the contents of the drawer. *Could it really be Ma's recipe book?* It had been so long since he – since anyone – had laid eyes on it. As he cautiously lifted it from the drawer, his strong hands began to tremble. With a catch in his throat, he mumbled, "It really is…*it!* But when…how…?

"Come. Sit back down and I'll explain everything.

Chapter 42

"The night the river flooded, Paulie set out to make his usual rounds. He had a bad cold and I begged him not to go. It was still raining hard and the temperature was in the fifties. But there was no stopping Paulie when it came to his responsibilities. I knew his normal route would take him along the banks of the creek and my only victory was to convince him to wear an extra coat under his rain gear and stay clear of the creek. He promised he would stay on the roads. I also knew that the diner was one of his stops. Even after Ma died, he still considered himself her night watchman; and he still had his key to the back door. By the time he got there, water was already in the diner and Paulie knew he had to protect Ma's recipe book, so he took off his raincoat, wrapped it around the book and came back home. By the time he got here, he was soaked to the bone and suffering from a chill. The following morning, he was running a temperature and I had to take him to the hospital. He ended up with pneumonia and was there for almost a week. When he came home, he never mentioned Ma's recipe book."

Miriam lifted her eyes to Dil's before continuing. He wasn't certain what he saw in those eyes, but felt she was looking for his understanding of what she was about to tell him.

"I think you know, Dil, that over the years, your mother and I became friends – mostly because of you boys. Since I worked during the day and she spent most evenings at the diner, we didn't see a lot of each other except on weekends when I was home. Your mother was a wonderful woman and it was easy to see why your father loved her. She would take care of the two of you during the day, as well as checking on my mother. I would watch over you boys in the evening and on weekends. It was a good arrangement for both of us.

"While Paulie was in the hospital, I took the recipe book over to your mother and explained how I came to have it. Her reaction was a total shock to me. She begged me to keep it – to hide it or destroy it. She said she was praying that it had somehow been swept away in the flood. The diner had been doing poorly since Ma's death and your father was spending more and more time there. She was certain that if he didn't have Ma's recipe book, he would give up the diner…and she was right. I think you know that your mother's health was poor and she wanted to move closer to her sister in Frankfort. They didn't need the income from the diner and the only reason Cliff had kept it going was to honor his mother. Mavis had always been – for lack of a better word – jealous of Cliff's devotion to his mother. Then when he began talking about her ghost haunting the diner, she knew she had to get him away from here. It took longer than she anticipated for him to make the decision, and I think he came dangerously close to becoming an alcoholic before she threatened to move to Frankfort without him."

Once again, a wry smile appeared on her face as she spoke.

"You do know that the mysterious light was Paulie making his nightly rounds. Even after Cliff boarded the place up and put padlocks on the doors, Paulie found a way to climb in through the smoker."

Dil explained how Karen had told them about Paulie's confession to her.

Miriam emitted a slight chuckle, before continuing.

"I've kept the book all these years, knowing that when the time was right, I would give it to you. I just didn't expect it to take so long for you to return to Farmers."

She ended her tale with a tired little smile, then whispered, "Look in the back pocket."

Dil carefully turned the binder over, reached in the pocket and pulled out two photos. Both were quite old, one more faded than the other. It showed the face of a smiling boy standing in front of a house. The second was a picture of him and Paulie, taken on Paulie's tenth birthday. Each had an arm around the other's shoulders. Cheshire cat grins covered their faces and they held plastic cups in their free hands, lifted as if toasting the world. The boy in the first picture looked almost identical to Paulie. As he studied the pictures more closely, he realized that he and Paulie had very similar eyes.

They sat in silence for several minutes and Dil didn't realize that tears were streaming down his cheeks until Miriam reached over and gently laid her hand to the side of his face, brushing a tear with her thumb. He tried to think of words to reassure Miriam that he would always look after Paulie… that he appreciated the fact that she had lived with her secret all these years, never attempting to interfere with his parents' marriage. That she had been a true friend to his mother and honored her request to hide Ma's recipe book, knowing that in doing so, she would likely lose the opportunity to be near the only man she had ever loved. Still trying to put his thoughts into words, he wondered if this is how Paulie felt each time he tried to express himself – mulling the words around in his mind before he could articulate them vocally.

When he finally found his voice, all he could say was, "Thank you."

Miriam smiled, and once again, Dil caught a glimpse of the lovely young woman of his childhood. The sound of the front door opening startled them both and Miriam quickly tossed the blanket over the recipe book which now rested on the bed next to her.

"I...I got you some of Karen's chicken rice soup, Mama. She made it fresh, just for you. That's...that's why I was gone so long. Dil said you'd eat this Mama. You need to eat."

Paulie's words came out in the nearest thing to a rush as he was capable of, bringing an affectionate smile to his mother's lips.

"Karen's chicken rice soup sounds wonderful Paulie. I do believe that I'm hungry for a change. Would you mind putting it in a bowl for me?"

As soon as Paulie left the room, Miriam anxiously turned to Dil. Tapping the blanket covering the book she said, "Do you think you could smuggle this out without Paulie seeing it?"

"I have my laptop in the car – if I empty the case, it should fit it in there. I'll run out and get it, and then we can tell Paulie we've been discussing some business matters."

Dil stood, and with a quirky smile added in a firm, concise tone, "Of course this means you'll *have* to finish your soup so we can get Paulie to take your *empty* bowl back to the kitchen while we make the transfer."

Margo looked up in surprise when she spotted Dil coming through the door of her office.

"What are you doing here?" she asked. "Is this some kind of banker's holiday I don't know about?"

Closing the door behind him, he crossed the room and pulled Margo into his arms.

"I'm here to take my girl to lunch and it is *this* banker's holiday."

Margo cocked her head, her eyebrows almost touching as her face contorted into a suspicious glare. "Have you been drinking this early in the day, Dil Krus?" she teased.

"Drunk on life," he quickly responded, planting a quick kiss on her wrinkled up nose. "I have an amazing story to tell you if you'll join me for lunch."

By the time Dil finished telling Margo about the morning's events, she was beyond stunned.

"I've always admired Miriam as a business woman – and her devotion to Paulie is unquestionable, but I certainly never knew that she was such an amazing woman. Not knowing her background, I've always wondered why she never remarried. I suppose she never stopped loving your father."

"You're probably right." He paused, a thoughtful look covering his face. "I hate the idea that she's refusing to fight this cancer. She's afraid of surgery and I understand how frightening it seems. Plus, the idea of radiation or chemo at her age doesn't make a lot of sense, but I'm going to talk to a friend of mine who's an oncologist and professor at the KU medical school. They're always coming up with new treatments and maybe there's something out there that could give her more time."

Chapter 43

During the drive to the airport, Jesse had bombarded Simon and Ken with questions about flying. Since Jesse had never flown before, Simon wasn't certain if his constant chatter was nervousness, excitement or fear. He hoped he would at least sleep through the nighttime portion of flight, but all indications said that wasn't going to happen.

Lizzie and Monica had said their tearful good-byes at the house. The mission jeep was too small to carry five passengers along with all of the luggage. Lizzie's final playful words to Jesse had been, "Don't break too many hearts, Son." Her attempt at humor had broken the tension somewhat, but Monica clung to her brother sobbing until Ken gently pulled her away.

They arrived at the airport three hours before the flight and by the time they cleared customs, checked in and finally arrived at the gate, they still had over forty-five minutes until the flight boarded. Jesse stood at the window fascinated by the various aircraft taking off and landing.

"I sure don't understand what holds them up in the air," he said, as a jumbo jet left the ground with the grace and ease of a tern taking flight.

"Sorry, Jesse, I don't know anything about the aerodynamics of flight. I've always pictured the hand of God picking up the plane and tossing it in the air, much the way a child does with a paper airplane. I know that's simplistic, but it comforts me when I fly. Of course I also pray – especially during take-off and landing."

Jesse turned to Simon with a gleam in his eye and laughter in his voice. "And of course God follows from airport to airport to always be with *you*."

"Of course!"

"Then I am lucky to be flying with you, Senhor Simon."

Jesse was silent from the time the plane left the gate until it was leveled in the air. When the roar of the jets signaled take-off, he had crossed himself and bowed his head. Glancing periododically out the window, he gripped the armrests until his knuckles turned white. Simon thought he was holding his breath as well and half expected him to pass out. He was glad to hear a slow exhale, followed by the uncurling of Jesse's hands.

"Are you okay?" Simon asked.

"Once my heart stops racing, I'll be fine. I think landing might be less frightening."

"It is," Simon assured him. "It feels more natural for something that's up in the air to come down – even when you don't understand how it got up in the air in the first place."

"So what do you usually do when you are flying for so many hours?"

"I read, or talk to the person sitting next to me. Sometimes I even manage to sleep."

"I don't think I can sleep – or read, for that matter. Will I bother you too much if we just talk?"

"I'll let you know if I get sleepy. Otherwise, I prefer talking."

And talk they did! For almost five hours straight. By the time Simon's eyes grew so heavy he couldn't hold them open, he had practically told Jesse his life's story, including all his ups and downs with Staci. With each detail he shared, Jesse would ask more questions, adding an occasional comment. After telling him how he had met Karen and sharing what he knew of her past with him, Jesse looked thoughtful for several seconds before saying, "My dad says that he and my mama were good friends for many years before they fell in love. He says it is much better to fall in love with a friend than to fall in love with an image of someone that is impossible for them to live up to. When you know everything there is to know about each other, there is much less room for disappointment. I think he is right about this – would you not agree?"

"Definitely food for thought, Jesse."

To change the subject, Simon started asking Jesse questions, prompting him to open up at last about his life in the dump. He even shared the few memories he had of his natural family. These stories were golden for Simon, and he knew with this new information he could continue writing the Jesse stories for years to come. Jesse, of course, knew that he was the inspiration for the books and often said he was "humbled to be represented so gallantly." He was also relieved to know that few people in the States knew Simon as the author – or him as his inspiration. He often told Simon, "I do not think I could possibly live up to such a courageous image."

Simon's nap lasted only around forty minutes and he awoke to find Jesse watching him.

"What's that smug grin about?" he asked, rolling his head to get the kinks out.

"You fell asleep before you answered my last question. I've been waiting a long time for the answer."

"What was the question? The last thing I remember is your asking something about…someone meeting us at the airport…I think."

"Yes, but then I asked if your friend Karen would be with your sister and you just said her name, then fell asleep with a silly grin on your face. I am thinking that you are anxious to see your *friend*."

"I am. But she won't be there. Belinda is the only one who knows when we are coming. I want to surprise my mother…and Karen. If I told Mom when we were coming, she would have driven to Cincinnati. I want *you* to be a surprise as well. Belinda is the only one who knows that you're with me."

"I'm sure glad Adam isn't here to see me drooling. That young man has to be the most gorgeous hunk I've seen since Enrique Iglesias became the object of my fantasies."

Belinda hadn't stopped staring at Jesse since their arrival. Simon was so engrossed in his little niece that it took him a moment to respond to Belinda.

"I'm going to pretend I didn't hear that, little sister – but then I knew he'd be getting that kind of reaction from all you googly-eyed females." Then, turning his attention back to Caitlyn, who was staring at him in fascination, he added, "Except for you, my beautiful little Caiti. You'll only have eyes for Uncle Simon, won't you?"

Joyfully kicking her legs, the baby began making little gurgling sounds, further enchanting her besotted uncle.

Jesse had been standing by the luggage carousel while Simon and Belinda hung back, not wanting Caitlyn to get caught up in the throng of people attempting to be the first to retrieve their items. Reluctantly, Simon kissed the top of Caitlyn's head, and then handed her over to Belinda. He joined Jesse at the carousel when he saw two of their suitcases coming through the opening and realized that Jesse was somewhat distracted. Three young women had managed to maneuver their way through the crowd, surrounding Jesse and engaging him in conversation.

"Excuse me ladies," Simon said, as he reached between one lovely blond and Jesse, to pull off a large duffel bag. Jesse promptly reacted and grabbed the suitcase just behind it. Shortly afterward, two more large cases were plucked from the carousel. As Simon and Jesse made their way back over to Belinda,

Simon couldn't help but notice the disappointment in the eyes of the three women as they watched Jesse disappear in the crowd.

"Already accumulating a fan club, Jesse?" Simon teased.

With his dark skin, it was hard to determine if Jesse was blushing, but Simon was pretty certain he was.

"Sorry, Senhor Simon. I am not used to the fair young women of your country. They are very…friendly."

Chapter 44

"Mom...how would you like to have some company for a few days?"

"That would be wonderful, dear. Is everything okay?"

"Everything's fine, Mom. Adam is in Tampa for his company's annual golf outing and won't be back until Sunday night. Caitlyn and I are getting house fever. The weather is supposed to be good – no snow in the forecast for the next week."

"Then by all means, come on down. We can do some Christmas shopping – maybe drive to Lexington and see Sandy as well."

The excitement in Margo's voice made Belinda feel a little guilty...almost. She knew that her mother would be even more excited to see Simon. As if reading her thoughts, Margo enthusiastically added, "Simon should be getting here any day now. He mentioned sometime around the fifteenth in his last letter. You haven't heard from him, have you? I'm not sure if he plans on going directly to Cincinnati to pick up his car or if he'll fly in to Lexington. He'll probably call when he gets to Miami."

Margo rattled on for several minutes about plans for them all to be together at Christmas, obviously forgetting that she had asked a question in the midst of her rambling.

Thank heaven! Belinda thought, inserting a comment when Margo stopped to take a breath. "I'll have my cell phone with me, so he'll be able to get in touch with me wherever I am."

"Of course, Dear. When will you be arriving?"

"Early tomorrow morning. If you have appointments, Caitlyn and I will make ourselves at home until you can get away."

"I wouldn't think of not being here. You know how slow it is this time of year. I'll be closing the office for the holidays on Friday anyway, so I'll just forward any calls to my cell phone in the meantime. I'm so anxious to see my baby. They grow much too fast at this age."

"Mom, it's been less than three weeks since you saw her. I doubt she will have changed that much."

"That's because you see her every day."

They chatted for a few more minutes before saying their good-byes. Hanging up the phone, Belinda turned to Simon. "Sorry that took a lot longer than I anticipated. You know how Mom gets when she's excited. This is going to be s-o-o-o much fun."

Margo watched as Simon's car pulled into the driveway, wondering to herself why Belinda had chosen to drive Simon's car instead of her own. As the big SUV reached the top of the hill, she saw Belinda's car pull in as well, and almost leapt over the counter getting to the front door.

Simon was immediately out of the car and whirling her around in an embrace. By the time he set her down, Jesse had emerged from the passenger side and was peering over the top of the vehicle. Margo's eyes widened as she glanced from Simon to Jesse and then realized who he was and let out a little yelp.

"Oh my gosh – you have to be Jesse," she said as she rounded the car, grabbing the startled young man in a welcoming embrace. "Oh Jesse, I feel like I know you. How wonderful to finally meet you in person. How long will you be staying? Did your family come with you?"

"Just us," Belinda said, her eyes sparkling with humor as she approached her mother. "You know – *your* family!"

"Oh Sweetheart," Margo exclaimed, reaching out for Caitlyn. "I didn't mean to ignore you." Then cuddling Caitlyn, she murmured in her sing-song grandmotherly voice, "I could never ignore my precious baby."

"Hope you don't mind that it's sort of frilly. This is my sister Sandy's old room. Mom keeps saying she's going to redecorate, but my sisters always comment on how great it is to come home to their familiar rooms, so she keeps putting it off."

"It is a most beautiful room, Senhor Simon. Monica would – how do you Americans say – *flip out* over such a room."

Simon laughed, saying, "Well I'll understand if you don't *flip out* over the accommodations, but I want you to make yourself at home. Needless to say, Mom is thrilled that you're here."

"She is a most welcoming senhora. I already feel very much at ease in her presence."

"She's a wonderful mother and that's her favorite job – mothering. Over the years I've brought home many people without even warning her, and she always makes them feel like special guests. That's her gift." Simon paused, and then added, "By the way, Jesse. You can drop the senhor and senhora. We are very informal here and you are now a member of our family."

"But I could not be disrespectful of your mother, sen…Simon." Jesse protested.

"Do you know what she would like the very best?" Simon asked.

"What is that?"

"If you would call her Mama Margo – or just Mom if you prefer. That would thrill her to no end."

Despite Simon's suggestions, Jesse asked Margo how she would like for him to address her. She reaffirmed Simon's proposal to call her Mom and seeing the joy in her eyes the first time he did so, Jesse decided it was the right choice.

It was late afternoon before Simon stepped into his home office. He expected to see a stack of mail awaiting him, but found only a single letter on his desk. The handwriting was Staci's.

"It came two days ago." His mother's voice startled him as he looked up to see her standing in the doorway. "The rest of your mail is in the center drawer."

"The address is her parents' house. Is she back in town?" he said, studying the envelope.

"She is. I ran into her last week at the drugstore. She looks…uuum… different."

"I know. I dropped in on her at her grandmother's on my way to Sao Paulo. It wasn't a very pleasant meeting."

Margo had stepped inside and closed the door behind her. The pain on Simon's face made her heart ache.

"You didn't mention that you would be seeing her before you left. Is…Is it something you would care to share with me?" Then she quickly added, "I'll understand if you don't want to talk about it."

"Actually, Mom, I planned on telling you all about it. I just didn't think it would come up this soon."

"Did you want to read the letter first? I can come back later. Jesse is asleep in the recliner, and Belinda is rocking Caitlyn. I can go down and start dinner."

"I was thinking we could go to the diner for dinner. I'm anxious for Karen to meet Jesse."

"And maybe a little anxious to see Karen yourself?"

"That too. Meanwhile, I'll tell you about my…uh…visit with Staci. I think I'll hold off on the letter 'til later."

Simon looked as if he was going to say something else and Margo wanted to wrap her arms around him but knew it would only bring his emotions to the surface. She sat quietly and waited for him to begin. He spoke continuously for over fifteen minutes, not only relating the conversation, but elaborating on what he considered the conclusion of their relationship. He ended by saying, "I can't imagine what this letter is about. I can only assume it's a rebuke for my leaving so abruptly. I got the feeling she might be getting back together with Blake."

"Well, at least it explains her attitude toward me at the drugstore. I had the feeling she was trying to avoid me and when we did speak, she acted nervous. I assumed that it had to do with her…um…new look. I probably inadvertently stared at first."

It was almost six and the dining area was filling up fast when Simon, Jesse, Margo, Belinda and Caitlyn entered the diner. Karen was busy in the kitchen, plating orders and singing along with the radio as she listened to an oldies station.

"If I can't have you, I don't want nobody baby. If I can't have you…uh-huh-ah!"

"I'd-a never pegged you for a Bee Gees fan."

Karen's head shot up at the familiar voice and she almost dropped the plate she had just finished garnishing.

"Simon!"

He opened his arms and she flew into them without regard to the stunned kitchen staff who had all turned to watch. Her hair had been tucked up into a chef's beret, which now lay on the floor. Burying his face in the now exposed mass of dark curls, Simon inhaled deeply. She smelled of fresh herbs and the sweet spices she had worked with all day. It took several seconds for Karen to realize they had an audience. Reluctantly pulling away, she said, "Welcome home."

Darrell, who had been working alongside her, made a loud "ah-hem," reminding Karen that several of her kitchen staff didn't know Simon. After introductions, Simon asked, "Can you get away for a few minutes? I have someone in the dining room I want you to meet."

"Go on. Go on." Darrell prompted. "We've got it under control here."

The minute she walked through the door, she spotted Margo and Belinda sitting in the corner booth. Jesse had his back to Karen, but had seen Margo's face light up as Simon approached, so stood to face her.

"Karen, I would like you to meet Jesse Castela Matheson."

"*The* Jesse?"

"The one and only."

"And you are Simon's good friend, Karen, who writes letters that make his eyes shine." Jesse said – his smile as warm as his face was beautiful.

Karen wasn't certain if it was his words or his extraordinary good looks that made her heart feel like it was going to pound right through her chest. He was much taller than she had expected and while the snapshots she had seen of him were over three years old, she could never have imagined that he would turn out to be the magnificent young man that stood before her. He was beyond Hollywood handsome. His intense brown eyes with their long thick lashes and perfectly arched brows could easily hold you captive; not to mention the model's build and stature. *I'm going to have to keep him away from Jeannie* – Jeannie being her newest waitress, a nineteen-year-old student at Morehead State who worked weekends. She was a pretty little round-faced pixie who loved to flirt with the customers.

"Can you join us for dinner?" Margo asked. "It looks like your customers are busy eating right now."

"Of course she can." Cricket's voice came from behind Karen. She was poised with her order pad, her eyes trained on Jesse. "Darrell said to tell you to take your time. The initial rush is over and the orders will be coming in at a slower pace now."

"Sometimes I wonder who's in charge here," Karen said, her lips curling into a mischievous smile.

Cricket's childlike, tinkling laughter had everyone at the table joining in. As Karen slid into the booth next to Belinda, she held out her arms to Caitlyn.

"You look very natural holding a baby," Jesse commented.

"Caitlyn and I became good buddies over Thanksgiving – didn't we, little angel."

Simon didn't realize he had emitted an audible sigh as he watched Karen over his shoulder. He couldn't help but remember her telling him about her *list*, which had mentioned "having a baby" as her top priority. *Is that still a priority for you, Karen?* He wondered.

They spent almost two hours at the diner and it pleased Simon to see the constant flow of customers that came and went. Several had spotted him and approached the table to welcome him home. By the time they returned to the house, Jesse was having a hard time holding his eyes open. Karen had beamed at his praise of the *Chef's Special*, which happened to be Granny's chicken enchiladas. It had become a favorite at the diner and was now a permanent Thursday special. He had eaten the entire generous portion, served with

Spanish rice and guacamole, and then topped it off with a piece of peach pie and ice cream.

Literally groaning as he rose from the table, he patted his stomach, saying, "I am afraid I have just committed the sin of gluttony. I will have to go to confession before Sunday."

"Get used to it Jesse. Everything Karen cooks is equally scrumptious." Margo said. "I have to limit my visits to the diner and then fast for several days in order to maintain my girlish figure."

Chapter 45

Jesse was again asleep in the recliner, while Belinda was busy putting Caitlyn down, when Margo followed Simon to his office. "Are you certain you wouldn't rather be alone while you read Staci's letter?"

"I wouldn't have invited you if I felt that way. I just can't figure out why she would write me a letter."

He sat there for several minutes fingering the letter, before he finally slit the envelope. It was a single page of scented stationary, with her initials embossed across the top. Taking a deep breath, he began reading.

> My Darling Simon,
>
> The past four months have been the most miserable time of my life. I have existed in a state of despair after your surprise visit at Grandmother's and my abhorrent conduct. I hope you understand that my behavior toward you was not representative of my true feelings. Needless to say, your appearance was upsetting for me because it ruined what I hoped would be a pleasing surprise for you. I was still recovering from my procedure and on medication when you arrived. I hope you understand that it was because of these conditions that I reacted so unpleasantly.
>
> You are completely correct, my darling, about my inability to share my personal hurts and disappointments openly. I was raised to believe that it was thoughtless to pass such burdens on to the ones you love. Knowing your life is filled with concerns over the problems of your family and church members, I never wanted my misery to add to your troubles. If it's important to you to know about my life with

Blake, I'll tell you anything and everything you want to know. My personal self-esteem has been at an all-time low since the divorce, and I am just now coming to terms with the finality of this part of my life.

Please call me as soon as you get home. I am begging for your forgiveness and understanding. We must talk, my dear Simon. I've missed you so very much.

All my love, forever,

Your Staci

Simon put the letter down and looked up at his mother. His face was pale and filled with confusion. When he spoke, he sounded so dejected that Margo had to fight off the years of anger and frustration she had withheld. Whatever the letter said, her son did not deserve this.

"I can't do this again, Mom. I thought it was over. Why won't she leave me be?"

Looking her son in the eyes, Margo reached over and touched the letter as if asking permission to read it.

"Go ahead."

Margo read the letter, her mother's heart raging with the closest thing she had ever experienced to hate. She forced herself to calm down before she spoke. "This makes no sense to me whatsoever," she said, as she threw the letter on the desk.

Shocked by her reaction, Simon said, "I'm not sure I understand, Mom."

Margo took a deep breath and stared hard at the letter. She didn't dare look her son in the eyes when she spoke, afraid that the rage inside of her would explode.

"When I saw Staci at the drugstore, she never inquired once about you. I asked her when she got home, and she said she was here temporarily. Her grandmother had asked her to come live with her permanently and she would be going back to Boca after Christmas. I'll be honest with you Son. At the time I was afraid she planned on talking you into moving there, so I asked if you knew about her plans. Instead of answering me, she got what can only be described as a disgusted expression on her face, looked at her watch and said she had an appointment. She then scurried over to the check-out without another word."

Margo paused, her mind in an angry whirl. When she began speaking again, her face was a combination of confusion and suspicion. "Something's changed, Simon. That letter is totally contradictory to her attitude that day. Maybe she had planned on getting back with Blake and he rejected the idea."

"Or maybe she *is* planning on asking me to move to Boca and knew you wouldn't be pleased."

"I really don't think that's it. Call it my motherly instinct, but I can't imagine being as passionate about someone as she appears to be in her letter and not attempting to contact them for four plus months. She has the address for the Mission – or if she lost it, she could have gotten it from any number of people. It just doesn't make sense to me."

"When has Staci ever made sense, Mom?"

Margo wanted to cry. Tears of sorrow? Tears of anger? Tears of pain for her hurting son? Maybe all three. When she spoke, her voice sounded defeated.

"I suppose that regardless of her motives, the important thing is to determine if you still love her. I don't understand her and haven't for quite some time. But I trust you, Simon. If you see something there that isn't obvious to me, then you owe it to yourself – and to Staci – to either pursue a permanent relationship or make a clear break. She obviously didn't see the confrontation at her grandmother's as the end."

"I know, Mom," Simon said, exhaling deeply as he spoke, and then adding, "I wish I knew what real love feels like. Whatever it is, I can't believe it carries this much turmoil with it. I know I have feelings for Staci – I'm just not sure what those feelings are anymore. What makes it even more confusing is the fact that I'm starting to have feelings for Karen. Feelings I'd like to explore, but I can't even think about that until I put my relationship with Staci to rest. I was so excited about getting home, introducing Jesse to the family, getting back to my writing – getting back to my life. And now…"

Tears were forming in Margo's eyes and the pain she felt for her son was as physical as it was emotional. She wanted to say something comforting, but the knot in her throat prohibited her from speaking. When Simon began speaking again, his voice trembled with emotion.

"Sometimes I wonder why God is leading me through this maze with Staci. I feel responsible for her happiness and yet I don't know how to make her happy. At least not without losing everything that brings *me* joy. Everything I value most - the simple things in life – pastoring my little church, spending time with my family and friends. I want children. I want to keep writing. Not for the money – for the love of knowing that it brings joy to those who read my stories. Is that selfish of me, Mom?"

Suddenly, her pent up anger took over Margo's emotions, enabling her to respond to Simon's question. "You, my Son, are the most unselfish person I know and I hope what I'm about to say will not be too harsh or add to your despair. If so, I ask your forgiveness in advance."

She paused, half expecting Simon to cut her off. When he continued to stare blankly at the letter, she began speaking as calmly as she could.

"There was once a time when I considered Staci your ideal match. Even when she started to change, I believed the sweet young girl you fell in love with still existed beneath her superior attitude. I considered her aloofness a way of hiding her timidity. I was angry when she broke your engagement, but seeing her genuine grief at your father's funeral gave me hope that the old Staci was back. When she walked out on you – again – I lost a large portion of my respect for her. Then when she popped back in your life after her divorce, I was completely distrustful of her motives. But I decided that it was not my place to interfere with your life, despite the fact that I felt like she was simply clinging to you while she searched for her next victim. I know that sounds cold, but I'm trying to be honest with you. I figured she had hooked up with someone in Boca and that's why she stayed down there. I was overjoyed that you never mentioned her in your letters, and prayed we had seen the last of her. When I first got that letter, I was tempted to destroy it, but you know I could never do that. Now I wish I had. Please Simon, think with your head and not your heart. You deserve happiness, and I don't see you *ever* finding it with Staci. Look at who she's become and not at who she was.

"She's all about glamour, excitement and having fun. Can't you tell that from the way she rattles on about her *fabulous cruises* and *exclusive resort vacations*? She's selfish, self-centered, self-indulgent and a card carrying member of the *me* generation. Wake up Simon! Please, I beg you. Give yourself the opportunity to explore your feelings for Karen – or any other woman you feel attracted to."

Throughout Margo's tirade, Simon's head remained bowed down, not looking at his mother; much the way he acted when he was being scolded as a child. When Margo stopped talking, he slowly began lifting his head. Margo cringed when she realized everything she had said, fully expecting Simon to ask her to leave. When his face revealed a silly grin, lips trembling as if containing laughter, it frightened her more than the expected reproof.

"Are you alright, Simon? I...I really didn't mean to get so wound up. I wouldn't blame you at all if you...why are you smiling like that?"

"You're somethin' else Mom. The last time I saw you that wound up, Sandy was seventeen and had just announced that she wanted to marry that – what was it you called him? – that 'hooligan' from Frenchburg."

"You aren't angry with me?"

"No…well, maybe a little. But only because I wish you had said something about the way you felt a little earlier. You know I respect your judgment and you might have saved me months of grief."

"You're right, of course. I should have said something. My only excuse is that I have no excuse. I told myself that I didn't want to interfere with your life."

"I'm guessing that Belinda and Sandy share your opinion of Staci." It was half question and half statement.

"Oh yes. Don't *ever* get them started on the subject – especially Sandy." Margo had finally begun to relax a little when a soft knock on the door gave them both a start.

"Is this a private conversation or can anyone join in?" Belinda's voice was deliberately soft as she stuck her head in the room.

"Come on in Sis. You might as well have your crack at trashing my love life."

The puzzled look on Belinda's face as she gently closed the door elicited a chuckle from Simon and a playful admonishment from Margo.

"Be nice, Simon!"

Then turning to Belinda she said, "I take it Caitlyn's down and Jesse's still sleeping."

"Yes. Now what's this nonsense about trashing Simon's love-life?"

Simon debated on whether he should let Belinda read the letter, then decided she might as well know the full story if she was going to offer an opinion. The three sat in silence while Belinda read the letter, then tossed it back on the desk in disgust.

"You know what Sandy would do if she read this, don't you?" Then she made the familiar gesture of sticking a finger in her mouth and gagging.

"So you think it's a phony entreaty as well," Simon said.

"I think it's a load of crap," Belinda stated bitterly. "What does she want from you Simon? Your soul?" Belinda's face glowed scarlet with rage. If the baby hadn't been sleeping across the hall, she would have screamed. After a moment of seething, she added, "It's not that you don't deserve to be loved that way, Simon. You definitely do. But after Mom told us about her encounter with Staci at the drug store, we all believed she was out of your life. Something's changed…unless she thinks she can coerce you into moving to Florida."

"I think you know that's not going to happen. I have everything I want right here."

"So are you going to call her?" Margo tentatively asked.

"You know what, Mom. I'm not – at least not until I've had a few days to enjoy my family without any distractions. Right now I'm going to call Lenny and let him know I'm back."

Margo couldn't quite read Simon's demeanor. The smile he wore contradicted the pain in his eyes. *Please God, give him your guidance. Protect him from his own selflessness.*

Chapter 46

"Who was that gorgeous guy with your boyfriend?" Cricket's exuberant voice had Darrell giving her a shattered look as she and Karen entered the kitchen together. Then looking over at Darrell, Cricket smiled sheepishly saying, "Not to worry, handsome. He's just a kid. A positively dreamy one, but I'm not into boy toys."

The only word Karen heard was boyfriend. *I wish!*

"Where did you get the idea that Simon is my boyfriend? He's a friend and the pastor of my church. Nothing more."

"He's pretty easy on the eyes too. But I'm not convinced, girlfriend. When you were holding that baby, he was looking at you like he wanted to eat you up," Cricket smugly replied.

"That baby is his niece and any adoration you may have witnessed was for her – believe me."

Cricket shook her head and rolled her eyes as if listening to a child's denial of the obvious. "That still doesn't tell me who tall, dark and dreamy is."

"He's sort of Simon's protégé. Simon met him in South America when Jesse was only twelve. He's one of the main reasons Simon goes back to South America every so often. Simon's also close to the couple who adopted Jesse. During his college years, he spent a lot of time with them. And now, Jesse is going to be attending college at either Morehead State or UK."

The dinner rush was over and Karen was pulling the steam pans from their wells in the steam table as she talked. Evidently satisfied with Karen's answer, Cricket, who had been replenishing the sandwich board as she talked, returned to the dining room.

After emptying the steam table, Karen began a new batch of chili for tomorrow, and then started the sauce for lasagna. While she cooked, her mind wandered back to the conversation at Thanksgiving when Margo told her,

Sandy and Belinda, about the brief conversation with Staci at the drugstore. She also mentioned that Staci had "suddenly grown boobs," as she put it, and then added, "Guess the Florida sunshine grows more than oranges – these were definitely grapefruits."

They had all laughed at Margo's humorous spin on Staci's obvious surgical enhancement, but Karen secretly hated the idea that the already gorgeous woman now had an even more desirable body. How would Simon react to the new Staci? But when Margo had added that Staci would be returning to Boca after Christmas, it had sparked a glimmer of hope in her. She tried not to think about the possibility of Simon joining her there.

Darrell's voice wrenched her out of her musings as he removed two large pork butts from the refrigerator. He began seasoning them for tomorrow's barbeque special, and then he asked Karen to hand him a large roasting pan. Karen reached over and placed the pan next to Darrell, his smug grin not going unnoticed. He obviously shared Cricket's belief that she and Simon were involved.

"Simon seems like a nice guy. How long have you known him?"

"He's the first person I met when I came here. He's the one who introduced me to his mother, who introduced me to Dil…so in essence, he's the reason I have the Krossroads."

Over the next few hours, Karen and Darrell talked and joked as they cleaned the cooking area and set up for the following day. By the time Karen finished all her prep, she was equally exhausted and exhilarated. She always had this euphoric high after a busy day, despite the fact that, except for the little time she had sat with Simon, she had been on her feet since five this morning.

"Would you mind closing up for me tonight, Darrell? I think I'm going to check on Goodness, take a shower and head over to Margo's. She asked me to come by as soon as I could get away. I'm anxious to hear all about Simon's time in Sao Paulo. He said he has a lot of pictures."

"You know I don't mind. I'd probably be hanging around 'til closing anyway."

"Knock, knock! Anybody home?" Karen called as she stuck her head through the front door of Margo's home.

"Back here," Margo's voice answered from the sunroom. Even in the winter it was the coziest room in the house. The small free-standing electric fireplace provided the perfect amount of warmth and gave the room a pleasant glow.

"You're earlier than we expected. Was it a slow night?"

"Anything but! It always slows down after eight on weeknights and Darrell said he would close up for me. I'm really blessed to have such a great crew."

Simon beamed as Karen entered the room, unaware that both Jesse and Belinda were watching him rather than their entering guest. Karen couldn't help but notice that Simon's eyes looked really tired. Maybe this was a bad idea.

"You look as fresh as a spring daisy. How can you possibly look this good after fifteen or sixteen hours at the diner?" Margo said as she greeted Karen with a hug. Her lovely compliment made Karen blush, adding soft color to her already radiant appearance.

"You're forgetting; I had a most pleasant break this evening." Her eyes drifted back to Simon as she spoke. Despite the tired eyes, his dazzling smile made her positively dizzy. She quickly looked away as she took a seat next to Belinda.

"I suppose it's too late to have some baby time. Honestly, Belinda, she is beyond adorable."

"Actually, she'll be awake any time now. I can't get her off her ten o'clock feeding, but she lets me sleep until around five or six after that, so I don't mind."

Twenty minutes later, Caitlyn was busy suckling at her mother's breast. Watching this bonding of mother and child always made Karen more than a little envious. She remembered experiencing the same feeling every time she was with Amy, who had breast fed all three of her babies. Caitlyn was a hearty eater and Belinda affectionately referred to her as "Little Miss Piggy" when she fed her.

The two women sat in silence while Caitlyn settled into her feeding. Curious, but not really comfortable with her unasked question, Karen reluctantly probed, "Has Simon talked to Staci yet?"

Belinda was tempted to tell her about the letter and both her and her mother's suspicion that Staci was up to something, but bit her tongue before answering. "I think he's waiting until he has a weekend with the family before he lets her know he's home. He wants Jesse to feel more settled in before he… uh…"

"I know. Staci demands his full attention when she's with him. I understand." Karen finished what she thought was Belinda's hesitant response, her heart sinking at the knowledge that he did intend calling her. *I suppose it's inevitable. Guess I was just hoping he would wait for her to call him – or better yet – not call.* Without realizing it, she emitted a deep sigh.

Belinda looked at her sympathetically. She was certain that Karen had feelings for Simon, but didn't want to give her false hope. Who knew where Simon's heart lay?

Deciding it was best to change the subject, Karen asked, "Did I hear Simon say that he would be introducing Jesse to Father Brian tomorrow?"

"You did. He called him earlier this evening. Simon thinks that with Jesse considering the priesthood, Father Brian will be a great influence on him. He's very straight-forward about the ups and downs of being a priest." With a hint of laughter, Belinda added, "I don't know how he's going to keep the girls from hanging all over him. Can you believe how gorgeous he is? Those huge, dreamy brown eyes are enough to cause any female to positively swoon."

Karen obviously noticed that Jesse was an extremely handsome young man, but somehow, with Simon in the same room, he didn't affect her that way. Belinda had finished feeding Caitlyn and was now trying to get a burp from her, so Karen reached over and asked if she could rock her for a while. Without hesitation, Belinda handed the baby over, traded chairs with Karen and watched as Karen skillfully managed to get a loud burp from Caitlyn, then began gently rocking as she spoke softly to her.

"You look like you have things under control. Do you mind if I go change by blouse? My Little Miss Piggy can be a really sloppy eater at times. I should know by now that it's best to just remove my top completely before nursing."

"We'll be fine. If you like, you can go on back downstairs. I'll settle her in bed once she's asleep."

Caitlyn's eyes were already drooping and within minutes after Belinda left, she was sound asleep. Karen continued to hold her and rock her for several more minutes, simply enjoying the feel of her. When she stood up, she was surprised to see Simon standing in the doorway watching her. There was such an adoring look on his face that it made her heart ache. *If only that look was for me. But it's all yours, Sweet Caitlyn. Do you mind if I'm just a touch jealous?* Kissing the top of her head, she laid the baby in her crib, tucking the covers around her and placing the little plush bunny that was always close by, next to her. Together she and Simon returned to the gathering downstairs.

Chapter 47

Around eleven thirty Karen said she had better be heading back home. Simon offered to walk her to her car, setting her heart racing and hopes soaring. *Stop it, you fool. He's simply being a gentleman. Nothing more.* When they the reached the car, he held the door for her, then gave her a *friendly* peck on the cheek.

"I'm glad you came by. I'll be tied up all day tomorrow, but maybe on Saturday you'll be able to get away for a while. I'm not sure what the family plans are yet, but..."

Karen cut him off, disappointment filling her voice as she said, "Saturday's not good. It's our busiest day, and things don't let up much all day. We stay open 'til ten on Fridays and Saturdays, but I'm off on Sunday. Your mom has already invited me to join all of you at Dil's."

Simon's voice sounded equally disappointed as he said, "Well I guess it'll be Sunday then. Drive safely."

Everyone had gone to bed except for Margo and Dil, who remained in the sun room, sipping wine. It was becoming harder and harder for Dil to leave the warmth of Margo's presence. Despite the fact that he still had a long drive home and it was going on midnight, he reveled in this alone time with her. He had already bought an engagement ring, but was saving it for a Christmas surprise. Knowing that Margo loved him as much as he loved her, there was no doubt in his mind that she would soon be his wife.

"A penny for your thoughts."

Margo's voice broke into his musings and he tightened his arm around her. "Just thinking about you – which is what I'm doing about ninety-five percent of the time."

Margo smiled, resting her head on his shoulder.

"Normally, I'm spending an equal amount of time thinking of you, but I have to confess that my thoughts have been somewhat distracted by my concern for Simon."

Soon she was telling Dil all about Staci's letter as well as Simon's visit with her before leaving for South America.

"Since I've never met the girl, I really can't offer an opinion, but from what you're telling me, it does sound suspicious. You say her name is Staci Perkins?"

"Perkins is her married name. Her maiden name is Winthrop. Her parents are both college professors."

"Is her father Everett Winthrop by any chance – the head of the College of Business at Morehead State?"

"Why yes! Do you know him?"

"He's on the board of directors for The Morehead Community Bank. That's where you and Simon do your banking, right?"

"Why yes it is. What are you thinking, Dil?"

"You said that Staci knows nothing about Simon's finances and when he hinted at it during their last meeting, she scoffed at the idea of him having sufficient income to support a wife with her needs."

"I don't recall putting it exactly that way, but yes. He's always wanted Staci to accept him for himself and not his money – or lack thereof. Where are you going with this?"

"As you know, my bank is in the process of buying Morehead Community. Winthrop was appointed head of the due-diligence portion of the auditing committee for the bank. As such, he has access to information on all the depositors and their accounts. It would be a serious breach of ethics for him to discuss any of this with his family, but perhaps he thought that Staci was aware of the fact that Simon is the bank's largest depositor."

Margo sat up straight, her eyes wide with excitement. "Of course! That has to be it. Every time she and Simon have been close to getting married, she backs off because she knows she can't live her life 'as a poor preacher's wife,' as she so often puts it. I'd be willing to wager money that her father mentioned something about Simon's account – maybe not in detail, but even if he just said something inadvertently, Staci may have picked up on it and made some inquiries on her own. She once dated the accounts manager of the bank. I'd be more willing to believe that Leroy Allen is the leak. I doubt Everett would ever deliberately do anything unethical."

"You know him that well?"

"I doubt that anyone knows the Winthrop's *that* well. They pretty much keep to themselves. Even when Simon and Staci were engaged, we only saw them a couple of times when we had them over for dinner. I don't know if you would classify them as anti-social, or even snobs, but they are very close-mouthed about their personal lives."

"You're probably right about Winthrop. The few times I've met him, he came across as somewhat pompous, but Miriam felt he was the most qualified for the task, and my auditors seem to have a great deal of respect for him. I think I'd like to know how Simon's conversation with Staci goes before I mention anything to Miriam."

Chapter 48

It was after ten before Karen sat down for the first time since the dinner customers started arriving around five on Saturday evening. Up until then there had been no real break from the lunch crowd. Sherry assured Karen that the day business was largely due to Christmas shoppers opting to eat out after busy days at malls in Lexington, Winchester and Mt. Sterling. There were lots of new faces that evening, but there was one very familiar face.

Toby came in with a lovely young woman who turned out to be a writer for the entertainment section of the Lexington Messenger. It was around seven-thirty when Cricket had stuck her head in the kitchen, saying, "A great looking guy is out front asking for you." Up to her eyeballs in orders, she nonetheless left her post, thinking it was Simon. Toby stood, greeted her with a peck on the cheek and introduced her to Carol Rogers.

"I've been telling Carol for the last month about the great food you serve and she's here to check out my boasting."

"I have to say, this is as good as anything I've had in Lexington," Carol said, offering her hand to Karen. "Where did you learn to cook like this? It's not what I expected from a diner."

Obviously looking for Karen to name some notable cooking institute or big name restaurant, she was taken aback by her reply.

"Mostly from my granny and my boss at the diner where I worked after high school – along with a lot of experimentation."

"Really? You never attended professional cooking classes?"

"Not unless you want to count endless hours of watching the Food Network. I learned a lot about technique and experimenting with different seasonings. Bottom line is, I simply love cooking – speaking of which, I'd better get back to the kitchen before Darrell gets covered up."

Disappointed that Simon hadn't come by at all on Friday, she was confident that he would at least drop in on Saturday – maybe not for a meal, but at least to say hi. By the time she finished showering and giving Goodness a little attention, she had convinced herself that it didn't matter. She would see him at church tomorrow and they would be together all afternoon at Dil's. After her two eighteen-hour days, Karen was too tired to get in a funk over Simon. Collapsing in bed shortly before midnight, she immediately fell asleep. When the alarm went off at seven thirty, she stretched alongside of Goodness, literally jumped out of bed, and hurried about her morning tasks. She wanted to arrive at church early, hoping she would get an opportunity to talk to Simon before the services started. Arriving at the church twenty minutes early, she spotted Margo and Dil right away, but no Simon or Jesse.

"Did you need to speak to them about something, dear?" Margo inquired when Karen asked where they were.

"Not really. I was just hoping to see them since they never came by on Friday or Saturday."

"Poor Simon has been running around like a chicken with its head cut off. He spent most of Friday with Fr. Brian, and then we all drove over to Lexington to surprise Sandy. Yesterday he was with Lenny and Gail planning today's service. Jesse is with Fr. Brian this morning. Simon drove him all the way over to West Liberty for mass after breakfast and is now in the office with Lenny."

"So Jesse won't be joining us today?"

"Heavens yes! Fr. Brian says mass in Owingsville as well as West Liberty. The timing is such that he will drop Jesse off on his way to Owingsville. They will begin the service at the regular time, but Jesse should be here before it ends."

Looking around, Karen asked, "Where are Belinda and Caitlyn?"

"Belinda wanted to get Caitlyn fed before church. They'll be here any minute. She's hoping you'll ride over to Dil's with her."

"Of course – I'd love to." Karen replied, hiding her disappointment that it wasn't Simon who asked for her company for the ride. *But then, he'll have Jesse with him so it's not like I would have him to myself.*

As if reading her thoughts, Margo added, "Belinda will be headed back to Covington early this evening, so you'll probably have to ride back with Simon. I'll be staying at Dil's. Miriam and Paulie will be spending the night as well. We're going to do some shopping together in Lexington tomorrow after Miriam sees Dil's oncologist friend."

They had been standing in the back of the church and others were starting to arrive. Each one stopped to greet them, several inquiring as to when Simon would be returning. It took only a brief conspiratorial look from Margo for

Karen to realize they were planning his return as a surprise – which explained why he and Lenny were holed up in the office.

Taking their seats in the front row, Margo, Dil and Karen were soon joined by Belinda and Caitlyn. Gail and her children were already seated across from them and all of them came over to ooh and aah over Caitlyn who was now fast asleep in Margo's arms. When Seth reached up to stroke her soft blond hair, Caitlyn emitted a sigh of contentment, prompting him to turn to his mother, announcing proudly, "She loves me, Mama. I'm her most favorite."

They had no sooner returned to their seats, when the organ began as it always did, with a loud crescendo; then more softly as the congregation began the opening hymn. Lenny took his place at the pulpit to say the opening prayer, followed by a reading, meditation and another hymn. As the congregation sat for his sermon, he announced that he had a "*very special speaker this morning along with a truly amazing young guest.*" This was Simon's cue to enter the sanctuary with Jesse. As the church erupted in a loud applause, Simon replaced Lenny at the pulpit while Lenny joined his family. It took him several minutes to quiet the joyful response to his return; and almost as long to calm them down after he introduced Jesse. Karen was certain she had heard numerous audible sighs from women when Jesse first appeared. She recalled a phrase that Leslie, a Catholic friend from high school, used to refer to any priest that was young and attractive. "Father What-a-waste." *Oh yea. If this one does become a priest, all the girls will definitely agree with Leslie.* But Karen had eyes only for Simon. He shared with his congregation about his time in South America, how he had met Jesse and that Jesse would be attending college here in Kentucky. When he mentioned that he was considering the priesthood, numerous moans replaced the earlier sighs. Jesse's dark skin masked his blushing face, but Karen knew from the way his feet shuffled restlessly, that he was uncomfortable with the praise Simon paid him, as well as the starry-eyed ogling from the female members of the congregation. She could relate to his feelings quite well, knowing that she was often equally discomforted when people gushed over her cooking. Over the years, she had learned to accept praise gracefully. Granny had taught her at a very young age to understand that whatever her accomplishments might be, they were gifts from God, and to deny them was a lie. Once she heard someone praise Granny for a beautiful cake she had made for their child's birthday. Granny smiled and said, "Why thank you very much. I'm very blessed that God has given me this talent." Over the years, she had used this line quite often.

Realizing that her mind had drifted, Karen forced herself back to the present just as Simon asked the congregation to stand and pray for Jesse's future success. As the service ended, a flock of people gathered around Simon and Jesse at the back of the church. The weather was cold and a chilling drizzle had started, keeping everyone indoors. Most left after welcoming Simon home and greeting Jesse with well wishes. Several young women had begun quizzing Jesse as to where he would be attending college, where he would be living and if he would be joining them every Sunday. Karen, Belinda, Margo and Dil stood back, waiting for the crowd to dwindle before approaching them. No one was paying much attention to the opening and closing of the door as people left, but when it was opened from the outside, everyone facing the door looked up as Staci let out a little cry and launched herself at a very startled Simon.

"Oh Simon; My darling Simon, you're home!"

Before Simon could brace himself for the assault, Staci had thrown her arms around his neck and was kissing him fervently. "You naughty man," she scolded in a low seductive voice. "Why haven't you called to let me know you were home? I've driven by every Sunday for the last three weeks to see if your car was here. Didn't your mother give you my letter?"

Simon didn't bother answering her question; he simply took her by the wrists and disengaged himself, saying, "Staci, this is hardly the time or place for such an exhibition." Karen wasn't certain if the red glow on his face was embarrassment or fury. She had never seen him angry, so assumed he was simply embarrassed by Staci's exuberance. She hadn't heard what Staci said while her face was buried in Simon's neck.

Stepping back, Staci slowly turned to face the group of people who were either uncomfortably attempting to ignore the scene, or snickering at Simon's obvious chagrin.

"I'm so sorry, Simon," Staci said, in an obviously fake penitent voice, "but I'm sure your friends understand how much I've missed you." Her coy smile was accompanied by a girlish batting of her eyes, which elicited mixed reactions. Belinda, who was standing to the side out of her sight, did the gagging gesture, for which she received a slap on the wrist from her mother. Margo was actually trying to keep from laughing at the expression on Jesse's face. The only way she could possibly describe it was "a deer in headlights."

Still standing next to Simon, her arm possessively around his waist, Staci maintained a sweet, innocent smile as Simon bid farewell to his friends. No one had noticed Karen slip silently through the door. On the verge of tears, she wondered if the temperature had actually dropped this much – or was it that her heart stopped pumping that caused the cold to penetrate her very soul. Shivering uncontrollably, she made her way across the parking lot toward the diner.

Chapter 49

"Dil, would you mind if Jesse rides over with you and Mom? I'll join you in a little while." Simon's voice was subdued and without emotion. It was just the seven of them remaining in the church. Margo led Jesse outside, with Belinda, Caitlyn and Dil close on their heels. Looking around, she asked, "Where's Karen?"

They all scanned the parking lot, searching for the familiar dark curls among the scattered group headed toward their cars. It was Jesse who spotted her crossing the street. "Is that her, Senora Margo?" he asked, pointing in that direction.

"She must have bugged out when Staci started her little show," Belinda said, not hiding her scorn at the interruption to the wonderful service they had just enjoyed. "I'll drive over and pick her up. You go ahead, Mom. Karen may have wanted to change clothes. Would you mind taking Caitlyn with you?"

Margo, who was now holding Caitlyn, gave her daughter a, *that's a stupid question* look, and headed for Dil's car.

"Don't be long," Dil said. "Gloria has a very special brunch planned for Jesse."

As soon as everyone had left the church, Simon led Staci to the front pew. "Sit down, Staci. We have a lot to talk about – but first I have to make sure everything is shut down and locked."

"Will we be joining your mother and her…uh…friend after that?"

"No!" he barked, then felt a flash of shame for having let the mounting anger he was trying so hard to suppress overtake him. "No." he repeated more calmly. "We are going to sit right here and talk."

"But Simon, this is hardly the place…"

"This is the perfect place, Staci," he said, wanting to add, *I need the strength of my church – of my God – to keep me from strangling you for that absurd performance you just put on in front of my family and friends.* Instead, he prayed to himself, *Lord, give me patience and understanding to deal with my weakness where this woman is concerned.*

After completing his inspection, Simon returned and sat next to Staci. When she attempted to move closer to him, he put up his hand and she withdrew. Giving him a questioning look, she said, "I take it you never got my letter."

"Oh, I got your letter," he replied, "I just didn't understand it."

"But that's ridiculous, Simon. I thought I made it clear that I was ready to set aside my personal needs and come to you without reservation. I'm ready to open up and share my life with you. Isn't that what you said you needed?"

There was a sadness in his eyes that alarmed Staci. She could deal with anger, but not this obvious pain. To show emotional pain was to show weakness and she never thought of Simon as a weak person. He had been her strength when she was lonely or frightened. He had been her comfort – her hiding place.

When Simon began speaking, his voice was steady, his tone defeated.

"It's too late Staci. I needed your honesty when I received an engagement ring by mail seven years ago. There was nothing else in that envelope – just the ring that held my heart. I had given both to you in earnest. Every time you've come back to me, I've convinced myself that the girl I fell in love with was somewhere within the shell of who you've become. I thought if I was patient, that shell would crack, and the Staci of my youth would be returned to me. But the shell has just become more impenetrable. That was obvious to me when I visited you at your grandmother's. That's who you've become, Staci – your grandmother – vain and haughty. You talk about your *personal needs*, of which I am obviously not a part, since you are willing set them aside to come to me. You don't need *me* Staci. I'm just your recovery zone when your life is upended in some way."

"That's not true, Simon – at least not completely true. Doesn't the fact that I keep returning to you show that I do need you? When I said personal needs, I was referring to material needs. But that's not a problem any more. I know you can provide..." She stopped mid sentence.

There it is. Mom was right.

"So how did you find out?"

Her instinct was to play innocent, but she knew he would see through her, so she said, "I overheard my father asking Mother why I never told them that my preacher boyfriend was a millionaire. Of course Mother was as surprised as I was. Mom said he must be mistaken – that whoever told him such a thing had to be referring to another Simon Crawford. I started thinking about what you said in Boca – about having another source of income and I…uh…made some inquiries. But what does it matter, Simon?" Her voice became animated as she continued. "We could travel. We could build a beautiful home anywhere we wanted. We could have all the things we've ever wanted. We could afford to have a family – I know how important that is to you, Darling. I'll sacrifice my body to bear your children. That's how much I love you."

Sacrifice your body! Who are you, Staci? Simon was too stunned to speak, but when she started to say something else, he knew he couldn't listen to any more of her drivel.

"Stop!" he commanded. "There is no *we* Staci. I thought that was clear when I left Boca. But then you weren't even willing to listen when I attempted to tell you that I did have the means to provide a very comfortable life for us. You simply dismissed me. However, you've just answered the question I asked back then. Money does make a difference and that's *not* what I wanted to hear. You don't understand me in the least, Staci, and I doubt you ever have. I'm perfectly happy in my present home, living a simple life as a pastor. I don't consider the excess money mine. It's a gift from God, and as such I will use it in ways that I feel will be pleasing to Him. I will use what I need to support my family, but not in the kind of extravagance you spoke of. Those are your needs, Staci. Not mine. I will use what's necessary to educate my children and what is left will be used to help others in need. Do you honestly think you could accept those decisions? I don't."

Simon had been looking directly at Staci as he spoke, but now lowered his head as he continued. "There is a part of me that will always love you Staci. But that love is reserved for the sweet, innocent girl of my youth – not the person you have become. I've held on to the image of that girl for too long and must now accept that *you* are not her." His voice was a choked whisper as he finished speaking and when he looked back up, Staci had tears in her eyes.

Slapping at the tears as if chasing away a pesky insect, she emitted a woeful sigh. In a low voice, filled with resignation, she said, "You're right Simon. We've never been friends, and as adults, we've never shared the same needs. I have always loved you, but I suppose it's not the kind of love that you need. I've always looked up to you as being…well…perfect. Too perfect for someone as imperfect as me."

Simon started to protest her last statement but she put her fingertips to his mouth, saying, "Don't bother correcting me. I'm not always honest about everything, but I can at least be honest about myself."

She attempted a smile as she said, "Can I ask you one last question, before I leave?"

"Of course."

"Where did the money come from? Did you win a lottery or something?"

Simon smiled, albeit a weary smile, for the first time since Staci had walked through the door. "I tried to tell you once before. Do you remember when you came by my office all excited about the job in Atlanta? I had asked you to come because I was going to tell you that we could afford to get married and stay right here. I had carefully placed a book on my desk for you to see. Well, it caught your eye alright. You picked it up and began mocking the absurdity of the concept behind the story. You asked who wrote such *tripe*. Well the answer is me. I wrote that book and have written numerous others since then. My pride wouldn't let me admit that I was the recipient of your scorn."

"Oh Simon, I..."

"Don't, Staci. It's too late for apologies. I was probably being more prideful than I should have been anyway; and you made me realize that. But just so you know, Staci, there *are* children who live in incredible poverty and unimaginable conditions, and they are filled with a joy you or I could never understand. I'm not saying that they are always happy with their circumstances, but there's a difference between being happy and being joyful. Happiness is fleeting, but joy comes from hope – and that is what sustains them – hope. Those children look beyond what is seen by others. I sometimes think that God has allowed them a glimpse of heaven, and that's the future they focus on to carry them past the hunger and pain of the present."

Staci's head was now bowed, as she waited for Simon to continue. She felt like she was listening to one of his sermons. His voice held the same passion he exuded when he preached. When he stopped speaking, she looked up to see him watching her intently. With as much poise and dignity as she could muster, she stood, saying, "Well I suppose this is it, Simon. I'll be going back to Boca after Christmas and I don't expect to return. Mother and Father will be retiring in the summer. They'll relocate to Florida as well. Mother says this place reminds her too much of her childhood on a small farm in South Georgia. I guess I've never told you how poor she was back then."

For the first time since his father's death, Staci's face held a sadness that tore at Simon's heart. He stood and pulled her into his arms. "You've never told me much of anything about your family, Staci. You've never shared the hurts that make you who you are. Maybe if you had, we wouldn't be where we are now. Try to be happy Staci. Find someone you want to share all of yourself with. Find joy."

Kissing her gently on the top of her head, he released her and watched as she slowly walked out. Out of his life.

Karen was still in her coat, sitting on the edge of her bed, when a knock aroused her from her stupor. She didn't know how long she had been sitting there. She wasn't even sure how she got there. She looked around as the knock became more of a pounding.

"Karen, it's Belinda and it's cold out here."

Throwing off her coat, she ran to the door. "I'm sorry, I must have dozed off. I didn't realize how tired I was. I hope you weren't out there very long." Then looking over Belinda's shoulder, she asked, "Where's Caitlyn?"

"With Mom and Dil. Did you know that Dil had a car seat put in his car just for Caitlyn? How sweet is that?" Belinda did a little shimmy as she removed her coat and threw it on the bed next to Karen's.

"Oops. That coat is wet. I probably shouldn't have done that."

"Just following my bad example," Karen said, but her tone held no mirth.

"I hate this kind of weather. That cold wet air just goes right through me. I wish the temperature would drop a few more degrees and turn this miserable rain to snow." Turning to face Karen she abruptly asked, "Are you okay? I mean, you aren't feeling sick or anything, are you?"

"Just tired. I probably shouldn't go to Dil's this afternoon. I'll just be a drag on everyone's good time. Do you mind driving over there alone?"

"Yes I do mind – and you'll be more of a drag by not showing up. Mom will be worried sick about you. You know she considers you as much her daughter as Sandy and me."

Karen had to smile at that thought. She knew she was blessed to be part of this wonderful family; and she knew she couldn't disappoint them. She would just have to get past her distress and face the reality that Simon was not, nor would he ever be, more than a friend. *Take what you have and be grateful for it KC. You're far more blessed than most.*

Simon had no idea how long he had sat in the church. His head was hurting from the emotional upheaval that engulfed his entire being. When he attempted to focus his thoughts, he could only summon a jumble of disconnected words and images. *Be still and know that I am God.* The words from the forty-sixth psalm flashed through Simon's head. It was the first cohesive thought he was able to put together and he grabbed at like a life raft. He said the words out loud several times before grasping their message. *Surrender yourself to the pain you are experiencing and know that I will carry you through it.* Simon choked back a sob and released the pent up tears.

Chapter 50

Everyone seemed to be watching for Belinda and Karen's arrival. Gloria met them at the door before they had reached the entry and all eyes were on them as they walked into the great room. Sandy was holding Caitlyn, who was sucking furiously on her pacifier.

"I think Little Miss Piggy wants to be fed. She's pretty much figured out that nothing's coming from her paci."

"Did you try her bottle of water?"

"She finished that thirty minutes ago and I've had to change her twice already. I think she leaks."

As soon as Belinda left the room with Caitlyn, Sandy stood and gave Karen a hug. "We missed you yesterday – but then you must have been busy serving your 'classic country cuisine with a big city twist.'"

Karen gave her a, *what in the world are you talking about look*, to which Sandy responded by picking up a newspaper and handing it to Karen.

It was the entertainment section of the Lexington Messenger and Sandy's finger pointed to the "Day Trippin'" article. It was Carol Rogers's popular byline that was featured every Sunday. The basic article was about all the Christmas activities featured in Kentucky that were an easy day trip worth checking out. In the middle of the article was a little blurb saying, "If you happen to pass through the Cave Run area in Farmers, don't miss a stop at the new Krossroads Diner. This sixty-plus-year-old landmark has been renovated and is serving some of the most marvelous food I've experienced in this area. The menu is classic country cuisine with a big city twist. While my date feasted on a plate of perfectly seasoned smoked baby back ribs (no sauce necessary – trust me, I tried them,) I devoured a generous serving of delectable herb-crusted lamb chops that was worthy of any fine dining experience, without the pricey tab. I'll take good food and happy chatter over candlelight and linens any day."

Karen felt light headed. She was almost in tears as she said, "Well bless his heart!" A puzzled Sandy said, "You do know that Carol Rogers is a woman."

"I was referring to Toby. You remember – the guy on the cabin cruiser that crashed our outing on the lake last summer? He's the one who brought her in. I met her briefly, but if I had known she was going to do this I would have spent more time with her, and picked up the check."

It was impossible for Karen to be in a funk when she was in the midst of this lively and loving family. Sandy *had* remembered Toby, referring to him as "the bare-chested hunk," which elicited a somewhat crude remark from Rick. Sandy immediately shot back that he had been more interested in Rick than he was in her. "A member of the Rick Hansen fan club as I recall." Soon the room was filled with lively chatter, teasing and laughter. It was almost two when Gloria came in to say that brunch would need to be served soon or several of the dishes would be ruined. They had planned to eat by one, but were obviously waiting on Simon. Dil looked at Margo for an answer, to which she replied, "I believe brunch is served."

Dil reached for Miriam's hand to help her off the couch. She immediately slapped his hand saying, "Don't start treating my like a helpless little old lady yet. I'm perfectly capable of standing on my own."

Her words were filled with teasing, prompting Dil to reach over and kiss her on the cheek. "Can I at least be a gentleman and escort you to the table?"

Relenting, she placed her hand on his crooked arm, then looking around asked, "Is Paulie still out at the stables?"

"He should be on his way in. Gloria called him on the intercom several minutes ago."

Soon they had all settled at the table. Dil said the blessing and everyone was busy filling their plates when Margo's cell phone rang. They all knew it was Simon calling as soon as she asked, "Are you okay?" Then she excused herself, stood and walked into the other room. When she returned, she had a worried look on her face, but forced a smile as she sat down.

"Simon will be here in about an hour. He said the weather forecast is for this rain to begin freezing soon after sundown. It might be best if everyone headed home before then." Turning to Belinda, she added, "I'm thinking that you should spend the night here, Sweetheart. Do you have time to get in touch with Adam before his flight leaves?"

Belinda looked at her watch. "He's already in-flight from Miami, but he said he would call me when arrives in Atlanta around four. Hopefully, this won't turn into something that will keep him from getting home on time."

By the time Simon arrived, the mood had returned to one of happy chatter. Paulie talked about Mountain Dulcimer like a proud father. "I'm learning to shoe the horses and Dulci likes it when I clean her hoofs better than when Scotty does. Scotty says I'm a natural with the horses and that soon Dil won't need him anymore. But I think Dil will always need Scotty because I can't be here all the time."

Karen found it fascinating that when Paulie talked about the horses, his mind seemed to work without the confusion that often accompanied his thought process. Dil said the same was true when he talked about anything mechanical.

When Simon walked in the room, he was smiling as he greeted everyone, but it was clear that his mind was elsewhere. It was as if a shadow hovered over his face, diminishing the bright green of his eyes. Karen felt that familiar heart-wrenching tug in her chest, but fought to maintain the cheerful atmosphere of the afternoon. *At least he didn't bring Staci.*

"How was the drive?" Dil asked, as Simon took a seat on the couch next to Belinda and Caitlyn. Reaching over to take his niece from her, he replied, "Nothing to worry about yet – at least not for us. I was listening to the weather on the way over and they said it's starting to get pretty nasty north of us. I hope you aren't planning to drive home tonight, Little Sister."

"We've already discussed that and I'm spending the night here. Adam's supposed to call me from Atlanta. He'll take a cab home if his flight isn't cancelled. Rick's been following the weather reports and they said there's ice on the runways at the Cincinnati airport."

The discussion remained on the weather while Simon cuddled and played with Caitlyn. When Sandy brought up the article in the Herald, handing the newspaper to Simon, he beamed with pride as he turned to Karen. "I knew you'd be a tremendous success. Congratulations. I already know what I'll be ordering the next time I'm there."

It was after five when Sandy and Rick headed home. Belinda had just finished talking to Adam, who thought his flight might be delayed, but was sure he would be home before morning.

"He said the storm had moved past the Cincinnati area so they would be able to salt the runways and renew regular service within the hour, so his flight shouldn't be too far off schedule," Belinda informed the group gathered at the front door to bid Sandy and Rick farewell.

After their departure, knowing that Margo was anxious to know the outcome of Simon's time with Staci, Dil steered everyone else back to den, while Belinda took Caitlyn upstairs. As soon as they were alone, Margo asked, "Are you really okay, Simon? You look so distressed."

"You were right about her knowing, Mom. She overheard her father say something to her mother about her *preacher boyfriend* being a millionaire. Then she put two and two together when she remembered the end of our conversation in Boca. I'm pretty sure I know where she got the rest of the information, I just don't understand how her father found out."

Margo explained about Everett's position with the bank and that Dil was in the process of purchasing it.

"A lot has happened since you've been gone. I won't get into all that right now. All I want to know is how your talk with Staci went. Not details, Simon, just the outcome. You know that whatever that may be, you have my love and support. The girls too. If you need Staci in your life to be happy, we will all stand behind that decision."

Simon had such love in his eyes when he looked at his mother that she wanted to weep.

"I know that, Mom. But I think you'll be relieved to know that it's over. It took a very wise young man to remind me that love without friendship is very vulnerable. I've come to realize that Staci and I were never friends. When I think of how little I know about her and her family, it sort of boggles my mind. Every time I've attempted to get her to open up to me, she would retreat further into her shell. I can't help but think that if I had demanded answers from her, she might have eventually realized that she could trust me with even her darkest secrets. But I always looked at her as being so fragile that I was afraid she would break."

Abruptly standing, Simon pulled his mother to her feet and embraced her. "I'll be fine, Mom – but right now I need to get Karen and Jesse safely home before ice starts forming on the highway. We'll talk more when you get back home. I love you Mom. You're the greatest."

Chapter 51

The ride back to Farmers was relatively quiet. Karen insisted on sitting in the back seat, claiming she might fall asleep, which wasn't entirely a lie. She was still quite full from the late brunch, when, upon Simon's arrival, Gloria had brought in a tray of cheeses, fruit and tasty Mexican breads, followed by a rich flan. Overeating always made her sleepy.

Simon appeared to be in a better mood after talking with his mother, so Karen was content to sit in the back listening to Simon and Jesse discuss plans for the upcoming week. The hum of the two deep male voices soon lulled her to sleep. When the car pulled to a stop behind the Diner, she awoke with a start. Simon jumped out of the car to open her door and insisted on walking her to the cottage. "There's liable to be ice on your steps. I don't want you slipping down."

As soon as the door was unlocked, she turned to thank Simon and found him observing her with a curious look on his face. Before she could speak, he brushed her cheek with the back of his hand, leaned in and gave her a gentle kiss. "Get some rest," he said as he turned to walk away. "You look... exhausted."

"Thank you...for the ride home." *For the kiss.*

Whatever fatigue had overcome her earlier, dissipated as she walked through the door. Goodness met her with the usual complaining "reeooow" that greeted Karen whenever she left the kitten alone for more than a few hours. Picking her up, she kissed her on the nose, cradling her in her arms as she dialed Amy's number. This had become a Sunday night ritual – a call to Amy followed by a call to her parents. Amy always let her know what she could expect when she spoke to her mother, who still didn't fully understand why she had to "travel half way around the world to get away from Chase."

"So are you done with all your Christmas shopping?"

"You're in a good mood. You sound rested." Amy had a way of keying in on the sound of Karen's voice and recognizing her moods.

"I am. We spent the day at Dil's ranch and I fell asleep on the ride home."

"We being…?"

Karen went on to explain that Simon had arrived home on Thursday and had a young man with him who would be attending college in Kentucky. All of Simon's family, except for Adam, was there. They talked for almost an hour before Karen said, "I probably need to give Mom and Dad a call before they think I've forgotten them."

"Oh, that won't be necessary," Amy promptly said. "They…uh…decided to go skiing up at Whistler. You know they never have their cell phones when they're on the slopes."

Hanging up, Karen wondered what prompted her parents to take their annual ski trip before Christmas. It had always been an after-Christmas event – usually in mid-January at Brighton in Utah. But she was in too good a mood to worry about it. If something was wrong, Amy would have said so. Looking around her little cottage, she decided that the only thing missing from her holiday setting was the smell of cookies baking. Her favorite recipe was granny's almond sugar cookies that literally melted in your mouth. They were the perfect accompaniment to eggnog – or Tom and Jerry's if the weather was cold enough. *Like now*! She had decided *not* to worry about the outcome of Simon's time with Staci. There was something in the way he had looked at her – and *the kiss* – that held a hint of promise. She would hold on to that and not allow any negativity into the celebration of this holy season.

After loading all her favorite Christmas CD's in her player, she began pulling out cookie sheets and ingredients for an evening of her favorite pastime. Sometimes, as she stood in the kitchen, she could feel Granny's arms wrapped around her and hear her voice saying, "You're doing a fine job, cupcake."

Chapter 52

Karen wasn't certain if it was the article in the paper or Christmas shoppers that resulted in the busiest Monday the Krossroads had experienced since opening. Whichever it was, she was grateful and totally exhausted when she headed to the cottage for her afternoon break. Having awakened to an ice forest out her back window that morning, she expected their usual slow Monday. By nine, the trees that had earlier appeared as fragile as her delicate crystal stemware had returned to their drab leafless winter attire. And now, bright sunshine had brought the temperature up to sixty-one, prompting Karen to forgo her afternoon catnap for a cup of hot chocolate and a couple of sugar cookies on the back deck. She had just poured the steaming hot chocolate into her Santa mug, when there was a knock on the front door. *Oh great! Already a crisis at the diner.* She knew her employees wouldn't bother her unless it was important – and it didn't happen often. Walking to the door, she said a quick prayer that it wasn't an injury demanding her attention.

"Mom! Dad! Ohmygosh!" Her parents were both embracing her at once. "What a surprise!"

"That was the idea," her father smugly responded. "We decided our Christmas gift to ourselves would be to come see what you found so enticing about this place out in the middle of nowhere."

"What an adorable little home you have here," her mother said, her eyes roaming around the cottage interior. "And I have to say that your diner is equally charming. When we told that woman behind the counter who we were, she greeted us like long lost family."

"Sherry. Her name is Sherry, Arliss."

"Right...Sherry. Lovely woman. If everyone here is that friendly, I can see the appeal."

"I assure you, they are," Karen said. *Well…almost everyone.* She forced the image of Staci out of her head. Then, looking around in panic, she added, "Oh Mom, as you can see I don't have much room…"

"Not to worry, Darlin'. Amy warned us and we are already checked in at the motel where she and Ronnie stayed. They were real friendly folks as well."

An hour later when Karen had to return to the diner, she reluctantly left her parents watching TV, with Goodness napping in her father's lap. Her first question to Darrell as she came through the door was, "What on earth am I going to do with them for the next week? I don't think they understand that…"

Darrell stopped her by finishing her sentence. "…you practically live in this kitchen?"

She looked at him with a totally helpless expression.

"We had a little meeting and everyone agrees that you need to have some time off with your folks. Once you do your morning baking and prepare the specials for lunch, we can handle the rest. I called Cricket and she said she would come in anytime we needed her and I'll work as many hours as necessary. Consider any extra time we put in as our Christmas gift to you. There's no room for argument here – even if you are the boss."

Tears began forming in Karen's eyes as she walked over and gave Darrell a hug. "The most blessed boss in the world," she said. "But I want you to clock in for every minute you spend here. You *will* be paid – and there's no room for argument in *that* decision."

When she released him, he was wearing his little lopsided grin. "Now if you'll mix up your magic sauces, Cricket will be here in a minute to take over the sandwich board and garnishing, and I can handle the rest. Why don't you bring your folks in for dinner. That way you can judge for yourself if I'm doing things right."

"I fully intend to. I already know that Dad will be ordering the grilled salmon with curried peach sauce. Just make sure the salmon isn't overcooked. Mom will probably order the shrimp pasta in Alfredo sauce and you prepare that as well as, if not better, than I do." While she talked, she was tying on her apron and was soon busy watching over numerous sauce pans. It was going on six and the dinner crowd had begun arriving when she led her parents into the diner. Sherry had taken a one hour break, and then returned for the evening shift. She greeted them with a huge smile, seating them and teasing Kathy about "taking extra special care of these folks."

As predicted, her father ordered the salmon and her mother the shrimp pasta. When they both commented that "this is as good as yours," Karen laughed.

"It is mine, Mom. Darrell does a great job of following my recipes to the letter and all my grill cooks are masters at the grill. I have an amazing crew working for me."

When they returned to the cottage after dinner, Karen called Amy. After giving her sufficient grief over her *lie* of the evening before, each of her parents took a turn at raving about the diner, "with its wonderful food and delightful staff." Her mother even admitted that she was quite taken by the charm of everything she had experienced thus far.

Her next call was to Margo. By the time she got off the phone, the remainder of her week was planned. It was a foregone conclusion that Karen and her parents would be joining them for Christmas Eve as well as Christmas day. Margo was as anxious to meet Karen's parents as Karen was for them to meet her and Dil…and of course, Simon. When Karen asked Margo to join them at the diner the following night, Margo insisted that she would cook dinner for all of them. "I've got to keep up my cooking skills and you need to spend some time away from the diner."

Karen had already sent gifts to Portland for her parents, but wanted to have something under the tree for them. The following day, she left her parents in Margo and Dil's care long enough to make a quick run to Mt. Sterling. By the time she returned, you would have thought the two couples had been lifelong friends. Walking into Margo's living room she found the four of them playing a rousing game of hearts – her father being the obvious winner. The playful scolding her mother directed at him sounded so familiar that Karen wished she could lock this moment in time. A feeling of contentment settled over her. *The only thing missing is the feel of Simon's arm around my shoulders. Aaack! Where did that come from? Stop it KC – no time for a funk!*

Setting aside her flash of longing, Karen walked up behind her father and put her arms around his neck, resting her chin on his head. Looking at her mother across the table she asked, "Is Daddy picking on you Mummy?"

"He always does," she replied, her mouth in a mock pout. "While you're over there, slap him up the side of the head for me."

Instead, Karen kissed the top of his head, and then turned to Margo saying, "Whatever you've got cooking smells wonderful. When do we eat?"

"As soon as Simon and Jesse get home. Everything is ready and they should be here by five-thirty. Would you like a drink – a glass of wine, maybe?"

"I'll get it. You go ahead and finish your game. Can I get refills for anyone?"

Dil had been idly shuffling the deck of cards and now set them aside saying, "I think we'll just declare Jimmy the winner if that's okay with everyone."

They had all settled in the living room with drinks when the sound of a car coming up the drive set Karen's heart racing. Her parents hadn't met Simon or Jesse yet and she was anxious to see their reaction to them – especially Simon. As soon as he walked through the door, Simon extended his hand to her father saying, "You have to be Karen's parents."

At the dinner table, the conversation was dominated by Simon and Jesse, who were alternately being bombarded with questions from her parents. Karen, Margo and Dil mostly listened as Simon and Jesse spoke between bites of the delectable pot roast dinner prepared by Margo.

Simon had them all in stitches as he described the dress rehearsal for the children's Christmas pageant to be presented at the Wednesday night service.

"Gail is doing a great job of directing, but getting the kids to follow a script is almost impossible. They tend to adlib when they don't remember their lines and even Gail wasn't quite prepared for the innkeeper's curt reply to Joseph's plea for a room. 'Can't you read? The sign says no vacancy.' Then he slammed the stage set door so hard, the entire inn fell over. Joseph reacted heroically and caught the falling inn before it could hit Mary or the two Roman soldiers who stood nearby. Then, as if it was part of the script, our Mary looked at Joseph and cooed, 'my hero,' throwing her arms around him and kissing him on the cheek, dislodging his beard. Unfortunately, Jesse and I were too busy laughing to appreciate Gail's frustration. She managed to get them through the scene on the second try, but I can't wait to see what happens tomorrow. We've yet to have a pageant that goes one hundred percent smoothly. It's the most joyful part of our Christmas services."

Back at Karen's cottage her mother confessed, "I so wanted to find you miserable and lonely and ready to come back home with us. I see now that isn't going to happen. You've obviously made a wonderful life here, Karen. I hope you are truly as happy as you appear to be."

"I am, Mom. I miss you and Dad, and of course, Amy and her family. But I really think that God led me here – with a little coaxing from Granny. You've always said that I have her *southern heart*, and I think you're right. I feel more at home here than I ever did after leaving my childhood home. Having my own business is beyond my wildest dreams – and someday, I'll have a family of my own – a husband who loves me for who I am and the children I've always wanted."

"Speaking of potential husbands, what about that charming son of Margo's? He seemed quite attentive toward you."

"Not gonna happen, Mom." *Unfortunately!* "He's already taken."

Oh!" she said, sounding disappointed. "He's engaged?"

"Not officially, but I'm sure it's just a matter of time. They've been on the verge a couple of times and she's the one who's always backed away, but I sense that she's ready to settle down."

"Humph! If there's no engagement ring involved, he's open game, Sweetheart. Unless of course, you don't find him as appealing as I do."

"I find him more than appealing, Mom. He's good and kind and thoughtful. He has all the qualities I've ever dreamed of, without Chase's arrogance. But the timing is lousy. I don't have the time or energy for anything other than the diner right now. It's only been seven months since my life was turned upside down and I don't want to make any decisions about my future out of loneliness. Simon has been a dear friend to me and there's no way I would jeopardize that friendship. If I tried to come between him and Staci, I would most likely lose not only Simon, but Margo and Dil and everyone connected to them."

Seeing the disappointed look on her mother's face, she took her hand and calmly added, "I'm only twenty-six, Mom – well, almost twenty seven. I'm not exactly an old maid yet and I have plenty of child-bearing years ahead of me. I figure God brought me this far and I doubt He'll turn his back on me now."

Breathing a deep sigh of acceptance, Arliss Christian moaned, "You're right, dear," then in a brighter tone asked, "Will we be meeting this...Staci was it?"

"Probably. I imagine she'll be around for some of the Christmas gatherings. She may even be at tomorrow's service."

Before her mother could say anything else, her father, who had feigned disinterest in the conversation, but obviously heard every word, stopped her. Standing abruptly and pulling her with him, he said, "I think that's enough, Arliss. We need to head on to the motel and let Karen get some rest. You can continue your motherly inquisition tomorrow."

Chapter 53

For the remainder of their visit, Staci's absence from the gatherings at Margo's and Dil's became more and more peculiar to Arliss. When she failed to appear at the pageant, Karen's explanation of "she and her family are members of a Presbyterian church in Morehead and are probably attending their services," seemed reasonable enough.

The following night when Margo and Dil met Karen and her parents at the diner for dinner, Simon and Jesse weren't with them. Karen hid her disappointment when Margo explained that Simon had a previous commitment and Jesse was with him. Later, Karen told her mother that he was most likely introducing Jesse to Staci's family.

Miriam and Paulie joined them at Margo's on Friday and Jesse was there, but again, no Simon. Margo said he would be joining them later, but offered no details of his whereabouts, so Karen again assumed he was with Staci. She expected her to be with him when he arrived late in the evening and was relieved when he came alone. She couldn't help but wonder if Staci was avoiding the gatherings because of her, or if she was embarrassed over her little show last Sunday.

Fortunately, her mother saved her inquiries until they were at the cottage. Karen explained that Staci had been out of town for several months and was "probably making up for her long absence by spending as much time with her parents as possible over the holidays." This prompted her mother to ask if Margo didn't get along with her parents. Exasperated, Karen replied, "I have no idea. I've never met her parents and have only seen Staci a couple of times. She's not a very open person and I imagine her parents are the same. I'm sure Simon has told them that you are here. They probably feel like they would be intruding on your visit."

If her mother planned on making any further inquiries, she was warned off by a menacing look from her father. The, *thank you Dad*, look Karen gave her father was rewarded with a knowing wink.

On Christmas day, when Margo opened her final gift from Dil, everyone watched with anticipation as she lifted the lid of the small box to reveal a beautiful engagement ring. Her gasp, followed by a tearful nod of her head was affirmed by a loud applause from everyone gathered. Soon they all joined her in tears of joy as they offered their congratulations to the beaming couple. Simon pulled Dil into a bear hug as he thanked him for "putting the sparkle back in Mom's eyes."

No one heard what the big man mumbled into Simon's ear just before releasing him. Simon had a playful grin on his face as he walked away. Karen, who had her back to Simon, didn't observe his sideways glance in her direction – but her mother did.

The Diner had closed at two on Christmas Eve and Karen gave a little party for her staff, passing out bonus checks and small personal gifts to each of them. Her parents had enjoyed the gathering as much as she had and when they left for the airport shortly after having a hearty breakfast on Monday morning, they hugged every member of the staff that was present. "We'll be back…soon," they promised.

As sad as she was to see her parents go, Karen was also relieved that they were leaving. Now she could return to her normal routine. It had been difficult to be around Simon with her mother's inquisitive eyes watching her every move. For Christmas, Simon had given her a gold charm bracelet filled with charms of pots, pans and cooking utensils. She loved it. In return, she had given him a silver fountain pen with his initials engraved on the cap. After praising her gift, he then scolded her for being so extravagant. "Look who's talking," she chided, jangling the bracelet, which she had immediately placed on her wrist. Each had honored the others God given talent. Her mother watched the exchange with a smug, knowing look on her face. Karen had caught the look out of the corner of her eye and hoped no one else noticed.

As expected on the day after Christmas, business seemed to have settled back to its normal pre-holiday pace, allowing Karen to take her afternoon break. The first thing she did when she reached the cottage was to call Margo and find out if they knew the results of Miriam's tests.

"Dr. Griggs said that she is in remarkable health for a woman in her eighties and she has the heart of a woman half her age. The tests indicate that it's an isolated tumor and confirm that it hasn't reached any of her vital organs. He believes she could easily withstand surgery to remove the cancerous part of her stomach along with any infected lymph nodes. She will probably require only minimal follow-up treatments."

"That's wonderful news. How does Miriam feel about it?"

"At first she told Dr. Griggs that she would have to see how much Medicare and her supplemental insurance would cover before she would consider the surgery. Dil assured her that that was the last thing she should be worried about. She said she wouldn't do it if it meant delving into Paulie's trust fund, but eventually agreed to go through with it. They've scheduled the surgery for January third. Can you believe she's never been hospitalized except for Paulie's birth?"

"That's incredible! Speaking of Paulie, what does he think about this?"

"Dil explained everything to him. All he really cares about is that his mother gets better. Dil even convinced them to stay with him after the surgery — at least until Miriam is up and about enough that Paulie can take care of her at home. He has no doubt that that will happen in just a few months."

"A few months meaning you two newlyweds will have the house to yourselves after the honeymoon?"

Karen could sense Margo's blush over the phone. She and Dil had set the wedding date for Valentine's Day and would be traveling to Europe for a month-long honeymoon. Belinda and Sandy immediately began planning the wedding, inviting Karen to join them. They had all giggled like school girls as the two daughters argued over which of them would give their mother *the talk* on the eve of her wedding.

"It really doesn't matter one way or the other," Margo said in response to Karen's chide. "That house is big enough for all of us, but I doubt Miriam is ready to give up her independence. I really wouldn't mind if they stayed permanently. Both she and Paulie are such delights to be around and Gloria adores them both. Paulie worries that he might be needed at the diner, but Dil told him you had everything covered until his mother is ready to return home. They'll be with us tonight when we come in. Do you think you could join us – for a while at least? I'm guessing Paulie needs your reassurance."

Try as she might, Karen couldn't stop her heart from racing as she replied, "Of course," then reluctantly asked, "Will…uh…Simon and Jesse be with you as well?"

"Oh my!" Margo exclaimed, her voice sounding distressed. "Didn't Simon tell you that he's headed for New York this afternoon? He's delivering his newest book in person and he has some contract issues to discuss with his agent. He was somewhat evasive about it and I try not to pry. I thought he may have mentioned it to you."

Covering her disappointment she asked, "Did Jesse go with him?"

There was a little chuckle in Margo's voice as she replied, "No. Jesse is staying with Father Brian while he's gone. I think Father Brian is trying to recruit him for the Glenmarys."

After hanging up, Karen did some laundry and attempted to take a cat nap. It was useless. Refusing to allow herself to get depressed, she headed back to the diner to find every booth filled.

"Honestly," Cricket assured her, "they just came in – all at once. From what I've overheard, it's mostly travelers returning home after Christmas."

Thank heaven there wasn't time to worry about who or why they were here. The orders were coming in fast and furious and she had to prepare several evening specials. By the time Margo and Dil arrived around six, things had settled back to a relatively normal Monday pace. Karen came out to greet them but had to return to the kitchen almost immediately. They were just finishing up their dessert when she managed to find a few minutes to sit.

"Have you heard from Simon – that is, did he have a safe flight?"

"Why yes, I did. I scolded him for not telling you he was leaving and he actually said, 'Oh crap!' *My* Simon, who has never used crude language in my presence – at least not since I washed his mouth out with soap when he was ten."

After everyone had a good laugh, Margo added, "He said he meant to say something to you, but with your parents here and the fuss over the engagement, he never had an opportunity to be alone with you."

"Simon doesn't have to account to me for his time, Margo. I was just surprised that he would be going somewhere so soon after his return from Sao Paulo." With a wan little smile, Karen stood, saying, "Now I better get back to the kitchen before Darrel thinks I've deserted him completely."

As Karen walked away, Dil noticed a scowl on Margo's face. Taking her hand, he asked, "What's wrong?"

"I don't think Simon has said a word to Karen about his breaking up with Staci. She's not the kind who would bring it up and probably thinks they're still a couple."

"So why haven't you said anything to her?"

"Because it's not my place. I told you that Simon said he has feelings for Karen and I don't know the extent of those feelings. If he's going to act on them, then he needs to…" She almost said, *get his rear in gear,* but she caught herself and finished by simply saying, "act on them!"

Dil was watching his fiancée with a wry grin on his face. They both seemed to have forgotten that Miriam and Paulie were with them until Paulie asked, "Who's Staci?"

Chapter 54

There was a look of panic on Cricket's face as she burst into the kitchen on Tuesday evening. "What am I supposed to tell these people who keep calling about reservations for New Year's Eve?"

"What have you *been* telling them?" Karen asked.

"That we're a diner and we don't take reservations – but some of them are getting pretty snippy about it and I don't want you to lose customers."

"I told Sherry to say that if they called ahead of time on New Year's Eve, we would put their name on a waiting list and they would have preference over walk-ins as long as they arrived at their given time. I thought she would have told you – but then you haven't really seen her since the calls started coming, so guess I'm the one who dropped the ball. Sorry."

"No harm, no foul. I just hope that satisfies some of the pushier ones."

Cricket was gone before Karen could make any further comments, but she couldn't control the excitement she felt with the knowledge of the diner's popularity. Everyone on the staff had agreed that they should stay open a little later on New Years Eve if necessary, but they didn't really anticipate too many late diners since they didn't serve alcoholic beverages. Hopefully, they would be able to close the diner in time for her staff to enjoy her planned New Year's Eve party. All of their family members were invited, along with Dil and Margo and their families. This might mean facing Staci, who would most likely accompany Simon, but Karen refused to let this occupy her thoughts. She was looking forward to preparing all the hors d'oeuvres she loved to make and would spend her afternoon break in the cottage kitchen.

On Friday afternoon, when Karen had not heard anything from or about Simon, she decided to call Margo. After chatting for several minutes, she casually asked, "When are you expecting Simon to arrive home?"

"Good question, and I wish I had a definite answer. His morning flight was cancelled and he's on stand-by for the next available seat. He said it's liable to be late tonight by the time he gets home. They have no direct flights to Lexington and usually you get routed half way around the world. Heaven only knows how many layovers he'll have to deal with."

Hanging up the phone, Karen picked up Goodness, and nuzzling her soft fur, said, "Well so much for having time with Simon without Staci present. I'll just have to deal with it." Lifting her arm, she jangled her bracelet in front of the kitten, who immediately began batting at the charms. "You love it as much as I do, don't you Goodness?"

By eight on New Year's Eve, Karen felt like she had just run the Boston Marathon. The madness started at five and there was no indication that it would let up soon. She and Darrel kept up a constant chatter as they coordinated their moves with the grace of a choreographed dance. In the midst of the pandemonium, Darrel wryly commented, "This madness reminds me of a sign I saw in a little seafood restaurant in Florida. *When you're up to your ass in alligators, it hard to remember your original intent was to drain the swamp.*"

Karen burst into a fit of laughter that was as much adrenaline based as it was reaction to Darrel's remark. Looking at the countless tickets lined up overhead, she shot back, "Well buckle up partner. This swamp is a long way from being drained."

Most of the early arrivals had been younger couples headed to Lexington for the big downtown celebration. The later diners appeared to be an older crowd who would either be attending house parties or heading home to greet the New Year. Sherry was in her element, managing the waiting list and supervising the staff, while Willie was entertaining the entire dining room. Over the past few months, he had honed his skills on the grill and loved to show off. He would flip a hamburger onto the bun, on a plate held behind his back, or a steak onto a plate while doing a little dance. Karen had seen him doing his little routine several times and wished she was out there watching as the crowd burst into applause numerous times throughout the evening. It was shortly after ten thirty when the last of the customers cleared out, leaving only the families of the staff and a few invited guests. Sherry flipped the open sign over with a flourish, announcing, "Okay gang, let's clean her up and then it's *party time.*"

Karen and Darryl had already cleaned the kitchen and were now cooking off the hors d'oeuvres to be placed on the counter. Just as they set the last tray in place, there was a tap on the door. Margo, Dil, Miriam, Paulie and Jesse came in shouting "Happy New Year." Simon wasn't with them. Karen tried not to let her disappointment show as she greeted her guests, but Margo could see her eyes searching the parking lot as she gave Miriam a hug.

"Simon will be here as soon as he can," Margo said. "He had a layover in Cincinnati and called just before we left the house. He was at the airport and should be here before midnight."

Karen sat for the first time since the evening rush had began, and despite the throbbing in her feet, she felt quite good. It had been an extremely successful evening.

For the New Year's specials, she had put a prime rib dinner, along with a couple of larger steaks on the menu. The prices were higher than her regular menu items and she was somewhat afraid that it might scare off some of the customers. She couldn't have been more wrong. When Sherry told her what the take for the evening was, Karen's jaw dropped several inches. It was more than they had taken in for the last four days and no one said a word about the prices. Fortunately, the bulk of the sales were credit cards, but it still left her with an uncomfortable amount of cash for the night drop. As she sat down, she spotted Kathy Hansen's beau, Manny Ortega. Manny was a Morehead policeman and still wore his uniform, having just got off duty at eleven. She decided right then that she would ask Manny to make the night deposit for her. She already knew that both he and Kathy were teetotalers and his presence in uniform would probably discourage any of the other guests from over-imbibing. She decided to relax and enjoy the rest of 2005.

Karen visited with everyone for several minutes before remembering that she hadn't checked on Goodness since before noon. Glancing at the clock behind the counter, she decided she had time before midnight to run over to the cottage. She also wanted to pick up the two extra bottles of champagne that were in her refrigerator. She probably had enough, but it was unthinkable to run out before everyone's glass was filled. Standing abruptly, she said, "I need to run over to the cottage to check on Goodness. Be sure you try the mini-crab cakes before they're all gone – and let me know what you think of the sauce. It's my own recipe."

As Karen walked by the counter, she did a quick check of the platters and made a mental note to replenish the stuffed mushrooms on her way back. Looking up, she caught a glimpse of her reflection in the mirrored pie case and thought; *I also need to replenish me.* She hadn't realized that when she took off her chef's cap, a large portion of her wild hair had escaped the clip that held it back. *I look like I just stuck my finger in a light socket!*

Goodness met her at the door, scolding her with a loud *meo-o-o-w* and almost tripping her as the she wound herself around and between Karen's legs. A quick nuzzle and a handful of kitty treats later, the disgruntled kitten was happily playing. Meanwhile Karen did a quick change from the t-shirt she wore under her chef's coat to a warm sweater, redid her hair and sprayed herself with a refreshing body splash. As an afterthought, she kicked off her clunky, rubber soled clogs and slipped her aching feet into a comfortable pair of flats. *At least I won't feel like a complete frump when Simon arrives. He'll probably pick up Staci before coming here.*

With the two bottles in hand, she headed back to the diner. When she reached the door, she tucked one of the bottles under her arm so she could open the door. It was fortunate there were no neighbors to complain about how loud Cricket had set the music. *I'll have to take it down a couple of notches to make the New Year's toast.*

Just as she pushed the door closed, a subtle rattle of pans startled her. Before she could turn around, a large hand came over her mouth and both bottles of champagne went crashing to the floor.

"I ain't gonna hurt you. I just don't want you to scream or do anything stupid – understand?"

I'm being robbed! Karen's entire body trembled as she shook her head, affirming that she wouldn't cry out. *No one would hear me anyway,* she thought. The man released her and she turned to face a large, burly man who smelled of alcohol and tobacco. He hadn't bothered to hide his face, which heightened Karen's fears. *Please God, don't let him hurt anyone.* He had a disheveled appearance with a scraggly beard and a wild animal look in his eyes. He had placed one hand in a pocket of the heavy leather jacket he wore, and appeared to be holding a gun pointed at her. Karen's eyes widened and she audibly gulped before asking, "Who are you? What do you want?"

"I'm Christine's husband and I want you to get her back here without causing any trouble."

Confused, Karen stuttered, "I...I don't know who Christine is. What... what does she look like?"

"Don't play games with me, bitch. I know she works here and I know she's out there hangin' all over some string-bean hick."

That's when it hit Karen. *Cricket! Her real name is Christine and this is her abusive husband.* Over the past months, Cricket had opened up somewhat to Karen about her past. She half defended her ex-husband, saying that he hadn't always been mean – just jealous. It was only in the last months before she left him that he became physically abusive, and then, only when he was drunk – and he had obviously been drinking. According to Cricket, the first few times he had hit her, it was more open handed slaps after she called him a fool for thinking she was flirting. So she stopped talking when he went into a rage, and somehow, that seemed to anger him more. It was after he actually slugged her with his knotted fist, sending her flying across the room and into the corner of a coffee table, that she knew it was only going to get worse. The following day, she filed for divorce and moved in with a friend. Remembering the ugly scar on Cricket's cheek, Karen was afraid of what might happen if she did as he asked. With a calm she didn't truly feel, she said, "Mr. Donovan… Ziggy…, don't you think it would be better if you spoke to her tomorrow when you're…uh...not so upset?"

"Look, Lady – this is none of your damn business and I'll talk to my wife when and where I choose. Are you gonna' do what I ask or do you want this to get ugly?" he snarled. "If *I* have to go out there, someone's liable to get hurt."

When he spoke, he jiggled whatever it was that he held in his pocket in a threatening manner. As frightened as Karen was for herself, she was more frightened for her guests, and especially Cricket. *Dear God,* she prayed, *please show me how to deal with this.*

She had no sooner finished her silent prayer, when the door from the dining room swung open and Simon appeared.

"There you are, Karen," he cheerfully said, "We were beginning…"

Ziggy turned around, grabbing Karen as he whirled to face Simon. Seeing the terrified look on Karen's face, Simon stopped.

"What's going on here? Who are you?" The anger in Simon's voice was a complete shock to Karen. She had no idea he was capable of this degree of fury. At the moment, he looked as if he was capable of tearing Ziggy from limb to limb. The only thing stopping him was the fact that she was being held hostage, possibly with a gun in her back.

Before Ziggy could say anything, the door opened again and this time it was Willie who walked in. "Darrel said we have some more of those…" He almost ran into Simon before he halted and quickly assessed the situation. Willie's voice was calm and controlled as he spoke, but the look on his face was pure menace. "I don't know what you think you're doing, Mister, but I recommend you leave…*now!*"

Karen couldn't see the fear on Ziggy's face, his eyes wide as he assessed his chances against two obviously angry men; the larger one being particularly intimidating. Slowly he backed toward the outside door, pulling Karen with him. Karen struggled against his strong grip, and with one quick motion, he pulled the door open and released Karen. As she lunged forward, she attempted to grab the work table, but lost her footing on the champagne soaked ceramic tile floor. Her feet flew up in the air and her head slammed into the stainless steel prep table, bounced off and hit the floor with a crash. She didn't hear Simon cry out as her world went black.

Chapter 55

Slowly, Karen opened her eyes and took in her surroundings. She realized she was lying in a hospital bed. Her head throbbed mercilessly and it felt as if she had been run over by a Mack truck. A nurse was hooking an IV up to the needle inserted in her right arm.

"I know you're hurtin' Honey, but now that you're awake, we might be able to give you something for that pain."

Trying to rationalize why she was here, Karen wanted to shake the cobwebs from her head, but just moving her eyes caused the pain to increase. With a concerted effort, she managed to ask, "What happened?"

"Well Honey, I'm not the person to ask. Maybe this lady can answer your question."

Stepping aside, the nurse revealed a very worried looking Margo sitting in a chair next to the bed. As soon as she realized Karen was awake, she stood and rushed to her side, picking up Karen's hand, careful not to disturb the IV.

"Oh, Sweetie, you're awake. Thank God you're awake." Tears streamed down Margo's face and her voice cracked as she spoke.

"What happened, Margo?" Karen repeated her question, adding, "How long have I been…sleeping?"

Margo burst into sobs. "You recognize me! The doctors weren't sure if your memory would be affected. You took a really nasty spill, Sweetie, and you've been unconscious for over three days. We've all been so worried."

Karen tried to assimilate Margo's information, but it made no sense. She closed her eyes and attempted to put her thoughts together. *Three days.* The first clear thought that came to her mind was Goodness. She didn't realize she had said the kitten's name out loud.

"Goodness is fine, Sweetie. She's at my house terrorizing Princess. She's obviously not used to having so much room to run around and Princess isn't used to having competition." Margo's voice was more composed now, obviously relieved that Karen appeared to have cognitive thoughts.

"I'm sorry," Karen mumbled.

"Why should you be sorry?" a confused Margo asked, and then realized Karen had taken her words seriously and immediately felt terrible. "Oh, Sweetie, I'm the one who needs to apologize. You're in no condition for my lame humor. You know Goodness is an absolute sweetheart. She's been entertaining your parents ever since they arrived."

"My parents are here?"

Before Margo could say anything further, Dr. Floyd Schaefer, accompanied by Natalie McKay, walked into the room. His deep pleasant voice drew Karen's attention away from her confusion. "Hi there, Beautiful – glad you decided to rejoin the world. Now I can resume the plans for our wedding."

Natalie immediately gave him a playful punch in the arm. "Don't mind him Karen – he has a warped sense of humor."

"You're no fun, Nat. One of these days I might get lucky."

The words of their playful exchange didn't quite sink in as two unfamiliar faces leaned over the bed. When Karen finally realized that it was Natalie McKay, she asked once again, "What happened?"

Natalie gave Dr. Schaefer a hesitant look, so he responded.

"You took a couple of nasty blows to your head and fell into some shattered glass. I'm just glad we didn't have to do surgery to keep the swelling down. I'd hate to have to cut off those gorgeous locks."

As he spoke, the doctor was examining Karen, shining a light into her eyes, and then gently touching her head. It wasn't until he moved over to her left side that she realized the upper portion of her left arm was bandaged. She had tried to absorb what he told her, but nothing made any sense and her eyes were growing heavy. It would be several hours later when she again opened her eyes to find Simon staring down at her, his beautiful green eyes cloudy, and rimmed with dark circles.

He tried to smile as he emitted a choked sob, his hand tightening on Karen's.

"Hi there," he said.

Karen's brow scrunched up in confusion as she attempted to make sense of why she was lying in bed with Simon standing next to her looking like he hadn't slept in a week. They had taken her out of ICU and moved her to a private room. Within seconds, three other faces appeared above her.

"Mom...Dad...Amy? What are you doing here? Where am I?"

Her mother's reaction had been the same as Margo's as she turned into her husband's chest and bawled like a baby.

"Hi, Sweetheart," he said, looking down at her, his own face streaked with tears. "You sure gave us all a fright."

Amy burst into heart rending sobs and James Christian pulled her into his embrace as well. Pulling away, she placed her hand on Karen's arm saying in what she hoped was a playful tone, "If (hiccup) you didn't (hiccup) look so miserable (hiccup) already, I'd (hiccup) deck you one. You scared the shit out of us."

The last was said with a weak little whimper that brought a smile to Karen's face. She was alert enough to recognize her sister's teasing and responded in a like manner. "You may as well, Sis. It couldn't make my head hurt any worse."

It was almost a week later when Karen was released from the hospital with the doctor's orders to "get plenty of rest and don't attempt to return to work for at least three weeks." She still wasn't clear as to how and why she had ended up in the hospital. She didn't recall the policeman that had come by to ask if she could identify "the intruder." Simon had told her everything he knew from the time he walked into the kitchen, but the last thing she actually remembered was leaving the cottage with the two bottles of champagne.

"I barely got a look at the guy," Simon said, "but Willie saw him. I just remember seeing you go sailing across the floor. When you slipped on the spilled champagne, your head hit that big stainless steel table and then bounced on the ceramic tile floor. By the time I got to you, all I saw was the blood and you were unconscious. Willie started to go after the guy, but when he saw you, he ran back to the dining room to get Natalie and tell Manny to call 911. Manny ran out the front door in time to see someone take off on a motorcycle. After he called 911, he alerted the police to be on the lookout for him. There couldn't have been too many motorcycles on the road with the weather as cold as it was, but he must have taken some back roads, because they didn't find him. It wasn't until Cricket heard Willie describing the man to the police that she determined it could have been Ziggy. When she showed Willie a picture she had in her wallet, he said he was pretty sure that was the man.

"Willie told the police that the guy he saw looked older and heavier, but the face was the same. Cricket said the picture was almost ten years old and verified that the last time she had seen Ziggy, he was about thirty pounds heaver than he had been in the picture.

Throughout her hospital stay, everyone from the diner had come by to visit; each assuring Karen that everything was under control at the diner. Darrell said that there hadn't been "too many complaints about my cookin'" and Willie assured her that Darrell was doing a "fine job." Cricket burst into tears when she came by and kept apologizing. "I don't know why I kept that picture. It was taken before he turned mean and I suppose I just wanted to remember him like that. I told the police they could keep it. I also told them that there's no way Ziggy had a gun. He was scared to death of guns ever since he shot a couple of his daddy's fingers off in a hunting accident when he was thirteen. Willie said it was the way he held his hand in his pocket that made them think he had a gun. I'm sure he was just faken' it."

While Cricket had rattled on, Karen kept trying to connect her words with what had happened to her, but nothing made any sense.

The three inch gash on Karen's upper left arm, along with numerous small cuts over her lower arm and backside, were all healing. The physical therapist and the speech therapist who had been working with her were both amazed at her recovery. Her short term memory was still a little off, but the doctor assured her that it would improve with time. Amy had already flown back to Portland, but her mom and dad planned on staying for another week. They would all be housed at Margo's upon her insistence. Jesse, who had been helping out at the diner, agreed to stay at the cottage since Karen would be in the room he had been occupying.

"There's no way you're gonna be on your own, Kiddo. Not until I'm convinced you're one hundred percent. No arguments."

When Margo had first made this statement, Simon wasn't present. Karen couldn't help but wonder how this would set with Staci. She and Simon under the same roof for three weeks or more? She waited until she was alone with Simon to voice her concern.

"Simon, I appreciate your mother's offer, but I don't want to cause any problems between you and Staci. I'm sure she wouldn't like the idea of me living in the same household as you. She doesn't care for me as it is."

It was the day before her release and Simon had lingered after visiting hours were over and everyone else went home. His head drooped and his brow furrowed as he began to speak. He reached over and took her hand, his thumb tracing small circles over her knuckles.

"I'm not sure where to start. I've wanted to explain this to you ever since I got back from Sao Paulo. Things just got sort of crazy and then with that scene Staci made; your parent's visit; my trip to New York…and this…"

His voice trailed off as he lifted his head to see Karen's eyes staring at him in confusion. *Will she even understand what I'm trying to tell her?* He wondered as he made up his mind to go on. *I'll tell her again and again if I have to – until it sinks in.*

"Staci and I are finished. I considered it to be over before I left for South America, but then Staci discovered that I have money. She always considered me to be a poor preacher who lived off his mother. I guess I never gave her any reason to believe differently. I've told you before how I tried to tell her about the Jesse books, and when I saw her in Boca before I left for South America, I had every intention of telling her then. I won't go into the details of that conversation or the one at the church right now. The most important thing for you to know is that Staci has moved back to Boca with no intention of returning to this area. For the first time in almost thirteen years, I truly feel free to pursue my feelings for another woman…for you. I know you consider me simply a friend and that means a lot to me. I just hope that with Staci out of the picture, you'll be able to look at me…a little differently."

Simon's mouth turned up slightly in a tentative smile as Karen continued to sort out his words. Her brain was still not processing all her own thoughts in a timely manner — much less the words of others. The speech therapist warned her that this could happen, so she tried not to appear totally perplexed by Simon's last statement. When she finally found words, it came out as a baffled question.

"Staci's really gone? For good?"

"Mmm-huh."

"That's good. I didn't like her very much."

Her honesty elicited a little chuckle from Simon.

"Do you understand what I've just told you?"

"I think so."

"Are you going to remember it tomorrow?"

"I think so."

"Good! I'm going to let you get some rest now. I'll see you in the morning."

He stood up, gave her a gentle kiss on the forehead, released her hand and turned to go.

"Simon…"

He turned back to face her.

"I know you told me that I fell on some broken glass and hit my head, but I still don't know how it happened or why Cricket thinks Ziggy was involved."

Simon paused before speaking, then said in his gentle pastor's voice, "That's partly because no one but you knows the whole story. When you're completely recovered, I'll tell you everything we know again and maybe by then you'll be able to recall the rest."

After leaving Karen's room, Simon stopped in the little chapel and said a prayer of thanksgiving for her recovery, followed by a prayer of petition for continued healing of her mind and body.

Chapter 56

Karen couldn't help but feel that there was way too much fuss being made over her release from the hospital. They had stopped at the diner on the way to Margo's house. A banner was strung above the counter saying "Welcome Home" and everyone in the diner, customers and staff alike, applauded when she walked in. One by one, the staff came over and gave her a hug. The last one in line was Cricket, who burst into tears as she sobbed, "I'm so sorry Karen. I'm so sorry! Thank God you're okay."

Karen's left arm was still a little sore and everyone else had been cautious with their hugs, but Cricket had wrapped her arms around Karen's shoulders in a near death grip. Karen winced, wondering why Cricket was so upset. *Had she somehow caused the fall?* She automatically began patting her gently on the back as she said, "I'm fine Cricket. It was an accident."

Pulling back, Cricket started to say something, but caught the warning look on Margo's face as she said, "That's right, Honey, it was an accident. No one's to blame."

By the time they arrived at Margo's, Karen was already exhausted and her mother tucked her into bed with instructions for her to rest for the remainder of the afternoon. They had eaten lunch at the diner and Margo said that dinner would be ready around six. Karen immediately fell asleep and awoke at five fifteen to find Simon sitting next to the bed, his bible in hand. Her mind flashed back to the first time she had met him, and with a clarity that had been missing since waking up after the accident, she realized her feelings for him were far deeper than mere friendship. Was that what he had been trying to tell her last night? Did he have those sorts of feelings for her as well? She remembered him saying that Staci was back in Boca, but she couldn't quite recall the reason. *Dear God, please let my brain start functioning properly. I need to know what's happening in my life!*

As if sensing that Karen was awake, Simon looked up and caught her staring at him with a curious look on her face. His first thought was that she didn't recognize him. *Had they over done her homecoming by stopping at the diner?* With his heart in his throat, he said, "Hi there Gorgeous. Did you have a good nap?"

Her smile assured him that she was aware of her surroundings and recognized him. He released the breath he had been holding and returned the smile.

"What time is it?"

"Almost dinner time. Would you like to freshen up before we eat?"

"I look that bad, huh?"

"You look perfect," he said, brushing back a curl that lay carelessly across her forehead. "I just meant you might want to splash some cold water on your face to wake up."

She sat up, stretched and yawned. "Good idea."

Everyone was sitting in the sunroom when Karen came downstairs. As soon as she walked through the doorway, Margo handed her a glass of lemonade.

"Sorry Sweetie, no wine for the next few weeks. Doctor's orders."

"That's okay. I have a feeling it would just put me back to sleep anyway."

As Margo rejoined Dil on the love seat, Karen realized the only vacant seat was next to Simon on the couch. His arm was stretched across the back as if waiting to embrace her. A little shiver ran down her spine. However, when she sat down, his arm didn't move. She hid her disappointment by taking a sip of the lemonade, and then placed her glass on the coffee table.

"Whatever you're cooking smells wonderful." Closing her eyes, she sniffed the air and added, "Let me guess – Lasagna."

"Close, but no cigar. Baked Ziti. Your mother did the cooking. She also made tiramisu for dessert," her father stated with obvious pride.

Karen gave her mother a warm smile. "You remembered my favorite."

"That and the fact that it's the only one of your grandmother's recipes that I ever mastered."

"Speaking of grandmother's recipes," Dil said, "I have something for you."

Reaching to the side table, he picked up a large binder and held it out to Karen.

"This belongs at the Krossroads."

Karen immediately knew what it was and held the binder with as much reverence as Simon held his bible. "But this belongs to you Dil. I couldn't..."

"It belongs at the diner. I know perfectly well that Ma would much rather see you with it than the likes of me. Gloria won't let me near the kitchen. She claims I could burn water."

Dil had told the story of how Ma's recipe book had been in the care of Miriam. The binder was falling apart and he had his secretary carefully laminate all the pages and put them in a new binder. It was the first time Karen had seen the recipes and as she opened to the first page, she burst into laughter. Almost choking as she spoke, she said, "No wonder Charlie Mae couldn't recreate Ma's recipes. Listen to this recipe for Flaky Buttermilk Biscuits. Two handfuls of flour, several dashes of salt, baking powder, and enough lard to make a crumbly dough. Add ice cold buttermilk until the mix is sticky, then..."

By the time she finished with the instructions, everyone was laughing.

"Poor Charlie Mae," Dil mused, as he wiped tears from his eyes. "She got a bad rap on all counts. I guess I should have looked at this myself before I gave it to you, Karen. It's probably useless."

"Oh no," she protested. "This is wonderful. I know enough about cooking that I'll be able to at least come close on her recipes. Real cooks rarely measure. They cook from instinct. Granny always had precise measurements on her recipes – probably the schoolteacher in her – but when she taught me to cook, she emphasized that I had to learn how to smell, taste and feel, as I cooked. Start with the basics and adjust as needed. It was like a mantra for her."

"I can already tell it's in the hands of the right person," Dil said, his face beaming.

"I was wondering what I could do with my time until you jailers release me back to my diner. I'll be testing Ma's recipes and you will all have to be my guinea pigs." As she spoke, she was paging through the book. "Now here's one I've always wanted to try. Mousaka! I had it once at a friend's house and it was delicious. Grandpa Rickles had an aversion to eggplant, so Granny never tried to find a recipe. I'd forgotten all about it until I saw this. Awesome!"

Everyone was watching Karen with expressions ranging from relief to pure joy. She was sounding more like herself than she had in almost two weeks.

Karen's parents hadn't rented a car this time. Dil had insisted on picking them up at the airport, fearing that they would be too upset to drive safely, and they used Karen's car to get back and forth to the hospital. Simon volunteered to drive them to the airport and Karen insisted on going as well.

"Are you sure you're up to this Sweetheart?" her father inquired.

"Of course I am, Daddy. It's not like I'll be driving, so if I get sleepy, I'll just sleep."

In her first week out of the hospital, Karen tried to spend more time awake than sleeping, but the longest she seemed able to go was about three hours. Her recipe testing had produced several successes along with several dishes she considered duds, although everyone assured her that all the results were delicious. Ma's recipes, with their pinches, dashes, dabs and dollops proved to be quite a challenge. She still wasn't sure what the exact differences were but tried to translate them to measurements just the same.

Simon wasn't home nearly as much as she had anticipated. He was still showing Jesse around and they had made several trips to UK in Lexington as well as to Dil's ranch that week. Karen knew that the trips to Dil's had to do with looking in on Miriam and Paulie. Miriam had done splendidly throughout her surgery and was now ensconced at the ranch under Gloria's watchful eye. She hoped they could swing by on their way back from the airport, certain that Miriam could empathize with her protective imprisonment.

Saying their good-byes at the airport, Karen felt a combination of sadness and relief. Her mother had hovered over her throughout the past week, constantly asking if she was tired or sleepy. They had arrived at the airport early, so with time to kill, Simon and her dad wandered off to get them something to drink.

Sitting in a waiting area, her mother watched as the two men disappeared around a corner, and then leaned in to her daughter saying, "He's in love with you, you know."

"I know no such thing, Mom. It's too soon after his break-up with Staci for him to even consider falling in love with anyone else."

"Has anyone told you that young man spent all of the first three days you were in the hospital either praying in the chapel or sitting next to you? Margo said he got away with a lot by saying he was your pastor – but that *was not* merely pastoral concern for your well being that I witnessed."

Despite herself, Karen allowed her mother's words to give her hope. She tried to temper her response saying, "But he is that caring, Mom – both as a pastor and a friend. It's what I..." When she stopped mid-sentence, her mother gave her a wry grin as she completed Karen's thought.

"What you love about him? That's what you were going to say, wasn't it?"

Karen could feel color rising in her cheeks and she had to return her mother's smile. "Yeah, Mom, I do love him. That's the first time I've admitted it out loud. I think I must have fallen the first time I saw him. I'm just not so sure you're right about him being in love with me. He said something about wanting to pursue his feelings for me, but I don't think he even knows what they are at this time."

Giving her daughter a condescending pat on the hand, Arliss Christian settled back into her seat wearing a smug knowing smile just as Jimmy and Simon re-appeared down the corridor.

Walking back to the car, Simon had taken Karen's hand as they crossed to the parking lot. He didn't notice the contented sigh she released as they settled in their seats for the ride home.

"I really like your parents, Karen," Simon said, as he buckled his seat belt.

"I can assure you that the feeling is mutual."

As he pulled out of the parking lot, he gave Karen a sideways glance. "You look tired. Why don't you let your seat back and take a little nap."

"I'm not sleepy – for a change. I'm just a little emotionally drained. I hated seeing them go, but at the same time, I'm relieved I'll be able to go to the bathroom without Mom hovering over me."

Simon let out a little chuckle, reached over and ran the back of his hand over her cheek. "You have a great family, Karen, and they obviously care a lot about you."

The feel of Simon's hand on her cheek was so sweet. Karen wanted to hold it there – *forever!* However he had to pull it away to execute a turn onto the highway.

"You know, Simon, I never did learn what your trip to New York was about – that is, how it went. Your mother said it had to do with a new contract or something."

"Actually, it was more than that. I'm afraid my anonymity is soon going to be a thing of the past. My agent was contacted by a production company in Los Angeles and they want to turn the first three Jesse books into a film with the potential for sequels if it's as big a hit as they seem to think it will be. I spent three ten hour days with a group of people from the studio. We met at my agent's office to discuss the screen play and negotiate a deal. It is way more than I ever wanted to get involved with, but they assured me that I could do most of the work from home. I have to go back in a couple of weeks to sign the contracts and they want me to fly out to L.A. in the spring. The money is more than I ever imagined. All I could think of was how I'd be able to add a much-needed wing to the hospital in Sao Paulo and get some updated equipment. There's also the possibility they'll do a large portion of the filming at the mission. I may go with them when they check it out. I think it would be good for them to see the children I write about and it would be a source of income for the area – especially if they end up making more than one film."

Karen didn't know if her mouth was gaping open or not. She sat in stunned silence, staring at Simon. "Why has no one told me about this before? It's…it's…Oh, Simon, I am so proud of you. This is so exciting." If it weren't for the fact that he was driving, she would have thrown her arms around him.

Simon's broad smile soon turned to a forlorn thoughtful look. "Actually, you're the first one I've talked to about it. Everyone, including myself, has been so concerned about you, that no one has asked. It all seems so unimportant when I consider…"

They had reached the interstate by now and Simon reached over and took her hand again. After giving it a squeeze, he continued in a brighter tone. "It's really way more excitement than I ever wanted in my life. I miss my congregation. Lenny's been doing a great job and knowing he'll be here when I have to travel makes it a lot easier to commit to this."

Shortly after hearing Simon's news, Karen had drifted off to sleep, her hand still in his, so they didn't stop by to see Miriam and Paulie. That evening he shared his news with Margo, Dil and Jesse.

Chapter 57

When Karen went for her final check-up with Dr. Schaefer, he said she should be fine to be on her own as long as *she* was comfortable with it.

Although Simon had never made any romantic overtures toward her while she was staying at Margo's, he often put his arm around her or held her hand while they sat on the couch conversing with others. When she brought up the subject of going back to the cottage, everyone but Simon expressed their concern over her being by herself. She wondered if he was growing tired of her constant presence.

On the day Karen arrived at the cottage, an eerie feeling came over her as she looked toward the back door of the diner. *Maybe I am afraid to be alone here.* Giving Goodness a squeeze, she said aloud, "But I'm not alone, am I baby?" The kitten's answer was a loud purr as she bounded out of Karen's arms the minute the door closed.

Karen had insisted that no one should come in with her right away, saying, "I just want to get the feeling of my home again – and I need to do it alone."

It was early afternoon on a Wednesday, and by the time she unpacked, checked the refrigerator and made a short grocery list, she was already tired. She made herself a cup of tea and sat on the couch. More than anything, she wanted to remember what had happened that night. With a concerted effort, she attempted to piece together all the things that various people had told her.

Margo said that the police in Dayton had arrested Ziggy based on Willie's identification from Cricket's picture. However, they weren't able to hold him because he had an alibi. Two friends claimed he was with them on New Year's Eve. They had all been in Lexington for the downtown celebration. After seeing the mug shots sent to the local police, Willie was certain that it was Ziggy he saw – but Ziggy's buddies wouldn't back down from their story. When Manny had brought the picture to Karen, she just shrugged her shoulders, the face totally unfamiliar.

Cricket was still certain it had been Ziggy. New Years Eve would have been their anniversary. "Comin' here is just the kind of stunt he would pull," she had said.

Cricket also knew the two men who vouched for his whereabouts. One was his brother and the other his best friend. According to her, they would have lied for Ziggy "anytime, anyplace." Unfortunately, the three men were able to back up their presence in Lexington with a receipt from the hotel where they stayed. It still didn't guarantee that Ziggy had been there the entire time, but it shed legitimacy to his story, so the police had to release him.

Cricket was furious. She said she called him with a warning that if he ever came anywhere near the diner again, she was going to take out a restraining order and start carrying a gun. "And I told him I'd aim low."

Karen determined that thinking about it was futile – and it made her head hurt. To take her mind off that subject, she decided to call her parents and Amy. They had talked almost every day over the past two weeks, but she wanted them to know that she was home and everything was fine. After making her calls, she realized she was hungry so headed over to the diner to have an early dinner. When she opened the back door, Darrell was standing behind the prep counter, but Karen saw a completely different man. The color drained from her face and she heard someone scream. She had no idea that it had been her own voice she heard as her knees buckled and she crumpled to the floor. When she awoke minutes later, she was surrounded by her entire crew. A cool cloth was draped over her forehead and someone had placed a bundled up coat under her head. Everyone let out a collective sigh when she opened her eyes and asked, "What happened?"

Fortunately, Darrell had made it around the counter and caught her just before she hit the floor.

"You tell us boss. I know I'm not the greatest thing to look at, but I don't ever remember scarin' anyone that bad."

A nervous laugh from the onlookers was followed by Sherry ordering everyone to get back out front. "Give her some air, for cryin' out loud. We've got customers out there."

Karen sat up, and in a dazed voice she said, "I think I remember what happened that night."

An hour later, she was back in her cottage with Margo and two police officers, one of them Manny Ortega. Simon was with Lenny preparing for the Wednesday night service, so Margo didn't call him.

After carefully giving them an account of the events that occurred prior to her fall, Karen asked, "What's going to happen now?"

"Well, with your testimony, they'll be able to hold Mr. Donovan on assault charges. They'll extradite him back down here..."

"What if I don't file any charges?" Karen interrupted.

The two officers looked at each other, and then Manny finally asked, "Why wouldn't you press charges, Karen? The guy put you in the hospital for almost two weeks. He could have easily killed you."

"It truly was an accident Manny. I don't believe he had any intention of hurting anyone. He even said he didn't want anyone to get hurt. As I was telling you what happened, I realized that he didn't push me. I was pulling away and when he let go, I started to fall forward. I was trying to right myself when I slipped. As far as him having a gun..." Karen closed her eyes as if picturing the scene before continuing. "When he grabbed me, I was pressed right up to him and what I felt could have easily been a small flashlight. After Cricket telling me about his aversion to guns, I have to believe that his pretending to have one was just a means of controlling me. I don't know what might have happened if Simon and Willie hadn't appeared, but I really don't feel he would have hurt *me*. My concern was more for Cricket."

Manny flipped his pad closed, obviously annoyed. "We'll still have to file the report, and then it will be up to the D.A.'s office to determine if they want to charge him with anything."

After the Wednesday service, Simon stood at the back of the church as he always did, surrounded by members of his congregation. Karen gave him a little wave as she exited, but someone had him engaged in conversation. He barely had a chance to glance up at her.

Margo had been observing her closely throughout the service and said, "You look exhausted, Karen. I think you've had a little too much excitement for one day. I'll walk home with you, and Dil can stay to let Simon know where we are."

"Thanks, Margo. It just hit me about halfway through the service that I've actually been up all day. I think I may have dozed off for a few minutes."

Margo smiled as she put her arms around Karen's waist, saying, "Simon will understand, dear." She had actually slept for almost ten minutes.

Karen and Margo were sitting on Karen's couch, sipping hot tea, when Simon and Dil arrived. While walking over to the cottage, Dil had filled

Simon in on Karen's memory returning, the visit with the police, and Karen's decision *not* to file charges. After visiting for a few minutes, Margo and Dil excused themselves, leaving Simon and Karen alone.

"Do you realize that other than our trip back from the airport, this is the first time I've had you to myself for three weeks?" Simon said as he took Margo's vacated seat next to Karen on the couch.

She turned to face him, and the look in his eyes was new to Karen. He took both of her hands in his and began speaking in a deep, emotional voice.

"Since the first time I saw you, I've been denying the feelings I have for you. Perhaps because on that day, as I watched you climb out of your car, I had this…stirring…something I hadn't experienced in a long time. I accused myself of being lustful, but now I believe what I felt was a moment of grace – God reminding me that I was only human, and as a man, such feelings are natural. I've fought those feelings long enough. I want to explore them…with you…for the rest of my life. I love you Karen."

Karen sat frozen – certain that her fantasies of this moment happening had pushed her over the edge. It wasn't until Goodness brushed against her leg, her loud purring matching the pace of Karen's heart beat, that she realized it truly was Simon sitting next to her, speaking the words she had ached to hear for so long. His face, *his beautiful face*, held a longing that matched the yearning she had tried to hold in check for all these months. She didn't attempt to stop the tears that slowly welled in her eyes as her hand slowly reached up and touched his face, as if confirming to herself that he was real.

"I fell in love with you, Simon Crawford, the moment you first smiled at me."

Then she was in his arms. The kiss that followed was far removed from mere friendship.

As the memory of her past hurts dissolved, her exhaustion dissipated as well. This was her future – a new beginning – and the conclusion of her crossroads journey.

Epilogue

September, 2009 – Portland Oregon

"On this episode of Diners Drive-ins and Dives, we're headed down south to visit Farmers, Kentucky, a little dot on the map in the heart of the Daniel Boone National Forest. This historical diner has it all, folks. History, romance, a ghost, and some of the best food you're gonna find anywhere. There's even a special kid's dish called 'Frank 'n Macdoodle" that I'm dyin' to try."

As Guy Fieri spoke, pictures flashed across the screen, and when Debbie realized who she was seeing next to the huge commercial stove, she almost dropped the cake pan she was carrying to the oven.

"*Chase!* You gotta' come in here and see this," she yelled in an excited squeal.

"Aw, Debs, my football game just started."

Instead of replying, Debbie Beckham marched into the den, grabbed the remote out of her husband's hand, and changed the channel to the Food Network.

"What the hell!" Her disgruntled husband said, as he grabbed for the remote.

"Oh, you're gonna' want to see this, sweetums."

The face of Guy Fieri, with his signature sun glasses, spiked blond hair, engaging smile and his arm hanging out the door of his red Camero convertible, filled the TV screen.

"Why would I want to watch one of your stupid cooking shows? Give me back the remote, dammit."

"Stop using that kind of language around our son," Debbie demanded. "So you'll miss the first few minutes of the game – trust me, you'll find this much more interesting."

Chase resigned himself to enduring whatever Debbie was so excited about. Folding his arms across his chest, he slumped back into the couch and stared at the TV, which had now gone to a commercial. He had to bite his tongue to keep from going into a tirade, but Debbie, sitting on the arm of the couch with her swollen belly, plus the presence of his four year old son, prevented him from expressing his rage.

When the host's face reappeared on the screen, he said, "Our first stop is in Farmers, Kentucky, where a transplant from Oregon took her love for cooking, along with her Granny's recipes, and turned a sixty-five year old diner that had been closed for over thirty-five years, into a new landmark in what was Rowan County's first settlement. Located fifty six miles east of Lexington, Kentucky, on highway 60, and walking distance to Cave Run Lake, Farmers was once the…"

Old photos began flashing on the screen as a brief history of Farmers and the diner was given. Chase started to say something just as the screen changed to the interior of a commercial kitchen and Guy was standing next to Karen – Chase's ex-wife, Karen – saying, "Meet Karen Crawford…"

His jaw dropped several inches as Debbie's mouth curved into a smug grin.

"Told ya you'd want to see this." Her tone was as self-satisfied as her grin.

Karen looked great in her short chef's jacket and jeans. Her hair was tucked under a beret-type chef's cap, and numerous wild curls escaped around her radiant face. She cooked as she talked about her Granny leading her to Farmers and the diner. Between descriptions of the dishes she prepared, Guy asked questions about the origins of the recipes, while tasting various ingredients and commenting on their heat, sweetness, and so on. The completed product looked like something served in a high class restaurant and drew raves from Guy. He even proclaimed the macaroni and cheese in the Frank 'n Macdoodle as "stellar," adding, "that dish is a real *wiener* – get it? *Wiener*;" and then mugged for the camera.

Flashes of customers enjoying different dishes and praising each as their *favorite*, alternated with shots of Karen and Darrell preparing the dishes. When the program again went to a commercial break, Debbie reached down and closed Chase's mouth.

"So do you want to go back to your game?" she taunted.

"But they said they was more about Karen's diner, didn't they? Something about her grill cook and her connection to the original owners?"

Debbie moved over to sit next to her husband, kissing him on the cheek as she burst into laughter. "I love it when I'm right."

Farmers, Kentucky

"Play it again, Mommy." Two and half year old Jimmy sat on floor in front of the TV and didn't bother turning around to make his request.

"Yeah, Mommy, play it again. Lizzie wants to see her beautiful mommy on TV one more time." Simon reached over and brushed a wayward curl from Karen's cheek after he nuzzled six- month-old Lizzie's partially exposed tummy.

"And me too, Daddy. I'm on the TV too." Jimmy said.

They had received a copy of the Diners, Drive-ins and Dives episode several weeks before it aired. Everyone was delighted with the results, but Karen still blushed every time someone mentioned it. While the first part of the segment had focused on her and Darrell in the kitchen, the second part focused on the front end of the diner. All the regulars had been invited to come in for the filming. Willie hammed it up for the cameras, challenging Guy to flip a hamburger onto a bun held on a plate behind his back. During the filming, Guy missed numerous times before he finally caught one. After he succeeded, he made a big show of Willie holding his hand high over his head for a *high five,* while Guy attempted to jump high enough to slap it. The cameraman almost dropped the camera, he had laughed so hard.

The final few minutes had Guy sitting around the table with Karen, Simon, Jimmy, Grandpa Dil and Grandma Margo, who was holding Lizzie. They talked about the family connection tracing back to the original owners. Karen told the story of how she met Simon, who introduced her to his mother, who introduced her to Dil, who had once dated Margo. Now Margo and Dil were married and by virtue of her marriage to Simon, there was still a family connection to the original owners. Guy feigned dizziness and pretended to fall out of the booth.

When the video ended, Jimmy wanted to see it again, but Karen cut him off. "No more tonight, Jimmy. It's time for your bath."

"But Mommy…"

Simon had his son in his arms with one swift move, threw him over his shoulder, saying, "No arguments."

An hour later, Simon and Karen sat snuggled together on the couch.

"Do you know how long you'll have to be in L.A. this time?" Karen asked as she lifted her head from Simon's shoulder to look directly at him.

When the first Jesse film was released, Simon had to spend way too much time away. Despite his celebrity status, he still considered himself first and foremost, husband, father, and pastor to a small community church. The media demands for interviews had died down by the time the first sequel came out, and thus far he had been able to keep his private life private. He and Karen now occupied the home he had shared with his mother. Karen had come to love it and thought of it as her own – never once demanding that they move to anything bigger and better. It was convenient to the diner and yet afforded them privacy.

As a wedding gift, Dil had marked the loan papers on the diner as "paid in full." The property itself remained in his name, but with no debts on the diner, Karen was able to maintain a staff that allowed her to spend more time with her family; and when Simon traveled, the children stayed at the cottage with a sitter while she worked. They had all accompanied him on several of his trips to L.A., and Karen had gone with him on his last trip to Sao Paulo.

"Three days – tops," He replied, kissing Karen on the nose and pulling her closer. "I've already told them, I won't be going to Sao Paulo with them for the third sequel. My babies are growing up much too fast for me to be spending so much time away – and I need *you* way to much."

The kiss that followed was as tender and inviting as it had been on their wedding night – the night Karen discovered there could be fireworks and earth-shaking passion associated with lovemaking. Simon stood, took her by the hand and pulled her into his arms. She sighed in peaceful contentment as he led her up the stairs.

Manufactured By: RR Donnelley
Breinigsville, PA USA
August, 2010